'We all share the same small planet, we all breathe the same air, we all cherish our childrens' futures and we are all mortal.'

John F. Kennedy. American University, Washington DC, June 1963

SEPTEMBER SONG

Gerry Hickey

Doon and Auburn

Dublin

Copyright © Gerard Hickey, 2020

First Published in Ireland, in 2020, in co-operation with
Choice Publishing, Drogheda, County Louth, Republic of Ireland.
www.choicepublishing.ie

Paperback ISBN: 978-1-913275-22-8

eBook ISBN: 978-1-913275-23-5

A CIP catalogue record for this book is available from the National Library.

In Memory of my Father
Called home too soon for those of us who loved him.

Acknowledgements

The author wishes to thank David Joseph in Massachusetts, Brian Thomas in Dublin, Deirdre Devine of Choice Publishing, Brian J Hickey, Cape Cod and Barry McCabe of MDG for their practical and constructive help with this book. Thanks particularly to Heilén for her help and support throughout this process. All errors are the author's own.

CHAPTER 1

Cape Cod
August 1963

The woman had less than five minutes to live when she walked briskly past me on Craigville Beach that Labour Day weekend. When I thought about her afterwards, I am certain that I felt there was something familiar about her but I can't honestly say I recognised her or even thought consciously about her. Maybe it was the way she was dressed that lodged in a recess of my mind. Although it was a beautifully warm sunny morning, she was wearing a navy blue windbreaker zipped up to her neck, tan slacks and white sneakers, a stark contrast to the other people on the beach that day. If I noticed that an attractive woman bustling along the beach looked preoccupied, that too was a fleeting half second thought instantly dismissed. The beach was crowded. It usually is on Saturday of the Labour Day weekend, the traditional end to the summer season on Cape Cod. Craigville beach in Centerville, just outside Hyannis, my home town, is not a glamorous place. It's wide and spacious but it does not have the same cachet as the bigger National Seashore beaches further up the Cape or of smaller more intimate beaches nearby. The people here had the look of a local crowd, with kids and dogs running around, laughing, barking or crying, their parents lying on the sand, reading or sleeping. Three teenagers close to where I was stretched out on the sand, positioned themselves in a triangle, noisily throwing a football to one another and taking up an unreasonably large chunk of beach territory. As might be expected there were a lot of people in the water. All in all it was a typically warm summer's day by the ocean, despite it being the last day of August and after the weekend, the official end of summer in my part of the world.

It was my old high school friend Tom Noonan who heard the shot. I didn't hear a thing over the cacophony of competing noises. We had both been swimming and were lying on our towels letting the warm sun dry us as we talked. Tom stood up suddenly.

'Hold it a second Jimmy, did you hear that?'

'Hear what?'

I had been lying back with eyes closed my head resting on the old canvas back pack I had used as a beach bag since I was seventeen. I looked up and noticed that the three football guys had stopped their game and were walking slowly away from us towards the water's edge. A mild hush had suddenly descended on the noisy crowd. The football guys were going in the same direction the blue windbreaker woman had gone, just a couple of minutes before. 'I didn't hear a thing.' I said.

'Are you deaf Flynn?' he said. 'That was a gunshot. No doubt about it, come on.'

I scrambled to my feet and followed Tom who broke into a slow jog ahead of me. I could see that quite a few others were doing the same. The noise on the beach had now reduced almost to silence, apart from the playful sounds of a few people still in the water. A crowd had gathered up ahead. Now I had no doubt that something was wrong. When we reached the growing group of people, Tom cut through a thick ring of onlookers who were staring at something on the ground and I followed him. 'Let me through please, I'm a police officer.' He said, in a tone I had never heard him use before. The crowd moved aside respectfully, despite the fact that Tom was wearing nothing but swimming trunks and obviously could provide no evidence of his authority. I followed in his wake. The woman in the blue windbreaker was lying on the ground close to the water which was ebbing slowly out. Even to my layman's eye she was clearly dead. There was a small neat hole in her right temple and a pool of what looked to me like black blood, seeping from the wound into the wet sand. Tom knelt beside her and felt for a pulse in her neck. He turned and spoke to the first person he saw, as it happens it was one of the kids who had been playing catch beside us.

'Go up to the Mama Turini's, the ice cream stand, there's a pay phone there. Call an ambulance and then call the Barnstable Police Department, in that order. Tell them there's been a shooting, a probable homicide. Tell them State Trooper Tom Noonan is at the scene, got it?' 'Yes,' the kid said, still staring at the woman on the ground but he did not move.

'Well go now,' Tom barked. The kid turned and sprinted up the beach. One of his buddies ran after him.

The transformation in Tom Noonan was a revelation to me. I had bumped into him the night before in the Brass Rail, a bar we knew well at the west end of town. He was a neighbour for as long as I could remember. We had once been good friends but after high school we went our separate ways as people do. Tom, much to the surprise of everyone who knew him as a pretty wild teenager, joined the Massachusetts State Police as a motor cycle cop and now was some kind of detective, based in Springfield in Western Mass. I took a different path. I went to college in Boston to study languages, so we rarely met after that. I was home for the weekend to visit my mother. Tom was also back in town visiting his folks. Our meeting on Friday evening in the Brass Rail was accidental but it turned out to be very enjoyable. Tom was there with two women, Linda Crocker, an attractive and unattainable beauty during our school days. She was with her pal Susan Becker. Linda and Susan still lived in town. The two of them had arranged to meet Tom for old time's sake. They chose the Brass Rail as the venue for the same reason I did. When we had been in high school a popular local crooner of the Johnny Ray variety, who went by the name of Gino Francetti, had a regular spot there. We were underage and had tried all the usual ploys to get in but were never successful. Although all of us were now closer to thirty, we still got some pathetic childish thrill going to the Brass Rail, now that we could, even if Gino was long gone, a mushy romantic ballad singer blown away by the hurricane of rock and roll and Elvis in '56. We asked another guy who happened to be in the bar to join us, a guy named Joe Davis, whom we all knew well from junior high and who used to do odd jobs with me when I worked as a gopher at the Hyannis Port Yacht Club.

The five of us had a great night, laughing, reminiscing and telling old war stories about difficult teachers and a variety of eccentric townsfolk. It was typical small town stuff, although the town of Hyannis and Cape Cod as a whole, is not really a normal place. This part of New England has a special resonance in the minds of many Americans because of its association with the Mayflower, Thanksgiving and the founding of modern America. Every summer without exception, the Cape is thronged with tourists from all over the eastern seaboard and further afield. Frankly, apart from the beaches and some quaint old houses, I always wondered what they come to see. The rest of the year the place is dead or at least it always seemed that way to us. But we accepted this never ending cycle of tourist feast and famine without thinking very much about it. Until, to our surprise, something happened in November 1960, which put our hometown on the historical map for reasons we did understand. For a brief moment Hyannis was not just at the heart of America but was actually the centre of the world's attention.

I remember my father and me driving to the South Street National Guard Armoury that November morning to see our most famous local resident, the thirty fifth President of the United States. The President-elect was there to formally acknowledge his narrow victory over Richard Nixon, accompanied by his entire extended family, including, for the first time since the election campaign began, his formidable father. JFK had come to accept the presidency of the world's most powerful nation. As my Dad and I drove to the armoury we listened to the electoral coverage on the Radio. The broadcast from the Ambassador Hotel in Los Angeles of the events the night before had a large crowd shouting repeatedly. 'We want Nixon'. My Dad laughed with a childish delight I had rarely seen in him before. 'Well they're not going to get Nixon, are they Jimmy.' For my Dad, like Kennedy, also the grandson of Irish immigrants to Boston, the election of John Fitzgerald Kennedy was an event of unparalleled joy. It did bother him a little that a majority the electorate of Barnstable County, where we lived, had voted for his opponent Nixon, despite the fact that the Kennedy's also lived here, on and off, since the twenties. But this did not really diminish his pleasure. He had a stupid grin on his face for at least a month afterwards. 'We have arrived', he would say, as he presided over the evening dinner table. 'Who can doubt we're as American as the Cabots and the Lowells now?' I pretended I had no idea what he was talking about and told him so. 'Never mind Jimmy', he would say smiling but never explaining. 'It doesn't matter anymore.'

It took less than fifteen minutes from the time the kid ran to the phone for the ambulance to arrive at the beach. While we waited, Tom started to ask people in the crowd if they had seen anything. He questioned anyone who said they were close to the woman when the shot was fired and told them to stand to one side and wait for the arrival of the police. He asked those who obviously knew nothing to move away or to go home but most didn't budge. No one seemed to want to miss the drama. We all waited patiently as two paramedics wheeled a gurney across the sand. When they reached us, one of them bent down to examine the body. He instantly confirmed what we all already knew, the woman was definitely dead. The two men then gently turned the corpse over on its back and brushed wet sand from her face. I looked at that face for the first time since she had scurried by me earlier. She was young, maybe twenty five. She seemed good looking, though it was hard to tell in these circumstances. She was the only dead person I had ever seen, apart from my father, who had died just nine months before. Once again, just as it had when she bustled past me earlier, a tiny inkling of recognition flashed through my mind. I knew I didn't know this woman. But there was something familiar about her. Maybe she was a neighbour or someone I'd seen around town. Maybe it was my imagination, maybe I was like all the other rubberneckers gathered round, I just wanted to have some connection with the drama myself.

We went back to where we had been sitting. Tom grabbed his clothes and dressed quickly. He told one of the Barnstable cops, who arrived just seconds before the ambulance, to take the names of the handful of people he had corralled who had been in the vicinity when the woman was shot.

'I'm going to go in the ambulance with the body, Jimmy. I'll be in touch. Here, take my car and leave it at my folks' place.'

He threw me his car keys and followed the cops and the paramedics, pushing the woman on the stretcher, the remaining onlookers bringing up the rear like some weird funeral procession on the beach. I picked up my own clothes and walked to the car park. I thought about the dead woman and the cruel untimely nature of her end. My father had had cancer. He had known for almost a year that he was going to die. Heartbreaking though it was for us, he had time to prepare himself and to some extent to prepare his family for what was about to happen. This woman was cut down without warning, in a split second she was gone. Perhaps that is one of the reasons murder is the most heinous of crimes. Victims have no time to reflect, to reassess or to prepare for whatever is to come next. I was intrigued by what I had just seen. I found myself envying Tom his official status and his inside track. I didn't know it then but as things turned out, Noonan's involvement in this case would end before Labour Day weekend was over, whereas the murder and its consequences would have a profound effect on me and on my life in ways that I could not have imagined as I climbed into Tom's '61 Buick and drove home.

CHAPTER 2

September 1963

As usual, whenever I was home for the weekend my mother insisted I take her to church. The Sunday morning routine had been the same in our house for as long as I could remember, Mass at eleven o'clock, in St Francis Xavier's, the neat blue and white clapboard church on South Street. Since I got my modest government job and moved to Washington, my mother saw all such occasions as an opportunity to impress friends and neighbours with what she imagined was my exalted status. From the way she told it you would imagine I was Dean Rusk's right hand man. In fact my job as an analyst and translator was a lowly specialist post, not considered worthy of entry to the coveted diplomatic stream of the State Department, where I worked. No matter how many times I explained this to my mother she remained undeterred and invariably introduced me to anyone who would listen as some kind of ambassador in waiting.

Since his election, whenever he was on the Cape and that was almost every weekend from summer to fall, the President continued to attend St Francis Xavier's regularly, just as his family had since he was a kid. As we walked from our car we could tell from the discreet Secret Service activity on the street and the conversational buzz from those making their way inside the church that this was going to be one of those mornings. We went in and took our usual place about three quarters of the way up on the left side. After a couple of minutes a sudden silence descended on the congregation. Without looking around, you could tell that the President had arrived. He walked briskly up the aisle heading for his usual place in the second pew. One of his sisters was with him, and two other men I took to be part of the Secret Service detail. It was understood that his wife was still recuperating from the loss of their third child just a couple of weeks earlier and so was unlikely to be here. He sat about four or five rows in front of us. My mother examined his face intently as he sat down.

'He looks tired,' she whispered. 'I don't think I have ever seen him so tired. He's aged since he took this job. The poor man, the baby's death must have been a terrible blow.'

From my angle I couldn't see his face just his back and the thick head of chestnut, almost red hair. An altar boy's bell rang signalling the beginning of the Mass, the priest emerged from the sacristy at the side of the altar, the congregation stood up and all further conversation ceased.

As he always did, unless his children were with him, the President left the church pretty quickly when Mass was over, everyone stood aside to let him pass. He then waited impatiently by the door as the priest rushed around from the back to the front porch to greet him. By the time my mother and I had shuffled out, he and his party had already gone back to Hyannis Port, less than a ten minute drive away. The priest stayed at the church porch, to greet us lesser mortals. Outside in the sunshine there was the usual after church mingling. I cooled my heels on the sidewalk, feeling like a ten year old kid, while my mother, as she always did, chatted to friends and neighbours. I heard a car horn honk urgently a couple of times and I looked across the street to see Tom Noonan in his white Buick, grinning in my direction. 'Hey Jimmy, thanks for dropping the car home.'

'No problem buddy, anytime.' I shouted back.

He leaned out of the car window and looked up and down the street like someone about to tell an off colour joke. 'Come here a sec will ya. There's something I want to tell you.' I glanced back at my mother, she was still talking. I went over to him.

'Hail to the Chief huh, was he here this morning?'

'Yeah, he just left.'

'That was something else yesterday, wasn't it?' He said excitedly.

'I never saw anything like it. Did you find out who she is?'

'I'm just about to go over to where she was staying. The body is still in the mortuary at Cape Cod Hospital, a single bullet, a .22, right in the centre of the brain. There's a lot of excitement about this for some reason. The Feds are in on it as well as our guys. They think the victim came from Canada. No matter what, I won't be on the case. It will be worked out of Boston. I'm going back to Springfield tomorrow anyway. But I am curious about the woman, so I'm going over to the Wianno Motel on North Street to take a look. They found a room key in her pocket along with a Canadian train ticket. Why don't you come over with me?'

I had to admit I was tempted. 'They won't let a civilian in will they?' I asked.

'It won't be a problem if you're with me. C'mon jump in.'

'But my Mom,' I started to say and instantly regretted it.

'My Mom,' he imitated in a mock baby voice. 'What are you Flynn, eight years old? Your mother's not handicapped. She can drive herself home. You've been to church, done your family duty, which is a lot more than I have, now come on, get in.'

'OK. Give me a sec, I'll just tell her.'

'Yeah, you do that Jimmy boy,' he called after me as I walked back. 'Check with Mommy, Mr big shot State Department guy.'

It didn't take us five minutes to get to the Wianno Motel on North Street. It was a single storey L shaped structure on a small lot. The rooms were referred to as cabins to suggest a rustic old New England image. It was low budget but respectable. There are dozens, if not hundreds of similar ones all over the north east. As we pulled into the car park Tom's confident tone of a couple of minutes before changed to one of mild anxiety. 'Now Jimmy, this is not my case, so strictly speaking I'm not supposed to be here, but my badge will get us in. You don't say a word. Just leave the talking to me. There's absolutely nothing to worry about but keep shtum, got it? Let's go.'

I couldn't resist a smile as we got out of the car. This was more like the Tom Noonan of old, always just barely on the right side of the line and always trying to put one over on somebody. It was obvious to us that the activity was in cabin seven. The door was open and we could see flashes from a police camera and hear the mumble of voices from inside. We walked over. Tom knocked confidently on the door frame and went in. There were five men packed into the small space, the photographer, one uniformed policeman, whose name I didn't know but who I recognized from around town and three men in suits. The obvious leader of the pack, a heavy set guy in his forties with a buzz cut, did not look pleased to see two new arrivals. 'Hi Rob, what's up?' Tom said to another of the suits, an older man named Rob Durand with a white moustache and a slight stoop, another Barnstable PD guy, who was also vaguely familiar to me.

'Oh Tom,' Durand said somewhat anxiously, 'Tom this is Special Agent Verling of the FBI and Agent Caulfield, indicating the other two. This is Detective Tom Noonan of the Mass State Police, it was Tom who was first on the scene yesterday and called it in.'

The old timer then threw me a questioning glance. Tom shook hands with the FBI men and said. 'This is Jimmy Flynn. Jimmy was at the scene with me yesterday.' The two unfriendly Feds gave me an imperceptible nod but did not reply or shake hands. The clear implication of what Tom had said was that I too was some sort of cop. I didn't like that but I should not have been surprised, it was a typical Noonan production.

'Dave, Officer Daniels, I think we got enough pictures, thanks, we'll be out in a minute.' Verling, the buzz cut agent said curtly, dismissing the photographer and the uniformed cop, thereby reducing the pressure on space in the small bedroom. I looked around. The room gave no indication of having been occupied. There was no sign of luggage or clothing of any sort. The bed was neatly made. As soon as the other two left, Verling turned to Tom. 'I believe you're based in Springfield. You're a long way from home. You probably know that this is a Bureau matter now, so you can sleep easy. We'll take it from here.' And then as an afterthought 'But thanks for the list of witnesses from yesterday, it makes our job a lot simpler.' The guy couldn't have been more condescending if he'd been talking to a shoe shine boy.

'Sure,' Tom said. Any luck identifying her? I hear she's Canadian.'

'Who told you that?' Verling asked with more than a hint of irritation.

'Dunno', said Tom, 'I must have heard it someplace. Didn't she have a

Canadian train ticket in her pocket?'

'Bus ticket to Logan from Rock Island Ontario.' Caulfield, Verling's sidekick volunteered, earning him a narrow eyed glare from his boss.

'We gotta get outa here.' Verling said quickly, moving towards the door. We all trooped out after him. 'Detective Durand,' he said, addressing the elderly Barnstable cop, 'we're going back to the station to make a few calls and then on to Boston. We have to make arrangements for the body. With a bit of luck we should be out of your hair for good by the end of the day. I take it we can still use your office?'

'Sure thing,' Rob answered.

'We'll see you back there then.' He and his partner walked briskly across the car park to a black sedan. They didn't as much as nod to Tom or to me and didn't say another word. As their car drove passed us, heading out on to the street, Rob, who had been deferential, even obsequious to the two FBI men just a few seconds before, gave them a stiff little wave, 'There go two twenty four carat shit heels.' He said through his teeth, his fake smile receding as the car drove away. It was hard not to laugh.

'So Rob, What's the big mystery?' Tom asked. 'Who is this woman, why are the Feds sitting on it so tightly?'

'She hasn't been positively identified yet. She had no luggage, nothing except the clothes she had on and she only had two things in the pockets of the windbreaker she was wearing, the key to cabin number seven here and a bus ticket. Rock Island is a border post between Ontario and Vermont. The FBI took over because of the Canadian angle. We and you Staties too, have been told in no uncertain terms, to butt out. The Bureau's Boston Field Office has issued a written instruction to that effect.'

'The hard ass, Verling, is he in the Boston office?' Tom asked.

'No. Funny thing is, he's from DC.'

'DC? What do they care about a murder on Craigville beach?'

'Beats me, they're playing this one real close to the chest. Verling's an SAC, very senior guy. He's so cagey his left hand doesn't know what is left hand is doing.' Rob chuckled to himself at his own little joke.

'The victim must have signed the motel register Rob, Didn't anyone check that?'

'No Tom, we never thought of that. You guys make me laugh. You think you wrote the book on detection. Of course we checked the name, first thing I did. But people sign any old name in a motel register, particularly when they're covering their tracks, as this girl seems to be.'

'Well what was it? Tom asked, 'what name did she use?'

Rob took a black notebook from his jacket pocket and flipped it open. 'Kircherr', Rob said. 'She called herself Elsa Kircherr, gave her address simply as Toronto, Canada.

'Elsa Kircherr,' Tom repeated the name. 'That doesn't sound like the kind of name you'd make up.'

The name hit me like a thunderbolt. I had heard it before and now I knew why the appearance of the young woman lying dead on the beach seemed vaguely familiar. I had actually seen a picture of her when she was alive. I had even read something about her background. But nothing I had read had anything to do with Hyannis. How could this woman possibly have any connection to a beach on Cape Cod? As I thought about it, I felt my face flush and my heart beat a little faster but the other two, still wrapped up in their own conversation didn't notice a thing.

'I'll bet you five bucks it's not her real name.' Rob Durand said to Tom. 'Although actually it's the second time she's used it.'

'How do you mean, the second time?'Tom asked.

'She was stopped by one of our uniform guys near Sea Street beach on Saturday afternoon, walking past the old lighthouse on Ocean Road. She was heading towards the ambassador's house. There's tourist traffic down there all summer long, women mostly, trying to catch a glimpse of Jackie. It was the same woman alright. She gave her name to the cop who stopped her. She said she was Elsa Kircherr.'

The ambassador's House, was the largest of the three houses clustered together at the end of a short street called Marchant Avenue that made up the so-called Kennedy compound. 'Aren't the Secret Service on duty down there? I asked, still trying to work out how coincidental it was that I knew anything at all about the dead woman.

The old detective looked at me properly for the first time since the conversation started. 'You Bill Flynn's boy by any chance?' He asked.

'Yeah I am,' I said.

'I can see him in you.' He said now eying me closely the way cops do. 'I played in a four ball with him at Sandwich a couple of years ago. He won. He was a nice man your dad, far too young to go. It was a tough break for all of you. How's your mother holding up?'

I was used to this question over the past nine months and I gave my usual reply. 'Fine thanks. She's as well as you might expect.'

'Jimmy is it?'

'Yeah.'

'To answer your question Jimmy, the President is not staying in the compound right now. He's renting a place on Squaw Island, a house called Brambletyde, better security there and more privacy. The Secret Service can take better care of Lancer there, so they're thin on the ground at the compound, which is why we only had one uniform guy on the beach.'

'Lancer, what's that?' Tom asked.

'That's the Secret Service code for the President,' Rob said, obviously proud of his insider knowledge. 'They always refer to him as Lancer. That's not public knowledge by the way. I shouldn't have mentioned it.'

Tom laughed. 'Lancer huh, how very appropriate,' he said. 'Someone in the Secret Service has got a sense of humour.'

Neither Rob Durand nor I had any idea why Tom thought the name funny. Squaw Island was just a few hundred yards from Hyannis Port. There's no through road, so unlike the road near the compound there is no passing traffic. The Island is a small enclave of about a dozen or so large houses separated from the mainland by a narrow causeway. I was still trying to figure out what possible connection there could be between the murder on the beach and what I knew about this woman. I spoke up then and almost immediately regretted it. I was simply showing off, trying to impress an old detective and my high school pal with a little insider knowledge of my own. It was egotistical and a little dumb but that had never stopped me before and it didn't stop me this time either.

'You'd lose the bet by the way, I said to Rob. 'Her name really is Elsa Kircherr. I know her, or at least I think I know who she is.'

Tom Noonan looked at me like I'd grown a second head. 'You know her. How the hell do you know her? You didn't say anything about this yesterday.'

'No. I didn't recognise her yesterday. I never actually met the woman but believe it or not, I recognise the name. Come to think of it, I know quite bit about her.'

'You do, how? Well what are you waiting for? Go ahead, spill.'

'Sorry Tom,' I said smiling at his frustration. 'It's confidential. Government information, I'm not allowed talk about it.'

Tom, who, up to this point had been leaning casually against the hood of his car, drew himself up to his full height. 'Confidential my ass, you'll talk to me about it Flynn. Otherwise you won't be going back to your fancy schmancy job in Washington. They'll have to dredge you up from the murkiest depths of Bass River.'

'Whether you tell us or not,' Rob said more soberly, 'if you have any information on this woman you'll have to tell the Feds. You'd better come to Barnstable with me and let them know whatever it is you know.'

'OK.' I said. 'You mean now?'

'Of course now, right away. You heard them, they won't be there for long.'

'Yeah', said Tom, with renewed enthusiasm. 'We'll go now. I'll drive him Rob and he can tell all me knows on the way there.'

Despite the kidding around I was not sure I could tell Tom or anybody else who was not involved in the investigation, what I knew about this woman now that I had an idea who she was. A peculiar feeling came over me but it wasn't one of foreboding. It was a tangible feeling of excitement that something strange and mysterious had happened and maybe I, Jimmy Flynn, and my boring, mundane life, might be part of it. I don't really believe in coincidence. From the little I knew about her it was hard to shake the feeling that this woman's murder was somehow connected to our town's most famous resident. I felt this killing was unlikely to be the end of a story it was bound to be just the beginning.

CHAPTER 3

Berlin

August 1961

The regional train from Dresden pulled into Alexanderplatz Station in Berlin at 11.00 am. It was on Monday, 21st of August. Klara Hartmann, who had turned twenty four, just a week earlier, was aware that she was coming to a city that was the talk of the entire world that summer. Only a week before, on the night of twelfth and thirteenth of August, the Communist Government of East Germany, began construction of the 'Anti Fascist Protection Barrier' otherwise known as the Berlin Wall, dividing the city in two and leaving its western half controlled jointly by the United States, Britain and France, a capitalist Island in a communist sea. Since Sunday 13th August, no one living in East Berlin could cross to the western part of the city. The city's eastern half was jointly controlled by the Soviet Union and its client state, the misnamed German Democratic Republic. The station in Alexanderplatz was a just short tram ride or a twenty five minute walk from the wall, although it wasn't quite a wall yet. At this stage there was more barbed wire than brick wall, but that situation was changing daily. The new construction was heavily guarded by an armed workers militia, with orders to shoot anyone trying to cross into the West. It was a warm late summer day as Klara emerged from the station, the kind of balmy warmth which raises the spirits from everyday worries. But Klara was unable to appreciate the weather. She held in her hand a letter bearing the name but not the address of the person she was to meet that day, Dr Armin Hoffman of the Ministry of State Security. It was the thought of that meeting and only that, which occupied her mind. She had been summoned to Berlin just three days earlier.

The letter from Dr Hoffman was hand delivered to her parents' apartment in Dresden, three hundred kilometres to the south east. The man who delivered it would not have been mistaken for anyone other than a representative of the 'organs of state security.' The summons was terse and to the point. It informed Klara that she was to travel to Berlin, go to the *Rote Rathaus, Alexanderplatz,* the old Wilhelmine red bricked town hall, with its conspicuous tower, just a few metres from the station. She was told to stand at the front of the *Rathaus* and await contact by a representative of the ministry. She was early, so she took a short stroll down the Leninallee heading west. She thought she might walk as far as the wall just to take a look. She liked walking, it gave her a chance to think about whatever was bothering her, but today she just wanted to postpone the inevitable for a little longer. Before long she turned back. Even in warm sunny weather there was no pleasure for her this particular morning. When she reached the entrance of the old municipal building, it was not yet 11.30. She was still twenty minutes earlier than the appointed time but she had no opportunity to loiter. An overweight man wearing a shabby tweed jacket with patches at the elbows, an open necked shirt and a leather cap approached her.

'Comrade Hartmann, come this way please.'

He could be anyone, Klara thought but apart from her mother, no one else knew she was here. She dutifully followed the man to across the square to where a black Wartburg car was parked. He opened the rear door and motioned her to get in. Within minutes they were on their way, driving north eastwards through almost non-existent traffic. Not a word was spoken. The further east they travelled the shabbiness of the streets in this part of the city increased. Sixteen years after the end of the world war, there was still plenty of evidence of the battle of Berlin in 1945 and of hundreds of Allied air raids. Badly refurbished apartment buildings, still pockmarked with bullet holes were more common than buildings which were wholly intact. There were tracts of waste ground where bombed out buildings had been demolished but not yet replaced. This kind of cityscape was familiar to Klara. Her home city Dresden had been entirely wiped out by allied bombs in 1945 and was still in the process of being rebuilt. The car reached the Genslar Strasse tram stop, about five kilometres east of Alexanderplatz. Klara's destination, though she didn't know it was a place which had not appeared on any map of Berlin printed in East Germany. It was known, if it was referred to at all, simply as the 'forbidden zone.' The car turned northwards on Genzlar Strasse and drove through a maze of narrow residential streets. Up ahead, Klara could see a high wall covered with warning signs. The Wartburg turned into a street signposted as Freienwalder Strasse and quickly came to a stop sign and a checkpoint manned by armed guards of the Ministry of State Security. Steel barriers blocked any further movement along the street. They had reached the main entrance to the forbidden zone. The guards recognised Klara's taciturn driver and waved him through with barely a glance at the passenger in the back seat. The car went through the metal gate, passing over a cobblestoned road.

The Hohenschönhausen interrogation centre was part of a bigger complex which included a prison and a specialist labour camp. As the car came to a stop, a uniformed officer, a man about Klara's own age, opened the door to let her out. 'I am Lieutenant Winkler,' he said curtly, 'follow me please.' They moved briskly into an administrative building of some kind. The young officer walked so quickly, Klara had difficulty keeping up. Once again not a word was spoken. They passed through a maze of corridors and climbed what seemed to Klara interminable flights of stairs. When they arrived at a carpeted corridor, the officer stopped at a door bearing the name Dr A. Hoffman but no job title, He knocked tentatively. 'Come' boomed a voice from within. The young officer opened the door and nodded at Klara to go in. She thought she detected just a hint of sympathetic support in his eyes, as she stepped past him. He did not follow her in, merely closed the door behind her. Klara stepped into a large corner office, sparsely furnished in modern Scandinavian style. There was a large desk of blond wood in the corner. Sitting behind the desk with his back to the only window was a man writing. He did not look up. Klara stood patiently inside the door, waiting for some acknowledgment of her presence. In front of the desk there was single straight backed chair and an identical one against the wall. In a corner of the room opposite the desk a sleek timber filing cabinet and the only other piece of furniture, a high stool. It was identical Klara thought to those she remembered from her school science lab on which pupils would perch precariously while conducting experiments. Two or three interminable minutes passed before the man looked up. He was heavy set and balding. He wore a green jacket and tie and had a short, dark goatee beard, identical to that of Party Chairman Ulbricht, whose photograph was to be seen on every street and in every public building in the Republic. Although he remained seated, Klara had the impression he was not very tall. He scribbled an initial or a signature on the paper in front of him and looked up again, replacing the cap on a fat fountain pen. 'You may sit Fraülein Hartmann, he said gesturing to the chair in front of the desk.'

She sat demurely on the chair. Hoffman examined her closely almost professionally, like a farmer appraising a horse.

'Yes, you are as pretty as I have been told. Tell me something about yourself, comrade. What is it you do?'

'I work on the assembly line in the Zeiss factory.' Klara answered, certain that the man already knew this and everything else it was possible to know about her.

'You may address me as Dr. Hoffman, comrade Hartmann.' Hoffman said a little sharply, as if irritated that this girl was not suitably in awe of him. 'You were I believe a clever pupil at school but you did not go to university is that so?'

'No I did not, Dr Hoffman. I was informed I would not be accepted.'

'Were you told why?'

'No, but I presumed it was because of my father's views.'

'Which are?'

'I am sorry?'

'What are they, what are you father's views?'

Klara was momentarily flustered. The last thing she wanted was to cause trouble for her father. A wrong word might have dire consequences for him. 'I am not sure. My father has no political views, Dr Hoffman. He is, as no doubt you know, a pastor of the Lutheran Church. I believe his views are entirely religious not political.'

'In our socialist state, comrade, everything is political. Do you think that your exclusion from university and your father's arrest were errors on the part of the security organs of the State?'

'My family were never told the reasons for my father's arrest Dr. Hoffman, so how I could I be expected to answer that question. I have no doubt that the security organs felt justified they were acting in the best interest of the State. I can only say that in my father's case I have never known him to speak of political matters.'

Hoffman smiled thinly at this response, like a school teacher not entirely pleased by a pupil's answer. 'Do you share your father's religious views comrade Hartmann?'

'No I do not.' She said quickly, instantly regretting her reply. Was this a betrayal of her father? Religion had been the only real bone of contention between them, but since her teenage years it had been a serious one and she knew that it was a matter of deep disappointment to her father.'

'So you have a fundamental disagreement with your father's world view?'

'I know him to be a good man and a law abiding citizen. It is not necessary to agree with everything someone else believes in order to recognise that and to respect one's parent.'

'Well said comrade, the family unit is important in a socialist state. But I would like to know, if this Christian philosophy your father espouses is so powerful, how come it had no effect on you, his own daughter, living under the same roof?'

'I do not know Dr. Hoffman, I can only say that after a certain age I was unable to bring myself to believe as my father does but that does not mean....

'I get the point Fraülein your loyalty is commendable there is no need to labour it.' He said sharply and then leaned toward her, his thick neck thrust forward in a combative manner. 'But let us talk about your own political beliefs. Do you believe in our socialist State comrade Hartmann? Are you proud of your homeland and its achievements?'

Klara hesitated for a few seconds before answering. On the train journey from Dresden she had considered that she might be asked this kind of question and had mentally rehearsed an answer.

'Yes Dr Hoffman, I am proud of what we have achieved in the GDR since the defeat of Fascism. We have built a society in which no one goes hungry, everyone gets an education and workers are respected. That is not the case in the West, where the rights of capitalist employers are all that is important.'

Hoffman's eyes narrowed suspiciously. 'Are you simply parroting something you heard someone say or is that a true reflection of your views?'

'I don't believe that one could challenge anything I have said as being untrue. I have benefitted myself from the generosity of our socialist system. I was well educated and I have the honour to work in a prestigious and important industry.'

'Would you not have preferred to have gone to university? You did apply to study history, isn't that correct?'

'I am happy Dr Hoffman to serve the Republic in whatever capacity the State thinks best. I consider my personal preferences to be irrelevant. Frankly, I don't believe that the study of history could be compared with the benefits to the GDR of working of the manufacture of precision instruments with a worldwide reputation.'

Klara noticed that Hoffman appeared to be mollified by this response, but not entirely. 'That is the correct answer comrade but I wonder if it is entirely sincere?'

'I can assure you, Doctor Hoffman, it is my honest opinion. I have no regrets whatsoever about not going to university.'

Without warning Hoffman's conversation changed tack. He leaned back in his chair. 'What would you say Fraülein Hartmann if I told you that the reason you have been brought here today is to be informed that your father has died while in State custody?'

The blood drained from Klara's face. She felt as if her stomach had fallen to the floor. For a moment she was certain that she would fall from the uncomfortable wooden chair. 'Comrade Hartmann.' Hoffman barked. 'I asked you a question.' The violence of his tone had the intended effect of preventing her from fainting.

'Is this true?' Was all she could whisper.

'As I told you, you will address me as Dr Hoffman. I ask the questions here comrade. It is your duty to answer.'

'What is the question?' she said conscious of the tears running down her face and having nothing but her sleeve to wipe them away.

'I will rephrase the question. If it was possible to bring your father back from the dead is there anything you would not do to bring this about?'

'No of course. There is nothing I would not do. Dr Hoffman.'

'Would you betray your country?'

Even in her state of extreme shock and grief Klara knew that there was only one acceptable answer to this question. 'No Dr. Hoffman, I could never do that.'

'Even for your father?'

Her crying turned into a howl of grief. She was unable to stem it to answer the question. Hoffman looked at her with the air of someone with other things on his mind tapping the big fountain pen slowly on the desk, as if he was accustomed to having distraught young women in his office. He put down the pen, leaned back in his chair while waiting patiently for her sobs to subside. When she eventually stopped he reached for the intercom to his right and pressed a button. 'Now Winkler,' he snapped. Within seconds the door opened and the young officer who had escorted Klara earlier appeared. Klara stood up assuming that the interview was terminated and that she was to be escorted out but when the lieutenant entered, he stood back to let another person into the room. A tall, thin, sallow faced man in his fifties, wearing a shirt and pants of rough gray cloth came through the doorway. He had dark circles under his eyes, and a tightly cut head of graying hair. He walked with slow shuffle. The man stared incredulously at Klara who was wiping the streaks of tears from her face with the palms of her hands. She turned to look at him. 'Please remain seated Fraülein Hartmann. Do not, under any circumstances, make physical contact with the prisoner.' Hoffman said.

Klara's tear stained face brightened into an uncertain smile. 'Papa, is it you?' The man's rheumy eyes looked at her.' Don't you recognise me Klara? Of course it's me.'

CHAPTER 4

August 1961

The prisoner's initial shock turned quickly to a look of concern. 'Klara my dear, Is everything alright? Has something happened to your mother?' He glanced at Hoffman as if seeking an explanation but Hoffman merely observed the scene in front of him as if he was watching a play. Along with his changed physical appearance, Klara noticed that her father's voice was raspy and weak, no longer the same strong calm baritone it had always been.

'No nothing has happened. Mother is fine. Just as she was on the day you left.' There was a code in this brief message because Klara's mother, whose nerves were never strong, had broken down in distress as her husband was taken away almost fourteen months earlier. Before any further conversation was possible, Hoffman interrupted.

'You may sit, prisoner 157.' Klara's father looked at the stool in the far corner of the room. 'Not there,' he shouted. 'Winkler, the chair,' he said, gesturing impatiently to the Lieutenant. Klara winced at Hoffman's tone to her father, a man who was normally used to deference from others and had an innate sense of his own authority. The young officer took the second straight backed chair from against the wall and placed it next to Klara directly in front of Hoffman's desk. There was now about a metre between Klara and her father, whom she had not seen since his arrest. Hoffman indicated with the palm of his hand that the prisoner could sit. As he took his seat, father and daughter simply stared intently at one another as if each of them were memorising every detail of the features of the other.

Hoffman then spoke, looking straight ahead as if he was giving a speech. 'You may regard this opportunity to see each other as a generous humanitarian gesture on the part of the organs of the State', he said. 'It is being granted because of the deterioration in the prisoner's health since his arrest, despite the quality of care he has received. We are not barbarians and we have therefore decided to permit this visit so that the prisoner's family can be assured of his continued welfare while he is in custody. The visit will take no more than ten minutes. The prisoner will then be returned to his cell and the ongoing investigation into his activities will be resumed.' Hoffman then stood revealing a substantial stomach which until then had been concealed below the desk.

'There is to be no physical contact between you of any kind and no objects or papers are to be passed between you. You will both be thoroughly searched afterwards and the severest consequences will follow, if you disregard my instructions. You have ten minutes, no more.'

For a portly man Hoffman moved with surprising agility towards the door, which was opened for him deftly by Winkler and they both left the room. Klara felt as if she was in a dream. A minute before she thought he was dead, now she was sitting in a room alone with her father. Just doing that, knowing he was alive, was a blissful relief to her. She did not feel that any conversation was necessary. Even in her distressed state she was happy just to look at him. Her father pointed at the phone on Hoffmann's desk and cupped his hand to his ear, indicating that the room was bugged. Klara nodded her understanding. Then he spoke, more rapidly than he normally did and she realised he was trying to pack as much as he could into the short time they had together.

'You look wonderful Klara as always, and you say your mother is well?'

'Yes, she is, as well as can be expected in the circumstances. Of course she is worried about you.'

'Tell her not to worry about me. I am fine. Please Klara do not describe my appearance to her.'

'Are you very ill Papa?'

'I have had a slight illness but it may be past now. I am feeling perfectly alright.'

'What kind of illness?'

'They say it's pleurisy, but it's just a bad cough really. I am already on the mend. As you can hear my breathing is almost normal, so nothing to worry about. And what of Anni, how is she?'

'She was on the western side, staying with a friend on the day the wall, eh the anti-fascist barrier was put up and she has remained there. We have heard nothing from her for two weeks but she has many friends on that side of the city, so she is probably alright. Do you know about the wall?'

'Yes, they don't tell us much here but they did tell us of that great socialist triumph. Klara,' he said glancing once more in the direction of the telephone. Lowering his voice to a whisper, he leaned towards her, 'they are going to ask you to do something for them in exchange for better treatment for me. Don't do it, whatever they ask.'

'What do they want me to do?' She whispered.

'I do not know but they are not letting us meet because of any humanitarian scruples. Whatever they ask of you cannot possibly be good for your immortal soul.' They looked into each other's eyes. It was this kind of religious talk that was always a barrier between them, the source of many of their arguments. She had not changed her views but when Klara looked into her father's sad eyes now, she felt ashamed of all of the angry words that had ever passed between them. 'Why don't they let you go Papa? What are you charged with?'

'They are preparing a case on the basis of a charge of slandering the State. It's to do with the Monday evening sermons I gave at St Magdalena's. Our government believes they were politically motivated, but as you know I have no interest in political matters.' His eyes glanced again in the direction of the phone. He was letting her know that he was speaking for the listener's benefit. 'You know I was a prisoner of the Nazis when you were a child Klara. I was in Flossenburg for almost a year with Pastor Bonhoeffer.' Klara nodded her acknowledgement, a story she and her family had heard many times before.

'Bonhoeffer was the finest man I ever knew. I saw him go to his death with a serenity I will never forget, praying and singing hymns with those who shared his cell. Even the Nazi guards were impressed. I was opposed to the fascists Klara, so how could I oppose a government like ours, which is the sworn enemy of fascism.'

Klara almost smiled at this as she remembered her father's most repeated saying in the privacy of their home. *'Not even a sliver of rice paper separates the methods of those who run our socialist state from those of the Nazi thugs'.* But she went on with the charade.

'Exactly Papa, you could not be an enemy of the GDR and an enemy of fascism, so what is the point of keeping you here?'

Before her father could answer he was overcome by a loud hacking cough which made his frail body shake and convulse uncontrollably. Klara could clearly see that her father was very ill, despite what he said just a few seconds earlier. As the coughing spasm came to an end, he put his hand to his mouth and spat a quantity of bloody phlegm into his palm. Klara was horrified as she watched him. There was nothing in the sterile room to use to wipe away the bloody mucus. Her father, embarrassed by the coughing, wiped the palm of his hand on the rough material of his trousers. Klara pulled her chair closer to his, reached across and rubbed her hand soothingly up and down her father's upper arm.

'Papa you are not well', she said. 'We will have to get you out of here.' Her soothing gesture seemed to have the desired effect on her father. His breathing became steadier. He looked out the window at the blue sky.

'I have been in this room before, but I have never sat here and seen so much of the outside world. They make those being questioned sit on that stool over there against the wall. You are not permitted to let your feet touch the floor. It's hard to remain balanced on it if you have to sit for hours. It is placed in a way that provides just a tiny view of sky through this window, which is meant to tantalise us and encourage us to answer questions.'

A disturbing thought occurred to Klara.' Papa, are you saying there is no window in the place you are kept?'

Her father looked at her, regretting saying what he had just said.

'It is all the more helpful as an aid to prayer, even the rooms of nuns are called cells.' he said a little unconvincingly. The pitiful look in her father's eyes gave Klara a brief insight into the real conditions in which he must live. She was certain, though he was only 56 years old, that he would not live much longer if he stayed in this place or anywhere like it.

'Why are they doing this to you Papa? What is the point of it all?'

'What they do to me is of no consequence Klara. But they have brought you here for a reason.' He leaned over to her, placed his hand on her shoulders and whispered in her ear. 'Whatever they ask of you do not do it. No matter what the inducement, please do not do it Klara.'

Before he had time to remove his hand from his daughter's shoulder, the door was thrown open and Lieutenant Winkler came into the room. His eyes widened in surprise when he saw the prisoner and his visitor, in what he took to be an embrace. 'Stand please', he snapped loudly with one eye nervously on the corridor, no doubt anticipating Hoffman's return. Klara stood, but she was shocked to notice that her father stood with difficulty, both hands by his side in military fashion. There was something about Winkler's nervousness and her own confidence in the effect that her beauty often had on men that emboldened her.

'May I say good bye to my father Lieutenant?' She asked. Winkler's eyes darted nervously from the hallway to Klara and back again. 'Quickly', he whispered. Klara's father embraced and kissed his daughter tenderly and held her close to him. 'It has been so good to see you,' he said, 'you don't realise how good. Give my love to Mother and to Anni.'

'I won't rest till you are free Papa.' She said, feeling stupid and melodramatic as she said it. What could she do?

They could hear approaching footsteps in the corridor. 'Stand to attention prisoner 157'. Winkler suddenly shouted. Hoffman came in, perspiring in the summer heat, wiping his brow with a large red handkerchief. 'Take the prisoner back, Winkler.' Klara's father turned to his daughter.

'Don't forget Klara, Romans Chapter 12 Verse 21. Let that be your guide.'

Winkler took Pastor Hartmann by the arm and escorted him out. When they had gone Hoffman, stared intently at Klara, closed the door and took his seat once more behind the desk.

'What was that piece of religious mumbo jumbo your father was spouting?'

'I have no idea, my knowledge of the Bible is sadly lacking.' Klara said, still standing in the centre of the room.

'Not sad at all Fraülein, it is a sign of true enlightenment, why waste your time on fairytales?'

'Am I to leave now Dr Hoffman?'

'No Fraülein you are not, at least not just now. Don't worry I will let you out of here in time to catch your train back to Dresden. I have no intention of keeping *you* here as a permanent guest. At least not at the present time.' he smiled at her, a mirthless broad smile which did not reveal his teeth, his eyes crinkling into narrow silts behind his glasses.

'I have come to know your father well. He is not a stupid man despite his penchant for religious fantasy. No doubt he told you that I might have some further matters to discuss with you and no doubt he advised you against entering into dialogue with me. Do you want to help your father in his current predicament or not comrade Hartmann?'

'Of course I do.'

'Good, that, at least, is a start. That and the fact that you do not subscribe to your father's medieval world view, may give us a basis for discussion. There may be a way that you can help your father and help your country at the same time. However, I assure you, you will not be forced to do anything against your will. That is not the socialist way. So, comrade, would you like to hear what I have to say or do you wish to leave now and return to Dresden? It is entirely a matter for you.'

'If I stay how will it help my father?'

Another mirthless smile, 'I think you may be rushing things comrade. We will get to that in due course. But first let us talk about you.' Hoffman paused for a moment and once again appraised Klara with a professional eye, an antique dealer examining a Ming vase. 'Have you ever wondered comrade, how the life of a person fortunate enough to possess physical beauty is so much easier than the lives of others not so fortunate?'

'No, I cannot say I have given the matter much thought.'

'I doubt very much if that is true. I suspect you have given it a lot of thought. I have no doubt that you benefit in a thousand small ways, every day of your life, from the way you look and you know it. The smiles of your colleagues, the favour of your teachers, the welcome your friends give you when you join them, the unspoken patronage of your supervisor at work. It all falls at the feet of the beautiful so effortlessly. Yet the strange thing is, that it is so undeserved, just an accident of birth really, like poor eyesight or bad feet. For example, consider the way you prevailed on Lieutenant Winkler to permit you to embrace your father just now, although I had specifically forbidden it.'

His eyes narrowed again but this time there was no smile. So, he had been listening, Klara thought, probably in the next room as it had taken him only seconds to arrive after her father had kissed her.

'Yes comrade, you are a fortunate woman, but maybe the German Democratic Republic can also benefit from your good fortune, undeserved though it may be. Let us begin then, please, sit down comrade Hartmann, you and I have a great deal to discuss.'

CHAPTER 5

Washington DC

September 1963

I took the five thirty TWA evening flight out of Logan on Labour Day, September second. I brought a paperback for the flight as I usually do, 'Seven Days in May', a bestselling political thriller written by two Washington insiders. It had been on my 'must read' list for about a year. It came highly recommended but I found it difficult to concentrate. The events of the week-end were still spinning round in my head, in the same way the mind can't let go of a college exam or a job interview. After our conversation in the motel car park the day before, Tom Noonan had driven me to the police station in Barnstable village where the two FBI agents were temporarily based. Sergeant Rob Durand followed us in his own car. When we got there Verling and Caulfield were using Rob's cramped office. He showed me in and re-introduced me. I could see that the two agents were getting ready to leave. Rob left me with them. I told them that I worked in the State Department. I'm not sure what I expected but I didn't expect the cold stare and the non committal grunt I got from Verling. His mood had not improved since the motel meeting earlier. Caulfield, clearly the subordinate, maintained an expression as rigid as Teddy Roosevelt's on Mount Rushmore.

They didn't ask me to sit down. I told them what little I knew. I said that some months before I had seen and translated a variety of confidential documents relating to a West German citizen named Elsa Kircherr. I mentioned that the documents indicated that deportation proceedings were being prepared by the Justice Department for this woman. I had returned the material I had translated to the official in Justice who had made the original request and that was it. I had no further dealings with the matter. Deportations are the responsibility of the Justice Department. State got involved because the documentation in relation to the woman was in German and had been provided by the West German Embassy in Washington, along with a background note in German on the woman who had been murdered yesterday on Craigeville beach. I said that there was a file in my office containing an official record of this work and copies of the material translated. Verling, who was packing his briefcase during this exchange, did not even look up as I spoke. To my surprise neither agent made a written note of anything I said. Verling asked just three quick questions. What was my grade? Where exactly in State did I work? And who was my boss? I was a little disconcerted by this. After all, this was not about me. Verling snapped his briefcase shut. With a stiff jerk of his head he indicated to Caulfield that it was time to leave and brushed past me as he headed towards the door, Caulfield followed. Verling opened the door, but before he went out he turned in my direction.

'By the way Mr Flynn, have you ever heard the name Ellen Rometch?'

I told him I had. When I reviewed the Elsa Kircherr papers, a similar collection of documents relating to a woman of that name had also been sent to me for translation from German to English. They also related to a deportation order. He nodded, acknowledging this information but said nothing. Then almost as an afterthought he pointed his index finger at me and spoke in an unmistakeably menacing tone.

'I would advise you not to divulge this information, or any other information you have relating to this case, to anyone else and that includes anyone in law enforcement,' he said, inclining his head to the outer office. 'This is a classified federal matter Mr Flynn and shall remain so. You are a federal employee, so I take it you understand the consequences of a breach of confidentiality?'

'Of course', I answered with a nonchalance I certainly didn't feel.

'I hope you do', Verling said.

The agents left without a thank you or a goodbye, shutting the door, leaving me standing in the room seething with anger. The fifteen minute ride in Tom's car, back to my mother's house in Hyannis, was not pleasant. He naturally wanted to know whatever it was I knew. I told him I couldn't get into it. His annoyance was understandable, particularly as he was a cop and we'd been in this little adventure together from the start. But I wasn't really worried about Tom just then. I was still smarting from the humiliating treatment dished out by Special Agent Verling and his partner. I guessed I was naive to think that the information I had to give would help crack a murder case but I had not expected implied threats or inquiries as to who my boss was. Their dismissive attitude played into my awareness of the growing chip on my shoulder about my lack of progress in the State Department but that was another story. There was something very strange about Saturday's killing quite apart from the fact that it happened at all. Murders were few and far between on the Cape, but since Saturday very few people were talking about this one. It hadn't been mentioned on local Radio or TV. Monday's copy of the Boston Globe, which I bought in Logan, carried a brief account of it on an inside page, saying simply:

"An unnamed Canadian tourist was fatally injured while walking on a beach in Centerville, Cape Cod, where she was spending the weekend. Her husband, who accompanied her on a Labour Day weekend break, is believed to be assisting the authorities. An official investigation into the incident is underway."

The beach where this 'fatal injury' took place was not mentioned. There were no names given, no mention of a shooting or of where in Canada the victim had come from and no further reference to her husband. The implication was that the mysterious husband was somehow connected with the fatality. An identical article appeared in the Labour Day issue of the Cape Cod Standard Times, attributed like the Globe article, to the American Press news agency. That in itself was strange. Labour Day weekend is always a slow news period on the Cape. Every Labour Day edition of the Cape Cod Standard Times I could remember growing up was the same. It invariably carried pictures of the final holiday weekend of the season on the beaches, reports on the level of business over the summer just ending and worries about the prospects for fall tourists and the coming winter. But this year there had been a murder, of all things, an unheard of occurrence, and nothing in the local paper but a news agency report. Where was the local colour piece? How come nobody asked Tom Noonan about it? He was after all a state policeman and a local boy. How come nobody asked for a comment from Barnstable PD or from any of the witnesses on the beach, or from me for that matter? I figured there were three possible explanations. The lack of news coverage might be explained by genuine worries that tourist business would suffer if people got the idea that Cape Cod was a dangerous place to take a vacation. Secondly, it might be a result of lazy journalism. Journalists must look forward to Labour Day weekend just like the rest of us. The third possibility was that the FBI had decided, for reasons which were unclear, to keep a very tight lid on it and that any reports would be kept to an absolute minimum. I was beginning to obsess about the whole thing. I was also trying to figure out if this obsession was justified by the events or if I was just looking for excitement in an otherwise dull life. Either way I knew it was none of my business. If what happened on Craigville on Saturday was connected to my job, no matter how tenuously, it would be unwise delve too deeply into it. Federal government departments are funny that way. They expect their employees to stick strictly to their own areas of responsibility.

Early Monday morning before I left for Boston, I drove down to Main Street. I parked and took a walk down Sea Street, following the route the dead woman Elsa Kircherr must have taken when she was stopped and questioned by a policeman near the yacht club. I had often been down that way when I worked a couple of summers at the yacht club. By turning left on Main Street and heading south on Sea Street anyone can stroll to Hyannis Port, a quaint but exclusive ocean front extension of the town of Hyannis, in just a couple of minutes. Since 1961 hundreds of people come by each week to get a good look at the now famous Kennedy compound. It always tickled us locals that tourists in their thousands drive down Irving Avenue to get a glimpse of tall hedges, closed gates and the rooftops of the Kennedy houses from the street, when there is a far better view on the seaward side. As Sea Street peters out and becomes Ocean Avenue there's a strip of usually deserted beach before you reach a long timber walkway and the stone breakwater in front of the yacht club, they both stretch a couple of hundred yards into the ocean. When I got as far as the timber walkway, almost directly in front of old man Kennedy's house, I spotted a familiar figure coming towards me.

'Hey Joe,' I called. 'How's it going?' Joe Davis was carrying a large canvas bag stuffed with sails. Joe had been in the Brass Rail with us Friday night. He had never really been one of our gang, but I had known him my entire life. Joe was not the academic type and never graduated high school but he was a genius of sorts, able to fix anything that was broken, from a pocket watch to the engine of an oil tanker. He had worked on and off in the yacht club since he was fourteen. He was a talented sailor and owned an old restored twenty eight foot sailing cruiser named *Hasty Pudding*. Joe was always in demand as a reliable crew member on the more competitive sail boats if there was a big race on.

'Hi Jimmy what's goin' on'. He dropped the canvas bag on the wooden deck to give himself a breather. He was wearing shorts and his hair looked strange and unruly in the stiff sea breeze.

'Nothin' much,' I said, 'just out for a stroll. I'm going back to DC this evening. I enjoyed those beers Friday night. It was great to catch up.'

'Me too.' Joe answered. An awkward pause followed as we both realised we didn't have too much to say to each other. Joe broke the silence. 'I hear you and Tom were on Craigville Saturday, when that woman was shot.'

'Yeah, we were, how'd you know?'

The Crockers are members here' he said, nodding in the direction of the yacht club, 'Tom told Linda, she told me.' That figured, Noonan had been trying to impress the beautiful Linda Crocker since we were in grade school. I had no doubt he gave himself the starring role in the story. Joe dragged the huge canvas bag over to a low rock and sat down taking out a pack of cigarettes. 'Smoke Jimmy?'

'No thanks. I've kinda quit.'

'Kinda?'

'Y'know one day at a time, my dad never kicked the habit and you know the rest.' He nodded his understanding and lit one for himself. I sat down on the sand opposite him. 'Actually, Joe that whole thing on Craigville has sort of bothered me. I never saw anything like that before. Someone told me that the woman who was killed had been down here a couple of days ago. You didn't hear anything about that, did you?'

'Not down here no,' He said with unexpected emphasis on the word 'here'.

'Why, did you see her someplace else?'

Joe answered my question with a question and then answered it himself. 'What did she look like Jimmy, the murdered woman? Taller than average, shoulder length blonde hair, perfect figure, nice face, wearing a navy blue sailing jacket?'

'Well, she was dead when I saw her, Joe, so I can't really describe her face or her height exactly, death kind of changes things, but I'd say that's a pretty accurate description. How did you know?' Joe took a drag of his cigarette and stared back out at the ocean without saying a word.

'Joe?' I said somewhat plaintively, trying to get him back on track.

'You know what I do for a living Jimmy. I mean you and me, we've never been best buddies but I like to think we're friends and we did work here together for a couple of summers.'

'Yeah I know. Although I could never do the stuff you could do Joe.'

He shrugged off the compliment. 'I work here at the club, I landscape rich peoples yards, fix their cars in the winter, do a bit of house painting or construction and believe it or not I do alright financially, a lot of cash in the hand if you know what I mean. The IRS is not as all- powerful as folks think.' He said smiling. 'But Jimmy, let's face it I'm a servant, just the help. The only way I survive is by not getting too close to any of 'em. I stay out of their business and they stay out of mine. That way the work keeps coming.'

He looked at me more intently through the haze of his cigarette smoke. "I can tell by the gleam in your eye Jimbo, you're up to something. You didn't just stroll down here to clear your head. And I can also tell you that Joe Davis doesn't want to get involved in it, whatever it is. So yeah, I do have something to say which might satisfy your curiosity and for old time's sake I'll tell you, *just once and only once*.' I don't want any follow ups, or for you to mention to anyone else, who told you what I'm going to tell you, deal?'

'Sure' I said.

'No Jimmy not 'sure', I want more than that. I tell you something and that's it. I don't want to discuss it again, agreed? And I don't want you to mention to anyone else, that I told you what I'm goin' to tell you. Is it a deal?'

'Yes Joe, of course it's a deal. I won't repeat it and no attribution of any sort.'

'I'm not exactly sure what attribution is but I guess it'll do.' He paused, took another deep drag laughed a little and said.

'After all that, I'm not sure I'm giving you very much but here goes. You probably know I work for Josh Meredith sometimes, at the compound. He's the guy who's been doing most of the gardening and handyman stuff for the ambassador since the forties. When he needs an extra pair of hands he calls me. You know there are three houses there right? The ambassador's house, right there, he gestured at the big house, its roof clearly visible from where we sat. 'The President's is further back, not small but it's smaller than his old man's and the RFK house, the Attorney General's, you can see the curved roof over yonder. Friday we were cutting down a tree in the RFK yard, about two in the afternoon. Not a very big tree but too big for old Josh to handle by himself. We had chainsaws and a trailer and we were logging and loading the trailer as we worked. I have a guy in Mashpee who'll buy the cut logs from me.

Anyhow, the main front gate was wide open, ready to drive the truck and trailer out when it was loaded, when suddenly in from Marchant walks this woman, the woman I just described to you, in her blue windbreaker and her stunning blonde hair. She was a looker Jimmy, I can tell you that. Usually there are about two million kids running wild around that house but not that day. They were on the Vineyard or somewhere, actually I think they were horse riding in Osterville. Meredith and me were the only people around and this beauty came through the gate, walked right up to me and asked if the Attorney General was home. I happened to know that none of the family was home so I said no. Then Josh Meredith appeared from behind the trailer and said to her very sternly. 'I'm very sorry Miss, you are not permitted on this property and we have no information on the whereabouts of anyone living here,' like he had learnt it from a prepared script, which maybe he had. Josh gives me an irritated look as he said this, just 'cos I said there was no one home. He's had years of practice keeping nosey parkers away from the place, so I guess he knew better. The woman then asked if the President was home. Before either of us could say anything two Secret Service guys, one in his shirtsleeves, the other wearing a suit, came walking very quickly across the lawn from the ambassador's house. They told the woman that she was on private property, had no business being there and was to leave straight away. Then the woman said to the agent in the suit. 'You know me I think, Mr Banner, I have private business with the President or the Attorney General, I would like to see them please.'

'The guy in the suit, Banner, walked over, took her by the arm and turned her around facing the other way, not roughly but firmly, he escorted her to the open gate. I heard him say. 'M'am you are not an authorised person, if you try to enter this property again you will be placed under arrest.' The agent in shirtsleeves walked beside them, his shoulder holster and gun on display. When they got her off the property they both stood in the gateway with their arms folded across their chests. The woman walked away down Marchant. When she was out of sight they turned back and came towards us. The guy in the shirt, a real hard case said, more to Meredith than to me;'

'Finish up quickly, get out of here and don't ever leave that fucking gate open again.'

'That was it Jimmy, that's all that happened. After being pushed out the front gate, the woman must have gone back to town and come this way down Sea Street to get in. That's probably when the cop stopped her.'

I looked at the empty strip of beach. 'How come there's no cop here now?

'Barnstable PD only put one here when the Prez is around. I heard he's being interviewed by Cronkite at the house on Squaw Island, or maybe he's already gone back to DC. Who knows?'

'That's some story, I said. How did she talk Joe, the woman? Do you think she was American?'

Joe threw away the remains of his cigarette, stood up from the rock he'd been sitting on and began grappling once more with the huge sail bag. I got up from the sand with a bit more difficulty.

'I gotta get back to work Jimmy' Joe said. 'I'm not like you government guys with all the time in the world.' He picked up the sail bag. 'Actually she spoke perfect English from what I heard but yeah, maybe there was just a hint of an accent but not much. I couldn't tell you what kind though.'

'And you say she knew the Secret Service guy?'

'No. I said she thought that the Secret Service guy should know her but he didn't admit that he did. She seemed to know his name though. There's nothing more I can tell you Jim.'

It was only then I took another look at Joe's hair. 'What the hell did you do with your hair Joe, what happened to your regular Elvis DA, you had it Friday night?

'Elvis is over Jimmy, yesterday's news. I can't take any more of the crappy movies he makes and the even crappier music.' He ran his fingers through his thick, newly cut hair with bangs over his forehead. 'This is English style, it's called a Beatle cut. They're a new group, really good plenty of old style rock and roll. They're going to be big, believe me.'

'Beatle? What kind of a name is that and since when can the English do rock and roll? I can't see that happening Joe.'

He heaved the huge canvas sail bag onto his shoulders and walked towards the yacht club. 'Mark my words buddy,' he shouted back. 'You heard it here first. See ya 'round Jimbo.'

The stewardess announced that we were ten minutes from landing at Dulles Airport and asked that all cigarettes be extinguished and seat belts fastened. The crackly airline speaker having roused him, my rumpled neighbour began to wake from his deep sleep. Yawning and rubbing his eyes with alarming vigour he glanced at the book on my lap. 'Seven Days in May' huh? Conspiracy at the highest levels of government. I saw the movie, Kirk Douglas, Burt Lancaster, not bad.'

I had almost forgotten the paperback, not a single word of which I had read since getting on the plane. I nodded at the man, fastened my seat belt and looked out the window at the Washington monument and the long reflecting pool. They were strikingly beautiful in the early evening light. What a weird weekend I thought but it's over now. Tomorrow it's back to the real world.

CHAPTER 6

January 1962

Today was to be the final ten kilometre run for the Adler group, the route as usual, was along the frozen cliff tops on the outskirts of the town of Sassnitz on Rügen Island in the Baltic. For Klara the run became less of a challenge the more she did it. She had come to enjoy it. It gave her time to think without distraction. Not for the first time she thought that the Adler Programme so far hadn't really been so bad, in fact it was a lot better than she had expected. More than once during her training she had found herself being seduced by the political idealism of some of her instructors and the enthusiasm of her fellow trainees. The language of socialism has the power to do that to people with an idealistic streak. Words such as peace, fraternity, dignity, abound in the Communist lexicon and they have power. It is one of its key attractions. There was little doubt that this idealism could be infectious. Occasionally, over the previous four months Klara thought that perhaps the GDR might even have a future as a benevolent democracy.

It was only the thought of her father, in captivity for no crime at all and the not too subtle blackmail of Dr Hoffman that brought her back to earth. The blackmail was clearly working. Her father's situation had improved since she had agreed to his proposal to join the Adler Programme and train for unspecified 'special work' for the Ministry of State Security. In fairness to him, the odius Hoffman had been true to his word. Within a week of her meeting with him in Berlin and her tentative agreement to accept his offer, Klara's mother had been told that her father was receiving treatment for a severe pulmonary infection and liver problems in his 'place of detention.' Only one month later she was told that he had been admitted to the Charité hospital in Berlin for two weeks, where her mother, for the first time since her husband's arrest, was permitted to visit and to talk with him under the eye of a disinterested uniformed guard. Three days before the New Year holiday, Klara's mother was informed that her husband was being transferred to a detention centre for low risk prisoners near Leipzig, where monthly visits would be permitted. Elsterklinik, a former sanatorium was a short train ride from her parents' home in Dresden and retained the characteristics of its original function. Each small improvement in her father's circumstances had the desired effect on Klara and spurred her to work harder.

She had read somewhere that soldiers in the heat of battle do not fight bravely for some ideology or even for their country, but for each other. She could understand that now. She could not deny that a genuine spirit of camaraderie had been created in her small group. There were seventeen trainees remaining from twenty who had begun the course. Three had been summarily removed at different times over the previous four months. It was never explained to the rest of them, the reasons for the expulsions. They occurred at different times without notice. Petra Hiller, an otherwise clever girl, had serious difficulties with the grammar and syntax and the others suspected that was why she had to go.

Only one of the expulsions was obvious to all. That was the joker Metzger, a slightly overweight, clever fellow who was popular with the rest of the group from the outset. Metzger did not hide his lack of respect for the pomposity of certain instructors. He pointedly failed to speak of Chairman Ulbricht and other important national party figures with the proper note of reverence, obligatory for everyone. One Friday evening in the dining hall, within the hearing of Colonel Gerstein, the programme Director, Metzger told a joke about the British Prime Minister MacMillan, who was Khrushchev's guest at his luxurious new villa at Pitsunda on the Black Sea. After Khrushchev had proudly shown his visitor all of the features of his new summer home, the swimming pool, the huge bedrooms looking out to sea and the gold plated dinner service, he asked his British guest what he thought of it all. 'It is most impressive Chairman Khrushchev,' McMillan replied. 'But what will you do if the Communists take over?' Metzger had laughed loudly at his own joke, his listeners, aware of Colonel Gerstein's proximity, grinned uncomfortably. Klara had caught the steely glare of the programme Director at his table across the room eating dinner silently with his equally silent secretary, Frau Delp. The following Monday morning it was announced that Metzger would no longer be part of the Adler Programme. No explanation was given and of course no questions were asked. Metzger was the son of an army general. If this could happen to him for telling a harmless joke, it could happen to anyone.

The privileged background of Klara's classmates, with the singular exception of herself, was a noticeable feature of this specially selected group. As the bond between all of her fellow students strengthened over the weeks and months, it became clear to Klara that most of her fellow trainees' experiences of life were very different from her own. They had lakeside country homes and lived in roomy city apartments. They were confident and casual in conversation about the organs of the state, whereas in Klara's cramped family apartment in Dresden, the unspoken understanding was that the government was not to be trusted and all its agents, from the postman to the policeman, should be avoided, if at all possible. Unlike the majority of the population of the GDR, these young comrades wore fashionable western clothes, owned English and American pop records and seemed to have read books unavailable to the ordinary citizen. As far as Klara could make out, apart from privilege, the most obvious common denominator among the entire class was their facility with languages. Each of them was a fluent English speaker and all had a very good knowledge of Russian. Most of them also knew a third language, Spanish being the most common, the language of Cuba, the newest socialist country and the first, it was hoped, of many more in the western hemisphere.

It was clear to them, from the content of the curriculum, that they were being trained for special tasks abroad but nothing specific was ever said. Klara's training over the past four months had involved the study of history, political science, code breaking and code transmission, the use of one-time pads for sending secret messages, target practice with pistols, interrogation techniques, survival in the wilderness, gymnastics and cross country running. But without fail relentlessly, for two hours every day, there was language training. In Klara's case it was American English. Others in the group specialised in British English which to the surprise of most of them, had many subtle and not so subtle differences from the American. Daniel Eichner, one of the group, was being instructed exclusively in the idiosyncratic way that Australians spoke English.

The cliff top run was almost complete. It would end as usual at a rectangular stone folly closer to Sassnitz known as the *kleine Schloss*. It had been adapted as rudimentary dressing rooms for the runners. Usually, Fischer, the physical education instructor waited for them at the schloss, stopwatch and clipboard in hand but there was no sign of him today, on the final run of them all. Klara could see a group of three or four people waiting up ahead. They wore heavy coats, hats and gloves and were bustling about stamping their feet the way people do when trying to generate heat. She could easily make out Colonel Gerstein in his military greatcoat and cap. The other three, two men and a woman were strangers. Their presence indicated that something out of the ordinary was in the air. When all the runners had reached their destination Gerstein asked them to wait and not to change just yet. With a low collective groan they huddled together for protection against the icy north wind. Gerstein took a piece of paper from his inside pocket and read out three lists of names The first six whose names were called out were told that they were to dress and to accompany party comrade Sundermann, a stern faced woman of about forty wearing a high fur hat, back to the Academy. Why on earth are they doing this here on the freezing seashore? Klara thought. Would it not have been better to let us change first and go back? The second group of six whose names were called were assigned to a portly man who, despite his heavy coat and homburg hat, was visibly shivering. He was referred to as comrade Bluchner.

Klara's name was called as part of the final group of five, along with one other woman, Hedwig Schaeffer, small and bespectacled with dark curly hair, known to everyone as 'Hetty' and three men, Daniel Eichner, Karl Christian and Dietmar Bauer. They were to change and accompany the third person and the youngest and tallest of the three, comrade Korten, who was wearing a well cut coat with an astrakhan collar and a black trilby hat, back to the academy. They all changed quickly and when they emerged from the two canvas protected segregated spaces that passed for dressing rooms, the three groups automatically gathered behind their assigned leader. They marched away towards the temporary academy operating out of a former grand hotel in Sassnitz, less than a kilometre away, Colonel Gerstein in the lead walking alone and each of the three civilians walking in front of their own selected groups, like three biblical shepherds with individual flocks of sheep. Klara thought she was beginning to understand the simplistic psychology of which Gerstein was so fond. This entire ritual on the cliff in the biting wind and the march back to the academy, behind the assigned leader up ahead, was intended to impress upon them that the three group leaders had become the guides and mentors of the group assigned to them. The short march they were now taking would be the beginning of a longer journey and each student was to be in no doubt as to who their particular leader was. First Hoffman in Berlin, then Gerstein and now it seemed clear to her that this man Korten was about to take over the management of the next stage of her strange new life. Standing shivering in the cold she hadn't really taken much notice of the man in the well cut overcoat.

CHAPTER 7

September 1963

I returned to work Tuesday after Labour Day in the same kind of mood I suspected everybody else in America did. It was a beautiful day and while summer was officially over, Washington weather was just coming into its own. The capital's clawing summer mugginess was receding. It was likely to be very pleasant for the next two months. I had very little vacation time left, so fall and winter spread out before me without much to look forward to until Thanksgiving. I shared an office in the State Department with two colleagues, Sylvia Dos Santos, a married woman in her late thirties and a specialist in the Romance languages, Spanish, French, Italian and Portuguese and Victor Chen, who had a comprehensive knowledge of five oriental languages including Korean and Vietnamese. Until a couple of years ago we occupied two rooms in the old Defence Department building. Since the refurbishment of the State Department and the construction of a grand new entrance on C Street, we were now housed with the diplomats and high flyers, while still being treated as below stairs servants. Dean Rusk, our Secretary of State, worked in the same building, in the section of Washington known as Foggy Bottom. But he might as well have worked on Mars for all the contact we had with him. In fact of the three of us, only Victor had ever actually seen Rusk.

Our little unit was called LAU2, an acronym for Linguistic Analysis Unit 2, a misnomer if ever there was one. Day to day work involved very little analysis. We provide translation services for the plethora foreign language documents which emanate from our missions and embassies anywhere in the world and from other government agencies if there is an overseas angle. The material we deal with ranges in importance from routine memos intended for foreign workers employed in US Embassies overseas, to sensitive briefing documents prepared for foreign politicians. For me, the most interesting part of our work was the very thing we got far too little of, that is analysing the true meaning contained in convoluted or complex documents, going beyond mere translation but requiring an assessment of the nuances of the language in question, identifying possible oblique or hidden aspects to whatever was being communicated. Documents of that kind tend to be both sensitive and highly confidential. But for me that made them all the more interesting. I craved that kind of work but it didn't come my way often enough. Victor Chen was given much more of this sort of stuff, because the languages he worked with, particularly Chinese and Japanese, lent themselves to more subtle forms of communication than is usual in the West. On the same corridor was LAU 1, five colleagues, each with an individual office of their own, working in fifteen other languages as well as the ones we dealt with. The LAU 1 people were on a pay grade higher than ours. The Department felt that their analytical work was of greater importance. I tried to convince myself that this didn't bother me. I knew that matronly Miss Sheppard, the senior person in LAU1, who worked in Russian and German, as I did, was a brilliant linguist. But the pay difference niggled at us in LAU2 nonetheless, more and more as time went on.

Of the three of us in the unit I was usually first into work most mornings. The other two had school going kids, which inevitably caused them delays. This morning, I was the one running late. It was nine twenty when I got to work and Sylvia and Victor were at their desks long before me. They looked up and greeted me as I came in but by the time I got to my desk I could tell that something was not quite right. 'You guys are kind of quiet, is there something up?' I asked.

They both looked a little sheepish, Sylvia answered first. 'Jimmy, I got here early this morning, Hector had to be at work earlier than usual today.' She paused as if that was all she had to say, though clearly there was something wrong. Sylvia gave a quick dry cough before she spoke again. 'Vern was here this morning Jimmy, with two other guys, they were going through the stuff in your desk and on it, and searching the filing cabinets behind you.'

'Oh, I see. What kind of guys, somebody from the Department?' I said, not sure what was coming next but I could almost have guessed.

'No Jimmy, not from the Department, policemen type guys. They didn't speak to me except to ask me to step outside while they were doing whatever they were doing. Vern was little embarrassed but he clearly wanted me to leave, so I left. I went to the ladies room, came back, I could hear them, they were still here so I walked up and down outside in the corridor for about five minutes. Then they came out carrying some files and Vern told me I could go back to work. The two guys said nothing more to me. They were only interested in your files Jimmy. They didn't take anything from me or Victor,' she said, reddening a little.

'Which files did they take?' I asked.

'Dunno, I couldn't see. The guy put them in a brown attaché case and literally held it close to his chest.'

'It was all over by the time I got in', Victor said, for no reason at all except to be part of the conversation.

'Was one of the guys a burly fella, about forty, maybe forty five, greying hair, like an ex-marine, the other younger, taller and thinner?' I asked Sylvia.

'Sounds about right, do you know them?'

'Not exactly but I may have bumped into them over the weekend.' They both waited for a fuller explanation from me, but I was in a kind of confused shock, I had no intention of saying anything else for now. In government service in Washington you can sometimes get away with stuff that might get you canned in the private sector but there are two things you cannot do. If you screw up with the taxpayer's money, not necessarily by wasting it but by putting any of it in your own pocket, you are dead in the water. Secondly, if you publicly embarrass the Department or its political bosses, there is no escape. You are either terminated or you have the mark of Cain on you for the rest of your miserable static career. That's why we have the reputation we have. If it's a choice between taking a risk that might result in a screw up or doing nothing, the second option tends to be the road most travelled.

The theory is that people may never remember if you do nothing but if you mess up royally, no one ever forgets. Sylvia and Victor had the sympathetic look of two decent people who were certain I had committed some terrible transgression. I could see that their kindly expressions were tinged with relief that it was me and not them. I would have felt the same in their shoes. The phone on my desk rang before anything else could be said. There was silence in the room, Victor and Sylvia looked at me, trying to read my expression as I picked up and listened. 'OK Vern I said, 'I'll be right there.' I heaved myself out of the chair with an involuntary sigh and headed for the door.

'Be right back,' I said with an attempt at jocularity I certainly did not feel. They both looked at me with expressions that would not have been out of place if I were heading up the steps to the gallows.

Vernon Granville Templeton the third, as he liked to style himself, was the epitome of old school State Department. His particular type used to be commonplace in the Department in the thirties and forties. By now it was not quite extinct but was definitely on the way out. Vern was 58 or 59 years old, from a distinguished family in Savannah Georgia, old money but not too much of it. His southern gentleman persona, which he tried to resurrect every now and then, with a pronounced but temporary southern drawl, had been diluted by spending his college years in northern schools, taking his primary degree from Williams College and a Master's in Politics and Philosophy from Princeton. This was followed by a diplomatic career which showed considerable early promise, with postings to some of the most challenging US missions abroad, including his most often mentioned career highlight, a stint as part of FDR's delegation to the Yalta conference in Crimea in the winter of 1945. Vern, as he was universally, even affectionately, known throughout the Department, appeared at one point in his career to be heading right to the top but somewhere along the way something went wrong. No one knew quite what. His career trajectory spluttered and finally fizzled out, to the point where he was on a seemingly permanent home posting with a ragbag of unconnected administrative responsibilities. He was popular with those who worked for him because most of us rarely saw him. Vern was very much hands off, weeks would go by without any significant contact with him.

A summons from him was a rarity and therefore all the more worrying. I pressed the button for the elevator to Vern's palatial office two floors above our own rabbit hutch. As I stepped into the empty elevator and watched the doors close, my knees were trembling involuntarily. Why was I worried, what was I feeling guilty about? I had done nothing wrong. Then again I had never heard of a colleague who had his desk searched by the FBI before. Whatever my emotional state, I was primarily irritated with myself for being such a chicken about it all.

Vern's large office, to which he was not strictly speaking entitled by virtue of his grade, was intended as a reflection of what he liked to think of as his patrician background. It was long, narrow and wood panelled, with eighteenth century English fox hunting scenes on the walls between the spaces left by two large glass fronted bookcases. The room had a long Persian rug partially covering a parquet floor and a brightly polished oval mahogany conference table surrounded by what Vern always referred to as 'Queen Anne' chairs. I had never sat at the conference table nor had anyone in the Department ever seen anyone, including Vern himself, use it for the purpose for which it was intended. But we were somehow aware that it was one of his treasured possessions and wild horses would not have succeeded in separating him from it. 'Come in Jimmy,' he called out in response to my knock. He was sitting at his ornate rosewood desk which would not have been out of place in the oval office, reading a memorandum, in a distracted way that indicated he was not reading at all. He wore his usual light beige summer suit, blue shirt and a green and salmon pink bow tie, an affectation we were all familiar with, indicating his membership of London's Garrick Club. Vern, like a lot of the old guard at State was a keen Anglophile. He had done a stint during the war at our embassy in London, the Court of St James, as he insisted on calling it. He liked to flaunt his knowledge of British history and its arcane institutions at every possible opportunity. As I approached the desk I could see that there was a tightening about his mouth and frown lines on his brow, a contrast to his usual air of insouciance. It was one of Vern's many affectations that he normally behaved like someone who believes that nothing in the world of work or international affairs is really important. Wine and art, literature and most of all classical music, were matters to be passionate about, but a crisis at work, in politics or on the world stage, even the Cuban missile standoff of just a year ago, which had the world on edge for two weeks, was dismissed as the 'merest storm in a diplomatic teacup.'

'Sit.' He said, indicating one of the two leather wing chairs that faced his desk. He placed the sheaf of papers he had been pretending to read in front of him in a neat pile. I could see now that it was a copy of the President's speech on world peace given in June at the American University here in Washington. The speech had been circulated to all staff in the Department within days of its delivery. As a keynote speech on the importance of avoiding a nuclear confrontation between east and west and the need for us all on this small planet to co-exist peacefully, it got plenty of press coverage at the time. Not all of it positive. Reading it now in September could hardly have been a matter of urgency for Vern. As usual, there were no other papers at all on his desk. He was strictly a clean desk man, a one task at a time sort of guy. I sat down and waited to hear what he had to say, I didn't have to wait long.

'I hope you had a pleasant Labour Day weekend Jimmy.' He said and then without waiting for a response. 'No doubt the departmental bush telegraph has informed you that we had visitors to your office this morning' he said, looking at me intently and raising his eyebrows by way of a facial question mark.

'Yes,' I said. 'I was told some files had been removed. I haven't had a chance to see which ones.'

He chuckled without a trace of amusement. 'Oh, I don't think you need to be Sam Spade to figure out which files, Jimmy. I believe you are already acquainted with Special Agent in Charge Verling and his slow witted pal, Agent Caulfield. In case you're in any doubt, it was they, not I, who rifled through your desk and filing cabinets. As you know I would never stoop to such methods, I can only apologise for their loutish behaviour. I received a call from Verling at home last night. I must admit I didn't care for his tone. He told me something of your adventures over the weekend and said it was essential to get access to your papers immediately. He actually proposed coming here to the Department, right there and then. It was 11.35 pm. I quickly disabused him of that notion, I'm usually tucked up by ten thirty, so Verling reluctantly agreed to a Gestapo style early morning raid instead.'

'I suppose he told you which files he was looking for and why.' I said.

'Well, he told me which files but not why', Vern said narrowing his eyes just a tad, 'the files relating to Miss Rometch and Miss Kircherr. I take it Jimmy you don't have any other documents relating to either of these flaxen haired maidens about the place, do you?'

'No I don't. Actually only one of them was flaxen haired. Rometch is a brunette. Kircherr is, or was, blonde.'

'No need to split hairs Jimmy,' Vern said, smiling at his own little joke.

'As I said I haven't yet checked what they took away but if they have the files relating to both of these women, then they've already got everything we had. There are no loose papers or anything like that, nothing that wasn't on file. What I don't understand though, is that the stuff we keep on file downstairs are just copies of the originals we got from Justice in the first place. The Bureau can get all the stuff they need from their own colleagues in Justice. And anyway, we only get the foreign language documents, whatever needs to be translated. Their own files must be far more comprehensive.'

Vern had been leaning forward with his elbows on the desk idly tidying the sheaves of paper comprising the President's speech into a perfectly ordered pile. At this point he picked up the only other item on his desk, a pearl handled letter opener. He leaned back in his chair and began examine the blade as if he had never laid eyes on it before. 'Tell me a little about your weekend Jimmy, I understand it was quite eventful. By the way, you never mentioned you were a neighbour of our esteemed Commander in Chief. I always assumed you were from Boston.'

'Hardly a neighbour Vern, my parents' house is half a mile away from his and as you might imagine it's a lot more modest.'

'Have you met him?'

'No. I've seen him around over the years but I never spoke to him.'

Vern was now testing the sharpness of the pointed blade of the letter opener with the tip of his index finger. 'Actually I have,' he said swinging his chair around and indicating with the blade of the letter opener, one of the photographs on the wall behind him. Every Washington office of anyone of status has a gallery of photos, usually taking up an entire wall. The photographs invariably show pictures of the occupant of the office taken with the celebrated, the famous or the powerful. Vern's was no exception, he indicated a picture of himself sitting at a dinner table with a younger and thinner John Kennedy and a third man, all three of them in black tie and tux. 'That was taken in '58 at Joe Alsop's place in Georgetown, just a stone's throw from my own, as I'm sure you know. That's Joe there with us. Joe is a good friend of the Prez and a very old friend of mine. The very best political gossip in Washington is to be heard at Joe's little soirees and as you may know, Jack the lad loves gossip.'

'No,' I said. 'I didn't know that.'

Vern swung his chair back to face me again and looked at me with an amused mixture of pity and condescension. 'The trouble with you Irish, Jimmy, if you don't mind my saying so, is that, because you think of our supreme leader as one of your own, you idolise him to such an extent that you consider him saintly rather than human. Take it from me, he is all too human and believe me, the milieu at Joe Alsop's is far more to his liking than any sawdust on the floor bar in Boston's North End, where he first cut his political teeth.'

I made no reply but I realized that I was mildly offended by Vern's tone which of course only confirmed the point he was making. If I was honest I did think, just like my father did, that Kennedy was first and foremost our guy. Who was Vernon Templeton of Savannah Georgia, to pass judgement? My eye was caught by one of the other pictures on the wall behind him showing a group of four men wearing heavy woollen overcoats. Three of them were also wearing hats, except for a much younger and smiling Vern still easily recognizable despite a full head of curly hair, now considerably diminished. 'Is that you with Molotov, the former Russian Prime Minister?'

Vern glanced at the picture behind him clearly pleased with the observation. 'Yes, well spotted, that's me, Yalta, February 1945. The picture was taken outside the Livadia Palace in the Crimea, where President Roosevelt was billeted during the conference. Do you recognise anyone else in the picture?'

I looked more carefully. 'The shorter man with the goatee looks like

Maisky, the Soviet ambassador to Britain in the thirties. The taller man also looks familiar but I can't put a name on him.'

Vern's face broke into a broad grin. 'Well done Jimmy, I didn't realise you were so well informed about the Russian leadership. Not many people, even around here, would have recognised Maisky. Yes, Molotov, me and Ivan Maisky, he was a special adviser to Stalin and Molotov at the conference because of his insider knowledge of British politics. The tall man on the right, who looks familiar to you, is the famous, or perhaps infamous, Alger Hiss, once the Department's supreme high flyer. The Department lost one of its best and brightest when they lost Hiss.'

'Did you know him well?'

Vern swivelled his chair back to face me again, for a split second I thought he looked at me with something like annoyance. Before I could decide whether this was my imagination or not his expression reverted to its usual affability.

'Not really no.' He said. 'A couple of month's preparation for Yalta and the conference itself was the only time I ever worked with him. I haven't set eyes on him since he left State in 1950. But in his day he was very impressive. He had an immense capacity for work and a brilliant intellect.'

'Do you think there was anything to the accusations of spying?'

'It's possible but I think it unlikely. He was never convicted of spying or of anything else. So if they had anything on him you'd think tail gunner Joe McCarthy, or someone like him, would have nailed him. I can't say I ever noticed any Soviet bias in the advice he gave to FDR or to Stettinius, our Secretary of State at the time. Stettinius was new to the job at Yalta, he depended, pathetically in my view, on Hiss's advice and experience. And mine too of course.'

'Yalta, the Riviera of Hades.' I said.

'Yes that was Churchill's graphic description and he wasn't wrong. Conditions there left a lot to be desired. But it was certainly one of the most stimulating experiences of my career.' Vern said wistfully.

'Weren't Hoover and Nixon convinced of Hiss's guilt?' I asked.

'Yes they were, in the late forties.' Vern answered with another chuckle.

'That oddest of odd couples, it's hard to tell which of those two self styled American patriots is more paranoid. Nixon was trying to make it as a politician in California at the time and he needed a *cause celebre* of national importance to latch onto, the Hiss case fit the bill perfectly. As for Edgar, he thinks that every organisation in America, from the Boy Scouts to the Daughters of the American Revolution, is riddled with commies. He prefers the Bureau to spend its time on that kind of thing than, God forbid, grapple with real criminals.'

Mention of the FBI brought my thoughts uncomfortably back to the morning's events and it seemed that Vern too was jolted back to reality.

'Speaking of the Bureau, Jimmy, he said with a sudden note of urgency, there is a strong possibility, even a probability, that we, the privileged denizens of Foggy Bottom, will hear nothing further from our visitors. They have, as you have assured me, got everything that we ever had on the two women of interest to them. But I want to assure you that if there is any little difficulty arising for you personally or professionally from this sequence of events, then you can rely on me for support, insofar as I can give it.' He looked me straight in the eye and nodded almost imperceptibly as if to confirm his resolve to be of help.

'Thank you Vern, I appreciate that very much. Do *you* foresee any professional difficulties for me in this thing?' I asked, a little more anxiously than I had intended. Vern leaned back once again in his chair and resumed his usual languorous conversational style.

'Not at all, more often than not, with this kind of thing, there is a consensus that certain matters should be consigned to the trash and well and truly buried.'

What exactly did he mean by 'this kind of thing'? I was tempted to ask but Vern didn't pause for breath. 'What I will do Jimmy,' he said, 'is keep you fully informed of any developments I may hear of, anything you need to be concerned about, assuming there are any. I have but one condition.' At this point he paused for effect and looked at me questioningly. I duly obliged. 'What's that?' I asked.

'That you do the same for me of course. If you hear anything further about this matter, either from our two flatfooted G men, or anybody else, you will let me know. Is that fair?'

'Of course.'

'Good. By the way Jimmy, have you ever come across a man called Bobby Baker? He works on the Hill, legislative assistant or something, used to be right hand man and general dogsbody to our boorish Vee Pee, Lyndon, when he was majority leader in the Senate.'

'No, can't say that I have, why?'

'Oh, it doesn't matter,' he said distractedly, suddenly he perked up. 'Well anyway we've all got a lot of work to do, so we had better get to it.' I got up to leave but Vern waved me with a flat hand back to my seat. 'Just one moment Jimmy if you don't mind, I have never liked operating in a vacuum, as you may know. I always need context. Perhaps you would be good enough to give me a blow by blow account, no pun intended, of the events of the weekend, on the Cape, as we now, in deference to our leader, familiarly refer to it. From your own perspective if you would. I should like to know the precise background to this morning's unannounced visit by our Bureau colleagues. Would you do that for me?'

'Sure, you mean right now?'

'Why not,' he said, 'no time like the present.' He pushed his chair back put his feet up on his desk, folded his hands on his lap like a man about to take a nap. Smiling to himself he said. 'Go ahead, Jimmy, tell me everything that occurred, omitting no detail no matter how trivial or irrelevant you consider it to be.'

I paused for a moment not sure where to begin. Then I thought of the beautiful young woman in the blue windbreaker brushing by me on Craigville beach just three days ago, and of her dark blood seeping from a small hole in her temple into the sand. I began my story.

CHAPTER 8

May 1962

Klara Hartmann sat in the cramped office she shared with her four fellow trainees, on the top floor of one of East Berlin's most prestigious government buildings. From this vantage point it was easy to see over the wall into the capitalist West and to observe at close quarters the most obvious differences between the two parts of the same city, the gaudy noisy automobile filled West and the shabby rundown seemingly empty East. Looking longingly into the West was not encouraged and could lead to trouble. Klara often took a sneaky look across the frontier to see if she would catch a glimpse of her sister Anni strolling by. It was not unusual to see families divided by the wall waving forlornly to each other across the frontier. It was Saturday morning, a working day in the GDR. The work Klara and her colleagues were currently engaged in was mind numbingly boring. Each of them was engaged checking different aspects of financial records and expenses claims from overseas missions of the GDR, which were mostly situated in fraternal socialist states. The work was contrived to give the group something worthwhile to do when formal training or lectures were not being held. It was an irony, not lost on Klara that the GDR, a vaunted bastion of communism, was the beneficiary of this magnificent Nazi edifice. Hermann Goering's former Air Ministry building on the Wilhelmstrasse was almost the only building in central Berlin to survive the allied air raids of World War II and the subsequent street fighting. When the entire centre of the city and a lot more beyond it had been reduced to rubble, this concrete and steel structure had been only slightly damaged. The building was quickly seized upon by the new communist government to house their rapidly growing army of bureaucrats.

Klara's band of seventeen trainees, who had become such firm friends while on Rügen Island, had been broken up on their return to Berlin. Apart from the four people in her group who were assigned to work with her in the old Air Ministry building, she only saw the other women in the group at breakfast and dinner in the shabby government hostel she shared with them in Gneisenau Strasse in the south of the city. Occasionally she caught glimpses of the rest of the others at special lectures given at Stasi premises in Berlin-Pankow or in Karlshorst. Each of the sub-groups were under strict instructions not to discuss their own particular assignments with any of the others and that included Klara's small group of five, comprising two women, Klara herself, the quiet and studious Hedwig Schaeffer and three men, more boys than men, in Klara's view, Daniel, Karl and Dietmar. The five had all been told that they were being assigned to the HVA, the East German foreign Intelligence service and it was confirmed to each of them that they would eventually be given assignments in the West. No other details were provided but they were not complaining. In a country which prohibited foreign travel except to other Communist countries, the prospect of travel to the west was an exciting one for each of them.

The work in the air ministry building, which is how everyone quietly referred to it, was a mixed bag. Klara considered the obligatory study of the works of Marx, Engels and Lenin to be a refined form of torture, just as she had when she had learnt them at school. There were two aspects of the work she really enjoyed. The first was the study of English literature, with a particular emphasis on modern American writing. The books which she was required to read included the works of authors like Steinbeck, F Scott Fitzgerald and Robert Frost, many of them banned in East Germany. But she was also required to read less distinguished writers, such as Raymond Chandler, Dashiell Hammet and Micky Spillane. They wrote about the dark side of American life, where murder, blackmail and deceit were everyday occurrences and everyone, it seemed, carried a gun and used it. Films were also shown to the group, intended to give them grounding in everyday life and speech. It was obvious to Klara that the films had been carefully selected to present a negative image of the country. Their themes were crime, addiction, mental illness and invariably, gangsters and their violent way of life. An exception to this diet of fictional corruption and violence was the showing of a film called 'A Wonderful Life'. It was intended to illustrate the evils of capitalism as practiced by a greedy money lender whose exploitation of people hoping to buy homes for themselves threatened a small community. Klara loved the film. She thought it the most uplifting and positive piece of cinema she had ever seen. She suspected from the glow on their faces following its showing that her four fellow students felt the same but they rarely discussed the ideas behind the movies they had seen apart from the language used or some new word or slang expression employed. Even after watching this charming story, they each kept their feelings about it to themselves.

The training that Klara found most stimulating was the study of American history and politics. This too was presented in a way which showed the capitalist world in a wholly negative light. She had no doubt that the examples of corruption and graft in US politics were true. It was very credibly demonstrated that it was impossible to be elected to high national office in America without a great deal of financial backing. Those who provided such backing always wanted something in return, once their man was elected. An example given in considerable detail by the course director Frau Krause, was that of the current American Vice President, Lyndon Johnson. Johnson had been to Berlin the previous September, following the construction of the wall. His visit was intended to bolster the morale of the people on the capitalist Western side. As a result he was now firmly in the sights of the GDR government for ridicule and exposure. Frau Krause outlined how Johnson, a poor Texas schoolteacher, had risen from obscurity to become a multi-millionaire, the owner of his own TV and radio stations, a vast ranch and the second most powerful person in America, while earning only a modest public service salary. Johnson's boss, the handsome young American President, was not spared this level of scrutiny either. His father was portrayed as a reckless criminal capitalist who had made a great fortune manipulating the stock market, by ignoring the needs of others who were less fortunate and in effect buying the presidency for his son. Klara was certain there was more than a grain of truth in the picture of American life they were given but she was smart enough to read between the lines. Newsreel film of violent anti-segregation marches in the American south, showed streets filled with large shiny automobiles, while private cars in East Berlin and in the GDR as a whole were a rarity. A film of striking western workers, intended to illustrate the chaotic nature of the capitalist world, pointedly contrasted with her homeland, a self styled 'workers paradise', where to go on strike for better pay and conditions would mean a long spell in prison for any worker foolish enough to take part. Overall though, Klara felt that she benefitted greatly by what she studied and each topic studied sharpened her natural critical faculties. It was the make-work intervals to the training that she found tedious.

The biggest change in Klara's life since the arriving back in Berlin from Rügen Island, was her all consuming distraction with thoughts of her assigned mentor Max Korten. Reluctantly she had to admit that the repulsive Dr Hoffman had been right when he spoke to her on her first day of this new life, of the advantages of her physical beauty. Klara had been aware of it from the time she was fourteen. Until then, she had never been thought of as more exceptional than her older sister or any of her contemporaries. As her teenage years progressed she realised she had come to possess some quality that other girls in her circle did not. At first this was flattering to her but has the years passed and her beauty, in the eyes of others seemed to blossom, it became more of a handicap. She had to endure the unwanted attentions of boys and men in whom she had no interest. Her admirers included the handsome but arrogant, over confident athletic types in school as well as shy, artistic boys who anonymously sent her poems that spoke of her beauty in overblown, laughable language and of the agonies of unrequited love. It didn't take long for Klara to realise that her attractiveness to the opposite sex also brought with it jealous and spiteful feelings on the part of many other women and not only girls her own age. Women teachers could be gratuitously dismissive of her academic work when it was clear that her work compared very well with that of her classmates. The same pattern repeated itself when she went to work at the Zeiss plant. Female managers often demanded more of Klara than they did of other workers and they did not try to hide their disdain for what they regarded as her arrogance.

From their first introduction and briefing after they left the cliff top on Rügen Island, on that freezing January day, the familiar signs of interest on Max Korten's part were apparent. The prolonged eye contact, the use of her name more frequently than those of the other four, the offers to clarify any aspect of the training programme she might find difficult. The seemingly casual touch of a hand on her arm or back as they went through a doorway. She had experienced it all before, she knew the unmistakeable signs. The problem for Klara was not that she did not know how to fend off Korten's unwelcome attentions. She welcomed them, and was anxious and excited at the prospect of every encounter with this handsome, debonair man. Max Korten was not a lecturer or an instructor. His job was overall supervision of the programme that Klara and her colleagues were engaged in. Korten obviously had other more important duties because his visits to the group were sporadic and unannounced. He called in on them without warning and left without any indication as to when he might return.

Korten had the air of a man totally at ease with himself and with his position in the HVA. The rigidities of the socialist state and the formality of the defunct, but still discernible Prussian world were not for Max Korten. He wore the clothes of a casual well dressed westerner, moving freely and without a care in a gloomy gray bureaucracy, populated by cautious unsmiling careerists, in identical readymade suits and poor quality Bulgarian shoes. Klara guessed Korten's age to be about thirty five or thirty six, at least ten years older than her. He did not wear a wedding band and never mentioned a wife but that was not surprising, as there had been almost no personal conversation between them. In the brief conversations they had, he left her in no doubt, that he was familiar with her family history including her father's lack of commitment to the socialist cause and his current status as a prisoner of the state. Apart from that depressing topic, Korten was always cheerful and helpful to all five of the group. In order not to appear to favour the obviously beautiful Klara Hartmann, he was particularly attentive and charming to Hedwig Schaeffer, the only other woman of the four. 'Hetty', as she was called by her fellow trainees, was smart enough to see exactly where Korten's true interests lay. Nonetheless she appreciated his thoughtfulness and his courtesy and like every other person who had known Max Korten throughout his life, Hetty liked him for it. As for Klara, for the first time in her life, she had met a man who was different from any other she had known, though she had not known many. This was the first time she had encountered someone whose looks and personality had overwhelmed her. She was irritated by the turmoil he created inside her. She was distracted and unfocussed, her concentration slipping, yet there was nothing she could do about it. She was not in a position to take any initiative. He was her boss, he inhabited a world of which she knew nothing and to which she would never have access. The divisions between them were simply too formidable to overcome.

As the group prepared to leave that Saturday afternoon, Korten arrived, unannounced as always, wearing a silver gray mohair suit and a blue open necked shirt without a tie, a most unconventional form of dress for a government official. He asked the group to join him in the all purpose conference room, used for lectures, for film showings, silent study and reading. They trooped in, concealing their resentment. It was warm and sunny outside. They were all longing to leave and take advantage of the good weather. 'Comrades,' Korten said as he took a single page from his inside pocket, reading it to himself before he spoke.

'I will be brief, I am sure you would all like to get out of here on this beautiful day. You will be happy to hear that we are coming very close to the end of our training period. Very soon, each of you will be given your assignments, which of course you may not, under any circumstance, discuss with one another. Before that I will take each one of you away from your routine duties and from each other for individual assessment. These discussions too must remain confidential and cannot be shared with any of other comrades here, relating as they will to your own particular assignments. The first such briefing will be with.' He paused as he consulted the paper in his hand, comrade Hartmann', He said, not looking in Klara's direction 'And will commence tomorrow, Sunday.' I am afraid my work schedule does not always allow me to take a rest day. I will be at the women's hostel in Gneisenau Strasse at 9.30 in the morning. Please be ready to accompany me, comrade'. Glancing fleetingly at Klara for the first time he said. 'My apologies for cutting into your free time.' He returned the paper to his pocket and addressed all five once more.

'That is all, comrades thank you for your patience, enjoy what remains of the sunshine.' He turned on his heels and was gone. Klara looked at Hetty Schaeffer and shrugged her shoulders as if to say, 'I have no idea what this all about.' The three boys, as she and Hetty always referred to them, had become good friends since they'd been part of the Programme. They laughed excitedly, congratulating each other on the news. 'This means we are close to the end', Daniel Eichner said excitedly to the other two, raising his two fists triumphantly in the air like a footballer who has just scored a winning goal. Klara had been aware for some time that 'the boys' assumed they were in a different and far superior league than their two female colleagues. Whatever the future would bring, they had no doubt that their work would be more important to the Communist cause than anything their two female colleagues would be asked to do. So much for socialist equality.

As usual every evening after work, she and Hetty walked to the U Bahn station, from there they took the train to the hostel at Geneisenau Strasse. The hostel was for female government workers only. The three boys, who always went for a beer together on Saturday evenings, were billeted in a similar establishment, solely for men, some distance away, in Kreuzberg to the north. The walk was pleasant on this summer evening. The streets thronged with families strolling leisurely in the sunshine, many of the children eating Ice cream, their parents smiling at them indulgently, relieved to be finished their weeks work. On evenings like this, it was possible to blot out the shabby rundown appearance of the buildings. The pleasant mood of the passersby was infectious. At such times Klara could very easily convince herself that there was a real future for her socialist homeland. That there was more truth to the slogans displayed on every other public building, than many cynics would care to admit. Hetty too, normally so serious, was uncharacteristically in a frivolous humour. She was excited about the prospect of the training programme coming to an end and of her first foreign assignment. She chatted animatedly as they walked, in a way that Klara had never seen her do before, speculating about possible postings, Paris being her preferred assignment as French was the language in which she excelled. Klara found it hard to concentrate on what her friend was saying, she could not think that far ahead. Since Max Korten had selected her to be the first of the group to be individually assessed, she had felt a knot of anxiety in the pit of her stomach, which even this beautiful evening could not entirely dispel. Tomorrow morning she thought. Why such short notice, why on a Sunday? But mostly she thought about the underlying reasons for this unconventional approach. She knew it was vanity or bigheadedness, or egoism, whatever it might be called, but she could not help wondering whether Korten's sole aim was to have some time alone with her and only with her. Maybe he had contrived the entire individual assessment project just to bring this about.

When they reached the station, she looked at the normally anxious Hetty, walking beside her, still glowing with the prospect of a new life of adventure in the exotic West. Who do you think you are Klara Hartmann? She thought to herself, the centre of the universe, the unattainable one, someone who can make important people concoct intricate plans, just to spend a day in your company? She knew her vanity was laughable. Then another thought which had recurred since she first went to Rügen for training. She presumed she was the only one of the full group of seventeen, all sons and daughters of the elite, who had a father who was regarded as an enemy of the State and was in prison. Why then had she been selected for secret work in the first place? Why did they tolerate her at all? She had not been permitted to attend university because of her father's ideological unreliability. Many people in the GDR who were even mildly critical of the State had found themselves and their family members being allocated menial jobs no one else was willing to do, their children's educational and employment prospects blighted for life. Yet she, the daughter of a perceived 'enemy', was being groomed for special assignment abroad. She had thought about this since her training began but had neither the courage nor the opportunity to question it. Maybe the issue would be raised as part of the appraisal with Korten. When she thought about it, Klara realised that her greatest fear was that she might be removed from the programme. There was nothing she could do about any of it. She had no option but to wait and see what tomorrow would bring.

As usual neither Klara nor Hetty had any plans for Saturday evening. They would read and study English, in Hetty's case French and Klara would take the opportunity of calling her mother this evening instead of Sunday as usual. This was a cumbersome process as Klara's parents did not, like the majority of ordinary East Germans, have a phone of their own. She had to call the apartment of the apartment block warden, Frau Schabovsky, a difficult woman with an antipathy for the Hartmann family, and ask her to fetch her mother. Frau Schabovsky always did this with bad grace and then made no secret of the fact that she listened in to every call that the tenants made. Klara made the call every week without fail, to comfort her mother and to check on the welfare of her father now detained in the sanatorium in Leipzig. She had told herself from the outset that all the work and training she was doing was solely for her father's welfare. But if she was honest with herself, she enjoyed the project for its own sake. Until she had been summoned to Berlin by Dr Hoffman, she thought and worried about her father continuously. But now days, or even weeks passed, without her giving him a thought. This was partly because she knew his circumstances were better but she could not deny that the real reason was she was more and more interested in her own life and her own welfare than his. Concern for her father had receded. The strange adventure she had embarked on was really no longer about anyone else but herself.

CHAPTER 9

June 1962

Max Korten arrived at the women's hostel in Gneisenau Strasse at 9.30 precisely, in a brand new sporty Volvo. A pleasant odour of new leather was apparent as Klara got in. Government cars in the GDR were inevitably unglamorous black Wartburgs. Driving a Mercedes or an Audi built in West Germany, was frowned upon and at the same time deeply envied. In any event few could afford such luxury. Typical of Max Korten, Klara thought, to have a desirable car like this beauty. Klara had been unsure how to dress for the rendezvous with Korten. She did not have many clothes to choose from, so she decided to wear something similar to her normal work clothes, a plain medium length navy dress with a high white collar and a belt at the waist, nylon stockings and flat black shoes. She had worn this outfit many times over the previous three months. She also carried a light gabardine coat, although there was every indication that the day would be warm and sunny. She threw the coat casually onto the back seat of the Volvo and noticed an amused smile on Korten's lips at this gesture of independence. They said a formal 'good morning' to one another as Klara sat in the car. Korten took off at speed, the Berlin streets, at this time on a Sunday morning were empty of people and traffic. They headed south toward the old pre-war ring road. Nothing further was said by either of them for some time. Klara glanced in Korten's direction. He was casually dressed in gray slacks, a navy blue blazer with silver buttons and an open necked check shirt. His slicked back blond hair was held in place by some kind of gel. Once again she observed, he looked like no other East German citizen but exactly like the pictures of fashionable

American executives Klara had seen in advertisements in Life Magazine and the Saturday Evening Post, required reading as part of her training. After five or six minutes, the silence was becoming a little too prolonged for comfort. Was she being tested she thought, perhaps to see if she would show any initiative? She decided to break the silence.

'This is a beautiful car Herr Korten, is it yours?' He smiled a broader smile this time.

'Not exactly, but I have use of it if ever I need it, he said. It's Swedish. A Volvo P 1800. The very latest model and very solidly built. The Swedes say it will last a lifetime.'

'The smell of new leather is very pleasant' she said, feeling foolish at the banality of her remark. 'Surely cars from socialist countries are far superior to these western makes?' she added provocatively.

This time Korten responded more sharply. 'You and I both know that is not true, comrade Hartmann. The best cars in the world are made by our separated countrymen in the Federal Republic, but the French and the Swedes and even the Italians make cars far superior to anything in the socialist bloc. That won't always be the way of course. We will very soon catch up with them and not only in the manufacture of automobiles but in many other areas as well.'

Klara glanced in his direction to see whether he was being cynical or serious but his expression gave nothing away. They continued south, out of the city at considerable speed on the almost empty streets. After a further period of silence Klara asked, 'Is it appropriate for you to tell me where we are going Herr Korten?'

'Yes I think it is. We will soon make a stop for a discussion about your future work for the Foreign Intelligence Directorate and I will tell you as much as I am permitted to, about the prospects for your first proposed assignment outside of the GDR.'

'Is that not something that could just as easily been discussed in Berlin?'

'One of the first things you must learn comrade, is not to question the decisions of your superiors. This is particularly true when it comes to your work in the field. Remember that, it might save your life someday. That is if it is decided that you are suitable for work in the field.'

Klara could feel herself blush at this pointed rebuke but she recovered quickly and decided to continue probing. 'Has it still to be decided then, whether I am a suitable candidate for a foreign posting?'

'Yes. It is still to be decided. In the case of the other four in your group the decision has already been made. But you are something of a special case. Frankly there are still concerns in high places about your reliability, because of your family background.'

She stared straight ahead, shaken by this answer and surprised that Korten had put it to her with such bluntness. The other four would be assigned but she might not. She knew she was at least as good as any of them in completing the tasks they had been given since the beginning of the programme. She knew too, that she was superior linguistically, in both writing and in speech to the other four in her own group. To be rejected for service, she began to realise for the first time, would represent the biggest disappointment of her life. Inwardly she did something she had not done for a long time. She cursed her father and his pious principles, which had caused nothing but heartache for her family. Everything they had ever tried to do, to get a decent apartment, for her sister and herself to go to university, for her mother to get better medical treatment, had always been blocked or refused because of her father's stubborn adherence to outdated beliefs. Klara remembered her childhood, lying in bed, brooding over some insult at school or some petty bureaucratic decision, taken because of her father's religious views. *'Why can't we just be normal like every other family, why does he have to make everything difficult for us?'* Korten's driving became faster as they crossed the poorly maintained Berlin ring road and headed into the open country side. After another lengthy silence, he said. 'Don't look so worried, there is a problem but nothing has been finally decided, you have not been expelled from the programme just yet.'

These were hardly comforting words. The unmistakeable feeling in the pit of her stomach was that a great opportunity was slipping away from her, that she would be left behind, while Hetty and the 'boys' went on to a life of adventure. A return to the Zeiss factory for her was probably the most likely outcome, if she was lucky. With a voice inside her saying *'what is there to lose?'* she spoke to Korten in a sharper tone than she intended. 'How long will today's exercise take Herr Korten, at what time will we return to Berlin?'

He glanced at her with an expression of amused surprise. As you can see, we'll soon arrive at our first port of call. We are going to Spreewald. Have you been there before?'

'No I have not. Of course I have heard of it.'

'It's rather a unique place, very beautiful. I have access to a *Laube* there. We will stop, have a cup of coffee and I will ask you some questions about the programme, about your attitudes to it and to your tutors and colleagues also. It's an important part of the process. All of the trainees will go through the same procedure, so you must be not think there is anything special about it, as far as you're concerned. Be as frank and truthful as you can because I will ask each of the others to do the same.'

Korten turned the car off the main road and drove through a rough sandy track with the wide river Spree on the left side and dense pine woods to the right. Within minutes they arrived at what looked like a small village in a large clearing in the woods. Korten parked the Volvo alongside six or seven other far less glamorous cars, in an orderly line, their front fenders facing a low stone wall and a row of stables, with half doors wide open, rotting on rusty hinges. At each side of the small cobble stoned village square and along the river bank was a settlement of *Lauben,* little wooden houses of a variety of shapes and sizes, set in their own small plots of land. The village itself, such as it was, consisted of a small general store closed on this Sunday, a beer garden without customers, containing a shuttered timber structure, a cluster of picnic tables surrounding it and a small patch of grass with children's swings and a wooden carousel. The only other substantial structure in the place was the ruin of a tiny nineteenth century Lutheran church, its surroundings overgrown with grass and weeds, its rotting wooden front door was firmly shut and most of the roof tiles missing. Close by was another single story building, also missing a roof, which had been a post office, the faded logo of the Prussian postal service, still visible. Klara looked at the remains of the church. Its ruined condition a sad reminder of her father's outdated beliefs. She put the thought out of her mind. 'What is this place?' she asked Korten.

'It's called Muggledorf, or it once was. It was an old mail coach carriage stop, before the railways got going in this part of the world. The track along the river used to be a main road at one time. The land was owned by some aristocratic family, who ran like hell when the Russians came in '45. It was taken over by the state after the war, follow me. We don't have far to go.'

He led her away from the ruined village along a sandy track between two rows of little houses. Some were merely garden huts and others more elaborate timber houses, painted in bright colours. People were permitted to be creative and individualistic in this environment, in a way that was not possible in other areas of life in the GDR. The buying and selling of these little houses and their tiny plots of land by their owners was tolerated if people had been granted them and had done something to enhance what they had been given. Each small dwelling had an identical space around it, which in some cases was being used to grow vegetables, in others the owners had laid smooth green lawns and created colourful flower gardens in the English country garden style. Klara trailed along the track in Korten's wake she could see people making most of the sunny morning, working or sleeping in their little private paradise. The noise of children playing or the preparation of Sunday lunch could be heard coming from open windows.

'All of the old estate is now state forest but this section has been allocated to people as *Lauben*.' Korten said. 'A very popular government initiative I might add.'

'Yes, said Klara without thinking, 'if you were well connected enough to be granted an allotment.'

'Ah Fraülein Hartmann, do I detect a note of criticism of our socialist democracy?' Korten said, seemingly amused by her slip up. Klara realised her error but before she could reply, he added 'Here we are, this is the place.' They had arrived at a very nicely constructed single story timber house, newly painted in a muted shade of green as if to camouflage it in the surrounding forest. It was on the left side of the lane, so the front of the house would look out over the narrow road they had just driven in on and over the water of the Spree itself. The entrance to the property was through a small gate in a flimsy green picket fence, intended for decoration more than security. The word 'Vogelsang' was etched into the timber of the gate. Korten lifted a flower pot beside the front door and withdrew a single large metal key.

'Birdsong' Klara said. 'What a nice name for a beautiful little house.'

Korten did not reply as he opened the door. 'Come through,' he said, 'make yourself at home, take a look around if you like. I will make some coffee and then we can get to work.' She did just that and was enchanted by the spotless clean, pleasantly furnished space. The little house had two bedrooms a bathroom and a single larger room which combined the functions of a kitchen a living room and a dining room. Klara sat on one of the four straight backed plain dining chairs, as she had guessed the living room window had a view of the water. The small size of the house and the homely surroundings increased her awareness of the intimacy of the situation she was in. Over the previous months she had occasionally day dreamed what it would be like to be alone with this intriguing man. Now that she was, she could feel her levels of stress increase perceptibly. Korten moved about the room with the agility and ease with which he seemed to do most things. Throwing his document case on the small dining table he opened front windows, letting a welcome cool breeze from the river dissipate the muggy air in the house. He removed his jacket, placing it carefully over the back of a chair and went over to the stove opening cupboards with the confidence of someone who had been here before and who knew where everything was. 'Coffee,' He said, taking the clean cups from the cupboard. 'There are also some small pastries here we can share.' Pastries, where had they come from? Klara wondered. And milk and sugar which Korten, who had his back to her as he prepared the coffee, had also conjured up. He brought over a tray containing two cups of coffee, a milk jug sugar and a plate of dainty pastries and set them on the table.

'Whose house is this comrade Korten?' It is very nice.'

'Like everything in the GDR it belongs to all of us, I am a socialist comrade Hartmann, I do not believe in private property.' She laughed despite herself.

'Why do you laugh, I suspect you don't believe me.'

'I don't mean to doubt you, but when I ask is this your fancy foreign car? You say no, I merely have the use of it. Is this your beautiful *Laube?* 'I just have the use of it.' For a man who does not believe in possessions, Herr Korten, you are surrounded by some very nice things.'

He gave her a friendly smile, not at all objecting to the personal nature of Klara's remarks. 'Drink your coffee he said, before it gets cold and eat something, we have long day ahead of us.' He said cryptically. She took a sip of the coffee which tasted exceptionally good. Korten continued. 'I suppose I am fortunate enough to have a very interesting job and with it come some interesting tools of the trade. But to me that's all they are, tools of my trade.' He looked at her as if deciding what to say before continuing.

'Klara, before we start our work there is something I wish to say.' Klara felt her face flush and knew she could not control it. He had never before used her first name. 'If you are selected for a work assignment for the HVA and it is my hope that you will be, you and I may have long working relationship. I will in effect be your case officer and your boss.' He stood up from the table and walked to the window, coffee cup in hand, gazing out over the water. 'Therefore I propose that when we are alone that we address each other with the informal *du* and use our first names. I find this increases trust between comrades. As you know there are no such distinctions in the English language and I think that is a great help in eliminating unnecessary barriers.' He turned around and sat once more at the table, smiling slightly as if amused by some private joke.

'So Klara is that acceptable to you? I call you Klara, you call me Max. When we are altogether with the others in the group we can revert to the formal mode of address, agreed?'

'I think I would find that arrangement a little difficult, Herr Korten, not that I have any strong objection,' she added hastily. 'It's just not that easy for me.'

He laughed heartily at her discomfort. 'Don't be so silly. Think of it as something, well something like this little house here, or the green Volvo, a useful aid to our work. Will you do that Klara?'

She hesitated only briefly. 'Yes, yes I will do that.'

'Perhaps you would say yes, Max.' He said picking up the document case from the table and removing a long thin writing pad. He spoke in a kindly almost diffident tone.

She smiled at him. 'Yes Max', she said.

'You see,' he said, taking a pen from the inside pocket of the jacket draped over his chair. 'That wasn't so difficult, now perhaps it is time to go to work.' He wrote the day and date on the top of the first page of the pad, then moved his chair back from the table in a way that would facilitate note taking but also make it difficult for her to read any notes he might make. When he spoke again his tone of voice had changed from one of casual amiability which he had used since they arrived in the cottage, to that of a professional speaking to a colleague. 'Klara I am aware that in 1956 your father applied for a *Laube* near the village of Mittleweg, outside Dresden, stating his wish to build a small hut, to grow vegetables and to share the space with other parishioners of St Magdelena's church. He was turned down.'

'Yes, that is so.'

'I presume that is why you made that remark earlier about only certain privileged people being given an opportunity to obtain a *Laube?*

'Perhaps, I wasn't really aware of why I said it.'

'Klara, in our work you must be careful of everything you say. We cannot afford the luxury of thoughtless remarks. Someday your life, I am not being melodramatic, could depend on saying the wrong thing.'

'How did you know about my father and the *Laube?*'

'Because I know everything there is to know about you and about your family. It is my job to know these things. But don't worry, I have your best interests at heart, if you realise that and work well with me you should not be disappointed. Now let's get down to work.'

He smoothed his thick blonde hair back over his scalp with his fingers, something Klara had noticed him doing before in moments of agitation. The 'work' as Korten referred to it consisted of Korten putting detailed questions to Klara about all aspects of the training programme since it began the previous October. His questions included her assessment of each of the classes and lectures she had taken, the effectiveness of both the physical training, weapons training and academic studies. But the most difficult part of the exercise was Korten's insistence on her specific views of the strengths and weaknesses of the course tutors and of each of her colleagues. Korten questioned her relentlessly about each person. He did not permit any carelessness or casualness in her responses. When she expressed a view about someone's skills or the lack of them, he pursued the question with a rigour that shocked her. He was particularly interested in her opinion of any deficiencies or weaknesses she felt her fellow trainees might possess. When she hesitated or baulked at expanding on her remarks, out of loyalty or decency to her colleagues, he pursued the point without any pretence at politeness. 'What exactly did she mean? Was she saying this person was unsuitable or incompetent? Would she recommend expulsion from the course, yes or no?' Gone was the friendly chatty tone he had adopted earlier. It was, it seemed to her, a hostile interrogation. It lasted almost two hours and Klara felt exhausted and bewildered when it came to an end. Had she said too much? Had she undermined her own colleagues, had she put someone in real danger? Korten seemed to read her mind. As he closed his notebook and returned it to the document case, he said,

'Don't worry too much about all this Klara your answers were good, clear and analytical. Remember that each of your colleagues must go through the same exercise and each one will be required to comment on you, on your strengths and your weaknesses as they see them. And I will be just as tough on them. In any event these notes are exclusively for the Adler Programme and for me. They will not be placed on your personal file. They will help us with the final recommendations as to assignments abroad. He favoured her with a broad smile and held out his hand. Are we still friends Klara?' She took his hand with some reluctance her anger at his earlier hectoring tone had not yet abated. 'Yes,' she said without enthusiasm 'still friends.' He held onto her hand just a little longer. 'I think you meant to say, 'still friends Max.' With great difficulty she answered 'Yes Max, still friends,' then to minimise her embarrassment she asked. 'What do we do now?'

'Now, now we go on a little trip South, through Saxony.'

He stood up from the table and put his jacket on. 'Let's get going, we have long drive ahead of us. I have heard enough about you for one day Klara, as we drive I will tell you a little about myself. I am sure you have been curious about me.'

She ignored this egotistical remark. 'What about the cups and the plates,' she asked.

'Don't worry about them, someone will come and look after all of that. We have more important things to do, come.'

CHAPTER 10

September 1963

My interview, if that's what you could call it, Tuesday after Labour Day with Vernon Templeton, was the final official word I heard about the events of Elsa Kircherr's last weekend. I lived in a little suburban town called Garrett Park, Maryland, about a twenty five minute suburban train ride from DC and a little longer, if I drove my white Dodge Dart to work, which I sometimes did. I shared the house with two other guys, both younger than me. Brad Toland, a post graduate political science student at George Washington University and Steve McKinnon, who was a law graduate from Butte Montana working as an unpaid intern in the office of majority leader, Senator Mike Mansfield from Steve's home state, while he prepared for his State Bar exams. For different reasons, neither of my two roommates was around that week so Sunday evening I had the place to myself. I had spent the afternoon walking in Rock Creek Park with Shelly Rogan, a former girlfriend I still met from time to time.

I had met Brad Toland, whose parents owned the Garret Park house, when I first came to DC and joined a thrown together basketball team made up mostly of government employees and enthusiastic college students, not good enough to play for their own colleges. Our team is called 'the Nebraskan Wheelers' for reasons no one can now remember. I think the name has something to do with covered wagons heading west. Steve came to the house just a few months ago, and also joined the 'Wheelers'. He'd been sharing the house with us for the summer and was planning to stay only until he took his bar exam in December. Garrett Park wasn't particularly convenient for any of us, but the house was spacious for just three people, well furnished and relatively inexpensive. Brad, who was studying for a PhD in George Washington, was an undemanding landlord. The big drawback was that Garret Park wasn't in the city. Rents were much higher in DC, but it was the only place to be, in a town that thrived on political gossip. Every date with a girl or a night out in Washington ended much too early with the same old refrain. 'I've got to go, gotta catch my train'. I had already decided to move back to the city as soon as somewhere suitable came up and I could manage the rent.

That night, I was lounging on the couch reading the Post's Sunday sports section and half watching an episode of 'The Thin Man', featuring a couple of glamorous Park Avenue sleuths with a cute dog. No more unlikely a combination really than most other fictional detectives. Earlier that day southern segregationists had planted a bomb in a Black Baptist church in Alabama and four children had been killed. The incident cast a gloomy shadow over the entire day. The anger I felt when I heard the news stayed with me. I found it hard to concentrate on anything very much. Steve arrived back from wherever he had been for the past week and called out a loud hello as he came through the door. Unusually for him, he sounded like he had had a couple of drinks. He was carrying a canvas holdall in one hand and a few bottles of beer in a brown paper bag in the other. He dropped the holdall noisily in the hallway, slammed the front door a little too loudly, came in and slouched down beside me. He took a bottle from the paper bag and threw it onto my lap and then took one for himself.

I didn't know Steve McKinnon that well. We were all busy with our own lives and he had only lived in the house since May. But he was normally an easy, orderly housemate and as far as I could tell, underneath a jovial exterior, a fairly serious type of guy. He was also a very good basketball player, six two, to my five nine, fast and really competitive when a game got going. Steve glanced at the screen. 'The Thin Man,' he said stifling a burp or something worse. 'Isn't this a bit light for you Jimmy, Peter Lawford, the presidential brother in law. I doubt if he'd o' got that job if he wasn't connected to who he is.'

'I'm not really watching it.' I said, folding the sports section and putting it away in order to deal with the beer. 'The bomb explosion in Alabama has upset me. I can't shake my mood. Where have you been, back home?'

'No, Chesapeake Bay, would you believe. A guy at work, Joe Michaelson, has a beach house there. Hell of a place, fantastic, his parents' actually, not his own. We had it to ourselves. Four guys, four girls, what a week, a nifty little speedboat too. But I am exhausted, and...' He burped loudly at this point. 'I think I may be suffering from alcoholic poisoning. Don't think I have ever had as much fun. Everybody there works on the Hill, Everybody, except for one of the girls, Melanie, she was eh, somebody's friend. What a week.'

Like some people who have had what my father used to call, 'a skin full', Steve was speaking more to himself than to me. I noticed he had opened his bottle of beer but had not touched it, and looked like he might not have the energy to raise it to his lips. 'What about you Jimmy' he said. Where you bin', you were goin' home weren't you?'

'Yeah, I went for Labour Day weekend but I have been back at work since Tuesday after.'

I didn't get much further, Steve was on a roll. 'You would not believe the scuttlebutt about politicians up there, I have heard over the past week Jimmy, stuff you would never believe. Make you think twice about the nature of the democratic system, I can tell you.'

'Winston Churchill said that democracy was the worst form of Government, apart from all of the others'. I said.

'Oh yeah, well I'm with old Winnie on that one, no question. I was pleased with one thing though, no one had a bad word to say about my guy.'

'Your guy?'

'His Honour, Senator Mike Mansfield, of the great state of Montana, a natural born gentleman if ever there was one and as it happens, a good pal of my old man's, hence my presence here in the nation's capital, Jimmy. In case you ever wondered about that.'

'The Thin Man' had ended to be replaced by 'What's My Line' a favourite show of mine though I didn't always like to admit it. I walked over to the TV and switched it off. I could see Steve's eyelids begin to droop. 'Hey Steve, why don't you come into the kitchen with me, I'll make us both a cup o' coffee and a sandwich? Something happened last week on the Cape. I'd like to tell you about it.'

'Cape Canaveral?'

'Cape Cod. It happened to me, not John Glenn. A sandwich how about it?'

'Sure,' Steve said. 'Food, that'd be great.' He put his arm out to me and I pulled him up off the couch. We left the beers on the coffee table and headed for the kitchen. I gave Steve a large glass of water first, which from personal experience I know is always a help in these circumstances. It didn't take me more than five minutes to make two BLT's on rye, my only culinary speciality, preceded by two large cups of coffee, extra strong in Steve's case. The effect of the water and the coffee succeeded, as I'd hoped, to bring the conversation back to normal. As I made the sandwiches and he drank his coffee, I told Steve the story of the shooting on Craigville beach. I also told him about my brief encounter with the FBI. I decided to leave out the part about me knowing the woman's name and nationality and having dealt with her documentation. I hadn't forgotten Verling or that my work was supposed to be confidential. When the sandwiches were ready, I put one in front of Steve and sat opposite him with the other. I'm not sure why I felt the need to talk but since my chat with Vern the thing had been on my mind every day. I couldn't shut it out. What was I doing, was I just showing off? Maybe the killing was less of a tragedy and more of a dinner party anecdote for me. As we talked, I realised that this was the longest conversation Steve and I had had since he arrived in the house four months ago. By the time I was finished my story, Steve had wolfed down his sandwich and was getting back to his old self.

'So what do you think?' I said.

He picked up his coffee mug and looked at me across the kitchen table. 'Jimmy I'd like to tell you something, with all the sincerity I can muster.'

'Yeah, what?'

'You tell a hell of a story, and may I add, you make a great sandwich.'

I must have looked a little disappointed at his flippancy. 'Hey I'm sorry Jimmy, I don't mean to belittle your story, but it seems, well fantastic, literally fantastic. I mean a shooting on a beach, did this really happen,

Labour Day weekend?'

'Yes it did.'

'Was it on the news?'

'No, I just told you, a tiny article in the Boston Globe and in my local paper, that was it.'

'Has anyone informed the woman's husband or parents?'

'No idea, I presume the FBI has by now. The whole thing seems to be under wraps. Or maybe not, maybe they've arrested someone but if they have they're keeping very quiet about it.'

'Jimmy, any chance of another cup of coffee, that one really hit the spot.'

'Why don't you get it yourself Steve, you seem to be on the mend.' I don't exactly know why I was so snippy with him. I could hardly expect a student and unpaid intern to provide me with any great insights into the 'Murder on Craigville', as I was beginning to call it to myself. 'Sure,' he said, without seemingly noticing my rudeness. He got up, went over to the kitchen counter for the coffee pot. 'You want one?' He asked.

'Why not,' I handed him my cup. 'Steve did you ever hear of a guy working on the Hill, name of Baker, Billy or Bobby, I'm not sure which?'

Steve had his back to me as he poured the coffee. He looked around very quickly as I said this, his expression was a mixture of curiosity and amusement. 'House or Senate?' he said, staring right at me.

'Senate I think. He might have had something to do with LBJ before he became VP.'

Steve came over to the table, two cups in his hands and sat down. He pushed mine over to me. I could see now that he had sobered up and was more focussed. 'Who mentioned Bobby Baker to you Jimmy, in what context exactly?'

I hadn't expected this reaction. 'Nobody mentioned him in any context. My boss, Vernon Templeton, asked me if I heard of Baker. He knows everybody in town. He's the kind of guy who could hear mouse squeak within a five mile radius of Pennsylvania Avenue. He said Baker worked in the Senate and I'm asking you 'cause you're the only one I know who knows anything about the Senate.'

Steve hesitated for a second with the expression of someone who was considering should he say this or should I not. I found myself mentally urging him to continue and he did. Jimmy, you're a public servant right?

'Right.'

'You cannot reveal official secrets to outsiders and you must keep absolutely confidential, anything you hear or learn in the course of your work. Am I right?'

'You know your right Steve, what is it you want to say'.

'What I am about to tell you falls into that category OK? You are not to repeat this to anyone. If he ever found out, Senator Mansfield would have me on the first bus back to Montana and my old man would kill me if I ever embarrassed the Senator. Do you understand?'

'Will you give it a rest Steve? I deal with sensitive material every day of the week. I know how to keep an official secret.'

'You know we interns, unpaid assistants, whatever you want to call us, are the lowest form of life in the Senate. Even the ushers are far more important than us. Actually, now that I think about it, the ushers are far more important than most Senators. Anyway, in the course of my duties, which by the way, are almost a hundred per cent to do with routine, not to say, dull constituency matters in Montana, I came across a note to Senator Mansfield, from Senator Dirksen, that's Everett Dirksen, the Republican minority leader from Illinois. It was a strictly off the record, hand written, personal note, unusual in itself. Dirksen was asking to meet Mike, to discuss a sensitive matter. He wanted to talk about a colleague, Senator Williams of Deleware. Williams is a bit of a stuffed shirt but straight as an arrow. Where was I?'

'Mansfield, handwritten note,' I said. 'Go ahead'.

'Yeah, well because it was handwritten it got into my pile of mail by mistake, a lot of the stuff I deal with is hand written by people back home. You can imagine the kind of thing, parents looking for college scholarships for their kids, or to get them into West Point, maybe overturning planning refusals for house building, that sort of basic everyday stuff.' Steve stopped for a moment as if considering for the first time the banality of his intern duties.

'The note Steve,' I said. 'What did it say?'

'Well'. He said moistening his lower lip with his tongue, looking as if he was one of those guys about to dive of that cliff in Acapulco. 'It was about this guy you just mentioned, Bobby Baker. From what I could tell, a serious issue has come up in which Bobby Baker features prominently. It relates to two things, underhanded financial dealings and something called the Quorum Club, operating out of the Carroll Hotel not far from the Capitol building. From what I hear this so called club is an informal, after hours place for Senators, Congressmen and others to get together for R and R, if you know what I mean.' Steve gave me a knowing stare. I looked at him quizzically, unsure what he was trying to say.

'Drinking, women and I guess a lot more. I don't have to draw you a picture, do I?' He said in an exasperated tone.

'No, I guess you don't. What has Baker got to do with this club?'

Well, the note from Dirksen was basically an invitation for the two Senators to meet, informally to consider what to do about this. It seemed to suggest that Baker runs the operation in the Quorum Club, that he provides the girls, as it were, that he knows what all these guys get up to in private and that he may be financially corrupt. It mentioned an allegation about Baker being on the take from some slot machine company or something and Senator Williams from Delaware is on to him and not too happy about it. But there wasn't any detail on that so I'm not sure what it's all about. Apparently it's the money angle that Williams is particularly interested in.'

'Vern Templeton said Baker was a legislative assistant. This doesn't sound like the kind of thing someone so junior would get into.'

'Actually he's a bit more than that now. That's what's so strange about you mentioning him. We were all talking about him in Chesapeake over the last few days. The guy's a legend on the Hill. Not that I mentioned Dirksen's note or any of this stuff to the people I was with, by the way. But they all know Baker and know quite a lot about him. Originally Baker was, as you said, an invaluable sidekick to LBJ. 'Mr Leader' was how Baker always referred to Johnson. There was no one better in the Senate than Lyndon Johnson when it came to preparing and drafting legislation and most importantly, getting it over the line. Lyndon never actually drafted it of course, he's not that kind of guy, but he was a horse trader *par excellence,* if you follow my French. That's why he was so successful as majority leader and it's also why he has been missed so much since he was kicked upstairs to the VP spot. Although I think he still does a bit of legislative cajoling on the side, even now. The phone rather than the pen is Lyndon's weapon of choice.'

'They say Lyndon finds the VP job pretty frustrating,' I said, trying to sound like someone who was in the know. 'Once he was king of his own domain, now he's playing second fiddle to a handsome, east coast millionaire, who never spent even an hour and a half working on legislation when he was in the Senate, more coffee Steve?'

'No thanks but I think I'll have a cigarette, I've got some in my bag. I'll go get them.' The stuff Steve was telling me was fascinating, but I doubted it had any relevance to my murder mystery. When Vern mentioned Bobby Baker's name to me that Tuesday morning, I thought I noticed a particularly meaningful glint in his eye. It lasted just about a second and a half and then it was gone. But given Vern's reputation as an all knowing Washington gadabout, there had to be something to his question. Steve came back carrying a pack of Camels and an expensive looking silver plated lighter. He sat down and offered me one. At that moment, for the first time in a long while, I had a real yen for a smoke and almost cracked 'Thanks Steve,' I said. 'But I haven't had one since my father died, lung cancer nine months ago. Docs say that smoking was definitely a factor. So I'm trying to quit, or at least giving it a shot.'

'Sorry Jimmy, I didn't know about your father. I guess you and I haven't really talked much since I got here. This makes a nice change.' He lit his own cigarette inhaled deeply and exhaled a cloud of smoke in my direction that almost had me on my feet and snatching the pack from the table top. My nostrils twitched with the forgotten pleasure of nicotine. If I hadn't just made the little speech, I would have started again right there, no question.

'We're certainly making up for lost time, tonight'. I said anxious to get my mind off cigarettes. 'So, we were talking about LBJ and his mastery of the Senate.'

'Oh yeah well, that's exactly what he was, master of the Senate. And through it all, Bobby Baker was his right hand man. He was even nicknamed little Lyndon. Just like your boss, the guy who can hear a mouse squeak for five miles, Baker knows everything and anything that moves on Capitol Hill. But now he seems to be in trouble. Somewhere along the line he has screwed up. And the Rules Committee, according to Dirksen's note, may have no alternative but to investigate, which naturally means all this 'Quorum Club' stuff eventually gets into the public record. Not the kind of wholesome image our public representatives want to project. I take it you've heard about the Profumo affair in England?'

'I just know the basics. A British politician John Profumo is alleged to have had a relationship with a woman who was also romantically involved with the Defence Attaché at the Soviet Embassy in London. Profumo has denied it and I think Macmillan, the Prime Minister, backs him up.'

'I'm impressed, actually until a couple of weeks ago I'd never heard of it, but Senator Dirksen's note to Senator Mansfield mentions it. He said something along the lines of 'I would hate to think that we would open a can of worms here that would have echoes of the current controversy involving War Minister Profumo, in London.' The British press has reported on almost nothing else for months and as they say, it ain't over yet. So you see Jimmy, I suspect what Dirksen and Senator Mike are thinking about in the exclusive gentlemen's club we call the US Senate, is circling the wagons to avoid the same kind of scandal here.'

'Because something like this could lead all the way back to LBJ?' I suggested.

'Maybe, it depends if he and Baker are still close. But think about all the other implications, not just for Johnson but for anyone who has been involved in this sleazeball club. The national security risks, the potential for blackmail or even one politician compromising an opponent. All because these guys decide to cut loose here in Washington like college freshmen, while their wives and families are safely back home.'

'I wonder is that how it started out, this so called club. Is that precisely what Baker was trying to do on behalf of his master, Lyndon?' I said. Subtle blackmail is bound to be a pretty effective way to influence votes.'

'I'm not sure it was as blatant as that. The impression I got was that this was just a money making racket for Baker and a whole lot of fun for the participants. But who knows?'

'What did you do with the note?'

'I put it in a pile of mail for the Senator's personal secretary. She's been working with him for a hundred years and knows her way around. She was away for most of August, as was Senator Mansfield. I presume she will pass it on to him. Nobody will realise I read it 'cause the place has been as quiet as a graveyard all through August, with only lowlifes like me left holding the fort. So when you asked me if I'd ever heard of Bobby Baker, I was shocked, I read Dirksen's note just ten days ago, until then I had never heard of Baker. Then his name came up on Chesapeake, the last couple of days, everyone impressed at his chutzpah and his easy access to everyone on the Hill.'

He stopped and looked across at me he seemed satisfied now that he'd got all of this off his chest. In a strange way Steve and I weren't that different, two small town guys who had moved to the big city and had a lot to learn about the way the real world worked. With all that had happened recently, I was beginning to be embarrassed at my own gullibility.

'So, what do you think, Jimmy?' He asked.

'Just like you Steve, all this stuff opens my eyes to a kind of political life I was unaware of up to now.' Before we could say anything further we heard the front door open and Brad, our roommate and landlord, called out. He came into the kitchen looking exhausted. Brad supplemented his college scholarship by working as an assistant manager and sometime waiter at Harvey's, a legendary Washington restaurant, a hangout for many of the State Department's top brass. Brad glanced at the kitchen table strewn with coffee cups, empty plates and a used ash tray.

'Hi you two, long time no see. Looks like you've have been wineing and dining. Love to join you but I'm bushed, been working every night this week. Good news is, I have the next three nights off. I'm going to hit the sack.'

I stood up too and said to Steve. 'Maybe we should wrap it up as well, work in the morning and all that.' Steve readily agreed. He now looked refreshed and alert. 'I enjoyed our chat Jimmy, we should do it more often. You go ahead I'll clear up here.'

Brad was already at the kitchen door. 'I take it you both heard about Alabama, the four kids this morning, of all places in a church? 'The country is tearing itself apart. God knows what will happen next.'

CHAPTER 11

September 1963

Work the following day turned out to be more eventful than I could have imagined. Two interesting things happened which led me to believe that maybe my hitherto boring life was actually beginning to brighten up. At about ten thirty I was called up to Vern's office to discuss what he referred to in his inimitable way as, 'a matter of some delicacy.' I fully expected to hear something in connection with the events of the Labour Day weekend, but in fact what Vern wanted to see me about was strictly work related and he did not even mention our conversation two weeks earlier. On his desk, clutched tightly in his hands, I could see a three or four page document in Russian. He explained it was top secret and I was to get to work on it immediately. He repeatedly emphasised its confidential nature. He said there was to be no discussion with Sylvia or Victor about it when I took it downstairs. Vern had not asked me to sit down so I remained standing. Looking at it upside down I could see that the name of the author of the document, the date it was written and the identity of the intended recipient had been blacked out. Only the text itself, the body of the letter, was visible. Vern told me that I was to translate it as quickly as possible and along with the completed translation I was to provide an additional note of my own, setting out what I considered to be any nuances of language contained in it. Was it friendly or hostile, vague or specific was it evasive, or frank and honest? Was there anything in it which could be construed in more than one way?

'You are to analyse and comment on that kind of thing, or anything else about the letter that may strike you as being relevant to the intention of the writer.' Vern said. He added that this was not the first time that a document from the same source had been translated by our office but the work had always been done by my senior colleague Miss Sheppard who worked in LAU1.

'Unfortunately, Miss Sheppard is indisposed and may be out for the rest of the week.' Vern said primly, with the kind of discretion Miss Sheppard herself would certainly appreciate. With some reluctance he passed the pages to me. There were five tightly spaced typed A4 pages of Cyrillic script. 'I need hardly say, Jimmy, that this is an important task and one which must be undertaken with a degree of urgency not usually applied in the language analysis unit. Can you finish and have the translation, along with your own remarks, back to me by'- He consulted the gold pocket watch he kept in the breast pocket of his jacket. 'Let's say 3.30 this afternoon?'

'Less than five full pages, I should think so, unless there is a lot of technical or scientific content. That can sometimes hold things up.'

'Judging by previous writings from the same source, that is unlikely to be the case, but I can't be sure. Thank you Jimmy that will be all, I will see you this afternoon. And remember, be as fast and as accurate as you can, the people waiting for the material are always in a hurry.' I headed for the door. 'I understand Vern, Secretary Rusk must not be kept waiting'

'Actually, this is not going to Secretary Rusk. In fairness to him, he rarely applies undue pressure. But he will undoubtedly hear about it from on high if it's not finished on time. By the way Jimmy, any other developments with regard to that matter we discussed recently?'

'No, nothing at all Vern, have you heard anything?'

He did not answer directly. 'I think we can safely say it has now been consigned to the scrap heap of history. See you at 3.00 pm Jimmy.' He said, taking a small leather note book from his desk drawer and proceeding to write in it. This was an invariable habit of his when giving an assignment. The implication being that he was writing details of what had been requested and the timeline. It managed to disconcert the person getting the assignment sufficiently to ensure they complied with it in the time allotted. I went downstairs to my own office very pleased with what I had been asked to do. My pleasure was combined with a smidgen of anxiety that I should do it absolutely accurately. I noticed that 3.30pm had become 3.00 pm in Vern's mind even, before I left the room.

I got down to it straight away. I worked all morning, right through lunch and finished what I had to do by 2.15. Almost five pages of Russian had become eight and a half pages of English. This included my own remarks and analysis, which took up two pages in addition to the translation of the original text. I set down what I felt the writer was trying to say in specific places where there was a certain ambiguity of language along with notes about the tone and of the writing and the overall mood the writer insofar as it was discernible. In all modesty, I thought my observations were incisive and would be genuinely helpful in interpreting the writer's intentions. The fascinating content of the document being translated was a great help in producing a high end product.

The writer was clearly someone at a very high level in the Soviet government, who appeared familiar and friendly with the person to whom he was writing. He opened his remarks by apologising that it was not possible for both, writer and recipient, to meet face to face "*as was once our normal practice*". The subject matter of the document was wide ranging, setting out the current state of Soviet government thinking, in light of President Kennedy's speech at the American University in June. The speech, probably Kennedy's most important since he took office, marked a watershed in post war relations between the Communist bloc and the United States. The Russian letter went into great detail about the pros and cons of the proposed nuclear test ban treaty, from a Soviet perspective and provided a good deal of fascinating background information on the attitudes of various personalities at senior levels in the Russian government. When referring to Russians the letter contained only initials of first names, patronymics and family names. Full names and titles were given only if someone in the west was referred to. Khrushchev, (NSK), was easy to spot, as he got most mentions and his views were clearly the ones being given most weight. It was clear from the document that there were two distinct factions emerging in Moscow, hawks and doves. The writer seemed to be on the side of the doves and to my surprise, according to the writer, Khrushchev was one of the doves. The letter made it clear that there was no shortage of opposition in the Kremlin, to a more conciliatory approach to the West. Some in the politburo did not like the way the relationship between the two countries was evolving. The writer said that the hawks regarded last year's settlement of the Cuban missile crises as a defeat for Soviet prestige. They considered that President Kennedy's successful push for the nuclear test ban treaty, was giving the US the high moral ground, thereby diminishing the reputation of the Soviet Union. An individual referred to as 'MS', presumably Mikhail Suslov, the chief ideologue of the Communist party, a little known, old style hard liner, was cast as a leader of the hawks. As far as the identity of the letter writer was concerned, I could not say. I could only be certain that it was not an obvious piece of espionage, the writer's tone and some of his views made clear that he was a patriot, a loyal supporter of his own government and a proud Russian. It was clear too that the paper was not addressed to the President, as Kennedy was mentioned in the third person throughout and in a mildly critical manner at certain points. It was fascinating stuff. The writer finished the letter by offering to do anything in his power to help the person he was writing to, in any way he could.

I delivered the completed pages and my own comments, along with the original document, to Vern's office at 2.45 pm. standing in front of his desk, I felt like a school kid, pathetically seeking the approval of his teacher. He took the documentation from me without comment. As usual he did not seem to have any other work on his desk. As I left the room I could see him, his head bent low, the turtle shell half moon reading glasses on, studying the translated text with a kind of intense concentration I had never seen him display before. I went back to my own office more than pleased with myself, one of my more interesting days at work since coming to the State Department. My feeling of elation derived not only from the opportunity to translate an interesting text. It also had to do with the content of the document in question. It presented an insider's view of the mysterious world of the Kremlin. It was high level secret stuff. That was a major part of the thrill, the pleasure derived from being on the inside track. It was a sweeter sensation than I would have imagined. About an hour later Vern called and congratulated me on a job well done. He told me that he particularly liked my own personal comments and clarifications which he 'had no hesitation in passing on with the translated pages' I thought to myself that maybe the old blowhard wasn't really so bad after all. My second thought was that I would love to do more of that kind of work. I had a definite spring in my step as I prepared to go home that evening. Both Sylvia and Victor noticed it but I had already told them I could not discuss the particular job I was given that day. I could sense their irritation as I worked silently through the text. They both left promptly at 5.30 with very perfunctory goodbyes to me. The phone on my desk rang as I was leaving myself. I got to it just as the caller was about to hang up. 'Hi', said a chirpy female voice, 'I was just about to give up on you. Is that Jimmy Flynn?'

'Yes it is who's calling?'

'Hi Jimmy this is Shirley Beaumont on the West German desk. I'm Greg March's secretary, we have met I think. I hope I didn't catch you as you were going home?'

'Of course I remember you Shirley, how are you?' I'm staying a little late this evening it's been one of those days. How can I help?'

'Jimmy, I am doing a major clear out here of miscellaneous correspondence and believe me we've got plenty of it. I have come across some papers here that we got from your office, about a month ago, copies of documents from Justice in relation to deportation of two German citizens, a Miss Rometch and a Miss Kircherr. As you know, Greg is a stickler for the German desk being appraised of all papers relating to our area of responsibility. But I understand the deportation process in both cases is now complete and as the papers relate to routine matters anyway, we have no further need for this material. I can return the documentation to you if you wish but you might prefer if we just dispose of the papers ourselves along with our own confidential waste. I am just about to send down a fairly large bag for incineration, is that OK with you?'

I could feel my pulse begin to race as Shirley spoke. How could I have forgotten? Greg March, a one dimensional Poindexter type, the bureaucrat's bureaucrat, asked months ago, for 'sight of anything no matter how trivial', which comes under, what he insists on calling, his 'purview.'

'Actually Shirley,' I said. 'As it happens, we could use an additional copy of those documents. For some reason I can't seem to lay my hands on the originals. 'If you like I can run up there to the fifth right away and get the stuff from you?'

If Shirley noticed my uncharacteristic enthusiasm to get my hands on routine paperwork she didn't show it. 'Well, I'm just about to leave for the day myself Jimmy, as you're working late I'll stop off at your office and leave them with you. Will that be convenient?'

'Of course, Shirley, if you really don't mind, I appreciate you taking the trouble.'

'You are more than welcome,' she said in the kind of robotic tone people adopt when they've used the same expression for the hundredth time in a single day. 'It's just one less piece of paper lying around here. We are drowning in the stuff. See you in about ten minutes.'

I took off my jacket, sat back at my desk and tried to look like I was doing something useful. Less than five minutes later a friendly blond haired lady in her forties, whom I vaguely remember from last year's departmental Christmas party came in, wearing her overcoat and carrying a purse on one arm and in her other hand, a brown manila envelope.

'There you go Jimmy'. Shirley said, looking around the empty room. 'I see you're the last one here. I will be sure to tell Vern Templeton what a dedicated officer you are next time I see him. Have a great evening.'

I wished her the same and mused how all the old hands in State knew Vern and spoke of him so fondly. When Shirley had gone I opened the envelope and took out a sheaf of badly Xeroxed copies of the papers I had last looked at in July. All of the documents that had been passed to me were in German anything in English relating to either of the women had obviously been retained by Justice. Included in the documents were Xeroxed copies of photographs of both women that were so dark and smudgy their features were unrecognizable. I put the Ellen Rometch papers to one side for the moment and concentrated on Elsa Kircherr.

The contents consisted of a copy of the photo page of Miss Kircherr's West German passport, issued in September 1962, a short report prepared following her official debriefing at the Marienfeld Refugee Reception centre in West Berlin on 17 August 1962. There was written confirmation of her employment as a receptionist in the Hotel Spitzug in Garmisch Partenkirchen, in Bavaria, from September 1962 to end of January 1963. Attached to the copy of her passport page, was a dog eared birth certificate, complete with Nazi official stamp, stating that Elsa Kircherr, father unknown, mother a nurse, was born in Königsburg in East Prussia on August first 1937.

Then I noticed something in the papers which I had read before but that had entirely slipped my mind, in all my idle musing about this woman since her death. How could I have forgotten it? It was a certificate issued by a city official in Munich, recording her marriage to a Sergeant Robert Lavelle, of the US Army, in January 1963. For the most part the material comprised the usual kind of bureaucratic paper trail that accompanies all of us through our lives. But there was one substantial document among the mundane, which I recalled translating in July. This was what had made a vivid impression on me at the time. It was almost certainly the existence of these reports, one each for Rometch and Kircherr, which justified the need for a translation and which prompted the Justice Department to ask us to look at the papers and to undertake the job. Someone named Herbert Kluge, a second Secretary, a mid-level diplomat, in the West German Embassy in Washington, provided the Justice Department with an analysis of the biographical backgrounds and status of both Ellen Rometch and Elsa Kircherr. Mr Kluge did so with typical German thoroughness particularly with regard to Ellen Rometch but the difficulty in Kircherr's case was that there was not a lot to go on in terms of biographical information. Rometch's position was somewhat different because she had lived in the United States for about seven years. I looked around the empty room, it was Monday evening. I had nowhere else to be until 8.00pm. Thanks to the FBI, I no longer had my own translation of this stuff to look at, so I settled down once again to read Herbert Kluge's brief description of the life of the late Elsa Kircherr.

Private and confidential: For the attention of Mr Malcom L. Windom, special assistant to Mr N Katzenbach, Assistant Attorney General, United States Department of Justice....

Miss Elsa Kircherr or Mrs Elsa Lavelle (the subject), current address: 1200, Apartment 3A, Cherry Tree Lane, Arlington, Virginia, was born in 1938 in the city of Königsburg East Prussia, then part of Germany, now Kaliningrad in the Soviet Union.

Born on 1st August 1937, subject's birth certificate indicates that she is the child of an unmarried hospital nurse, Eva Kircherr of Königsburg. Subject's father's identity is stated as unknown on her birth certificate. Like almost the entire population of two million people then living in East Prussia, the subject and her mother appear to have fled their home region in the winter of 1945 in a mass exodus, prior to the arrival there of the Red Army. Her mother would, of necessity, have accompanied her on this journey. It appears that the subject became separated from her mother as the two of them were about to board an overcrowded passenger ship, the 'Wilhelm Gustloff' at the Baltic port of Gotenhafen. The vessel, carrying in excess of 7,000 passengers was sunk by a Soviet submarine on 30 January 1945. The death toll from the sinking, more than 5,000, mostly civilians, including hundreds of children, represents the largest single loss of life at sea in maritime history. The child Elsa, who remained on shore, was cared for by a refugee family who had failed to board the ship. The family took the child and travelled on foot for a period of weeks, to the small city of Görlitz in Saxony, where she was handed over to the civil authorities and eventually placed in state care. She remained in Görlitz, residing at different times at two state run homes for orphaned children and attending schools in that city. The subject was in a position to provide documentation to officials at Marienfelde Refugee Reception Centre in Berlin, certifying her place of residence and her attendance and graduation in 1957, from a Gymnasium (secondary school) in Görlitz. On leaving school she obtained employment in a factory manufacturing bone china in the town of Meissen in Saxony. While the factory in which she worked was closed in August 1962, for its annual two week vacation, Miss Kircherr travelled to Potsdam, south of Berlin arriving on 5th August. She had with her a rucksack containing, a small amount of clothing, toiletries, and personal documents, such as her birth certificate and her employment and school records. Subject alleges that she spent the night of 5th August sleeping under a tree in the grounds of the Sans Souci Palace in Potsdam. On the night of the 6th/7th of August, she entered the water of the Havel River on the GDR side and swam more than 200 metres to the other side, safely reaching the American Sector of West Berlin. Subject says she was spotted in the water and a number of shots were fired at her by the border guards when the alarm was raised on the GDR side. She presented herself to a West Berlin policeman on routine patrol, stating that she had just escaped from the GDR and was seeking asylum in the West. She requested that she might be taken to Marienfelde Refugee Centre. The police officer who examined the contents of the wet rucksack Miss Kircherr carried, noted that the paper documentation it contained had been carefully protected from the water by being placed in a small homemade black rubber bag.

Following her processing at Marienfelde, the subject was permitted entry to the Federal Republic of Germany and given a residency permit. She had expressed a wish, during the course of her interviews at Marienfelde, to travel south to Bavaria and to work in the tourist industry. She left Berlin by air for Munich on 13th August. The airline ticket and a small financial subvention were provided by the government of the Federal Republic. She arrived in the resort town of Garmisch Partenkirchen on 15th August 1962. Miss Kircherr obtained employment as a receptionist in the Hotel Spitszug, a small hotel on the outskirts of Garmisch, popular with US Army personnel.

Miss Kircherr's school records indicate that her knowledge of English is excellent and that she has consistently obtained the highest grades in that subject. In September 1962, Miss Kircherr met US Army Master Sergeant Robert Lavelle, aged 33, who was a guest at the Hotel Spitzug. Sergeant Lavelle had been serving with the US Army in Munich since November 1959. His tour of duty was due to finish at the end of 1962. A romance developed between Miss Kircherr and Sgt.Robert Lavelle. Because of his imminent return to the United States, Sergeant Lavelle applied to his commanding officer, on 29th October 1962, for permission to marry Miss Kircherr, without having to complete the normal waiting period required by US Army regulations in respect of soldiers overseas *wishing to marry non US citizens. Permission was granted and the civil wedding took place in Munich on 2nd January 1963. The only witnesses to the ceremony were officials employed in the city of Munich, civil registration offices. On his return to the United States, with his wife on 28th January 1963, Sergeant Lavelle was assigned to duty in the Pentagon in Washington DC.*

There are no independent sources of information relating to Sergeant Lavelle's wife (Miss Kircherr) other than what she herself has provided. A great displacement of population took place in central Europe after 1945. The mass movement of refugees involved the displacement of as many as twelve million people, combined with the extensive redrawing of political borders. It resulted in millions of German citizens and others, losing contact with the places of their birth and with the official records of their pasts. The opportunity for individuals in such circumstances to invent new identities and to create a more desirable personal biography was facilitated by this situation. It should be emphasised that the Government of the Federal Republic of Germany has no evidence that Miss Elsa Kircherr is anyone other than the person she states she is. It is understood that consideration is being given by the United States Justice Department to deport Elsa Kircherr, for reasons which the US government has chosen to keep confidential at this time. If it is the opinion of the government of the United States that such action is deemed to be in its national interest, The government of the Federal Republic of Germany raises no objection.

Herbert Kluge

Second Secretary

Embassy of the Federal Republic of Germany

Washington DC 1001.

27th July 1963.

Good old Herbert whoever he is, I thought. He made quite a nice little story out of it, even with so little to go on. I couldn't help being amused at the ponderous bureaucratic language of the text. Apparently it isn't only the State Department that goes in for this kind of stuff. I re-read the note again before putting it down. I had no doubt that someone in the West German Embassy thought that Elsa was a possible, if not a probable spy. They just didn't have any evidence to prove it and didn't want to say it out loud. That might explain why a Second Secretary was allowed put his name to the note. If there was a problem with its veracity or if the speculation about 'hostile intelligence agencies targeting the United States' proved to be unfounded, the Embassy bigwigs could blame any errors or misjudgement on the naiveté of a junior official. After reading this document, the question in my mind remained the same one I had on Labour Day. Who exactly was Elsa Kircherr? Even the German Embassy didn't seem to be certain they knew the answer. I turned to the package of documents relating to the other deportee, Ellen Rometch. It was far bulkier than Elsa Kercherr's and the accompanying note, also written by Herbert Kluge, was a lot longer and less speculative. It took me almost an hour to go through this material. The West Germans made it clear that they did not think that Ellen Rometch was involved in espionage but they did not raise any objection to her deportation from the States. I had expected some mention of a connection between Kircherr and Rometch, but there was none.

It was now seven thirty. I was tired as I often was on a Monday evening. But there was a Wheelers game I was due to play in at 8.00 in Georgetown University. Playing basketball after a busy day always had the effect of waking me up again. I gathered up the two separate sets of papers. I remembered what I had told Vern just a couple of weeks ago, that I had no further documents in my possession relating to these two women. It was true at the time but I decided I wasn't going to tell him about this stuff, which had accidently landed in my lap. I had always been the kind of guy that did things by the book but lately I'd been thinking, where did it ever get me? Elsa Kercherr's's murder had nothing to do with me but the whole business on Craigville beach continued to gnaw away at me, like nothing had ever done before and I knew it wasn't going to stop. I decided there and then that I was going to find out who killed this woman and why. I wasn't naive enough to think that there might not be a cost if I stuck my nose into something that was none of my business. I had something to lose, a good secure government job for a start, which for my family, had more value than a winning sweepstakes ticket. But my career was in a rut, my love life had run into the sand, someone was mysteriously murdered and no one seemed to care. I put on my jacket, gathered up my stuff and headed out. On the drive to Georgetown, the basketball game was the last thing on my mind. If I was going to do this thing, I had no doubt as to where I should start. I needed to talk to two people. One of them was Herbert Kluge, author of the notes on Rometch and Kircherr. Herbert was undoubtedly the initial drafter of the biographical notes on the two women, but his superiors would have put their own imprint on them before the material ever saw the light of day in the Justice Department. Those changes would show more caution, more restraint be far less speculative than Herbert was likely to be in his first draft. That was government the world over, particularly if something was being shared with an outside agency. What did Herbert really know and how much, if anything, would he tell me? Kluge is the German word for clever. How clever, I wondered was this guy Herbert and how forthcoming would he be? I intended to find out. I parked my Dodge in the Georgetown University student car park and got out taking a slim document case containing the papers relating to the two women I had removed from the office. I went to the trunk to get my sports bag and carefully concealed the document case beneath the soft fabric covering the trunk. From tomorrow I said to myself, maybe my humdrum life will get just a little more interesting. It was only much later I asked myself what it was that Robbie Burns said about the best laid plans of mice and men.

CHAPTER 12

June 1962

By late evening on Sunday 10thJune 1962, Klara Hartmann was certain of one thing. She knew she was in love and knew that she had never felt about anyone the way she felt about Max Korten. It was strange when she thought about it, because she had not felt the same way early that Sunday morning as she got into Korten's swish green Volvo. But the trip south into Saxony was the beginning of a real change in her feelings towards this enigmatic self-confident man. As they left the *Laube* on the Spree and headed south, Korten told Klara something about his life, his past and even his political philosophy. As he spoke, he drove considerably slower than he had on the first leg of the journey from Berlin to Spreewald. He was a Berliner he said, born in the working class district of Wedding, thirty six years ago. His father was a trade union activist, a sheet metal worker and later a full time Communist, his mother a housewife. His father had been a Communist member of the Reichstag for less than two years before the Nazis came to power. He was arrested in 1933 after the Reichstag fire, along with many other Communists and spent almost a year in Oranienburg, a concentration camp near Berlin. Young Max had no siblings.

When he was ten years old he and his father secretly left Berlin for Moscow. There they lived for a time with other exiled German communists, including Walter Ulbricht himself, in the comfortable Hotel Lux on Tver'skaya Street in Moscow. Max was the only child there amongst the older comrades, so he became a kind of mascot to the serious minded, not to say dull Communist exiles. He was academically clever but not industrious. He was admitted to Model School No 25, near Pushkin Square, attended almost exclusively by children of the elite of the Soviet government, including those of Stalin. In 1945 after the Red Army had captured Berlin, the entire German Communist leadership, including Korten's father and Max himself, were brought back to the city by the Russians and instructed to establish a new socialist order in the Soviet occupation zone of Germany. Max's father had contracted tuberculosis in Moscow. He survived only eight months after their return to Berlin. By that time, the 18 year old Max was on the closest possible terms with the men who would assume the leadership of the new Communist German Democratic Republic, when it was created in 1949. He was a child of Communist privilege and remained close to the centre of Communist power in East Germany. Because of his pedigree, he had his choice of jobs when new government bodies were being established. He chose to join the HVA, the Foreign Intelligence Directorate of the Stasi, because it promised a certain amount of glamour and excitement.

'And this has turned out to be very much the case', he said with a wink, glancing at Klara as he drove. 'Go ahead he said ask me anything else you'd like to know. My life is an open book.'

'Oh yes, even though you are a spy,' she said laughing.

'I would never confess to being a spy, even to you Klara. I work for our government and I simply do whatever is asked of me.'

'What happened to your mother?' Klara asked.

His face suddenly became serious and he was quiet for a moment before he spoke. 'When my father was in Oranienburg we were penniless, so she got a job in a clothing factory. The owner discovered she had a talent for managing and supervising others so they promoted her. She was well paid and she liked her work. Of course when my father was released he objected to her working as supervisor in a capitalist concern but she had begun to enjoy her independence and refused to leave. Because she was now better off she also began look more positively on the Nazi system which appeared to bring stability to the country. When my father and I left for Moscow in'37, she stayed behind. I tried to track her down after the war and discovered she had been killed in one of the last American air raids on Berlin in February '45, only a few months before my father and I returned to the city.

'I am sorry,' Klara said.

Korten shrugged.' The war brought heartache to everyone. I was luckier than many others.'

'Did you ever marry?'

'You'd make a good interrogator Klara, you know how to wrong foot a suspect.'

'Are you avoiding answering my question, suspect?' She said with mock officiousness.

'Well, if you insist on an answer, yes, I was married once. To a Russian officer stationed in Karlshorst. I was twenty and she was a year older. The foolishness of youth I suppose, we divorced three years later. She was transferred back to Russia. I have not heard from her since 1951.' He paused briefly. 'There are no children by the way, in case that was going to be your next question.'

'Actually it was.'

'Well, you'd better think of another one then, Interrogator Hartmann.'

'Alright then, where do you live?'

'I live in a two bedroom apartment also in Karlshorst. There are three apartments in the building and a good communal garden, the house was once the home of a single family. I also have a small country house, although I very rarely use it.'

'You do? Where is it?'

He smiled knowingly. 'Can't you guess?

'No. How could I?'

He looked over to her waiting for the penny to drop, it only took a second. 'The *Laube* in Spreewald,' she laughed. 'I knew it, so it was yours all along. I told you it was only the elite who are permitted to own these places and of course I was right.'

'Did you like it?' he asked.

'Yes very much. Why, did you think that I didn't?'

'No, it's not that. It's just that we might visit it again sometime, if you would like to.' He took his eyes of the road again to gauge her reaction to this proposal.

She stared straight ahead, hoping she didn't seem nervous and said quietly. 'Yes I think I would like that very much.' Neither of them spoke for some time after that. Then Korten said.

'It seems you've run out of questions for me Klara. Have you found out all you need to?'

'Not exactly Max,' she said addressing him familiarly by his name for the first time since they left the lakeside cabin. It was not so difficult this time, she thought to herself. 'Can you tell me where we are going? It is almost three thirty in the afternoon. We are a long way from Berlin and it seems we are heading further away with every minute.'

'Where do you think we're going?' He asked.

'You seem to answer a lot of questions with a question of your own. It looks to me as if we're on our way to Dresden. I hope I'm wrong.'

'As is so often the case with you Klara, you are not wrong. We are going to Dresden, your home town. As a matter of fact we are going to visit your mother.'

Klara was stunned. When she spoke her tone was a mixture of pleading and anger, her voice far louder than before. 'Max, I am not going with you to visit my mother. Why didn't you say this is what you had in mind? My mother is not in good health. If we arrive at the apartment unannounced, she will have great difficulty handling the situation. Her nerves are not good. You couldn't possibly understand something like this. Please turn around now. Let us go back to Berlin.'

'Klara, we are at most only thirty minutes from Dresden. I have no intention of turning back. Anyway we will not arrive unannounced. Your mother knows we are coming.'

'How could she possibly know?' She said, almost shouting.

'Please Klara, calm down. She knows because I spoke to her on the phone yesterday.'

'You couldn't have, we do not have a telephone.'

'No, but your block warden, Frau Schabowsky has one. She fetched your mother for me.'

'And you spoke to her?' Klara asked, fearful but much quieter now. 'Who did you say you were?'

'Of course I spoke to her and of course I told her the truth. I said I worked for the Foreign Ministry, that I was your boss and that as your period of probation is almost over and you may soon be assigned abroad, it is customary for a senior member of the Ministry to visit the families of junior staff. So I would be visiting her today and you would accompany me.'

Klara was almost tearful now. 'Why didn't you say any of this before? You tricked me. I am not ready to visit my mother and I don't want to. And I don't want you to be there when I do.'

'Oh, why not? What's so terrible about me?'

'You know perfectly well why not. Ours is a tiny, badly built apartment in a dismal part of the city and look at you, with your fancy clothes, your green Volvo and your stupid *Laube*. My mother simply could not handle a visit from you. It will be embarrassing for me, and you know it.'

Korten laughed at her outburst. 'I have already told you Klara, the Volvo is not mine. As you also know, personal privacy is merely a manifestation of the kind of bourgeois sensibilities we are trying to eradicate. We do not need that sort of mentality in a socialist state. Furthermore you should not be ashamed of living in a modest working class home.'

'If you knew as much about my family as you say you do you would know that because of my father's religious convictions, we were allocated probably the worst apartment in Dresden and in one of the shoddiest buildings. At school it was embarrassing to invite my friends there.'

'I know that your father has caused many difficulties for your family. You are fortunate that you have a chance to do something which can change all that.'

'I will not speak badly of my father. I did not always agree with him but at least he was always true to his own beliefs.' She then asked in a calm almost subdued voice. 'How did my mother sound when you spoke to her?

'She was a little tense at first, but she improved as the conversation continued. She finished by saying she would be happy to meet with us today.'

'Well of course she would say that to you, 'Klara said, after some reflection she added. 'My mother's nerves were never good. She should never have married someone like my father, whose principles brought her so much hardship and worry. She would have been more suited to a calm, steady, even dull husband but she got something quite different.'

'Does she resent your father?'

Klara considered this for a moment. 'No, strangely enough she doesn't. Actually, she thinks he is the most wonderful man in the world, exasperating but wonderful all the same. I think it is you who's the skilful interrogator, Max. You managed to get me to say things about my parents that I never even thought about until now.'

Korten smiled but said nothing. They drove on in silence. Then Klara said.

'Max, I know you have said that a decision has not been made about my assignment abroad and of course I have to accept that. If I am honest I will admit to you that the prospect of real work with the HVA is the thing I most ardently wish for.' She paused to let that sink in. But I have to tell you that I will refuse to undertake any assignment overseas if my father is not released from custody before I go. My father's health is so bad that he may die before being released. I simply could not leave my mother alone in that damp flat without her husband or either of her daughters. She could not survive that. She is only 48 years old but as you will soon see, she looks ten years older.'

Korten's reply was sharp and to the point. 'Refuse, comrade Hartmann?' Are you saying that if you are ordered to carry out a duty for your country for which you have been trained at great expense, you will disobey that order?'

'Klara looked at him but the only emotion she could discern on his face was irritation or genuine anger. 'Of course I would prefer not to but I feel I have no choice.' She said.

'You know that your attitude alone is enough to rule you out for permanent duty with the HVA or with any organ of the state. We don't take kindly to people threatening to disobey orders'.

'Should I abandon my mother here in Dresden to loneliness and penury? Is that what the state demands of me?'

He was genuinely angry now. 'The state demands, comrade Hartmann, that you do your duty, that you obey your superiors and that you accept that personal feelings do not have any place in how you carry out the work which is assigned to you.'

Klara stared out the car window at the familiar partially rebuilt streets of her home city. At one time but no longer, Dresden was one of Europe's most beautiful cities, famed as the Florence of the north. That was until the dark February night when the bombers came. She thought it better not to continue the conversation. She had been planning to say what she had just said, for some time and had been waiting for the right moment. Obviously she had badly miscalculated, maybe her career was already over, before it had even begun but she felt a burden lift from her all the same. She could not in good conscience have left the country and left her mother without any family support. Klara had not been too young to remember the night of 23rd February 1945, when everything changed for the Hartmann family and for Dresden. Neither would ever be the same again. Klara's mother had taken her and her older sister Anni to the circus that afternoon, to take their minds off their absent father. The children were told some months before that he had gone off to the war. Anna was eight years old and Klara just six. Their mother had told no one that her husband was a prisoner in Flossenburg concentration camp, because of his association with the anti Nazi Pastor Dietrich Bonhoeffer, who had also been arrested. The family visit to the circus had been a great success, but the British and American bombers came in their hundreds that same evening and the next. The two young girls, their mother and everyone else in Dresden spent the next forty eight hours in a living nightmare. They cowered in the basement of the St Barnabas church, and when that was ablaze, they had no choice but to stand in open parkland with hundreds of others, expecting a bomb to fall on them at any minute. They were kept warm on that freezing winter's night by the raging heat coming from the burning city around them.

When it was over two days later, the Hartmanns were still alive but more than thirty five thousand Dresdeners were dead and the beautiful city, the so called Venice of the North, had all but disappeared. In the days of that followed, the adult survivors, including Klara's mother, were ordered to help gather up and stack thousands of bodies on huge funeral pyres. They were to be burnt to prevent the spread of typhus. As she collected the decaying and burnt corpses, the thought occurred to Helene Hartmann that perhaps she had died in the bombing after all and had arrived in hell. An imagination has vivid as Dante's could never have conceived such a scene. Klara's mother was never the same again. The trauma of the raid, fleeing with two children from the blazing church, days spent collecting and stacking corpses and the worry of knowing her husband might be executed at any time or may already be dead, brought about a nervous collapse from which she never really recovered. The war ended just a little more than two months later and Flossenburg was liberated. When her emaciated husband eventually returned to the devastated city, Helene Hartmann was not the same person she had once been.

Korten and Klara had reached a cluster of six high rise prefabricated concrete apartment blocks set on untended scrubby wasteland. They were a considerable distance from the centre of the city. Korten parked the Volvo on the street. There were no other cars to be seen in the seemingly deserted neighbourhood. 'Let's go in' he said, curtly. Klara followed him out of the car and watched as he walked briskly towards the building where her mother lived. She noticed that Max Korten knew exactly which building to head for. Either he had been here before, she thought, or he had done his research very thoroughly. She caught up with him just as they reached the graffiti daubed entrance to block number four. 'You go on up,' he said, I wish to have a word with Frau Schabovsky.'

'Schabovsky, do you know her?' Klara was incredulous. Frau Schabovsky had long been a particular *bête noir* of the Hartmann family, Klara's father being a pastor, made him automatically suspect. The family had long suspected that the woman entered their apartment when there was no one home, in order to snoop around.

'I told you I spoke to her on the phone when I called your mother. Go ahead.' There was a tattered sign on the elevator door which Klara had last seen at Christmas, indicating that it was under repair. She took the stairs to her family's third floor apartment, glad of the chance to see to her mother alone before Korten joined them. As soon as the door to the apartment was opened Klara could see that her mother had made a special effort with her dress and her hair. She embraced her mother who reciprocated with her customary stiffness, then smiled nervously at Klara. 'Mama, you look wonderful' Klara said. 'I am sorry not to have told you about this visit. I only heard about it earlier today.'

She could see her mother was tired and anxious, despite the carefully applied make up. Klara could not remember a time when her mother had ever worn cosmetics.

'Where is he, the man?' Her mother whispered, once the door was closed.

'He's with Schabovsky. He will be here in a moment. 'How is Papa?'

'Schabovsky, what's he doing with that witch? Come in and sit Klara. Your father is a lot better since they put him in this sanatorium. They say it's a sanatorium but it's more of a prison than a hospital. I saw him yesterday, he sends you his love. You look so well Klara. Have you any news of Anni?'

Klara glanced quickly around the little apartment. Everything was neat and tidy. There was a distinct smell of furniture polish. The table was set with a white tablecloth, her mother's only china and a selection of savouries. 'Did you do all of this, Mama?' She asked indicating the room and the perfectly set table.

'Some people from the church helped me with it. They have been so good to me since your father went away. What is this Klara, about you being sent abroad? Is that likely to happen? I can hardly believe such a thing.'

'I'm not sure that it will happen now. It's possible but not certain.'

'Klara, if the opportunity is presented to you, don't turn it down. Do not worry about your father or me. Go, if you can. You and Anni can be a support to each other over there. Do you hear me?'

Klara had rarely seen her normally passive mother so vehement about anything. She glanced at the door wondering how long Korten would take to arrive. 'Mama, I won't go anywhere if you are likely to be left here alone, so don't worry about that.'

'Don't be such a fool child. I can take care of myself, as you can see. We have the small group at the church and we all support each other.

Anyway, they can't keep an innocent man like your father in that place forever. Klara darling,' she said in a more measured way. 'If you have a chance of something better than the life your father and I have had. I beg you, grasp it with both hands.'

Before she could finish, there was a firm knock on the apartment door. Klara was dreading the following inevitable encounter, but there was no way out of it. She rose and went to let Max Korten in. When he entered he looked around the cramped space with the air of a visitor admiring the ceiling of the Sistine Chapel. Klara did not get a chance to introduce her mother.

'Frau Hartmann, it is so good to meet you at last.' Korten smiled and extended his hand. 'I am Max Korten, we spoke on the phone. As you know I am a colleague of your very able daughter here.' He indicated in Klara's direction. 'I hope you are proud of her. We in the Ministry certainly are.'

Klara was unexpectedly pleased with this flattering introduction but she was more amazed by the transformation it brought about in her usually reserved mother. She favoured Korten with a kind of coquettish smile Klara could never remember seeing before.

'Very nice to meet you Herr Korten, you are most welcome, please sit down. It is so good of you to take the trouble to visit us. I haven't seen Klara since the New Year. I hope you will stay for a while and have a little something to eat.' Korten sat in the only armchair in the room, crossing his legs with his usual nonchalance. He gave Frau Hartmann a brief appraising look. 'I can see now where Klara gets her great beauty. She has clearly inherited her mother's flawless features.'

Klara was shocked to see her mother actually blush at this complement. She put her hand to the back of her hair as if checking that everything was in place. Despite Klara's worse fears the afternoon tea, which is the only way she could describe this strange occasion, was a great success. Max Korten charmed her mother in a way she had never been charmed before. Even confiding in her how he himself had been deprived of his mother at a young age. Watching both of these very different people in conversation, Klara marvelled at the chameleon like quality of Korten, whose mood had changed from barely suppressed anger less than half an hour before, to the personification of charm and good humour now.

She looked with some amazement at her mother, she could see the years of worry and anguish slip away as she served tea, passed pastries around and cut slices of fruitcake for the three of them. She told Korten of her idyllic upbringing on a small estate in rural Silesia and the difficulties of raising two small children during the war. She recounted the story of the catastrophic bombing of Dresden eighteen years before, but this time she described it as if it were an incredible wartime adventure, not the defining traumatic event of her life. The afternoon passed without any awkwardness or discomfort and Klara found herself filled with immense gratitude to this man, for making her mother happier than she ever remembered seeing her. Her mother laughed heartily at some of Korten's stories about the vagaries of stodgy Berlin bureaucracy. Klara could hardly remember when she had ever heard her mother laugh in this apartment. He spoke frankly about his own unusual family history and the difficulties for a German, even for a German Communist, living in Russia as a child. As often happens when conversation is going well, the time slipped by without any of the three of them noticing. It was almost six when Korten mentioned it was getting late and perhaps they should begin the journey back to Berlin. As he said it, Klara could see her mother's genuine regret that the visit was coming to an end. Korten and Klara stood up to leave.

'Frau Hartmann, I have had a wonderful day, I cannot thank you enough for your kind hospitality.'

Helene Hartmann beamed at the complement. 'The pleasure was all mine, I assure you Herr Korten. I hope you will take good care of my dear daughter when you both return to work.'

Korten looked over at Klara and gave her a kindly smile, then turning to Frau Hartmann he spoke in a more serious tone. 'Of course I will but I assure you that she is more than capable of taking care of herself.' He paused briefly and then said. 'Perhaps I should have mentioned this earlier but as you know Frau Hartmann, there is a good chance that Klara will be given a foreign diplomatic posting in the near future. If that is the case you may be concerned about being left alone here in Dresden.' Frau Hartmann looked at him, her expression suddenly tense as she wondered what was coming next.

'I have it on good authority, from the organs of state security, that the investigation into your husband's alleged anti-government activities, has found no serious grounds for concern. While it is not my department and of course I have no direct involvement in these matters, I am confident that you can expect to hear quite soon that a date for your husband's release from the sanatorium near Leipzig has been set.' He paused briefly for this news to sink in then continued.

'I think you may have to prepare for his return by the end of July, early August, at the very latest. I have no doubt he will be glad to be home.' Korten ignored the look on the faces of mother and daughter as they took in what he was saying.

'I will leave you both now, to say your goodbyes. He took Helene Hartmann's hand and kissed it in the manner of a nineteenth century aristocrat. 'Gracious lady', he said, 'I had a most wonderful afternoon. It was a great pleasure to meet you at last. I look forward very much to our next meeting. Klara, I will wait for you in the car, there is no need to rush.' As soon as the apartment door was closed, tears flowed down Helene Hartmann's face as she embraced her daughter. 'Did I hear correctly Klara? Your father is coming home? I can hardly believe it.' She sat down on the armchair as if she thought she would faint and put her two hands to her face. 'Who is this wonderful man you have brought to see me? I feel he has transformed my life in a single day.'

Klara sat on the arm of the chair and held her mother. She too was relieved at the good news about her father and overjoyed that her mother seemed so much better. In her euphoria she had put aside the thought that her father, a sick man, had been detained without charge for more than a year and a half, innocent of any crime. So why should they feel grateful to the government which would now release him? Klara stayed in the apartment for a further ten minutes, helping clear away the dishes before leaving.

In the desolate street below, Max Korten sat in the Volvo and smoked a cigarette. Just as he finished the Volvo's passenger door opened suddenly, momentarily startling Korten and Klara got in. For the first time in many months she felt truly happy but she still had a bone to pick with Korten.

'You must have known all along that my father was to be released yet you made me go through all that pleading with you. Why could you not have told me that he is to be freed?'

He started the car and then had second thoughts, switched off the ignition and looked intently at Klara. 'Because, the information I had in relation to your father's detention was for your mother, not for you.' His expression was not unfriendly but it his words were sharp. 'And frankly I was not happy with your attempt at blackmailing me. 'I won't serve unless....' That is not the socialist way Klara, as you well know. Your feelings and those of your family are unimportant. I should not have to say this to you: we serve the collective not ourselves. You must never put personal considerations ahead your duty. That is the basic tenet of all our work. Frankly, I was disappointed that you forgot it so easily.'

Klara was so incensed by this reprimand that she was about to grab the door handle get out of the car and walk away. Before she had a chance to move, Korten spoke again in a gentler tone. 'I meant what I said about you to your mother.' He indicated the shabby apartment block. 'You are very able, your training record is excellent and we in Adler are proud of how you have progressed as part of this programme. I too am also proud of you and I have no doubt you can be a success. That streak of independence you possess is unfortunate but it may, at some point, prove helpful out in the field. Someday you may have to make a crucial decision on your own, very quickly. It might even save your life. But within the service independent thinking is almost always viewed negatively.' He favoured her with one of his most winning smiles as he started the car once more and pulled away from the kerb.

'Try to separate the two in your mind, you will find it's important for your survival. By the way, your mother is an impressive woman, I liked her. I hope she did not find our visit a strain.'

'I think she enjoyed it very much, Klara said, mollified now by Korten's subtle flattery. 'Thank you Max sincerely, for being so nice to her. I have rarely seen her so happy.'

'It was nothing. I was more than happy to do it'.

Klara looked at him and a thought occurred to her.' I think I know the kind of man you are Max Korten.'

'I doubt very much that you do.'

'You are the kind of person who has charmed people all his life. Probably from the time you lived as the only darling child with all those boring gray men in the Hotel Lux in Moscow. You think you can talk to anyone and persuade them of anything. You think that there is no one on earth from Chairman Ulbricht to my poor mother who will not succumb to your charms, if only you have enough time with them to work your magic. Am I right?'

He laughed out loud obviously flattered by her assessment. 'No you are not. I can assure you Chairman Ulbricht does not easily succumb to anyone's charm. As for your mother, it is very easy to be charming with such a charming woman.'

'I am certain that I'm right, I believe I have the measure of you Herr Korten'. She said, laughing.

As they drove along Dresden's potholed roads, Klara could not help speculating whether he was working the same charm on her. She could not decide whether Max Korten was a sincere and thoughtful person or a master manipulator of others. So often during this long day, his conversation had oscillated between strict admonitions and friendly sharing of personal, even intimate information. Sincere or not, she knew that her mother had benefitted greatly from his visit and from the attention he paid to her. She realised now that her mother's mental health had been more of a worrisome burden to her than she ever admitted to herself. That burden had partially been lifted, thanks to Max. She also had to admit to herself that she very much enjoyed his company and looked forward to getting to know him a lot better. They drove in silence heading northwards again, when something else occurred to Klara.

'Max, you spoke to our building warden Frau Schabovsky, Was there any particular reason for that?'

He seemed not at all offended by her natural curiosity.

'No nothing in particular.'

'I see,' she said a little petulantly.

He decided to put her out of her misery. 'Klara, as you know comrade Schabovsky is not a particularly nice person. But such people are useful, even necessary to the orderly running of society. It may or may not come as a surprise to you but this woman has been your enemy and your family's enemy for many years. She has reported negatively on your father's opinions and even on yours and your sister's morals.'

'Our morals? I can assure you that my sister and I are probably the two most upright women in that ever lived in that apartment block.'

'Calm down, the State can determine what's true and what are simply flights of a more than fertile imagination. Actually it was this woman's reports about your alleged anti- social activities which brought you to the attention of the security services in the first place. That is how we began to assess you for suitability for the Adler Programme.' He watched her closely as she took all this in.

'Are you surprised?' He asked.

'No I can easily believe it. But Schabovsky does not actually know anything about me and certainly not about my morals, as you call them.'

'No?' I think you'll find she does. That's her job and she is good at it. She made quite a number of negative reports on the Hartmann family over more than ten years, in fact for all of the time you have been living in that apartment. I think your family became quite an obsession with her. The reports mostly concerned your father but they were also about you and your sister Anna. Strangely your mother was barely mentioned. The file grew quite large, so thick in fact that a couple of years ago the local Stasi office in Dresden forwarded all the material to Berlin for instructions. That file, which admittedly contained many inaccuracies, was brought to the attention of Dr Armin Hoffman, whom you have met. Dr Hoffman was aware of my involvement in the Adler Programme, so he brought your academic record and your exceptional language skills to our attention in the HVA. In a way you could say that you owe your involvement in the Adler Programme to Frau Schabovsky.'

'Oh yes. And do I owe the arrest of my father and his imprisonment for a year and a half to the same heroic Frau Schabovsky?'

Korten seemed irritated by the question. 'I don't know that there is any connection. The decision to arrest your father was for different reasons and would have been taken at a higher level. I might add that it is in your own interest Klara, not to inquire further into that particular matter. May I remind you that you are now a servant of the State. Furthermore you don't want to do anything which would jeopardise your father's eventual release.'

Klara looked at him to see if she could tell whether this statement was meant to be a threat or a piece of helpful advice but his expression had reverted to one of casual friendliness. The chameleon-like change of mood once again.

'Of course we always knew Frau Schabovsky disliked us.' Klara said bitterly. 'Her manner, particularly to Anni and me, made that quite clear. My father actually helped her in small ways once or twice over the years but nothing could melt that stony heart, if she ever had a heart.'

'Klara, forget about her. I'm sorry I mentioned it. I can assure you she is no longer relevant. I spoke to her in the strongest terms today. She won't be bothering the Hartmann family again. You can be assured of that. When your father is released your parents will have nothing to worry about. By the time he returns home, Frau Schabovsky will have been assigned to another apartment block, in a better part of Dresden.'

'She will? That's a great relief, thank you. Although I find it difficult understand why you are being so good to us. Will you treat each of the others on the programme with the same consideration?'

'Of course I will', he said smiling. 'I hope you don't think that you have been singled out for any special treatment. I am being 'good' as you call it because Klara Hartmann is a potentially valuable asset to the HVA. That is all. They drove in silence for a few minutes then Korten looked at this watch. I'm afraid we are running late, Klara, he said casually. It's been a long day all this driving is beginning to tire me. We may have to return to the *Laube* at Spreewald and stay the night there. Would you object to that?'

He asked glancing over to her and this time she could see that his expression betrayed a flicker anxiety despite the casual nature of the question. An unfamiliar tingle of apprehension and excitement passed through Kara's body.

'Won't that make us late tomorrow morning? And I have no overnight things with me.' She said.

'You let me worry about that. But I won't insist on stopping if you object. Do you?'

She was about to make a momentous decision and they both knew it. If Klara was honest with herself she had thought about this possibility or something like it for many months. But that was merely fantasising. Now the moment had arrived, she was frankly scared. But she knew she would only give one answer. 'No Max, I don't object. If you think that it is for the best then let us stop at Spreewald.'

'Good, that's settled then. I should have mentioned there's chicken, sweet potatoes and Georgian wine there, so we won't starve.'

Yes, Klara said almost to herself. 'Chicken, sweet potatoes and Georgian wine, that is convenient.' Korten pressed his foot tentatively to the accelerator. Klara noticed a slight increase in the speed of the Volvo, as it headed northwards.

Chapter 13

Summer 1962

The following two months, the happiest of her life, seemed to Klara to pass in the blink of an eye. Her first real love affair began on that early summer night in the little timber house on the water in Spreewald. At the same time Adler Programme training intensified as the team prepared for its completion and the confirmation of their individual assignments. Following the night they spent together in the *Laube*, Klara did not hear a word from Max Korten for five anxious days. On the following Friday, Frau Krause, the course Director, called Klara to her office and without ceremony, confirmed to her that she was indeed likely to be sent abroad on assignment and that she should plan to be ready to complete all necessary training by early August. She would not be informed of her precise destination or of the nature of the assignment until later. Klara wondered how, in that case, she was supposed to plan her departure. Was she permitted to tell her mother? She got the distinct impression from the cold dispassionate way that Frau Krause conveyed the news to her, that she disapproved of the proposed assignment. During her training, she had never felt any hostility from Frau Krause but on this occasion she was certain she was not imagining the older woman's disapproval. As ever, she knew better than to ask any further questions.

Thoughts of Max Korten were all that had occupied her mind since the previous Monday morning. She could not properly concentrate on any task, she couldn't read or study and she was certain that on their daily walks to and from the train station, Hetty could not have failed to notice her distracted state. She wanted to see Max and to be with him.

His silence was like a subtle form of torture. If this is what real love is she thought, it is far more painful than joyful. As she left Frau Krause's office, she realised that she did not actually care any longer if she was given a foreign assignment or not. All she wanted was Max. She would be happy to remain forever in the GDR if she could be with him. But he was nowhere to be seen. That Friday evening, as he had the previous Saturday, Korten arrived just as the team was preparing to leave for the day. Once more he gathered the five trainees into the conference room. Korten remained standing at the top of the room so the others did the same. Klara could feel her face flush and her heart beat faster as he spoke to them. He was careful not to make any obvious eye contact with her as he told the team that he would undertake the next assessment on the following day with comrade Hedwig Schaefer, and that it would take the entire day. 'You need not worry about the process comrade'. He said cheerfully to Hetty. Comrade Hartmann has already completed it and she has survived to tell the tale, is that not so Klara?' This time he looked her straight in the eye. It was the first time he had ever addressed any of the team by their first name and the faces of the others registered their surprise.

It was all Klara could do to blurt out a response. 'Yes,' she said looking at Hetty. 'It is not difficult.' What was happening to me? She thought. My face is burning. I am falling apart. Can they tell what's going on in my mind, why is he doing this to me? But the conversation had already moved on, Korten continued. 'By now Course Director, party comrade Krause will have confirmed to each of you that you are to be assigned and posted abroad before the end of August. Each of you will have separate and distinct assignments, so for the next two months, at the very most, there will be a little less group work and more individual training. This form of training is intended to address the needs of each of your specific assignments. Some people may be absent from the group for a day or so from time to time. These absences are to be respected and not inquired into by others. You are not, at any time, to discuss the nature of your own individual assignments or the details of your particular training with each other. That is a strict injunction, please adhere to it. It is not just for the sake of internal security, but it is important when you are abroad that you are not aware of the activities of other operatives in the field, unless it is essential for your mission. Remember, knowledge that you do not possess cannot be extracted from you. That is all for now. Comrade Schaefer, I will call for you at the women's hostel in Gneisenau Strasse at 9.30 in the morning and we will begin our assessment. The rest of you will be expected to report here tomorrow as usual. Thank you, you are dismissed.' Hetty beamed with pleasure at the prospect of her assessment. Klara could not help wondering if Hetty would also be taken to Spreewald for Max Korten's special brand of training. But she knew it was unlikely that little curly headed Hetty, with her thick spectacles and studious nature would be Max's type. As the group trooped out of the room, Korten removed some papers from his document case and placed them on the table in front of him.

'Comrade Hartmann'. He called to Klara as she passed by. 'One moment please, I have that paper by Professor Siegenthaler I promised to give you last week.' She stopped and looked at him not knowing what he was talking about. He handed her a copy of an academic treatise with a mind numbing title: *Significant Economic Advantages to the GDR and the Greater Socialist Bloc, of the Construction and Permanent Maintenance of the Anti-Fascist Protection Barrier.*

'There is a note inside indicating some of the most important points contained in the paper. I suggest you read it carefully.' He gave her the briefest of smiles, looking away quickly as he closed his document case and left the conference room. Klara returned to her little desk across the corridor in the room that all five trainees shared. Daniel, Karl and Dietmar said their goodbyes quickly and left for the evening together as usual, with the noisy enthusiasm of children being let out of school. The boy's club, thought Klara, as she heard them clatter down the stairs. For all the lip service paid to socialist equality in the GDR, she knew that no woman had ever reached beyond the rank of Colonel in the security services and even that was rare, most languished in the most junior grades and were given the 'softer' jobs. 'Klara, I need to use the bathroom, will you wait for me?' Hetty asked, just as she did almost every evening before they left.

'Of course.' As soon as Hetty left, Klara opened the paper Korten had given her. A note in clear neat hand handwriting was clipped to the second page, it read:

My Dear Klara,

I hope you do not interpret my silence since Monday last as indifference. Nothing could be further from the truth. Thoughts of you have occupied my mind every waking moment since we parted, I long to see you. If you can be at the main gate of the Humboldt University at 8.30 pm tomorrow evening, I will pick you up. Not the green Volvo this time but the official Wartburg! Bring whatever you need for an overnight stay. I hope I am not mistaken in thinking that my feelings for you are reciprocated. I shall soon find out. If you are at the gate of the Humboldt tomorrow evening, I will have my answer. As a first lesson in efficient tradecraft, please destroy this note. Let us ensure that our special friendship remains in the private domain. (How very bourgeois of us!) No need for it to interfere with our work.

Until tomorrow

Yours

Max.

He had not forgotten her. He was thinking of her constantly, he said, as she was of him. She was excited at the prospect of another rendezvous. On a second reading she was mildly disappointed that the letter contained no romantic endearments, no 'darling', no mention of the word 'love', only the phrase 'our special friendship.' Was that not a little dry? She consoled herself with knowledge that the letter showed a certain amount of anxiety that his feelings were reciprocated. Before she had a chance to read it a third time Hetty came back into the room. 'Are you ready to go Klara?' She asked as she took the papers from her desk and began to put them in the secure steel cabinet in which they were all required to lock them, each evening.

Klara folded Max's note and put it in her bag, smiling to herself. It gave her some kind of anarchic satisfaction that she had just disobeyed Max Korten's instruction to destroy it, within three minutes of having been told to do so. 'Let me just put my stuff away.' She said getting up. 'I see our three gallant comrades once again haven't bothered to tidy their desks or to lock their papers in the steel press.'

'Perhaps we should do it for them,' Hetty said. 'In case there's trouble.'

Klara gathered up her own papers and brought them to the cabinet slamming the steel door with a loud clang and locking it with a single movement. 'You know Hetty, maybe just for once we won't. These guys treat us like we're maidservants not their equals. C'mon let's go. I'll leave the key in Frau Krause's office on the way out.'

Her friend obediently followed her out of the room but Klara knew that like any good German, compliant Hetty was most uncomfortable breaking the rules.

The more intimately Klara got to know Max Korten throughout that summer the more she liked him. After some time she realised, that no matter how familiar she was to become with him, she never became blasé about his physical attractiveness. Each time she saw him, it seemed as if she was seeing him for the first time. If she thought he was unaware of being observed, she looked at him and admired his natural grace and beauty for the sheer pleasure of it, his head of thick blonde hair combed backwards but always held in place. Yet it was not his looks which won her over. As she got to know him she could see that he was kind, amusing, intelligent and observant. He was very widely read, making no secret of the fact that he read many books not available to ordinary citizens. He never spouted socialist platitudes and was often critical, in a measured way, of certain government policies, if they struck him as particularly absurd. She noticed that he never crossed the line between robust constructive criticism and anything which would be construed as a betrayal of the socialist cause. For example, he said he never doubted for a moment the necessity for the construction of the wall the year before.

The new training arrangement, whereby the trainees had been allocated time for individual instruction, facilitated their love affair. The cosy timber house by the water in Spreewald became an idyllic home from home for both of them in the summer of 1962. Klara loved the place and found it almost physically painful to tear herself away when the time came to leave it. She became just as familiar with Korten's spacious and luxuriously decorated apartment in Karlshorst, to the south east of Berlin. Karlshorst was a semi rural residential area built at the end of the previous century. It was now an enclave of the Soviet military. When the Russians arrived there in 1945 they liked what they saw. They set up their military headquarters in the Prussian barracks. It was not lost on Klara, that by the standards of ordinary citizens, Max enjoyed a privileged life. Not for the first time she wondered at the hypocrisy of an elite, who preached self denial, prescribed harsh medicine for others but did not actually share any of the pain themselves. Her disloyal moods were fleeting. She would not permit anything to hinder the joy of her first real love. She surprised herself at how easily she put aside such inconvenient thoughts.

Klara came quickly to the conclusion that a litany of lies and subterfuge inevitably goes hand in hand with an illicit love affair. The relationship with Korten was no exception. She told her four fellow trainees, that each time she was absent from the programme, there was a legitimate training reason. Apart from both their absences at different times for individual training, Klara and Hetty continued to live in the women's hostel in Gneisenau Strasse. Klara was under strict instructions from Max not to give her friend or anyone else, even the merest hint of their romance. Yet she found it impossible to hide her obvious happiness and perpetual good humour. Hetty had noticed this and had commented in a friendly way on Klara's good mood. In response Klara attributed her contentment to the prospect of the completion of the Adler Programme and her eventual final assignment abroad. Ironically, it was now the assignment abroad which was her principal cause of worry. She reluctantly admitted to herself that she did not want to go now that she had fallen in love. How could she walk away from this man now? But opting out of the foreign assignment was not a possibility. Hetty herself was no longer as chatty as she had once been. She was knuckling down to her studies, concentrating on the final phase of her training and as a stickler for rules, kept rigidly to the stipulation that there was to be no discussion between them about individual training.

On the final Sunday of July, Klara woke in Max Korten's apartment in Karlshorst. She could hear him moving about in the kitchen. She had told Hetty that she was going to Dresden that weekend to see her mother. She felt guilty about this particular lie because Max had told her earlier in the week that her father had been released three days earlier from the Elsterklinik, the sanatorium where he had been incarcerated and was now back home in Dresden. Even that momentous news was not going to separate her from Max. She was happy now and who knew how little time they both may still have together.

'Good morning, sleepy head' Max said, as she came into the kitchen wearing his warm white towelled bathrobe. The table was neatly set for two. Max was at the cooker turning down a saucepan of boiling water. He was wearing his best suit a white shirt and polished shoes, unexpectedly formal wear for a Sunday morning. 'We have some ham, some cheese, warm fresh bread straight from the Russian bakery down the street and even boiled eggs from the batch we bought in Spreewald a few weeks ago. Go on sit.' He said.

Klara did as she was asked. 'I should never have had so much wine last night. You look like you are going to work, how long have you been up?'

'Long enough to collect the bread from the bakery, actually I am going to work and so are you. I want you to wear the blue dress you wore last night and the same shoes. You and I are going to meet someone important and we don't have much time.'

A flicker of concern came over Klara. 'We are not going to see my father in Dresden.'

'No, not that, although I am a little surprised that you have not insisted on seeing him as you were so anxious to have him released.'

'He needs some time with my mother first.' She said, trying but failing to convince herself that her motives were not selfish. She knew that if she met her astute father, he would quickly discern the nature of her relationship with Korten and an inevitable scene would follow.

'So where are we going then?' She said as she sat at the kitchen table and put a slice of ham between two pieces of fresh warm flowery bread. Max came to the table with a coffee pot and filled cups for them both.

'We are going to meet with the second, or truthfully perhaps, the third most important man in the GDR, no less a person than Comrade General Markus Wolf.'

'General Wolf, you are not serious. Why would he want to see you?'

'Yes, General Wolf, the very same, our chief. He is the head of the HVA, he can see whomever he wishes and he wants to see *us*, you too, not just me.'

'Why me?'

'He is not in the habit of giving reasons to his subordinates, nor does he need to explain the time he chooses to see them. So let's be quick with breakfast. We leave in an hour and you must look your usual beautiful self when we get there.'

An hour and a half later, Korten's black Wartburg had already passed through the first of two security cordons around Wandlitz, a secret rural enclave, built three years before for the GDR political leadership. They were less than twenty kilometres to the north of Berlin. Wandlitz was closed to ordinary citizens. Klara had never heard of it. As they drove there, Max explained what she could expect. There were about twenty modest looking but luxurious country houses spread throughout the area, which contained a special shop for the residents, swimming and leisure facilities and a well stocked nuclear fallout shelter. The whole area, comprising five square kilometres, was ringed by two guarded security fences. Max described the place with a certain amount of pride. Klara could not resist challenging him.

'Don't you think that this kind of facility is contrary to the principles of socialism, Max?'

'To each according to their needs, Karl Marx said.'

'Surly these people already living in luxury in Pankow, don't need the hard pressed workers to provide them with country homes as well?'

He pursed his lips with obvious irritation but before he could answer they came to the second security fence about three metres high, stopping at what seemed to be the main security gate. The armed guard who came over to the car recognised Korten, saluted, raised the barrier and waved him through, without looking at the identity pass he was about to present. Within the perimeter, the place was beautifully landscaped. The rustic style houses, surrounded by woodland were modest in size, neat and trim. Each house was a little different from the other.

'Does Ulbricht live here?' she asked.

'Yes, Chairman Ulbricht does live here.' Max answered pedantically. 'And please try to resist asking any provocative questions of our host. He is a very clever man. He is meeting you because you are a potential agent of the Foreign Intelligence Directorate. If he feels that you are in any way ideologically unsound, you can say goodbye to any possibility of further participation in the Adler Programme. I should point out, Klara, that these facilities are not luxuries for the sake of it. Each member of the leadership living here in Wandlitz has suffered great hardships in the past for our cause. They created this country. They are all, as our Soviet friends call them, 'responsible workers.' They bear heavy burdens in their jobs and they are always at risk, either from Western agents or from some of our less enlightened fellow countrymen. So bear that in mind when talking to General Wolf.' He stopped the car, looked at her and smiled. 'OK we're here and that's the end of my little speech. Let's go and let us both be on our best behaviour.'

A tall slim man in his early forties with a broad mouth, brown hair and intelligent, sharp eyes, answered the front door of the half timber house, Klara could see now that the house was a bit more substantial than it had looked from the road. Marcus Wolf wore tan pants, brown shoes, a white open necked shirt and a gray sweater. In his hand he held an open book, his index finger marking the page he must have been reading. He smiled pleasantly at them both. 'Max how are you, please come in. 'Hello Misha'. Max said casually, as he shook the other man's hand. Korten introduced Klara formally as they stood in a wide vestibule.

'It is a pleasure to meet you comrade Hartmann, Max has tells me that you are one of the brightest stars of Adler Programme.'

Klara was more nervous than she had expected now that she was face to face with this legendary spymaster. His handshake was firm 'I would like to believe that is true, comrade General, but I think all of the participants in the programme possess exceptional qualities. I cannot see how mine would have stood out.' Wolf nodded approvingly.

'An excellent answer Fraulein, demonstrating admirable socialist modesty but believe me your talents have not gone unnoticed. Please come through both of you.' Marcus Wolf led them into a well furnished rustic style living room with a large stone fireplace stacked neatly with unlit logs. He sat on a brown leather chair which he had apparently been occupying before their arrival. He indicated the couch and Max and Klara sat down side by side. Wolf marked the page he had been reading with a leather bookmark and placed the book on a side table by fireplace. Klara noticed it was a German translation of Theodore H. White's, 'The Making of a President, 1960.'Marcus Wolf saw Klara reading the book's title and she noticed him noticing. She looked away quickly. He doesn't miss much she thought.

'Do you know this book, comrade Hartmann?'

'Yes General, I've read it in the English edition as part of my studies.'

'I see. And what is your opinion of it?'

'I thought it was a fascinating insight into the inner workings of the American political system. It was far more open about the various qualities of individuals in the US political leadership than I would have expected. But frankly I thought the author's bias in favour of Kennedy over the other candidates was a little too obvious. In my view it lacked genuine objectivity. I think that weakens it somewhat.'

Wolf smiled broadly.' I am two thirds of the way through it myself but so far, I concur with your view. Do you think it tells us all we need to know about the American system?'

Klara became aware that she was the subject of an in-depth interview from a master interrogator, the process disguised as a Sunday morning social call. She cursed herself for her naivety for not expecting this and silently cursed Max for not telling her in advance what was about to happen. 'No comrade General,' she replied. 'It's clearly a book aimed at the American middle class. It is not quite a scholarly work, so its scope is limited. I would say that it does not do anything to lift the lid on the real darkness behind the political system in the United States, corruption, the role of money in political life and the backroom deals which have to be done to achieve any real change.'

Marcus Wolf nodded, seeming to approve of this answer. 'In the course of your studies for Adler, are there any aspects of American life you could say that you wholeheartedly admire?'

This was a dangerous question and Klara and Wolf both knew it. Just at that moment Max chose to interrupt. Klara could not tell whether this was by accident or design. Misha, I'm sorry to interrupt you but I wonder if I may use your bathroom? It's been a long drive.' He addressed Wolf with the informal *du* and called him Misha. He was obviously not in any way in awe of his host.

'Of course, Max, you know where it is. Maybe you would look into the kitchen on your way back and ask Frau Baumann to bring the coffee.' Max nodded in acknowledgement and headed for the stairs.

'Max and I go back a long way.' Wolf said. 'He likes to tell people that we're more like brothers than colleagues, although I am undoubtedly the older brother. Do you recall my question comrade?' He said quickly putting the conversation back on track.

'Yes, of course General. Is there anything I admire about America? I can only say that America seems to foster a genuine self confidence in her people, about themselves and their place in the world. There appears to be a real sense of energetic patriotism there, which has to be admired. I think it is this feeling of superiority which is responsible for the American tendency to lecture the rest of the world about how we should live. They ignore the fact that they treat millions their Negroe fellow citizens with contempt and that there are swathes of poverty and deprivation in many parts of their own country. They are very slow to acknowledge their own flaws.'

'Do you think if you were ever assigned to work in the United States that you would be seduced by the materialism of the country?'

'No General, I do not. I hope I am too much of a realist to be taken in by superficialities. The Adler programme has thought me a lot about America, good and bad. But what has shocked me most about the United States during my training is its irresponsible foreign policy. America's unequivocal support for dictatorships and reactionary governments throughout the world, such as in Panama, Chile, Paraguay, the Philippines, and its support for the apartheid regime in South Africa. US foreign policy simply does not make sense for a country that describes itself as the land of the free. Support for despots is combined with opposition to progressive states such as Nasser's Egypt, North Vietnam, or Cuba, surely tells us that there is no real moral core in US foreign policy.'

'That is all very well but I'm asking about domestic materialism in the US. How can you know that you would not be taken in by America's material riches in a day to day context?'

'Because, comrade General, only a shallow person would succumb to materialism which they know to be underpinned by the abuse and exploitation of others, domestically and abroad. Thanks to what I have learnt on the Adler programme, I know something about the basis of American material wealth. I would like to think that I am not that shallow.'

Max Korten came back into the room followed by a middle aged woman who carried a tray with a coffee pot, china cups and milk and sugar containers. Korten resumed his place next to Klara.

'Just leave everything here please Frau Baumann. We will manage ourselves'. Markus Wolf said to the woman as she placed the tray on the coffee table. She nodded curtly to her master and withdrew to the kitchen. If Wolf was happy with the answers Klara had given, he gave no indication of it.

'Now that Max is back with us, comrade Hartmann, there are some things of importance I wish to say to you.' Wolf began pouring coffee for all three of them and passed the cups around. 'Help your selves to milk and sugar', he said as he sat back in the leather chair, coffee cup in hand and crossed his legs. It occurred to Klara that this self confident man was like an older version of Max. Then in the same instant the realisation came to her that it was the other way around, that Markus Wolf is exactly who Max Korten aspired to be. *'We are more like brothers than colleagues'.* The reverence with which Max always spoke of the 'Chief' said it all. Superficially Max surpassed his mentor. He was certainly better looking and made greater efforts with his western clothes. But Wolf seemed to have a keener intelligence and was supremely at ease with his place in the world. He wasn't as eager as Max to please others. He waited until Klara and Korten had taken their coffee and were ready to listen before he began.

'Comrade Hartmann, you are intelligent enough to know that you are an unlikely candidate for assignment as an HVA operative. Your father's opposition to our socialist world view and to our system of government would of itself, normally rule you out for state service.' Klara sat upright intending to speak in her defence. The General, foreseeing this, raised an open palm in her direction. 'Please comrade, hear me out. I know you will say that your father's beliefs are not yours etc. etc. and I accept that. You have never subscribed to his religious practices but neither have you ever shown any noticeable Communist zeal. For example, you were never a young pioneer, never a member of the SED, you never went to university. You never debated in school or stood out as a positive advocate of socialism, either at school or later at work in the Zeiss plant. In short comrade your appointment as a HVA operative is, from our point of view, a high risk proposition.' Wolf replaced his coffee cup on the tray and sat back once again. It was clear that he had more to say.

'On the plus side, your grades in school were excellent. You were never actually in any trouble. No anti social incidents in your youth. Your linguistic ability is exceptional. And I suppose if I were charitable, which as Max will confirm, I rarely am, obedience to your father when you were young, may have prevented you from playing an active part in communal activities. I understand that you were a very good worker at Zeiss and I am aware that you have excelled in all aspects of training and development during Adler. So, it might be said that all of the negative influences in your life stem from your father's unfortunate adherence to, well, let's call it an outmoded philosophy. However, in weighing up the pluses and minuses, personally I would have opted not to take the risk and to drop you from the programme.' Klara could feel the flush of heat coming to her face which must have been all too obvious to the two men. At this point Wolf looked at Max.

'Your strongest advocate all along, even before your selection for Adler, has always been the man sitting beside you, my old friend comrade Korten. He has already chided me for my caution and tried very hard to persuade me to take the risk and to approve your assignment. I have considered the matter very carefully and have come to a decision. I am informing you officially this morning, that I am giving my approval and that you will be confirmed as an agent of the HVA with the intention of sending you on mission to the United States.'

There was a brief silence as this news was permitted to sink in. 'Thank you comrade General,' Klara said. 'Your faith in me I assure you will be fully justified.'

'I sincerely hope so.' Wolf said, looking again somewhat pointedly at Korten. 'Max has always shown great skill as a talent spotter, in fact exceptional skill. There is no one better and I hope his selection in this instance will be no exception.'

'Thank you Misha,' Max said. 'You can be assured that comrade Hartmann's talents are exactly what are required in the context of the mission that is envisaged.'

'Good,' said Wolf. 'Now I think it is time we discussed some practical matters. As I have said, comrade, you will eventually be sent to the United States. In order to accomplish this we are confronted by two particular obstacles which must be overcome. The first is relatively simple. That is to provide you with a credible biography before you leave the GDR and to get you safely and legally into the Federal Republic, without any suspicion attaching to you. We have decided for the sake of authenticity and credibility that you will leave the country ostensibly as a refugee from the GDR. Max has already prepared a plan and will provide you with details of how this will be done. When you have been processed 'over there' as we say, you will leave Berlin. This will happen because you will express a preference for a particular location in southern Germany. You will be informed where that is later.'

'Comrade General.' Klara interrupted. 'Are the authorities in the West really likely to send me to any place I simply say I wish to go?'

General Wolf's expression indicated he did not care for the implication of her question. 'Our experience is that yes, they will,' He said curtly. 'The second more substantial hurdle to overcome is that we must get you to the United States. That too will be achieved legally and in a manner which will not raise any suspicions on the part of the American security services, although it may take a little longer. Max will of course outline to you in the coming days how that part of the plan is to be achieved. When in America you will not be alone. You will have a case officer assigned to you who will guide and advise you at all times.' He paused for a moment as if he was deciding what to say next. 'Comrade Hartmann, what I have to tell you now is most important and is a strict condition of your assignment. Firstly, you will be permitted only one visit to your father before you leave the GDR. That should take place as soon as it can be arranged. Naturally, you will not tell him or your mother, anything of your intended destination. You will not have to lie. You will say you are simply to be assigned to a foreign posting for a period of less than three years. Is that understood?'

'Yes of course.'

'Secondly, you have a sister Anna Hartmann, currently employed in the KaDeWe department store in West Berlin, whom you have not seen since before the anti-fascist barrier was constructed. You are almost certain to be sent to the Marienfelde Refugee Centre when you seek 'asylum', as they call it on the other side. Marienfelde is not very far from the Ku Damm. You are forbidden to make any contact whatsoever with your sister while in West Berlin. No phone calls, no visits, not even a postcard. Is that understood? For operational reasons it is absolutely essential.'

'Of course General Wolf, that is understood.' Wolf looked at her intently as she answered, in an effort to discern the sincerity of what she had just said. Klara did not look away.

'Finally, as Max will shortly tell you, you will operate abroad under a new identity. You will have a new biography to learn and a completely new family history. It will all be properly documented of course. You must make yourself as familiar with that new identity as you now are with your own. Making a mistake in relation to it could cost you your life, it has happened to others in the past. Please don't for a moment think that I exaggerate. Have you any questions comrade Hartmann?'

'Just one question, comrade General, I wonder if I may be allowed to know when all of this likely to happen? When will the mission begin?'

'My apologies, I thought you had already been informed.' Wolf stood up from his chair to indicate that the meeting had come to an end. 'Details of your new identity will be given to you by Course Director Krause, first thing tomorrow and you can begin to familiarise yourself with them. Max will brief you this coming week on all of the matters we have discussed today. It is now almost the end of July. I would expect that within three or four weeks you will have arrived in West Berlin and the first stage of your mission will have begun. After that you are unlikely to have any further contact with your fellow trainees at least not until you return to the GDR. I suspect you will not see comrade Korten again for many years.' He said this with a smile that Klara thought contained more than a hint of cruel satisfaction. A hardnosed bully beneath the polished veneer was briefly visible. Klara and Max stood up too, in deference to their boss.

'I won't walk you to the door comrade, 'I need to have a brief word with Max about other matters. Perhaps you would wait for him in the car.'

Klara turned and left the room feeling strangely awkward and conscious of the hard edge to Markus Wolf as he dismissed her. He did not shake her hand nor wish her luck with the mission. She knew her status had changed since she came to his house. She had entered as a trainee and was leaving as a *bona fide* agent of the German Democratic Republic, just another of Markus Wolfe's many subordinates. Out in the bright sunshine away from the intensity of the encounter with 'the man without a face' as he was known, she experienced the sensation of momentarily having forgotten where she was. The pine woods of Wandlitz and the nearby homes of the Communist bigwigs made the surrounding countryside look like a scene from a children's book of fairy stories. The workers state, she thought to herself. When she was a child her father had given her sister Anni a dog-eared copy of George Orwell's Animal Farm, a forbidden and dangerous book. It was Klara's first introduction to English writing and had been thoroughly read by all the family before being passed on to someone else. *'We are all equal but some or more equal than others',* one of the animal characters says in the book. A glance around this sylvan paradise left Klara in no doubt what Orwell was trying to say. She remembered her sister asking her father why a book about talking farm animals was considered dangerous. 'Because it is true', her father answered without any further explanation. Klara sat into the Wartburg, glad of the chance to reflect on everything Markus Wolf had said. Only three or four weeks left before her new life began. A visit to Papa, a new identity and incredibly, going to America. She would be 25 years old in a few weeks time, finally joining the adult world. She could hardly remember ever being so frightened. Max remained in the house for longer than she expected. She wondered what Wolf saying to him. When he eventually emerged and got into the car, he looked tense and tired.

'I know you must have stuck your neck out for me Max. He didn't really want to take me did he?'

'Not at first no, but as you now know, he's going to. I know how good you are, Klara and I know you can do it. He'll find out too, eventually. Anyway, you heard what he said. I'm the master talent spotter.' Even as he said this Klara could see that the talk with Wolf had taken something out of him. *More brothers than colleagues,* she thought, that was just a vanity of Max's. Wolf looked like he would turn Max into minced meat if her mission, whatever it was, went wrong.

'Three or four more weeks together Max.' She said. I don't think I want to go, I will miss you too much.'

Max turned the key in the ignition and pressed the starter button. The Wartburg's engine growled into life. 'It's far too late for that I'm afraid, my darling. There is no way back now, for either of us. The Chief just told me that if this goes wrong then it will be my head on the block, and the fact that he and I are old comrades won't save me. So to some extent Klara, my future, as well as yours, is in your own hands.' Rubbing his eyes with his palms, he sighed with apparent frustration.

'Let's go home.' He said. 'Suddenly I am very tired Klara. I will drop you at the women's hostel. We'll talk later in the week. Don't mention to Hetty or the others that you have met General Wolf. You are the only one on the programme to be granted that rare privilege.'

Hetty? You have never called her that before. You always refer to her as comrade Schaeffer.'

'Just be sure not to mention it, OK. I don't want to create jealousy in the group.' They had soon left the leaderships' rural idyll and were on the road back to the city. 'How exactly am I expected to get to the West, Max? Will you simply drop me off at Checkpoint Charlie and let me walk through?'

'No. Of course we could do that, but to ensure that your credibility is enhanced and that your cover story is fully accepted. We have contrived an escape plan.

'You're joking.'

'No I am not. There is a plan. You're going over the wall Klara, just like any traitor to our socialist homeland.'

'How do I know the Grepos won't shoot me?' She joked.

He looked at her without amusement. 'Actually my plan does call for some shots to be fired but of course, we hope they'll miss.'

CHAPTER 14

September 1963

Setting up a meeting with Sergeant Robert Lavelle proved to be a lot easier than expected but the call I made to arrange the meeting produced a shock I hadn't anticipated. I looked up Lavelle's's name and telephone extension in a copy of the Penatagon directory. Lavelle answered his phone after the first ring. He spoke in a polite, educated east coast voice, of a kind I had not expected from a non- commissioned officer, this guy was no Sergeant Bilko. I introduced myself and told him I would welcome a chance to meet and talk to him about an unofficial matter. Not surprisingly he asked me what it was about. I said it was to do with his wife. I expected him to ask, as anyone would, some follow up questions but he simply said he was not available at weekends that he could meet me in Arlington any Wednesday. I suggested the following Wednesday, the twenty fifth and he agreed. I asked him to suggest a location. He suggested a small coffee shop called General Lee's, close to the main gate of Arlington National Cemetery. We agreed to the time and location. I thanked him but before hanging up, I simply said.

'My condolences Sergeant Lavelle, on the death of your wife, this must be a difficult time for you.'

There was a lengthy silence before Lavelle said. 'Excuse me, what did you say?'

'Your wife, Elsa, I believe she recently passed away.'

There was another long pause before Lavelle spoke again. This time his voice betrayed his shock. 'I have not been informed of any such event.

'Did this take place in Germany?'

'No. It happened here in the States. I'm very sorry, I thought you knew.'

Lavelle's shocked voice suddenly rose with anger. 'Who exactly are you? My wife no longer lives in the United States. I believe your information is inaccurate. If you work in the State Department I would have thought you would be better informed. In any event, I fail to see what anything to do with my wife has to do with you. You specifically said this was not an official matter.'

'No, it's not official, although I do work for the State Department. I assure you Sergeant Lavelle this is not some kind of hoax. I was a witness to your wife's death, that's what I wished to speak to you about. I am very sorry to be to one to tell you this. I assumed you knew.'

'When?'

'When what?'

By now he was almost shouting but the genuine grief in his voice was unmistakable. I couldn't say I blamed him. 'When did this happen, when do you say my wife died?'

'Labour Day weekend, Saturday August 31st.'

'That's impossible, she had returned to Europe by then.'

'Listen, Mr Lavelle, Sergeant, I am very sorry. Of course I thought you knew, otherwise I would not have sprung it on you like this. Maybe if we meet next Wednesday as arranged, I will tell you as much as I know.'

Lavelle seemed unable to reply, after another silence he spoke almost inaudibly. 'I don't know, I really don't know. I'm sorry I just can't continue with this conversation.' The line went dead.

I had made the call to Lavelle before either Victor or Sylvia got to work. There were very few opportunities during the working day for any of the three of us to have a private conversation in our small shared office. With that in mind, as soon as I got home to Garrett Park I decided to call Herbert Kluge of the German Embassy. His home address and number were in the phone book. It was listed as an apartment in Alexandria. A woman answered, I asked for Herbert and I could hear her calling to him in German, saying she had no idea who was calling. When he came to the phone I spoke to him in German, hoping I might ingratiate myself with him but irritatingly he responded in accented but precise English, which meant that he had instantly recognised me as an English speaker. When that happened my ego was a little dented. I flattered myself that my spoken German was flawless. I told him out straight who I was and that I wanted to talk to him about the notes he had written regarding two women recently deported to Germany. He remembered instantly the names of Rometch and Kircherr and to my surprise said he would be happy to meet with me and asked would I be available for lunch tomorrow. There was no hard sell required on my part, he sounded almost enthusiastic. Tomorrow was a lot sooner than I expected but what could I say, I had called him. He suggested Harvey's on Connecticut Avenue, coincidentally the same place my roommate Brad worked part time. The place was a well known watering hole for the diplomatic crowd and senior government officials. It had starched linen table cloths well dressed waiters, good wine and was very much out of my normal price range. Herbert Kluge was being so cooperative I could hardly say no. We agreed to meet at 12.30 'To get in ahead of the busy Friday lunch crowd.' Herbert said. For a foreigner he seemed to know something about the lunching habits of the DC elite.

I got to Harvey's ten minutes early, gave my name to the maitre d' who, to my surprise, told me my guest had already arrived. I knew all about German punctuality but more than ten minutes early was pushing things. The maitre d' escorted me to a table for two by the window. Herbert Kluge was there but to my surprise there was somebody else sitting at the table opposite him, a pretty young woman, stylishly dressed with not quite shoulder length golden blonde hair. Herbert rose and shook my hand warmly. He looked to be the kind of German that a movie director might request from central casting. He was tall, over six feet, broad shouldered, with a shock of unruly fair hair. The black horn rimmed glasses he wore added an academic air to the overall Teutonic effect. The woman stood up from her chair and introduced herself. She had a warm friendly smile and seemed tiny next to Herbert's lanky frame.

'Hello, you must be Mr Flynn. I am Gabriella, Herbert's fiancée. Don't worry I am not staying. I just came to collect some keys. I have to get back to work. I work for the American Red Cross we can't afford to eat in places like this.' She said, laughing as she looked around. I introduced myself and shook her hand. Herbert leaned down to kiss her goodbye and she turned quickly towards the door. We both sat down and waited while the busboy poured iced water and Herbert, who was about my age or maybe a year or two older, got the conversation going.

'Very nice to meet you, apologies for Gabriella, she is from Switzerland, we are recently engaged, frankly we are at a stage when can't see enough of each other. And sorry for bringing you here, I know it's a bit chic.'

'Don't worry about it, it's not a problem and please call me Jimmy, everybody does.'

'Of course and you must call me Herbert. I hope you won't mind but I insist on picking up the check when the time comes. You see I have an expense allowance which I never use, so this is my big chance. We are actually encouraged to use it.'

'I won't hear of it Herbert, I invited you and frankly I was hoping our conversation today could be considered private, just between us. No memo to the ambassador when you get back to the office. Is that a problem for you?' He hesitated and then said:

'To be honest Jimmy, you are the first State Department official I have had lunch with since I arrived in Washington in January. So if I can be the host on this occasion, you'll make me look good. And yes of course, we can talk completely off the record. Let us call it a quid pro quo. As I am sure you know, being a Second Secretary I am only required to cultivate contacts. Serious policy discussions are for those further up the ladder.'

'I should tell you Herbert I'm not in the diplomatic stream myself. In fact I'm pretty far down the food chain.'

'I know exactly who you are Jimmy, I looked you up. It won't surprise you to know that our embassy has a very detailed directory of all State Department staff. It even mentions that you spent a year at Heidelberg University. I did my post graduate degree there also. I was there in fifty seven and you in fifty eight.'

'I am flattered.' I said unconvincingly. I hadn't intended to lie to Herbert about my status or the lack of it but I was a little embarrassed about being rumbled so early in our meeting.

'So, let us begin, he said. Miss Rometch and Miss Kircherr, what is it about them that intrigues you, Jimmy?'

Before I could answer, the waiter came and took our order, pan fried sea bass for Herbert and rack of lamb for me. Herbert also insisted on us sharing a bottle of Riesling, on the grounds that it was produced in a vineyard close the small city of Trier, where he came from.

'Well.' I said, finally answering his question once the ordering was done. 'I read your briefing notes on the two women. I had no choice because I was asked to translate them along with other documents in German, in preparation for the deportation. They were very comprehensive, particularly the one on Rometch. You seemed to know an awful lot about her.'

'Yes we did. Her husband was attached to our embassy for a while as an army sergeant.'

'That's a coincidence, Kircherr's husband was also a sergeant.'

'But Rometch's husband was a German army sergeant.' Herbert said.

'Of course, that makes sense. I thought from reading your note on Kircherr, that you were a little sceptical about the reliability of her story.'

Herbert smiled a little nervously at this remark, so I knew that I had hit a nerve. 'You may have a point Jimmy, but before I answer, could I ask you what is your interest in all of this, if it not official? Presumably you have done your job insofar as the translations are concerned and the matter is now closed, unless you have a personal reason. Did you know either Rometch or Kircherr or both?'

'No, I never met either of them. Insofar as Rometch is concerned, I found her story absorbing but that's all. However, it's Elsa Kircherr's story I am more interested in.'

'Oh, any particular reason for that or is it just because she's beautiful?' Rometch is beautiful too you know but in a different way.' Herbert sipped his water in a totally relaxed fashion and it was only then I realised that he did not know what I knew.

'No it's just because I was there when she was murdered. I saw her just seconds before she died.' The look on Herbert Kluge's face confirmed what I had thought.

'I'm sorry. What did you say?' He said, in a kind of strangulated whisper.

The place was now filling up with the lunchtime crowd, some of whom I recognised as senior players from State. I also lowered my voice. 'When she was killed I was there. I didn't see who did it but I heard the shot. You didn't know she was dead, did you?'

Herbert put down his glass, a worried frown on his face. 'No. I did not know. 'Did this happen in Germany? What were you doing there?'

'No Herbert, it did not happen in Germany. It happened right here in America, on Cape Cod just three weeks ago. Elsa Kircherr was murdered and I am amazed that neither the West German embassy, nor her own husband has any knowledge of her death. You probably know she was deported at the end of July but at some point she came back to the States, probably via Canada.'

Herbert had begun to regain his composure. 'I confess I am shocked Jimmy, more than shocked. I don't fully understand. Why were you there when this happened? I thought you said you never met her. What has it to do with you?'

'It has nothing to do with me except that I was there. It happened on a beach. I was simply having a swim, Labour Day weekend. I'm from Cape Cod. My being there was just a coincidence, nothing more. But since it happened I have begun to think that her death and particularly its aftermath, has something of a mystery about it. It was hardly reported in the press, there was no funeral that I know of. Her husband wasn't informed that she was dead. And even the German Embassy doesn't seem to know that one of its citizens re-entered the country illegally and was murdered. That's all pretty weird, don't you think?'

Herbert was not able to answer because at that moment the sommelier arrived with the Riesling and went through the usual ritual of opening it and letting him taste it before pouring and then setting up a stand and silver ice bucket to keep it cool. The sommelier had no sooner left, when a waiter arrived with the lamb and sea bass. The two of us sat in awkward silence while these culinary rituals were going on. The food was beautifully presented but we hardly noticed, both of us straining at the leash to continue the conversation.

'Because I don't know anything about this doesn't mean that the embassy doesn't know.' Herbert said finally. To use your own expression Jimmy, which is new to me, I am quite far down the food chain myself. But you said something about Elsa Kircherr's husband not knowing. Have you met her husband?'

'No, I spoke to him on the phone. Naturally I assumed he would know about the death of his own wife. So I mentioned that I would like to talk about it and I'm afraid I gave the guy a terrible shock. He knew nothing about it either. After that he was unable to say another word. I asked to meet him but I'm not sure that he wants to now.'

'This sea bass is very good.' Herbert said. 'Go ahead Jimmy don't let your lamb go cold. You know Harvey's was the place Kim Philby and James Angelton used to meet to exchange intelligence gossip in the early fifties. You may have heard that Philby has recently gone missing from Beirut. He is almost certainly in Moscow. So it looks like he was in fact the legendary 'third man' after all. Some say this restaurant was where the CIA passed on its secrets every week, directly to the Russians.'

'Yes, so I've heard. It doesn't seem to have damaged Angleton's career any. He's still a very big wheel in Langely.'

Intelligence gossip was all very well but I was anxious to get the conversation back on track. 'Herbert, do you mind if I ask you why you were suspicious of Kircherr's credentials?'

'I see you were able to read between the lines of my report or maybe I was unable to sufficiently disguise my personal views. My first draft would have left you in no doubt about what I thought.'

'I can imagine. I know the way the system works. 'I amend therefore I am' as Descartes didn't quite say. I suspect that's the way public services work all over the world.'

'Precisely, the report you saw was considerably watered down before it got to you. To answer your question there were two things that made me suspicious of the Kircherr narrative. Firstly, there was the timeline around her coming here to the States. It was far too tight to be accidental. Secondly, there was convenient neatness of the story of her childhood and youth. Take the timeline, look how quickly the whole thing moved along. She goes over the wall in August of last year, only one year ago. In that time, she has worked in Bavaria, meets and marries an American serviceman, comes to the US, and not to Idaho or North Dakota, but right here to Washington DC. She gets a job at the Carroll Hotel, a place frequented by a large number of Congressmen, Senators and other influential types. She operates as a 'hostess' in the Quorum Club for three or four months and whatever she does there, she raises enough suspicions in the minds of the FBI to be deported. That's a lot of action for one person in a single year, don't you agree?'

'And she was shot dead here in America, a little more than a month after her deportation.'

'Yes, well, as I said, this is very fresh news to me. Then of course there is the matter of the personal history.'

'It sounded pretty straightforward to me.'

'That's the point it did, but the *Wilhelm Gustloff?* What a very convenient way to get rid of an inconvenient mother. I mean inconvenient in a fictional way. The sinking of that ship in the Baltic, in 1945, was the world's worst maritime disaster. Far more lives lost than on the Titanic. Yet almost nobody outside of my country has ever heard of it because it was one more terrible event among so many terrible events in the last months of the war. The death of the mother, one of more than five thousand people on that ship who died, leaving her child on the quayside, accomplishes two things. It elicits sympathy for the daughter and ensures that the identity of the mother cannot be verified. Then the child is, also conveniently, taken to a state run orphanage where her medical and school records are the responsibility of the East German government and therefore can be altered at will or even created anew. Her schooling was followed by work in the state owned Meissen factory. There are no private industries in the East, so no one to contradict the official record. Then there was a successful jump over the wall, in her case a swim across the Havel. I checked on that too by the way. Two or three shots were fired at the escapee but miraculously they missed. As you say here in America Jimmy, I just don't buy it. But my superiors tell me that they do and that I should keep my suspicions to myself. So I don't really have a choice do I?'

Hebert was getting so wound up he had forgotten to eat. 'With all this talk it's your lunch that's getting cold Herbert not mine, eat up. You're right about the wine, it's very good. For what it's worth, I agree with you but then, who am I? By the way, are you saying that Elsa Kircherr was a call girl? She certainly didn't look like one.'

Herbert had resumed eating with some gusto. He looked at me, clearly amused. 'What's that supposed to mean? What does a call girl look like?'

'Well, I don't know exactly, I'm not an expert. Let's say when I saw her she looked to me to be a classy dame.'

'I'm only guessing what you mean by a 'classy dame', Jimmy, it is not a term I am familiar with but I think you are probably right. I saw photos which were taken of her at Marienfelde Refugee Centre. It would not be an exaggeration to say that she was a great looking woman. But that would not rule out her being a working girl, although, like you I know very little of such matters myself. He paused for a moment and took a sip of the Riesling before continuing. 'I take it you know all about the Quorum Club.'

'Well I've heard of it and I have a good idea what goes on there.' I said, exaggerating my knowledge unashamedly.

'And this man Baker. You know about him?'

'A little.'

Herbert put down his knife and fork and rested his elbows on the starched table cloth. 'We don't know each other, so I trust that what I say does not end up on the desk of Secretary Rusk.'

'As I have already said Herbert, I am only trying to satisfy my own curiosity about a murder. I am not working for anyone else. In fact I have been instructed to keep my nose out of this matter. If Dean Rusk or anyone else knew what I was doing, I don't think I'd have a job.'

'This seemed to satisfy him. 'OK then, I will tell you the view inside our embassy about the two deportations. What I am telling you is just speculation but it's what you might call, informed speculation.' Herbert then looked furtively around the crowded restaurant and leaned forward slightly, lowering his voice. 'This man Bobby Baker is a long time associate of your Vice President Mr Johnson. There has been much speculation about the presidential election next year. Does the President want to keep Johnson as his running mate in 1964? It is well known that the Attorney General Robert Kennedy dislikes Johnson and apparently the feeling is mutual. Johnson hates his present job but he does not want to be humiliated by being, do you say given the ticket?'

'Given the boot maybe but taken off the ticket, I think you mean.'

'Yes, taken off the ticket. Johnson thinks that Bobby Kennedy wants the Senate to get Bobby Baker accused of corruption and of running the Quorum Club with Johnson's knowledge, in order to cause trouble for him. If there is a public scandal involving Baker, Johnson will also be damaged and then he may no longer be suitable as Vice President. Johnson sees the moves against Baker as the work of Bobby Kennedy, who never wanted Johnson as Vice President in the first place and now has a chance to get rid of him.'

'How do you know all this Herbert? How does your embassy know all this?'

'We don't know but we are well informed, so we are guessing, that is, my bosses are guessing. And I would say they are guessing very well.'

'So Johnson thinks Bobby Kennedy is orchestrating all of this stuff about Baker so the Kennedys can bounce him from the ticket for next year's election.'

'Exactly.'

'How does any of this tie in with the deportations of Rometch and Kircherr?'

'That's a different matter. But it seems to me that if Rometch and Kircherr are out of the country and long gone when an investigation about Bobby Baker's activities begins, it will be less embarrassing for everybody concerned, for the Senators and Congressmen and anyone else who used the services of the club. If all of this goes public it would be too good a story for the press to resist. Politicians, sex and an espionage angle, as both women once lived in the GDR. The public would eat it up, just like the Profumo business in England.'

Unimaginatively, considering where we were, we both ordered Boston cream pie and two coffees. I was thinking about everything that had been said. When the waiter had brought the pie, I said to Herbert.

'There is something I haven't told you about the weekend of the murder.'

'Oh what's that?'

Now it was my turn to speak softly. 'Elsa Kircherr called into the Kennedy compound in Hyannis Port the day before she was shot. She asked to see the Attorney General or the President. Needless to say she was turned away. Hyannis is my home town. That's how I heard about it. She was shot on a nearby beach the following day.'

This news had the desired effect on Herbert. I could tell he was genuinely shocked. He stopped eating his pie, said nothing for quite awhile. Then he spoke. 'I'm glad you told me that Jimmy because I have told you a lot and to be honest I was afraid I was saying too much. You have my word I will not say a thing about this to my authorities. And I will tell you one more thing before we finish and then maybe we could change the subject. We, the West Germans, know for a fact that Elsa Kircherr paid at least two visits to a certain house here in Washington on two days in June this year and we have good reason to believe that she met with the principal resident there.'

He looked at me with an expression which seemed to say, 'How do you like them apples?' I looked blankly at him and said. 'I don't get you Herbert, what exactly is your point?'

He glanced around the room. The number of diners had thinned out a little but he wasn't taking any chances. He spoke in German. 'It wasn't just any old house Jimmy.' he said with exasperation. 'It was the big one on Pennsylvania Avenue. You know the principal resident, the guy who spends a good deal of his time in your home town. Now do you understand?'

I stared at him slowly realising what he was telling me. I was beginning to feel a little embarrassed that a junior diplomat from another country, who'd been here for all of nine months, seemed to know a lot more of what was going on in my country than I did. When I failed to reply he took another piece of pie and said in English. 'Take your time Jimmy' He said, laughing, amused by how slow I was on the uptake. 'There's absolutely no rush.'

CHAPTER 15

September 1963

The General Lee Cafe was five or six hundred yards from the Memorial Bridge entrance to the National Cemetery in Arlington. It was a cosy place, its walls covered with an interesting collection of civil war photographs along with formal portraits of 19th century politicians and soldiers from both sides of the Mason Dixon line. I got there at 10.00 am, had pancakes and two cups of coffee. I brought the Washington Post for company, but by 11.30 it was clear to me that Robert Lavelle was not going to show. I decided to go home. I had parked my Dodge Dart just down the street and when I reached it I remembered that, according to the documents I had removed from the office, Elsa Kircherr and her husband Robert Lavelle lived at 1200, Apartment 3A Cherry Tree Lane Arlington. I walked back to the Cafe and asked the guy I presumed to be the owner, if he knew where Cherry Tree Lane was. He did, it wasn't far and he was kind enough to draw me a map on a paper napkin. I thanked him and asked if he knew a customer of his called Robert Lavelle but he said no, most of his customers were tourists, visitors to the cemetery so he rarely saw them twice.

I decided to leave my car where it was and walk. The cafe owner's map was clear and accurate and within fifteen minutes or so I had reached 1200 Cherry Tree Lane. The house was one of two identical three story Victorian houses, on a single lot, obviously once fashionable mansions now converted into apartments. 1200 and its neighbour had seen better days, both needed a paint job. The house was a contrast to surrounding swish Arlington. Apartment 3A was on the ground floor. There was a mailbox on the wall with the names Lavelle and Powell. I rang the bell and waited long enough to ring a second time. Before I could, the door was opened by a man in his thirties, clean shaven and wearing a white undershirt and dark pants. 'Yes, can I help you?' He said, with a just a hint of annoyance.

'Hi. I'm looking for Robert Lavelle. My name is Flynn, Jimmy Flynn. I called him earlier in the week.'

'Yes, I remember your call. It came as something of a shock. I am Robert Lavelle. Actually I decided not to meet with you today but I had no idea how to contact you. Is this some kind of official inquiry? You said you are with the State Department. Am I obliged to talk to you?'

'No. It's not official. And you are not obliged to talk to me. I happened to be present when your wife died. And I wanted to talk to you about it that's all. I apologise for breaking the news to you last week, in that way. I never imagined you wouldn't have heard already.'

'Why would you want to talk to me about it? What has my wife's death got to do with you?'

It was a good question. Herbert Kluge had also asked me something like it and I didn't really have a valid answer. What had it to do with me? Absolutely nothing, the whole thing was none of my business. Yet for some dumb reason I knew I wasn't going to let it go.

'It's just that she died in rather unusual circumstances.' I said. 'I thought maybe I could tell you how it happened.'

He was standing erect in the doorway, his arms folded in a defensive pose. He had the physique of a gymnast, broad shoulders, flat stomach and narrow hips. 'I'd rather you didn't come in if you don't mind but you have piqued my interest. I will talk with you, if only to satisfy my curiosity. If you'll wait on the street I'll join you in five minutes. We can walk to the cemetery and talk there, is that OK?'

'Sure.' I said. He closed the door and as I walked back to the sidewalk I thought I heard muffled voices coming from inside the apartment. After loitering on the street for less than five minutes Lavelle came out, wearing a short tan jacket over a green army tee shirt. Apart from his tight military haircut he had an uncanny resemblance to the actor James Dean and the same moody demeanour to go with it. On the way to Arlington cemetery I told him of the events of Labour Day on

Craigville beach. By now I had recounted the story so often it was becoming easier to distil it down to its essentials. Robert Lavelle listened intently without interruption. A pained expression appeared on his face when I described his wife's body lying motionless on the sand. When I had finished he was silent for a moment, his eyes moistened but he simply stared impassively ahead. 'Did she suffer?' He asked almost inaudibly.

'I wouldn't think so. She died instantly. Apparently it was a small calibre bullet a .22. The wound was just a tiny hole in her temple. The strange thing is that even with so many people around nobody saw an assailant or the shot actually being fired. The guy I was with, Tom Noonan is a cop and he heard the shot. I was right there beside him and heard nothing.' Lavelle then began to question me about my own interest in the killing. I told him about the papers relating to Elsa Kircherr I had come across, in the course of my work. I explained that it was this coincidence which had sparked my interest in the murder. 'Of course I had never been that close to a murder before.' I said to Lavelle by way of an additional explanation but I could see by the expression on his face that he was already preoccupied with something else. We reached the entrance to the cemetery.

'I often come here.' Lavelle said. 'It's so peaceful among the thousands of dead and yet so very private. It's a great place to walk and to think. You can learn an awful lot just by reading the headstones. Each one is a little history lesson carved into stone.' He laughed quietly to himself. 'I'd go so far as to say it's probably my favourite place in the world. How sad is that?'

'I can think of worse places.' I said. 'It's quite beautiful. Maybe when your time comes you'll rest here yourself, you are a serviceman after all.'

'Not me.' He said. 'I'm the last person they'll let in here. I want to ask you something. Jimmy, you don't mind if I call you Jimmy do you?'

'Not at all.'

We started to walk along the narrow path between the graves. It being mid week there weren't many others doing the same thing but the expanse of the place was such that each group wandered among the gravestones in isolation 'What is it you want to ask?' I said.

'The documents you translated, did they tell you anything about Elsa's past?'

'A little, yes. They mentioned her origins in East Prussia, her mother dying in the war and her upbringing in a children's home. Not much detail, it was all fairly general. There were copies of documents, a birth certificate, employment record, asylum application and a copy of her passport, that kind of thing.'

'What about her escape to the West?'

'Yes that was mentioned. She had to swim to safety. Apparently some shots were fired at her but as we know, she made it to our side.'

'What about me? Is my name in there?' He asked with a look of concern.

'Yes it is. The documents mentioned that you were a regular guest at a hotel GI's frequented in Bavaria, that you met her there and married within a few months, a regular whirlwind romance by all accounts.'

Lavelle ignored my levity. 'Anything else, about me, I mean?'

'Only what you might expect, your army rank, your transfer to a job in the Pentagon, your address here in Arlington, routine stuff really.'

'Was there any mention of Elsa's motivation in coming to the United States?' He asked, with a quiet intensity as if he was afraid of the answer.

'You mean security concerns?'

'Yes.'

We had come to the majestic white steps leading up to the Tomb of the Unknowns. There was a bench nearby. I suggested we sit down. 'You know Robert I'm already in breach of government confidentiality regulations by telling you what I have already told you. But you're in the service yourself, so you know all about that. Anyway, although I am not quite sure why, I'm going to tell you a little more and I hope you'll understand that what I have to say is for your ears only.'

'I understand.' He said simply and quietly.

In less than ten minutes I had laid most of it out for him. I didn't mention Herbert Kluge's name or my meeting with him but I told him in full, the contents of the West German Embassy paper relating Kircherr. I told him of the West German suspicions that his wife was a spy. I even mentioned Bobby Baker's Quorum Club. I had to be circumspect about how I described it, as I was talking about this man's wife. I told him that I'd been warned off the case in no uncertain terms by the FBI. He listened carefully. I could tell he was paying close attention. I was being reckless, talking this way to someone I did not know and who I had met less than an hour before. I justified the indiscretion to myself by thinking this was a man who had recently lost his wife and he had no idea why. But there was something about Lavelle which made me trust him, some other worldly detachment in his demeanour which seemed to indicate that he did not have an angle that he simply wanted to know what happened. When I had finished he looked thoughtful for about thirty seconds and then said.

'I can do this a little better if we walk, do you mind?' We stood up. With headstones stretched out ahead of us, seemingly as far as the eye could see, we began to stroll again. He spoke and his voice was so low it was like that of a shy schoolboy. I had to strain to hear him.

'You called me last week and told me Elsa was dead. You can imagine how much of a shock that was. I assumed she was home in Germany. Whether it's a coincidence or not I received a call the following day from the FBI. A fellow named Caulfield. He told me 'officially' that my wife had returned to this country illegally. That she had been killed, 'in Boston,' as he put it, in suspicious circumstances and that the matter was being investigated by the FBI. He said there were, as yet, no suspects or any obvious motive for the killing, except a possible robbery. Caulfield said Colonel Taylor, he's my CO in the Pentagon, would be kept informed of developments and that if anything of significance emerged he would pass the information on to me. Caulfield advised me not to discuss this matter with anyone other than Colonel Taylor or himself, Agent Walter Caulfield. He didn't come across as much of a charmer, if you know what I mean. He then gave me both his office and home numbers. He was just about to hang up when I asked him about Elsa's remains. 'Thanks for reminding me.' Caulfield said. He told me that the body had been cremated in Boston 'for logistical reasons' and that an urn of her ashes and some personal effects would be sent to me next week. He said the cremation was necessary because initially, her identity was unknown and therefore I, as her next of kin, could not be contacted. Apart from another warning about not discussing the matter with anyone and the inadvisability of holding any kind of a memorial service for her, that was it'.

Lavelle's matter of fact rendering of this story surprised me. He didn't seem particularly disturbed by the manner in which federal agents had taken over his wife's funeral arrangements, not to mention the offhand way they seemed to treat the investigation of her murder. 'You know you could raise hell over this, don't you? It's not the FBI's business to conduct funeral services for your family members. Frankly Robert, I'm surprised that you're not a hell of a lot angrier about this than you seem to be. I mean who do those guys in the Bureau think they are?'

Lavelle stopped walking and looked at me for what seemed like a long time before he spoke. 'I'm going to take you at face value Jimmy. I'm sticking my neck out. Hoping you're not FBI yourself or CIA or any other spook outfit. I am hoping your exactly who you say you are. A federal employee intrigued by the identity of a woman he saw killed on a beach in Massachusetts. Am I being naive or dumb in making that assumption Jimmy?'

'No you're not. That is exactly who I am. I'm a middle grade State Department employee. I am nothing more than that.'

'OK', He said. We resumed walking. 'I liked Elsa Kircherr a lot.' Lavelle said. 'You might say I even came to love her. But she was my wife in name only. We were married in Munich just after Christmas and she returned to the States with me by the end of January. Dozens of GI's all over the world do the same thing every week, there's nothing unusual about it. But I was prevailed upon to marry Elsa, which is funny because she was such beautiful girl. It really shouldn't have taken much persuasion.'

'Who prevailed on you?' I asked.

'Believe it or not I don't know. But I could take a pretty good guess. Let me put it this way Jimmy. I know for a fact that she was instructed by someone to get a job at the Carroll Arms Hotel. I appreciate your delicacy in describing it as a social club but actually I know exactly what it is. Elsa was told to make contact with Bobby Baker, the head honcho of the Quorum Club and to make sure she was introduced to specific national legislators, with a view to obtaining information from them or putting them in compromising situations. The kind of thing could possibly be of interest of the CIA for example, but I suspect it's more likely to be of interest to the other side, our cold war enemies, don't you think?'

'Yes I do think but how can you not know? I mean you married someone at their behest. Didn't they introduce themselves?'

'No they didn't. They just made it clear to me it had to be done.'

'How did they do that?'

'Before we get to that let me tell you about Elsa. She was not a willing participant in this caper any more than I was. But she had a much harder part to play than I ever had. I only had to pretend to be married. She actually had to meet these sleaze ball politicians, drink with them, laugh at their jokes, flatter them and as you can guess, do practically anything else with them, they felt like doing.'

'So why did she do it?'

'Firstly, I doubt if she had much choice. I don't know much about her life in East Germany but I got the impression she still has family there. Secondly, I don't think she fully realised what she would have to do before she was ordered to do it.'

'Did you discuss her life as a spy with her? Because clearly that's what she was, there can be little doubt about that now. Did she tell you who she was working for?'

'No she didn't talk about it. She said the less I knew the safer I would be. So I never really asked. We weren't really a married couple in the normal way, as I've said.'

'I'm still not clear how you got into this. Why did you agree to take her on and bring her to the States?'

He gave me a look which was a mixture of pity and wry amusement. You know Jimmy, you don't seem like a bad guy but where the hell were you brought up, with Jimmy Stewart in Bedford Falls? You remind me of a kid in a Norman Rockwell painting.'

'I don't get it.' I said.

'I know you don't, that's precisely my point. Do you know the Tennesse Williams play, Cat on a Hot Tin Roof?'

'Sure, it was made into a movie with Paul Newman and Elizabeth Taylor.'

'And did you understand it? Do you know what Tennessee Williams was getting at?'

'There's no need to patronise me, of course I got it. It's about repressed homosexuality. Paul Newman is married to Elizabeth Taylor but is infatuated with his football playing buddy. I forget his name.'

'He was called Skipper. Paul Newman played a guy named Brick. Well Jimmy, I am a version of Skipper or of the Paul Newman character, if you prefer. People like us do exist you know, maybe not in Norman Rockwell land where you come from but in the real world.'

'Oh. I see.'

There was no low talking now. Lavelle was getting angry and his decibel level increased accordingly. 'Good. I'm glad you see. Well you won't be surprised to hear Jimmy Flynn from Main Street USA, that people like me are not tolerated in the United States armed forces or in sensitive posts in government or in lots of other places either. I'm a Yale graduate for God's sake, summa cum laude and I'm a Sergeant in the US Army and unlikely to progress any further.'

'I take it no one in the Pentagon knows this about you?'

'I'm not sure about that. My education and my ability would normally mark me out as officer material. But here I am. So somebody somewhere in the service certainly suspects something. The 'condition' as a doctor I know called it, severely limits your career options. Someone in Munich, I am guessing the KGB or their stooges from one of their iron curtain satellites, found out about me. It's not hard to do. They followed me to the kind of bars and clubs in Munich that cater for people like me, took pictures, intercepted my correspondence and asked me, politely, in the interests of my future career and my parents' peace of mind, to do a relatively simple thing. Marry a beautiful woman named Elsa Kircherr, no conjugal duties to be fulfilled on my part. Bring her back to the States as my legitimate bride and ask no further questions either of her or of them. It was blackmail, pure and simple but I did exactly as I was asked and I was left alone. Then a surprising thing happened. I got to know Elsa pretty well and got to like her quite a lot and I believe she got to like me.' He looked over at me and smiled his mood suddenly calm and serene. 'You're blushing Jimmy. I'm sorry. I can see I'm embarrassing you.'

'No, I'm not embarrassed.' I said unconvincingly. 'I'm just trying to take all this in.'

'Yeah sure. Any hoo hah, we became good friends, real friends, she and I but never lovers. She never told me her true back story. She was apparently ordered by her masters, whoever they are, not to and she herself seemed to think the less I knew about her real life, the safer it would be for me, what with me working at the Pentagon. She never once asked me anything about my own work, which is dull anyway and absolutely unclassified. But she told me something about the characters in the Quorum Club and did not hide her distaste for them. She only started working there in April and was deported at the end of July. That was long enough for her to find out that our much vaunted democracy has its flaws too.'

'Do you think she might have been killed because of something to do with the Quorum Club?' I asked.

'I suppose it's possible. From what she told me, the clientele are a bunch of low life rats. I think it was set up to influence the votes of particular members. Baker is supposed to be close to LBJ. But frankly I think that a murder emanating from that quarter would be a little melodramatic. I do believe this though, Elsa's assignment here in Washington had some urgency to it. I believe she was asked by her controllers to do something quite specific in the context of her work in the Quorum Club. She wasn't intending to be some kind of long term sleeper, no pun intended, who was to report back Moscow or East Berlin or wherever, solely on chickenfeed gossip she gleaned from a Governor from Arkansas or a congressman from the Bronx.'

'What makes you say that?'

'I just gathered from certain oblique things she said that she was on a mission. I can't be more specific. As I said she was careful about how much she told me. Listen Jimmy, if you don't mind, I'd like to stop this now. No offence but I'm a little tired and still very upset about everything you've told me. People like me can and do love women you know and I loved her. If you want to talk to me another time that's not a problem but how about we take a break? I'd just like to walk on my own for a bit. I have a lot to think about.'

'Sure Robert.' I said. You've been more than frank with me and I appreciate it. Do you mind if I call you sometime next week when you receive Elsa's personal effects from the FBI? I'd be curious to know what they are.'

Lavelle gave me a bemused look. 'I hope you're not thinking of digging deeper into this thing. This is not a suitable case for an amateur detective. Elsa was either a real life foreign agent or else she was a CIA operative. You work for the State Department. You could lose your job, or your liberty or both. Stay well away from it is my advice. Anyhow, I've already told you about as much as it's possible to tell. Now that you know who she is, your mystery is solved.'

'Maybe you're right.' I said. Forget it.'

'That's not what I mean. Feel free to call me next week if you want. Here, I'll give you my home number.' He scribbled his number on the back of a bookshop receipt he took from the inside pocket of his jacket. You're welcome to look at whatever it is the FBI may send me but I doubt it will be of much interest. As I said my strong advice is to let it go.' We shook hands and went our separate ways. He walked on alone, further into the heart of the cemetery and I headed back towards the same gate we'd come in. I had learned an awful lot about Elsa Kircherr that morning. Robert Lavelle was right. There was not very much more to know. Maybe it was time to leave it alone.

Outside the cemetery I headed for my car passing the General Lee Café once again. I was tempted to go in, have another coffee and ruminate on what I had just heard. I looked in the window to see how big the tourist crowd was and if there was a seat free. It was almost full so I decided to skip it. I walked to my car and sat in. It had been an interesting morning. Lavelle seemed decent enough but I was smarting a little about the Norman Rockwell remark. It was not all that different from Herbert Kluge's implication that I was some kind of innocent abroad. I was learning fast and nothing I had learnt made me feel any better about my own country or about the way politics really works in this town.

CHAPTER 16

August 1962

Klara Hartmann had undergone three days of fairly benign interrogation in West Berlin's Marienfelde refugee reception centre. She was questioned in turn by West German security officials and by two men who, judging by their accents and poor German, were from American military intelligence. They were there because Klara had arrived in the city's American sector. A representative from the refugee centre sat in on each of the interviews as a kind of guarantor of the refugee's rights. The accommodation at Marienfelde was adequate and the food was not bad. On her third day there she was a given a U Bahn ticket and permission to go into the city centre on condition that she would return by 5.00pm. It was almost noon when she got off the train at Zoo station. She still had about an hour to kill before she could do what she had come to do. She had decided to walk through the Tiergarten and to take a look at the Brandenburg gate from the western side. She was missing Max terribly.

They had spent their last night together in a small hotel in Potsdam which catered almost exclusively to Soviet army officers. They were booked into adjoining rooms in conformity with socialist modesty. They left the hotel in the early hours of their second night there. The mock escape was supervised by Max, a Major Stern, of the Volkspolizei and a young corporal who carried her rucksack. Klara was brought by car to a pre arranged spot on the banks of the Havel. She and Max said their formal goodbyes standing on the sandy river bank. Dawn had not yet broken but there was already a glimmer of bright sky to the east. Max shook her hand and wished her good luck, as he would to any agent he was about to dispatch on a mission. Major Stern, who was watching this scene, reassured her for the second time about the four shots that would be fired into the water near her as she swam. The corporal handed her the rucksack containing all of the worldly possessions she would take to the new world she was about to enter. This was it, she thought to herself. This was the adventure she had trained so hard for and wanted so badly. It was at that very moment she knew she did not want it at all. She was inwardly heartbroken as she entered the cold waters of the Havel. She was aware of the eyes of Max and the other two Vopos on her, as she shuddered at the first touch of the cold water before swimming away. She had trained for this over the previous three weeks in a pool reserved for Stasi operatives at a recreational facility in Berlin-Pankow. But she was surprised at the slow progress she seemed to be making. When she was almost mid point across the river, searchlights on the south side lit up the dark waterway, flashing forward and back along the river but deliberately never picking her out. Simultaneously a siren started up, shattering the quiet August night. A cacophony of guard dogs barking accompanied the siren. A minute or so later four shots rang out. Klara could clearly hear the bullets plop into the water some distance away. The fourth shot hit the water only two metres from where she swam. The Vopo Major had told her this would happen and assured her that she was in no danger of being hit. After four minutes of noise and light, the siren stopped and the searchlights were dimmed. Klara swam the remaining third of the river in an almost leisurely rhythm, her body becoming accustomed to the water, which by now felt almost warm.

The journey was longer and more tiring than she expected, taking more than thirty minutes. When she reached the far shore she pulled herself out of the river on to a stony rubbish strewn patch of ground. She walked across the stones with difficulty, panting with exhaustion, crawling up the shallow embankment, her wet clothes and rucksack weighing her down. When she reached a grassy surface she sat down, leaning her back against a metal post. She sat there motionless for three or four minutes until she felt the cold water permeate her skin. Then she removed light tennis shoes from the rucksack and put them on without socks. She stood up and took of her jacket and the woollen sweater she wore underneath. Thankfully the night was warm. She put the sweater and Jacket in her rucksack but was still wearing wet navy blue slacks and a tee shirt. By now her eyes had become accustomed to the dark, helped by the first intimations of the coming dawn. She stood up and looked at the sign atop the metal post she had been leaning against. It said in English German and Russian: 'You are now entering the American Sector of Berlin.' Inexplicably, the sign faced the water as if it had been placed there to greet incoming escapees. It was only ten paces from where Klara stood, to the sidewalk. She walked for less than a minute until she was blinded by a bright flashlight carried by a lone policeman who seemed to emerge from the shrubbery planted along the grassy bank. He ran the flashlight down from her face over her wet clothes. 'Are you alone Fräulein?' he asked. To her surprise he spoke with the strong Saxon accent of her home region, which some Germans find comical.

'Yes.' She said, 'it's just me.'

'Are you the cause of all the noise over there?' he said indicating the far side of the river. He had obviously been down on the bank looking across.

'Yes, I suppose I am.'

'Welcome to free Berlin, Fräulein. You are a brave girl. You are my very first. Come, I will bring you somewhere we can dry those clothes for you. We can talk there, it's not far. You have just given me quite a bit of paperwork to do.'

They crossed the empty street, as they walked to the police station Klara had the disconcerting sensation of wishing that she had actually escaped from the GDR and that she was truly free. But she knew she had a long period of servitude ahead of her. 'What is your name?' The friendly policeman asked and where are you from?'

'I am from Görlitz, Klara Hartmann answered. 'My name is Elsa Kircherr.'

'Ah Saxony,' said the policeman. 'Me too, as you have probably guessed.' He said smiling.

On her first free afternoon in the West Klara walked through the wooded Tiergarten, past the Victory column, and eastward to the Brandenburg gate. The gate was just barely on the Eastern side of the wall, an archway that generations of German soldiers had marched under but through which nothing could now pass. It was a sad symbol of a dysfunctional city. About a hundred metres to the right of it, a timber viewing platform, resembling a church pulpit, had been constructed and it was possible to climb the steps and look into the East. Klara waited patiently for some French tourists to finish doing so, before taking her turn. She mounted the steps and looked across at the now divided Potsdamer Platz and the wide empty space of the former government district. A heap of rubble in the centre of waste ground marked the location of Hitler's Chancellery and the bunker buried beneath, his suicide there bringing an end to six years of unprecedented death and destruction. To her right Klara could clearly see the air ministry building where she had worked until just five days ago, even the windows of the fourth floor offices were visible.

The experience of seeing the city from this perspective was surreal. Was Frau Krause, the Adler Programme director, up there now sitting at her desk? Where was Max, what was he doing now? What of Hetty? They had last seen each other just a week before, at a reception in Normannenstrasse, marking the completion of the Adler Programme, hosted by Erich Mielke, Markus Wolfe's all powerful boss. During the reception Max indicated that he wanted a final word with comrade Schaeffer before she was assigned and asked her to come out to the corridor. When she returned, Hetty, as arranged, whispered the words *'Au revoir ma cherie'* into Klara's ear. It was obvious that she was very happy. The words were a pre-arranged coded reference to the location of her assignment which they had both agreed on. Max must have told her she was being assigned to Paris or some other French city, as she had hoped. Telling Klara was an untypical breach of security by Hetty. The following morning, Klara looked for her at the women's hostel but Hetty's possessions had been removed and she herself had already left. Klara knew better than to ask, but she hoped she would meet her studious friend again, perhaps someday on a sunny boulevard in Paris.

Gazing at the strange ugly structure in front of her, she thought of the folly of building the wall, the sheer madness of cutting a great city in half and separating its people with bricks and guns. Three days here, she thought, and I am already thinking like a traitor. A polite cough behind her told her that a small line had formed of others waiting their turn in the wooden pulpit. She turned away from the wall, descended the steps and headed west.

A half an hour later she was walking down on the Ku'Damm. She passed the prosperous looking clientele sitting in the sidewalk cafés of the busy shopping street. When she arrived at Berlin's most prestigious department store, the legendary KaDeWe, she checked her reflection in the plate glass window, straightened her hair, took a deep breath and went in. At the cosmetics counter on the ground floor, three or four well dressed women were blocking access and talking animatedly to glamorous assistants behind the counter, seeking advice or deliberating as to whether a particular product was effective and worth the price. When one elderly dowager, wearing a sable coat moved away, Klara took her place at the counter. The assistant came towards her. 'May I help you Madam?'

'Hello Anni, greetings from Mama and Papa. You look well my darling. It's so good to see you.'

Anni Hartmann had to hold her hands firmly on the counter top to avoid fainting. The two sisters simply started at each other's faces for a long time. The customers at the counter suddenly stopped talking, aware that something unusual was taking place. Anni blushed when she realised her colleagues too, were also staring at her.

'It's my half day off today.' Anni said quickly to Klara. 'I will be free in less than an hour. Can you wait?'

Klara nodded, still staring at her sister but said nothing. Anni suddenly reached across the counter, took her sister's head in her hands and kissed her with an intensity that surprised Klara. 'You don't know how happy this makes me.' Anni said as she held her.

'And me too,' Klara answered, tears coming to her eyes. 'Can you get away? I will wait for you at the main entrance.' She slowly disengaged from the embrace gripping her sister's hand as she did so, then turned and walked away. The other women, customers and colleagues alike, looked at Anni with a mixture of amusement and curiosity. Anni smiled at them all, her heartbeat slowing gradually. 'My sister.' she said finally, 'From the East, over the wall. I don't know how she got here but as you can see I wasn't expecting her.' The customers smiled and nodded approvingly, one or two applauded politely.

Forty minutes later the two sisters were on a train heading to the strand at Wansee on the western outskirts of the city. The train was full of family groups going in the same direction, like generations of Berliners, taking advantage of the warm August day for sunbathing and swimming in the lake. The sister's conversation on the train was constrained by the fact that they were surrounded by potential eavesdroppers. Neither Klara nor Anni had brought any swimming clothes. When they arrived at Wansee station, they walked along the wooded lake shore. Klara told her sister everything that had happened to her since her visit to creepy Dr Hoffman, almost exactly a year before. Klara omitted nothing, including the intensity of her romance with Max Korten. Anni, the older 'serious one' of the two listened almost in silence. When Klara had told her story and Anni had satisfied her curiosity, they bought ice cream from a vendor and sat on a grassy mound overlooking a narrow strip of lakeside beach, thronged with bathers.

'I find it hard to get used to the noise and bustle on this side. Everything is much quieter on ours.' Klara said. It was obvious that her sister was still digesting all she'd been told and wasn't listening.

'I cannot believe all you are telling me Klara. It sounds like something from James Bond. You won't know him. He is big sensation on this side.' Anni said. 'At least you got Papa out of prison. I suppose that is the main thing. But it seems to me that you have put yourself in a very dangerous situation. Does Papa know who you are working for and what you have to do?'

'No. He knows that I work for the Foreign Ministry, which is technically true. As for what I have to do, I don't know that myself.'

'So what happens next?'

'Assuming I am granted asylum and get out of Marienfelde, I will go to Bavaria. I think there will be a job arranged for me there. After that I must wait to be approached by someone, who will tell me what I must do next. I can only guess from the kind of training I received, the long term intention is to send me to the United States. But I cannot be absolutely sure.'

'It sounds exciting the way you say it, far more exciting than the cosmetics counter at KaDeWe.'

'At least you are truly free Anni. You can do what you like and go where you like. No case officer for you. To be honest, I'm not sure I will be able to do whatever it is they want me to do for very long. Ideologically my heart is not really in it. As you know, I never liked to be controlled.' They both laughed at this obvious truth. 'Do you like it here in the West Anni?' Klara asked.

'Yes. I do. It's an exciting and interesting place. But honestly I have not been able to enjoy anything knowing that Papa is in prison and Mama is stuck in that flat. I am so glad that he is home. Thanks to you, a huge burden of worry has been lifted from my shoulders. I hope you don't have to pay too high a price for his freedom.'

'Any price is worth it. He would have died Anni, if they had kept him in Hohensconhausen or any place like it.'

'Did they ever get my letters?'

Klara shook her head. 'No, there is an official policy of not forwarding the mail of 'stay overs' to their loved ones.'

'How kind our leaders are.' Anni said. 'Actually Klara, I don't think it's all bad in the East. It's not a perfect paradise on this side either. But the pettiness and spitefulness of the system over there is hateful. Imagine throwing letters sent to a woman living alone in a damp flat, into the garbage, just to punish her because her daughter chose to work where she wanted to.'

Klara interrupted her sister. 'Remember, they read them before they destroy them. Anni I have something serious to tell you, please listen to me carefully.'

'Of course, go on, I'm listening.'

'I am breaking all the rules by making contact with you like this and telling you all I have told you. If they knew they would recall me or Papa would be sent back to prison or perhaps both. Please do not repeat anything I have said. Not to anyone no matter how trustworthy you think they are. In fact don't mention me at all, nothing about the so-called escape. Remember I am supposed to be another person. Just keep what I have told you to yourself, will you do that?

'Won't your friend Max get you out of any trouble you might get into?'

Klara noticed a slight edge to Anni's question. A vestige of sisterly rivalry still lurked there under the surface. 'No, he won't because he and his boss are the ones who told me I was not permitted to see you under any circumstance. He was adamant about that.'

'And you disobeyed that order at the first opportunity?' Anni said, laughing.

'Yes, I suppose I did. But I promised Mama and Papa I would try to contact you. Now I have to find some way of letting them know I met you and that you are alright.'

Anni took her younger sister's hand and spoke to her more seriously. 'I'm very glad you did, Klara. This is such a happy day, perhaps the happiest of my life, if only to know that Papa is now free.'

'So you couldn't care less about my daring escape across the icy river?'

'I think you know exactly what I mean, *Liebchen*.' Anni said standing up. C'mon lets walk a little further. We don't have much time if you have to be back at Marienfelde by five.'

It was almost four by the time they got back to the Zoo Station. The two sisters parted company and promised to meet one more time before Klara left Berlin. Anni Hartmann shared a rented apartment in Charlottenburg only a couple of UBahn stops away. To avoid being late, she gave Klara money for a taxi ride to Marienfelde. Because of heavy traffic it was just five by the time Klara got back to the refugee centre. Within ten minutes of her arrival she received a summons from the deputy director Herr Lange. 'I'm in trouble now' she told herself. But when she reached the deputy director's office, she was faced with all three of the men, including Morton, the senior American intelligence officer, who had questioned her and taken extensive notes over the previous few days. Surely this can't be about being late, she thought. But there were no stern looks on the faces of the men in front of her. In fact they all had tentative smiles on their faces. It was Herr Martinus, the representative of the Ministry of the Interior in Bonn, who spoke as the other two smiled benignly at her. Martinus had a thick buff envelope on the table in front of him.

'Fraulein Kircherr we have good news for you. In fact we have been waiting some time to bring it to you,' a not so subtle reference to her lateness. 'You are to be granted asylum in the Federal Republic. You are free to leave here as soon as it is feasible for you to do so, to begin your new life. You may leave tomorrow if you wish. I have here an envelope containing all of the documentation you will need. You will be free to apply for a West German passport as soon as you are settled in your new location in Bavaria. There is comprehensive information here about all aspects of life in that part of Germany, how to open a bank account, welfare and health matters, that sort of thing. The envelope also contains a small sum of money to tide you over in the coming week or so. Once you have decided when you wish to leave please inform the office here and an airline ticket to Munich will be purchased for you. I should add that you will be billed for this ticket and required to repay the value of it, to the Ministry, once you are settled in a job. It only remains for all of us to congratulate you Fraulein Kircherr, on your courageous and daring escape across the frontier and to wish you all the very best in your future endeavours.'

All three men now beamed pleasantly at Klara. Herr Martinus stood up and formally presented the bulging envelope to her as if he was giving her a military decoration. He then shook her hand, followed by the other two men. Klara found herself strangely moved by the little ceremony. Tears began to fill her eyes and she had a recurrence of the feeling she had when the policeman had welcomed her as she emerged from the water of the Havel. If only this were true. If only the whole thing was not part of an elaborate charade. That night she lay on her bunk bed clutching the bulging envelope, wondering whether she was really good enough to follow through with the job she would be given. This is really happening, she thought, everything falling into place, just as Max had predicted.

The following day she took bus to the Ku'damm but not before nervously requesting the Marienfelde secretariat to purchase an airline ticket for her, from Berlin to Munich, as she had been told she was permitted to do. She would leave Berlin the following day but she had one more thing to do before she left the city. The bus stopped outside the ruined Kaiser Memorial Church, hit by a British bomb in 1943 and never rebuilt. Its clock stopped at precisely the time the bomb had hit. She got off the bus, bought a copy of the International Herald Tribune from a newspaper kiosk and made her way through the crowd of shoppers to an expensive looking restaurant called 'Café Hennig.' It had sidewalk seating, providing an excellent view of the entrance of the KaDeWe department store on the far side of the street. Klara sat at an outdoor table and ordered coffee. She had half an hour to kill before Anni took her fifteen minute morning work break and came out to meet her as they had planned the previous day. She sat in the sunshine and began to read, occasionally stopping to watch the passing parade of well to do shoppers. As she read she became aware that someone had quietly sat down at her table. She looked over to see the face of the very last person she expected to see.

'Good morning, Fraülein Kircherr.' Max Korten said, staring intently at her. 'Not thinking of going shopping across the street I hope. It's very expensive, far too expensive for a poor refugee from the East, don't you think?'

Klara took a full ten seconds to respond. Korten was wearing a well cut light summer suit, white shirt and red tie. 'Max.' she said, lowering the paper. 'What are you doing here? How did you get here?'

'You don't need to know how or why Klara, or should I say Elsa. But you should know that I can. Anytime I wish in fact. Now please don't speak and listen to me very carefully.' A waiter came over to take an order but Max waved him away with a dismissive gesture. 'As we are in a public place I will speak in a low voice but don't let that delude you into thinking that I am not within an inch of terminating your service with the HVA right now, with all the consequences that will entail for you and your family. I gave you a specific instruction not to contact your sister because it could put this entire mission in danger. You recklessly disobeyed that instruction at the very first opportunity. Your expedition to the lake yesterday with a woman named Anni Hartmann, when you are Elsa Kircherr from Gorlitz, someone who does not have a sister, is about as irresponsible from a security point of view, as it is possible to be. Are you so naive to think that the authorities on this side don't follow people or check up on them, just as we do, particularly someone who has so dramatically arrived in their own jurisdiction?'

Klara folded Herald Tribune carefully to recover from the shock of being so easily caught out and to give her time to think. She could feel her face turning a bright crimson.

'She's my only sister, how could I come here and not even lay eyes on her?'

Max spoke quietly, through clenched teeth. 'Because you were ordered not to, that's why. How many times have I told you, you are not free to follow your own childish whims, you obey orders and you obey them to the letter. They are for your own safety as much as they are intended to progress an operation. Your stupid sentimental wishes are entirely irrelevant. Are you so obtuse that you can't understand that? I see now this whole project has been a mistake. It seems those who had doubts about your suitability were right and I was wrong after all.'

Annoyed by having her intelligence insulted, Klara could not resist a whispered instant retaliation. She looked around to ensure there were no eavesdroppers seated nearby.

'If you're so concerned about someone following me on this side Max, what are you doing sitting here on the Ku'Damm in broad daylight talking to me? You're a senior officer from an enemy service, walking about openly in West Berlin. If anyone is watching me, then surely they would want to know who exactly you are. If we are discussing cleverness Max, that doesn't seem very smart to me.'

She could see that Max was seething with anger and she was sure she had gone too far. He said nothing for some time as he tried to control his anger, his fingers tapping anxiously on the table. When he spoke his voice was as cold as ice. 'For the moment and very much against my better judgement Fraülein Kircherr, you may proceed to Bavaria as planned. You will be informed within the next two weeks whether we intend to proceed with the proposed operation. Personally I think it unlikely. I assume you selected this restaurant because of its proximity to KaDeWe. I suppose you have planned yet another rendezvous with your sister.'

'I only wanted to say goodbye to her.' Klara answered.

'Well, that is not going to happen. Now think very carefully about the instruction I am about to give you. You are going to get up from this table and walk away on this side of the street, past the front door of the department store on the far side. You will go to the U Bahn station. You will take the next train back to Marienfelde and stay there until you leave for the airport tomorrow.' 'Yes.' He said noticing her surprise at his knowledge of her travel arrangements. 'I know exactly when you are leaving for Munich. You will not contact Anni Hartmann ever again, either by letter or by phone or by any other method. Believe me I will know if you have. Now give me that newspaper and get out of here. I will be watching. If you as much as glance sideways across the street into that store, you're service with us will be terminated immediately, with obvious adverse consequences for the rest of your family. Don't say another word. Just go. And remember, if I can come here, I can just as easily get to Garmisch. Don't ever think for a moment that you are out of my reach.'

Klara had great difficulty keeping her own anger in check, seething that she had been so easily found out. She passed the paper across the table and stood up. She leaned down, bringing her face within inches of his. 'I would have thought, in view of our very recent personal relationship Max, that you would have the decency not to use my parents as a bargaining chip. Perhaps our friendship wasn't so personal after all, perhaps it was all strictly business.'

Korten grabbed her wrist tightly before she could walk away. A few people at neighbouring tables looked over, aware there was an argument in progress. Korten spoke with venom but not loud enough for anyone but Klara to hear. 'I put my career on the line to recommend you for this, Klara, the daughter of an enemy. I pulled you out of the gutter and opened the world to you. This is how you repay me? You disappoint me more than you will ever know. Go and if you know what's good for you, don't look over there and don't look back at me.'

Klara walked away, her emotions in turmoil. So, she thought, this is how true love dies. Yes, it does hurt. What a fool I have been, I should have known. When she reached the point on the street directly opposite the main door of KaDeWe, she kept her head facing forward but attempted to glance in the door anyway. There were too many shoppers blocking the entrance for her to see anything. Anni would come out for her break any minute. Her eyes clouded with tears as she walked toward the UBahn station. Back at the Café Hennig, Max Korten feigned reading the International Herald Tribune, as he carefully observed his protégé walk down the street. He had been hard on her. The confrontation had taken a lot out of him. He needed a drink. As he raised his hand to get the waiter's attention, the waiter noticed it was shaking.

CHAPTER 17

October 1963

I spent most of Tuesday morning working on a translation of a lengthy and tedious document written by a bureaucrat in the Soviet Ministry of Foreign Trade and sent to its Cuban counterpart, on the subject of sugar imports to Russia and reciprocal exports of heavy machinery from the Soviet Union to Cuba. Like thousands of communications of this sort it was easily intercepted by US Intelligence. This kind of material helped to build up a picture of the true state of the economies of the two very different countries, considered the most important to the US from a foreign policy point of view. Re-reading the turgid stuff, I was glad I only had to translate and not analyse. I had finished it by four thirty when Vern called to say he wanted to see me urgently. Since Labour Day I had seen more of Vernon Templeton than I had in the previous nine months and I was getting a little tired of it. When I got to his office I knocked, then walked in as usual. The first surprise I got was had was that Vern was sitting, not at his desk but at his mahogany conference table, a sight few at State had ever seen before. The second surprise was that there was someone with him, an elegantly dressed slim man who looked to be in his mid forties.' Ah, Jimmy, come in, come in,' Vern said when he looked up. His tone of comradely bonhomie had a phoney ring to it obviously for the benefit of his visitor. 'Jimmy, this is Elliot Markham, of whom you have no doubt heard, special advisor to Secretary Rusk.' I had heard of Elliot Markham, everyone at State had but I'd only seen him from a distance. He had been seconded to the Department from the Rockefeller Foundation, where Dean Rusk had come from. His Job was to do the tough jobs and to ask the hard questions that an introverted academic like Rusk didn't want to do. Like all temporary interlopers, Markham was despised by the career diplomats in the Department. State considered itself the best and most exclusive club in the world. As far as the diplomats were concerned, guys who were parachuted in like Markham were sidelined and hung out to dry at the first opportunity. Markham however had a reputation as a tough cookie. Apparently he wasn't remotely fazed by the self regard of those at the top tier in the Department no matter how exalted they felt themselves to be.

'Hello Mr Flynn, sit down please.' Markham said. Not rising and not offering his hand. He sat at the top of the table in the Chairman's seat while Vern, whose office it was after all, sat immediately to his right. I sat a little further down the table to Markham's left. Vern, I noticed was not looking his usual cool, unperturbed self. There was a glisten of perspiration on his forehead and a look of concern in his eyes. He smiled at me with what he intended to be a benevolent manner but he couldn't quite carry it off. Somebody, probably Markham, had done or said something to unsettle him before I came in. Vern spoke first.

'Jimmy, Elliot and I want to discuss a matter of some delicacy with you. It's in connection with a job I assigned to you recently. You may recall a document you worked on in connection with developments in Soviet government thinking *viz a vis* the United States.'

'Of course I remember. It was one of the most interesting things I have worked on lately.' I said, looking at Markham in what I hoped was an expression of enthusiasm for my work. It made no impression whatsoever He looked back at me impassively and then looked at his watch. Vern was about to continue but before he had a chance to, Markham raised a hand to stop him.

'Mr Flynn, Vernon tells me that you have not been made aware of the intended recipient of the document you translated, is that so?'

'Absolutely, Vern insists that we in the Language Analysis Unit operate on a strictly need to know basis.' In my peripheral vision I could see that Vern was nodding appreciatively, relieved by this fiction. I didn't know what was going on but I knew my boss was in some kind of trouble. Elliot Markham looked at me with an expression implying that that is exactly how it should be. Close up I could see his suit was tailored and expensive, his face had the weathered suntan of a yachtsman and his swept back perfectly cut dark hair had streaks of silver at each temple.

'That's good to hear but now it appears that you do in fact need to know.' Markham went on. 'So let me tell you confidentially and I will remind you that everything said in this meeting is strictly confidential. I would appreciate it if you would listen carefully to what I have to say, we don't have a great deal of time, so maybe you would leave any questions until I am finished.'

'Yes of course'. I said, looking at him with what I hoped was a sufficiently serious expression. I had no idea what the hell this was all about. The only thing I was sure of was that I didn't like this guy at all.

Markham continued. 'The end user of the document you translated was none other than our Attorney General. The author of the document is somebody who was once assigned to the Soviet embassy here in Washington. He has since been recalled to Moscow. His name is Georgi Bolshakov. The Attorney General and he developed a close, if somewhat unorthodox personal relationship when Bolshakov was *en post* here. This relationship was so close in fact, that it became at one time a back channel between the Soviet Embassy and the White House. As an official of the State Department you will be aware that this kind of *ad hoc* arrangement tends to complicate the efficient making of foreign policy. Simply put, the Secretary of State and his senior advisers need to know what's going on, and in this instance they didn't. The State Department cannot be run effectively in this way. Foreign policy, with all due respect to the Attorney General, conducted by amateurs, is fraught with all kinds of dangers.' Markham took a breath and glanced down at the folder in front of him. 'You apparently did a very good job translating and analysing the document Vernon gave to you. At his point he looked over at the still uncomfortable looking Vern. 'Although it might have been preferable if a more senior officer in the diplomatic stream had handled something of this sensitivity. No offence intended but I doubt if, at your level, you have had much experience with material of this sort, have you?'

'Some, but not as much as I would like.' I said, a little too forcefully. I didn't care how it sounded. In a Department with no shortage of prima donnas, Markham was as obnoxious as any I had come across. He opened a neat buff folder on the table and took out a sheaf of papers. 'This is the original Russian text from Bolshakov along with your translation and the accompanying notes. I must admit that I do agree they are somewhat insightful, if perhaps a little over imaginative. I can see why they might be of interest to Mr Kennedy.'

Thanks for the backhanded compliment, I thought to myself. He closed the folder again and pushed it down the polished mahogany to me. 'Have you any questions at this point?' He asked.

'Yes.' I said, 'just one. You mentioned that there was some urgency about all of this and you're returning the papers to me. Has there been a development that I am supposed to be aware of?'

'The Attorney General himself was in touch with Secretary Rusk. He wants to speak with the person who translated Bolshakov's original document and provided the analysis. Secretary Rusk is in Geneva right now and it was suggested that I or one of the Assistant Secretaries might meet with the Attorney General. However, Mr Kennedy insisted that he speak with the analyst himself, in this case you Mr Flynn, as unconventional as that may be.'

Obviously Markham felt that he should be the one to talk to Kennedy, not some lowly upstart like me, par for the course in bureaucratic power plays. Access to the one with power is everything, even if, as seemed to be the case here, the power holder is despised by the person seeking access. No one is resented more than the one close to the power source. This time, if only accidentally, it seemed I was going to be that person. This explained why Vern was in the doghouse with Markham. He should not have assigned such an important document to me. Vern's action inadvertently led to Robert Kennedy asking to see the lowly translator in person. Markham didn't like that at all.

'Me?' I said. 'Is there any particular reason he wishes to speak with me?'

'Not that we can tell' Markham said. More amateur antics I presume. Anyway he does, so there is not much we can do about it. In fact he wants to speak to you this evening. You're expected in the Justice Department at six.'

'Six? That's not a lot of notice.' I looked at my watch. 'It's already ten after five.' I said. 'I'll need to refresh my memory in relation to the notes.'

'You can do that in the car Jimmy.' Vern said. He seemed eager to make a further contribution to the discussion. 'We have provided a car and driver to take you there. You'll have to make your own way back.'

Markham made a slicing hand gesture, cutting Vern off once again. Looking at me, he spoke with increased emphasis 'The main purpose of this meeting is to warn you not enter into any wide ranging discussion with the Attorney General about departmental policy matters. He may be curious, in fact he's bound to be, but don't tell him anything. Just stick to the subject at hand. The more I think about it perhaps it's fortunate that you do not have much experience at the higher levels of the Department. You'll get into less trouble that way. I would like to speak to you again in the morning to debrief you, as it were. I want a verbal report of whatever may transpire, first thing. You can submit a written report in the usual way, up the line through Vernon here, as soon as you get a chance. Shall we say 9.30 in my office tomorrow morning? There's no need to bother you with all of this' He said to Vern. 'Mr Flynn can fill me in himself.'

This guy was some piece of work, insulting me and blatantly humiliating Vernon in front of a subordinate, without any attempt to conceal it. He turned back to me. 'So then, hadn't you better be going? 'As you say, there's not much time to refresh your memory. Good luck and remember, no inside stories from Foggy Bottom. Confine all discussion to the subject at hand. In case you don't know Mr Flynn, the correct form of address with the AG is General.'

'Oh it is? I didn't know that.'

'That's all, you may go.'

I was dismissed. I walked out of the office leaving a forlorn looking Vern with about the most objectionable person I had met so far since coming to DC. State being what it is, that's up against some pretty stiff competition. At five minutes to six and with little chance to prepare, a State Department driver dropped me at the Justice building on the corner of Lexington and Constitution. I was shown up to the Attorney General's floor and left waiting in a conference room for thirty five minutes. This was standard treatment by the high and mighty of a junior official, but I didn't object because it gave me a more time to re-read Bolshhakov's report and my own analysis of its contents. I was as ready as I was ever going to be by the time a middle aged woman put her head around the door and said. 'The General will see you now.' I was shown into the adjoining room, a spacious well furnished office which might have been impressive if it was neat and tidy but the place was a mess. There were kids' drawings and paintings scotch taped to the walls, a huge goldfish bowl, complete with fish, sitting in the middle of a round conference table and what looked like dog hairs on the carpet. The Attorney General sat at an ornate desk, similar to Vernon Templeton's, but this one was strewn with so many papers that its surface was barely visible. He was wearing glasses, which he never wore in public. His jacket was draped over the back of his chair, the sleeves of his white shirt rolled up and his tie pulled loose from the shirt collar. As I walked to his desk, he was reading something with deep concentration. He looked up, removed his glasses and stood up in a single movement. 'Mr Flynn, thank you for coming.' he said, shaking my hand casually but barely making eye contact with what seemed like shyness rather than rudeness. He was about my height but a little thinner and with his slightly dishevelled sandy hair, he looked younger than his years. 'Please sit down.'

'Hello sir, thank you.' I said as I sat. I realized I was not going to be able to call this man General. It just didn't seem to fit. Kennedy was all business no preamble.

'I read your document with interest Mr Flynn. I just have a couple of questions about it, I won't keep you long.'

It was strange hearing that familiar voice. I was reminded of the popular First Family comedy recordings by Vaughn Meader, making fun of the Kennedys and their mode of speech. The press always called the President's voice a Boston twang. The AG's was similar to that of his brother's but more staccato and rapid fire. My parents were from Boston and I have lived in Massachusetts all my life, but I have yet to meet anyone there who speaks quite like the Kennedys. They're a family with an accent all of their own.

'Are you aware who the author is?' Kennedy asked.

'I believe it's a Mr Bolshakov, formerly on the staff of the Soviet embassy here in Washington.'

That's right. Georgi Bolshakov. I know him well. I want you to give me your opinion of what he's written. Firstly, do you think it's genuine?'

'Yes I do. It's written in the style of a letter to a friend, familiar and informal. Not at all like an official Soviet document or even like an informal Soviet communication between colleagues, both of which I have seen and read many times. It's more like a letter someone would write to their brother or sister.'

He was leaning forward now, elbows on the desk, listening carefully. 'What do you think his motivation is for writing this just now?'

'Well as I said in my notes, he appears to be a worried man. The signing of nuclear Test Ban Treaty is imminent, the President's conciliatory American University speech in June and the prospect of better relations between Moscow and Washington have obviously brought divisions over there to the surface, between what you might call the hawks and doves in the Kremlin. He refers particularly to a serious rift between two people referred to throughout as NSK and MS and to the real possibility that NSK could lose out. We can safely assume that NSK is Khrushchev, that is Nikita Sergeivich and MS is probably Suslov, Mikhail, the last of the hard line Stalinists.'

'Any doubts in your mind which side Bolshakov is on?'

'None at all assuming that the document is genuine. He's definitely one of the doves. He writes very respectfully about NSK which leads me to think that Khrushchev may even have asked him to write to you or at the very least he was going to read what Bolshakov had written. He is far more negative about Suslov.'

'How can we be sure that MS is Suslov?'

'I'm not sure sir, but if I was a betting man, I'd put ten dollars on it. At one point Bolshakov uses the term 'the lanky one' about him. Suslov is tall and thin. But he also refers to MS as "formerly one of Koba's young cubs." Koba was Stalin's revolutionary nickname in Georgia before the revolution. It is thought that Suslov was being groomed for bigger things when Stalin died in '53.'

'Is Georgi in trouble, would you say?'

'Hard to tell, I doubt it, because he still has Khrushchev's ear. But he's definitely worried about recent developments. As long as Khrushchev is in charge he is probably OK. Frankly sir, I am not the best person to provide you with that depth of analysis. There are people in Langley who would give you a far more accurate picture of all this than I ever could.'

None of what I was telling Kennedy was particularly new or insightful but I could tell that he was impressed and pleased with what he was hearing. 'Yes, I know.' He said tersely. 'But I have reasons for not involving the CIA just now.'

Suddenly the conversation took a different turn. Have we met before, Mr Flynn? You look kind of familiar? Are you from Boston?'

'No, not Boston, my father was. Actually I'm from Hyannis. And we have sort of crossed paths. In college I used to work summers at Hyannis Port yacht club. I saw you and your family there many times in the fifties.'

He smiled a kind of toothy smile, leaning back in his chair, visibly relaxing for the first time since we spoke. 'I thought I recognised you. Didn't you operate that little beat up motor launch, bringing crews out to boats before races, you and that blond kid?'

'Joe Davis, that's right, I'm surprised you remember.'

'Well how about that, good to see you again. Sorry I've forgotten you're first name.'

'Jimmy.'

'Well nice to meet you again Jimmy. I remember Joe Davis a little better. He still does a little yard work and that kind of thing around our place on the Cape.'

'Yes I know. I saw him on Labour Day, still the same old Joe.'

I decided to risk a question on a subject I had intended to avoid up to then. 'Actually sir, there was a woman killed on Craigville Beach last Labour Day weekend. I happened to be there at the time. Not the kind of thing we're used to on the Cape, is it?' I watched him closely to see how he would react to this information but he looked almost disinterested.

'Really.' he said. 'A drowning, was it?'

'No, the woman was shot. Nobody saw who did it?'

This time he showed more interest, he was either a good liar or the information was news to him. 'Shot? I'm surprised nobody ever mentioned it to me. The President was on the Cape that weekend and not very far away. It's the kind of security matter we should be told about.' He shook his head in exasperation. 'No question but we're becoming a more violent country.' He then abruptly changed the subject back to the business at hand.

'Mr Flynn, or may I call you Jimmy, I intend to write back to my friend Bolshakov and I'm considering having the reply sent to him in Russian rather than English. I was wondering whether you would translate my reply to him, as soon I've written it. I have to consult a higher authority first, about what to say and whether it's advisable to write at all.' He gave me a conspiratorial smile as he said this. Then he suddenly stood up and of course I did the same. The guy was definitely wired, no standing on ceremony. He grabbed his jacket from the back of his chair and walked quickly towards the door, which I noticed had a dartboard hanging on it, with three darts stuck in it.

'Perhaps, Jimmy, we could keep the matter of my reply between ourselves. I would prefer to answer this letter in my personal capacity, so there is no need for your people at State or Secretary Rusk to get involved. He looked me in the eye. 'Unless there's any ethical problem for you doing so, is there?'

'Of course not I said. 'If we're talking about a personal letter, then not at all, I'd be happy to help.' I tried to suppress any thoughts of Elliot Markham and my debriefing meeting with him in the morning. Kennedy opened the door for me. In the large outer office, the woman who had shown me in was sitting typing at her desk. There were two other desks in the room both with typewriters covered. Their occupants presumably had already gone home.

'Maybe you would leave your contact numbers with Mrs Fitch. I'll be in touch when I can.' He put his jacket on without rolling down his sleeves. 'Excuse me but I have another pressing engagement, nice to see you again, Jimmy.' He said with another shy half smile, no handshake. 'Goodnight Mrs Fitch.'

With that he was gone. I left my office and home phone numbers with Mrs Fitch, my address in Garret Park and the phone number at my mother's house in Hyannis. Out in the empty corridor I waited for the elevator. When it arrived I got in but before I could press the button I heard a deep voice shout 'Hold that elevator.'

Two familiar figures slipped through before the elevator doors closed, FBI agents Verling and Caulfield. I tried not to look shocked when I saw them. 'Which floor?' I said in a voice as calm as I could make it, indicating the panel of buttons.

'Basement car park,' Verling said. He seemed as surprised to see me as I was to see him but he recovered quickly. 'What brings you here, Mr Flynn?'

I pressed first floor for me and the car park for the two amigos. 'I could ask you the same question, Agent Verling.'

'In case you don't know, Director Hoover's office is in this building and as I'm sure you recall we work for the FBI.' Verling said, with as much unfriendly sarcasm as he could muster. The guy was a natural born bully. I couldn't resist ragging him a little.

'About that fellas, any further progress on the Cape Cod murder case? I don't remember reading about any arrests in the papers, maybe I missed it.'

Verling's face coloured at my remark. But there was no time for him to reply before the elevator reached the ground floor. I made to go out but Verling reached across to the button panel to hold the doors open, partially blocking my exit at the same time. 'You didn't answer my question Mr Flynn. What are you doing here?'

'I'm a federal employee, as you know, Agent Verling. The State Department has business with many government departments. Our work is not always secret but it's usually confidential. Now if you will excuse me.'

I placed my hand gently at his elbow in order to manoeuvre my way around him. Caulfield stood silently in the far corner of the narrow space. Verling's face was red with rage but he reluctantly moved, just enough to allow me out. I began to walk away but my anger at his heavy handedness got the better of me. I turned back and placed myself in the gap before the elevator doors closed.

'I notice you didn't answer my question about the murder either.' I said. 'I presume that's because there's nothing to report. That's a pity. I was sure you guys would have wrapped that one up in no time. Maybe you should hand it back to the Mass State Police. I hear they're pretty hot.' I let that sink in. 'A pleasure to see you both again.'

I pulled back and the doors closed immediately, before Verling could burst through them and wring my neck, which I have no doubt he was dying to do. Outside the fresh air was a welcome relief. I walked down Constitution Avenue in the balmy autumn evening, thinking about Bobby Kennedy, how normal he was and how eager I was to please him, even to the point of disloyalty to my own colleagues. Was it because all those years ago, I envied those preppy sailing types at the yacht club and secretly wanted to be one of them? Was I so pathetic that I wanted the so called 'second most powerful man in Washington' to like me? Or was it an ingrained resentment of State Department types like Elliot Markham and Vern Templeton? Either way, I could see I was turning into a guy with a chip on both shoulders. Something I would never have imagined when I first came to Washington, full of ambition and hopeful dreams. My nerves had not quite recovered from the encounter with Verling and Caulfield. I glanced over my shoulder now and then as I walked. I passed a little bar called the Montecello, made a quick U turn and went in for a beer in order to calm down. The two agents were not just bullies they had an air of dangerous menace about them which was palpable. Verling particularly, could have carved out a successful career for himself in the KGB, the Gestapo or any other organisation of state sponsored terror. Sitting in the bar entirely alone, something I don't think I had ever done before, I thought about Rob Durand of the Barnstable police and what he said about our two G men that Sunday morning at the Wianno Motel. 'There go two twenty four carat shit heels.' I laughed to myself at the thought. Old Rob was not wrong but 'shit heels' is a too polite a term for those two. That set me thinking about Elsa Kircherr's stay in the motel. Did anyone ever question the staff or the receptionist there? Did Elsa Kircherr have any visitors while she was there or did she make or receive any phone calls? Were normal investigative procedures followed in the case? I had absolutely no idea why I but I suspected that when the FBI left Hyannis that Sunday, they never looked back and they never went back. I was going back to the Cape in two weeks time for a pressing social engagement, my five year old nephew, Kevin's, birthday. I decided would call in to the Wianno Motel and see what I could find out. Apart from that, all I had to decide now is how much of the conversation with the 'General' would I tell the pompous Elliot Markham at nine thirty in the morning.

I asked the barman where the payphone was and he helpfully set a phone down on the bar in front of me. I called Herbert Kluge at his home number. A friendly woman answered who I assumed was Gabriella, his Swiss fiancée. She handed the phone to Herbert. I told him about my meeting with Robert Lavelle and in the empty bar I felt able to confirm to him that his suspicions about Kircherr were largely correct. He was interested as usual and asked some questions which I answered but he had no further info for me. I left the bar after the call, to catch my train for Garrett Park. On reflection, I probably shouldn't have goaded Verling and Caulfield about lack of progress in the case. If they were visiting J Edgar Hoover presumably they were highly regarded in the Bureau. Verling seemed so volatile that any remark which called his competency into question was like poking a grizzly bear with a short stick. The chances of doing so and getting away with it were slim.

CHAPTER 18

October 1963

My interview with Elliot Markham the following morning went without a hitch. I told him most of what had transpired with the Attorney General the night before. Emphasising the fact that he had been in a hurry and the meeting had been very brief. As I expected he would be, Markham was pleased to hear this. The rules of the game are that if someone like me gets an audience, one to one, with someone high up the totem pole, while edging out the Markhams of this world, it can be tolerated as long as the meeting is brief and there is no time for the schmuck in question to make a real impression. It's hard to believe that well educated and sophisticated people at senior levels in government play these petty games but they do. Attraction to power and to those who wield it does strange things to the human soul, as Machiavelli I have no doubt must have observed. I did not mention to Markham that the Attorney General asked me for help with his reply to the Bolshakov letter, nor of course that I had agreed to give it. That information would ring alarm bells right away. Markham would certainly have vetoed any further involvement by me. I had crossed a loyalty line with the State Department by omitting to tell what Kennedy had asked and I knew it. It was unprofessional of me. I did it anyway, out of sheer ego. I simply wanted to be an insider myself. I wanted to know something that smug, self important people like Elliot Markham didn't know. Secrecy has a powerful pull and I certainly didn't have the willpower or, if I was honest, even the desire, to resist it.

As a courtesy to Vern, I called into his office directly after leaving Markham's. I had no intention of leaving my own boss out of the loop, particularly as he had seemed so down the previous day. I told him everything I had already told Markham. I did however also tell Vern that Kennedy had recognised me from my days as a part time 'step'n fetch it' at the local yacht club, because I knew that Vern loved those kinds of inconsequential social snippets. He was genuinely appreciative that I had filled him in, in view of Markham's dismissive remark that he could wait for a written report. To my surprise though, Vern was in no better shape than he had been the day before. He was agitated and distracted. Invariably immaculately dressed, this morning he had a dishevelled look, his beige suit rumpled and two tiny bits of tissue paper stuck to his cheek to stem the flow of blood from shaving cuts. Normally any discussion of a meeting with a person of importance in town was grist to Vernon's mill, but not today. I could tell he was only half listening to me.

'You OK, Vern?' I asked when I had finished my account of the meeting. 'You seem to be a little under the weather.'

'No, I'm fine Jimmy.' He said distractedly. I've got a lot on my mind, on the home front, you know.'

Vernon's marriage to a woman known by everyone at State as 'Bunny T' was the subject of much speculation. According to office scuttlebutt, Bunny Templeton, formerly Bunny Fairchild of Williamsburg Virginia was the one in the marriage with the money. In the early years of their marriage she featured regularly at State Department functions and prominently on the wider Washington social scene. However, when it became clear that Vernon's career had stalled, she was seen less and less in Washington and seemed to divide her social life between the horse country in Virginia and Manhattan, with regular forays, accompanied by Vern, to various cultural centres in Europe, Venice being their favourite. They had no children. Vern's frequent references to his wife were always those of a hard pressed husband who was a long suffering victim of his wife's unreasonable demands and lack of understanding. His complaints were the source of great amusement because it was clear to everyone that Vern was rarely stressed and that his life was an almost continuous round of dinner parties and foreign travel at his wealthy wife's expense.

Now though, I could see he was genuinely under pressure but I knew better than to pursue the matter, whatever might be bugging him. 'Thanks very much for filling me in on last night's meeting Jimmy I do appreciate it.' He said picking up the only file on his desk and opening it as a signal of his desire to be left alone.

'You're welcome.' I said getting up to leave. 'I'll do a short written note and have it up to you this afternoon.'

As I reached the door, Vern asked. 'Jimmy, I take it there have been no further development's arising from the incident last Labour Day weekend, have there?'

'No, Vern, none at all that I know of.' I said lying to his face and feeling bad about doing so.

'Good.' He said. 'No news is good news.' He gave the briefest of smiles but was unable to dispel the worried look from his face. When I got back to my own office Victor and Sylvia looked at me inquiringly. With all of my comings and goings lately they were beginning to wonder what exactly I was up to. I could see that they were irritated by my frequent absences, and my many mysterious trips upstairs. I can't say I blamed them.

'Aren't you a little late?' Victor said, knowing full well I had come to work before he arrived.

'I had to meet with Elliot Markham on the fifth floor and brief him about something.' I said this knowing that it would not be enough. None of the three of us had ever been within a mile of Elliot Markham up to now. I owed my closest colleagues some kind of explanation for my recent erratic behaviour.

'Oh my, Elliot Markham,' Sylvia exclaimed as if I'd said Elizabeth Taylor. She looked up from whatever she was doing. 'You are moving in exalted circles Jimmy.'

'You must be bucking for promotion, Jimmy. You seem to be up on the fifth more than your here,' Victor chimed in, not bothering to disguise a note of envy.

'Look guys, I know I've had a lot going on lately and that I haven't really told you anything about it.' No sooner had I said this than the two of them stopped what they were working on and sat back in their chairs like it was show and tell at elementary school. They were going to be disappointed.

'A couple of weeks ago I was asked to translate a confidential document that Mrs Sheppard in LAU1 would normally have been given but she had flu or something. Anyway, Vern and the fifth floor made a big deal of this material, although it seemed pretty routine to me. They've called me back a couple of times for clarifications on particular passages. Somehow Elliot Markham got to hear about it and showed an interest on behalf of Secretary Rusk. Vern expressly told me not to mention it to anyone. He was worried that Mrs Sheppard might be offended that she wasn't given it, even though she wasn't here at the time.'

'German or Russian?' Victor asked quickly, as if he doubted my story.

'Russian' I said, all of it economic stuff, statistical data about the shortage of grain in the Soviet Union and their need to buy a lot more from us and from Canada. Seems it's all very important strategically. So they keep asking me back to make sure I got every comma and full stop just right, nothing more sinister than that.'

'We never said it was sinister Jimmy.' Sylvia said. 'It just doesn't sound like the kind of thing Elliot Markham would get involved with.' Sylvia wasn't buying my story.

'Apparently the Soviet economy is a special area of interest of his, since his days in the Ford Foundation.' I said, almost believing this myself.

'What's he like, Markham?' Victor asked.

'As far as I can tell, he's exactly like his reputation, only worse. He obviously thinks that people who do our kind of work are beneath contempt. No handshake when I was introduced, no first name, no hello, goodbye or thank you ma'am'.

'It figures.' said Victor morosely, but I could tell he was beginning to be mollified.

'How's Vern doing?' Sylvia asked, still fishing. 'I haven't seen him in quite a while.'

'Not too good right now as far as I can tell. Unlike the three of us, with money troubles, Vern seems to be suffering from a bad case of Bunny troubles. Not that he provided me with any specifics.' They both smiled knowingly and by general agreement the topic of my recent patterns of behaviour was set aside for now. I didn't want to risk any further inquiries so I waited until lunch that day when the other two had left the room, to call Robert Lavelle, as I told him I would. I wanted to see whether Elsa Kircherr's personal effects had been sent to him by the FBI. The phone was answered very quickly by a man with a distinct southern, perhaps Texan accent, obviously not Lavelle. The voice on the other end sounded tired. 'Who is this please?' I gave my name and said that I had spoken with Robert the previous week about a personal matter and had told him I would call again.

'I'm sorry, but Robert is not available and this is not a good time to call.'

'Oh I see, do you mind me asking who I'm talking to?'

There was a weary sigh before he answered. 'I'm Richard Powell. I'm Robert's roommate and I know who you are. He told me something of your conversation last Wednesday. Robert Lavelle is dead.' There was a long pause. When he spoke again Richard Powell sounded tearful. 'I still can hardly believe I'm saying this. His body was taken from the canal last night. He was walking along the towpath of the Chesapeake and Ohio in Georgetown and somehow fell in. The police say it was suicide. There was a severe head injury from something in the water. Drowning is the official cause of death' There was a long pause I didn't know how to respond, Powell continued.

'I identified the body myself last night and I haven't slept since, as you can imagine. I have had to call everybody, including his poor parents. You'll forgive me if I end this call now I have a lot to do. Good bye.' The line went dead. It took me some time to replace the receiver.

Robert Lavelle dead? A man falls into a canal a little more than a month after his wife had been murdered. How coincidental is that? But I wasn't as sceptical as Richard Powell about it not being a suicide. I expect he led a stressful life. It had to be a strain for guys like Lavelle constantly pretending that you are something you're not, especially in the service, where your job is at risk if anyone ever finds out. Although I didn't really know Robert Lavelle, I was genuinely sad to hear he was dead. He had spoken so sincerely about his love for Elsa Kircherr. If I had met him in another context I think we might have been friends.

I filled in the afternoon with routine work and as soon as five o'clock came around I was the first of the three of us out the door. I hadn't driven to work, so I had no alternative but to take a cab from the State Department to Lavelle's address in Arlington. I wasn't sure why I was going but I put any thought of my motivation to the back of my mind.

I rang the bell to the ground floor apartment. After a long delay the door was opened by a heavy set man in his forties, with dark circles under his eyes. He wore an ill fitting dark suit and black necktie, loose at the neck, the top shirt button open. I guessed he was not normally a suit wearing guy. I could hear the muffled sounds of others in the apartment. I introduced myself to Richard Powell.

'Come in please, I'm Richard. Yes we spoke earlier today. I'm sorry I had to cut you off. You wouldn't believe what a day it's been.' The man sounded as subdued as he had on the phone and looked exhausted. He ushered me into a small living room where five or six other people were standing around drinking tea or coffee. They all looked like they'd been crying and seemed to know Robert Lavelle a lot better than I did. On the threshold of the open doorway, neither in the room nor outside, stood a middle aged army officer in full uniform, detached from the rest of the group, giving every appearance of a man who was uncomfortable in this milieu and looking for the first opportunity to leave. Not wanting to intrude on the genuine mourners, I stood at the open doorway beside the officer. The military man introduced himself.

'Colonel Walter Taylor, Sergeant Lavelle's CO. I guess I should say I was his CO. He was a good man, he a friend o'yours?'

'No not really. I only met him once.'

'Those gals,' he said, indicating two crying women in the far corner of the room. 'They worked with Sergeant Lavelle. They're civilian secretaries in the Pentagon. They seem pretty cut up about this business.' The Colonel seemed to find this fact surprising. Powell took up a position in the centre of the room and tapped his coffee cup with a spoon. As intended, the buzz of conversation ceased.

'Thank you all for coming at such short notice.' he said. We were all good friends of Bobby's and I believe we all loved him very much.' I glanced sideways at Colonel Taylor and I thought I saw his lip curl.

'As you can tell, I haven't gotten over the shock and I doubt if I ever will. I have talked with Mr and Mrs Lavelle and I understand they want him to be buried near their home in Hartford, where he grew up. I'll pass on any funeral details I get, as soon as I have them. Everybody in this room has been asking what happened. The short answer is I don't know, but I will tell you as much as I do know. Bobby had an appointment in Georgetown late yesterday afternoon, I don't know who with. I only know it had something to do with his job.' Taylor visibly bristled beside me when he heard this but no one noticed. Richard continued.

'He left Georgetown at about 7.15. He walked along the towpath by the Potomac. Somewhere along the way he met with an accident, he either fell in the river or was pushed.' Richard stopped, took a large red handkerchief from his pocket, dabbed his eyes and blew his nose loudly. I could hear an exasperated sigh emanating from Colonel Taylor. When Richard regained his composure he continued.

'A woman walking her dog along the towpath at about 7.40 saw a body floating in the water and rushed to the nearest phone booth to call the police. As I have already told some of you, the police quickly came to the conclusion that this was a suicide. As most of you know, I reject that theory. There was a severe injury to his skull, which according to the police, came from a sharp rock or stone impacting his head as he hit the water. They say he lost consciousness and drowned.'

One of the women in the room stood up and embraced Richard. Then to my surprise Colonel Taylor spoke up. He spoke with an accent not unlike Powell's.

'Excuse me Mr Powell, but how can you be so sure it wasn't a suicide? I mean the police know their business about this kind of thing. I knew Sergeant Lavelle very well. He was a good man. One of the best administrators I have ever come across in the Army. But it has to be said, Sergeant Lavelle, God bless him, was a sensitive soul. He felt things keenly. He was, and I don't think I'm telling tales out of school here, very easily offended. And as people here might know, his wife left him and returned to Europe just a couple of months ago, which can't have been easy for him. So maybe he was depressed and maybe as he was passing that body of water, he simply became overwhelmed. Who knows?'

You could hear a pin drop in the small room as Taylor finished. But Powell still had some fight in him. 'I'll tell you who knows Colonel

Taylor, I do. You will know he had quite a bit of leave coming. As it happens he and I were just about to take a long promised trip this weekend. We were going to do a week's hiking in Yosemite. He loved the outdoors and he was determined to convert me too. Lord knows I could use the exercise.'

A polite giggle went around the room, obviously to those who knew him Richard was not one of nature's outdoorsmen. His genuine anger at the accusation of suicide was now obvious.

'For your information Colonel, Bobby called me here in the apartment at exactly 7.25 last night. During a short conversation he told me a number of things. He told me that he was calling from a phone booth on N Street in Georgetown. He told me his meeting had just ended and he was planning to walk along the towpath to clear his head. He had bought the airline tickets for San Francisco from a travel agency in town that very afternoon. We planned on leaving Saturday morning and he said he had bought some books about the trails in Yosemite which he wanted to show me when he got home. He told me how much he was looking forward to our trip. When the police asked me to identify the body last night, the Airline tickets, purchased yesterday afternoon and the Yosemite books were still in his jacket pocket. That doesn't sound to me like someone planning to end it all.' Richard, obviously heartbroken, began sobbing helplessly and had to be helped to sit on the couch. Colonel Taylor looked a little embarrassed, and I was too, he turned to me and said.

'I gotta go. Do you need a ride anywhere? I'm heading into town.' I weighed up my options. It was obvious that this small get together was for Robert Lavelle's close friends, which clearly did not include me. Everyone there appeared to be upset by this unexpected tragedy and I felt like an intruder. I decided to accept Taylor's offer. I went over to Richard, expressed my condolences, shook his hand and told him I was leaving. He barely acknowledged me. I could see he thought of me as some kind of ally of Colonel Taylor's. He didn't get up and didn't see either of us out.

Taylor had an army issue, olive green ford sedan parked outside the apartment house. When I sat in, he said. 'These kinda folks can't really take much pressure, that's why the army has no use for them.'

I was about to say that he had just said what an outstanding soldier Sergeant Lavelle was, but before I could, I was startled by a sudden knock on the car's passenger side window. It was Richard Powell holding a large cardboard package. I lowered the window, to speak to him. 'Here he said, this is presumably what you came for. Bobby said you might drop by. I don't know what's in it and to be honest, I couldn't care less.' The package was too large to fit through the window so I opened the car door took it and placed it on my lap. The words 'Special Delivery from Federal Bureau of Investigation,' were printed clearly on the front.

'Thank you Richard.' I said. 'I did actually come to pay my respects. I really was upset when I heard what happened.'

'Sure you were.' Powell said curtly, turning away quickly and walking back to the apartment house.'

Taylor turned the key in the ignition and began to chuckle. 'Oh boy,' he said. 'If looks could kill you'd be a dead man by now and no mistake.'

'Colonel, are you aware of any Pentagon related business Robert Lavelle would have had in Georgetown that evening?' I asked as we drove away.

'None that I can think of, I certainly didn't send him there and I can't think who would. We are engaged in the maintenance of the world's biggest building. We rarely have cause to go socialising in Georgetown. But Lavelle was the kind of guy who guarded his privacy. He could have been there for any number of reasons. He was not the type to take kindly to anyone sticking their nose into his personal affairs. He was the touchy type, if you know what I mean.'

'Did the FBI or anyone else inform you that Lavelle's wife died recently in suspicious circumstances?'

Taylor looked over at me suspiciously. 'Mr Flynn, you are skatin' on thin ice. I don't mind giving you a ride back to town, but what the FBI say to me and what I say to them is between me and them. I have no intention of discussing that kind of thing with you or anyone else. So let's just leave it at that.'

We drove on in silence. Taylor, by his folksy response confirmed what I suspected he was the Fed's eyes and ears on Robert Lavelle.

CHAPTER 19

May 1963

Klara Hartmann heard the conductor tell an elderly couple that it would be a half hour before the train would arrive at Grand Central Station. Klara had taken the same train from Union Station in Washington on the last Saturday of each month since February. Each month she met the same man but always at a different location. She knew the person she was meeting only by his last name Kosenko. He seemed friendly and supportive and although he was Russian, or more correctly Belarussian, his German was impeccable. He seemed to Klara to be more like a kindly old uncle than a professional intelligence officer. Kosenko was employed at the Belarussian Mission to the United Nations. Belarus was one of three, purportedly independent countries of the Soviet Union along with Russia and Ukraine, which were member states of the United Nations. As East Germany had no diplomatic status in the United States, Belarus, in a spirit of Communist solidarity, looked after its interests in New York.

Each month a plain brown unstamped envelope, addressed to Mrs E. Lavelle, was left in the mailbox of apartment 3A, 1200 Cherry Tree Lane, Arlington. The envelope contained a white slip of paper with a typewritten message simply stating a location in Manhattan and nothing else. Washington Square and the Bronx Zoo had been two previous meeting places. Klara would arrive at the location at 2.30pm on the appointed Saturday and Kosenko would always be there ahead of her. This time the note had said simply, 'Tavern on the Green.' The location surprised Klara because it was a well known restaurant, lately fashionable with a certain kind of well heeled New Yorker. Klara's training had emphasised the importance of less conspicuous places for a rendezvous, favouring open spaces with anonymity provided by large crowds and with a variety of exit points.

As the train slowed rhythmically on its final run into Grand Central, Klara had come to her decision. She had made up her mind that today she would tell Kosenko she would not continue with this mission. Her cover as a 'hostess' in the Quorum Club could not disguise the fact that she was only half a rung away from working as a prostitute. The so-called members of the Quorum were superficially friendly, as she now understood most Americans were. But the collection of politicians who gathered in the Carroll Hotel, just a stone's throw from the Capitol building, were, almost without exception, crass, ignorant men, without any refinement or culture. Their lack of knowledge about the world outside the United States had astounded her. As for obtaining worthwhile intelligence information from such men, Klara had yet to meet a single Senator, Congressman or state Governor who knew anything of any value, unless it was connected to their home state or congressional district. It was the physical demands of the assignment which she found most repulsive. The persistent mauling and groping which the club members felt was their entitlement. The lewd remarks they found so amusing to make, liberated as they were from social constraints back home. Klara knew that she did not operate very well in this kind of environment. Bobby Baker never gave her any specific instructions. But it was clear that it would not be possible to avoid sleeping with these men if they insisted. On the one occasion Klara had done so, with a well known Senator, she felt soiled and ashamed to a degree she would not have thought possible. The image of her father and his strict moral code was never far from her mind when she thought about that particular encounter. Baker, an observant man, had noticed her reluctance and had gently encouraged her, in his pleasant way, to try to be 'a little more sociable,' as he put it. He was nice about it, with no hint of aggression or coercion. But Klara knew she could not do this job and she was also certain that, as an intelligence gathering exercise, it was a complete waste of time. She had no idea of the repercussions of her decision as far as HVA was concerned but she was certain that she could not go on. She would tell Kosenko as soon as she met him.

She took a cab from Grand Central Station to Columbus Circle and walked the short distance to Tavern on the Green on the western edge of Central Park. She went inside but there was no sign of Kosenko and the large Saturday lunchtime crowd seemed to be in no hurry to leave the main restaurant. It was the first time that she had arrived at a rendezvous before her controller. Klara went outside and stood at the main entrance looking anxiously around. The bulky figure of Kosenko was nowhere to be seen. She was suddenly startled by a familiar voice whispering in her ear from behind. 'You've changed Klara. I would never have believed it. You already look like a real American.' She did not have to turn her head to know that Kosenko wasn't coming and that somehow Max Korten had managed to get to America. Her knees suddenly began to tremble. She turned to look at him.

'Can I take it that the man I was expecting to meet will not be coming?' She said.

'You can, I hope you are not too disappointed to have me as his replacement. It's good to see you Klara, come let's take a walk.' As they headed into the park he reached into the pocket of a green gabardine coat he was carrying over his arm and produced a diplomatic passport with the words 'Soviet Socialist Republic of Belarus', written in gold Cyrillic lettering on the cover. 'I am on temporary assignment to the Belarussian mission to the UN, just for a few days. I arrived yesterday and go home on Monday.'

They walked into Central Park. There was a considerable number of people already there, enjoying the first taste of real warm summer sunshine. Klara took a good look at the man she had loved. 'You look well Max, but you seem little more anxious than you used to.'

He ignored her, staring at the impressive buildings surrounding the park on all sides. 'This city takes my breath away. Photographs or films don't do it justice.' Klara was amused see that for once, cool sophisticated Max Korten was impressed, even awestruck, by the Manhattan skyline and he could not conceal it.

'I was looking forward to lunch with Kosenko, I am a little hungry. Do you mind if we get a hot dog or something?'

'Not at all,' Korten answered. 'I'll have one too. But let's talk in English. We will be less conspicuous that way.'

Klara went to the nearest hot dog stand, Max Korten following in her wake. As she negotiated with the vendor asking Korten whether he wanted mustard or ketchup, she realised that he was unsure of himself, the way tourists often are on their first day in a new country, just as she herself had been when she arrived in Washington five months before. Hot dog stands and the noisy vibrancy of Central Park on a sunny day were a far cry from the plodding predictability of East German daily life. They sat on a nearby bench in order to consume two very large and unwieldy hotdogs. Klara had not seen Korten since the fraught meeting the previous August on the Ku'damm in Berlin. It had not been a happy encounter and Max certainly had the upper hand then. But now she thought she sensed vulnerability in him or perhaps it was a greater confidence in herself.

'So what brings you to New York Max? Is it something you can talk about?'

'Oh yes. I can talk about it alright, and that is precisely what I am here to do.'

Klara noticed his English was heavily accented and a little laboured, not at all as fluent as her own. 'Before you say anything, Max, I should like to say something to you. I was going to say this to Kosenko but as you are here, it is better that I say it directly to you. May I?'

'Of course, go ahead.'

'I do not feel that the mission our government has assigned me to is in any way effective from an espionage point of view.' She paused. Korten said nothing and waited for her to continue.

'Mainly because of the kind of second rate politicians that frequent that so called club where I work, if you can call it work. There is very little, if any, worthwhile intelligence to be gathered from men of that kind. Also, you may not be aware what it is I am required to do there. Max. My role there is no better than that of a common streetwalker and I'm happy to say that I don't have the talent for it. I doubt very much if you or General Wolf had that in mind when you sent me here. And finally, I don't find it acceptable from a personal point of view that I should have to, in effect prostitute myself, in order to obtain what amounts at best, to trivial political gossip.'

Korten listened intently as he finished the hot dog, saying nothing slowly using the paper napkin to wipe the remnants of ketchup from around his mouth. Klara waited for his answer.

'Is that it?' He said, in a voice that did not conceal his displeasure. 'I must say Klara, I am very disappointed that you do not yet trust your superiors, myself included, to have some inkling as to what we are doing. We do have a plan you know. We did not go to all of this trouble to train you and to send you here just to socialise with second rate politicians, as you call them and to enjoy yourself. You are on a mission. As I have said before, it is not for you to question the methods we use. You will wait to be told what to do, like every other agent.'

'What do you mean enjoy myself? If you think I enjoy a single second of this kind of life, you are very much mistaken.'

'Klara, It is immaterial to me and to the HVA whether you enjoy yourself or not. You're on an assignment in this country, not a vacation. As for General Wolf, you may be in no doubt that he knows the exact nature of the activities taking place in the Quorum Club and so do I. It's our business to know. You have been sent here specifically for this kind of work and you are expected to do it without complaint. If you have any intention of telling me what you were intending to tell Kosenko, that you want to be re-assigned, you can put such thoughts firmly out of your mind. We trained you for this work. There will be no reassignment and certainly no change in plan. Am I making myself clear?'

Klara was enraged by Korten's words. He spoke to her just as he had on that last morning in Berlin. Before she could answer Korten stood up.

'Come, let's walk a little, I have something important to tell you and it's better to keep on the move.'

They threw their hot dog papers and napkins in a nearby trash bin and began to walk northwards. Klara had not yet gained her composure from Max's verbal onslaught. They were both silent for a moment, Klara thinking how best to respond. Then Korten spoke again, this time reverting to German, perhaps because he was more persuasive in his native language. In a calmer more soothing voice, he said.

'This is not a long term mission Klara, at least the part of it you are enduring right now. We are not heartless, we don't intend to leave you forever languishing in that hotel and living with a man like Lavelle. I fully realise that it's not congenial for someone such as you.'

'Living with him is quite congenial. He's fine, he's not the problem.'

'As I said there is a plan and if it works you will not have to continue as you are now for very much longer. In fact that is why I am here. I have come here specifically to talk to you about the next phase of the mission. Before I tell you more, I want to stress how important and sensitive this next phase is. That's why we couldn't let Kosenko meet with you today. I selected you personally for this mission, Klara, because I know you have the attributes needed to succeed. I chose you. It was not Hoffman, Wolf or Mielke but me. I chose you, not for your natural beauty but for your intelligence, your sharp mind and for your empathy. You will see what I mean when I come to explain the next phase of the operation. Before I do I need to be sure that you will be committed to it one hundred percent. Can I still be sure of that Klara? I'm very concerned at the doubts you have already expressed about this assignment.'

She did not answer directly but put another question to him. 'Are you saying that the next phase will mean putting the life I've been leading since February behind me?'

'Yes, it certainly will. Although not immediately. But if we succeed you will begin to move in far more rarefied circles than you do now. I have hopes that you will become the most important agent that any socialist country has in the West. Then you can say good bye forever to those second rate politicians you seem to despise.'

'How long before I can leave the Quorum Club?'

Korten smiled. 'You haven't lost your natural impatience Klara. You seem more interested in leaving that place than in being socialism's greatest intelligence asset.'

'Quite honestly Max, I am. You would not believe how humiliating it is.'

'I can imagine.' He said unconvincingly. 'But as I said it will come to an end. How soon, though, depends not on me but on you. In this phase of the operation you will be in the driving seat.'

'I can't understand how that could possibly be Max.'

He tried to hide his irritation with her. 'I know you don't but if you have patience I will explain. So listen carefully. Do you know a man named Charles Brewster?'

'Yes I do. I have seen him at parties. They call him Chip. He was once a Senator from Florida, a handsome charming man, not unlike you Max but older.'

'Very good Klara, do you know anything else about him?'

'They say he's a friend of the President.'

'Do they? Well they're right. He is. Do you know what the basis of that friendship is?'

'I believe the President's father has a home in Florida. They refer to it in the press here as the Winter White House. Brewster may know him from there.'

'That's partially true, he is from Palm Beach. The two men have a closer bond. They served in the Senate together when they were younger, single and both keenly interested in the pursuit of women.' He glanced in her direction to gauge her reaction. Does that surprise you, Klara?'

'No, I can see what Brewster is like. The President is different. I have heard rumours about him but I don't believe them. He is happily married to a beautiful woman.'

Korten laughed out loud. 'How can you be so naive? Don't be fooled by the man's good looks and smooth charm. Believe me, it's merely to impress idiotic American voters. That's the way this so called democracy works. Kennedy was a legendary womaniser in the Senate and still is today. On a scale that is difficult to believe. It's a scandal that would shock the gullible public in this country, if they ever knew about it.' He paused a moment to let this information sink in. 'Fortunately for us, the President's weakness is our opportunity.'

'I think you're wrong about Kennedy, Max. He's a good family man. I saw him with his wife and daughter once, they looked very happy together.'

'How could you have seen them?' Korten said.

'I was simply curious.' she said hesitantly. Robert Lavelle, you remember him Max? My husband, he mentioned that the President and his family regularly attend church at St Matthews Cathedral in Washington. I simply went there one Sunday morning, not long after coming to Washington, and saw them come to church just like any other family. I thought they were the most handsome couple I have ever seen.'

'Oh were they? Korten raised his voice in genuine anger. 'I am truly shocked at your stupidity, Klara. Let me tell you something, I have access to information about Kennedy's personal life which would make your head spin. I happen to know Kennedy is reckless, foolish and shallow. He is almost certainly suffering from some kind of personality disorder. The image you see is just that, an image. The man is an utter charlatan. How could you think otherwise?'

Klara was surprised by the strength of Max response. Was he jealous of the President? She answered him with genuine indignation. 'Because he has a quality about him I have never seen in another politician. There is sincerity there and real idealism. I don't care what you say.'

'Oh Klara, Klara, I never thought that someone so smart could also be so dumb.' He looked at her for a moment as if looking at her for the first time.

'If what we have planned works out, you may have an opportunity to test out your theory about his caring nature for yourself. I think you will find that all is not as perfect as it seems in the bosom of the so called First Family.'

'What exactly are you talking about Max?'

Korten looked around him before answering. 'I can't explain here.' He said. 'Come with me.'

The park was crowded now with strollers, sunbathers and children playing. Korten looked around for a private place. He took Klara by the hand and led her across a broad meadow of grass beneath a copper maple tree which no one else had occupied. It provided a modicum of isolation among the throngs enjoying their day in the park. It was the first time they had physically touched since they said their goodbyes in Potsdam before the charade of the escape. He spread his gabardine coat at the base of the tree and they sat on it.

'What I am about to tell you, Klara, is the reason for your being in the United States and the reason for my coming here to talk to you. It's what all of your training and coaching has been about. I need hardly tell you that what I am saying to you is top secret and cannot ever be revealed to another person. That goes for your make believe husband too. Do you understand?'

'Yes, of course.' Klara said.

'Good. You can ask questions when I have finished. For now just listen and listen carefully.' Klara nodded her assent.

'Senator Brewster will approach you soon. He will ask you whether you would like to visit the White House and meet a very important person. Of course you will agree to do so. Brewster will escort you to the White House himself on an evening of his choosing. I cannot say exactly when but it will be soon, within two or three weeks at the most. You will of course agree to go and Senator Brewster will introduce you to the President. Yes, to President Kennedy himself.'

Klara opened her mouth to speak but Korten put a finger to her lips. 'Quiet please, listen now, questions later. The assignment for you, Klara, is to impress the President and to ingratiate yourself with him. Your beauty will impress him, that goes without saying but you must also impress him with your mind and your knowledge. For all his interest in women, he has very little regard for their intellect. He does not expect intelligent conversation from a woman and he's not really looking for it either. But this man is an insatiably curious person. He will ask lots of questions. If you answer intelligently he will be impressed. You excelled during the Adler Programme training with your knowledge of United States history. You will remember that there was a lot of material provided relating to the minutiae of this administration. You will need every bit of that knowledge and more to ensure that this single meeting with him will not be your last. We want him to be so impressed with you that you are asked back. In effect we want you to become this man's friend, not his lover. I will provide you with a list of books you will have to read before any meeting takes place. Kennedy is a great reader of history and biography. He recently provided the press here with a list of his favourite reading. The autobiography of Britain's Lord Melbourne in the last century is apparently his favourite. But he also likes less intellectual reading such as Ian Fleming's James Bond novels. I will provide you with far more sensitive information about the President and his administration. We will study it carefully together, here in New York this weekend.'

'Wait a minute Max, can you hear yourself? Are you mad? You actually think that I, Klara Hartmann, can meet with the American President and what? Become his friend? You must all have gone crazy over there in Berlin.'

'Once again you disappoint me. You show so little faith in your superiors. We are not amateurs, this is our business. We know what we are doing. Now listen once more to what I am saying and when I have finished, instead of arguing in that irritating emotional way, ask me some specific questions about the operation and I will answer all of them. This is not a game Klara. So listen. As I said, you will be approached by former Senator Charles Brewster of Florida and asked if you would like to come to the White House. He will think that you have a genuine interest in meeting the President. You will say yes. When you go to the White House, Brewster will escort you in. He won't stay long but he will introduce you to the President of the United States.

The President will almost certainly engage you in conversation. You will be your own charming and intelligent self when you talk to him. You will impress him but you will be subtle, not pushy or over familiar. You are not expected to get any information from Kennedy on this occasion but you will be so charming and interesting to him that you will be asked back again and a genuine meaningful relationship with this man will be initiated. That is your mission Klara. That is what all of your training in the Adler programme has been about. It is what this operation is about. We know it will not be easy but I have faith in you and you will be strongly supported along the way. Once you have made a real connection with the President you will withdraw from the Quorum Club and additional money will be provided to allow you to live comfortably in Washington and to concentrate solely on this operation. It will have absolute priority with us. So now, no outbursts just questions. Ask me what you want I will answer.'

Klara said nothing. She stood up and walked slowly out from under the canopy of the maple tree staring across the park. Korten sat watching her, resting his back against the trunk of the tree. She walked slowly away for about twenty yards before turning and looking back at Korten. She stood still for a full minute before coming back to him and sitting down on the coat once again. Her expression was serious and focussed. Korten waited patiently. Her first question surprised him.

'Is Brewster a spy for our side?'

'No. He's a loyal American, patriotic. But he has been indiscreet, as you know a great many of these American politicians are, so we will be able to persuade him to do this small favour for us. But he will have no idea who is asking the favour or what it's about. If he did I doubt he would cooperate. We never approached him before and we never will again. He is merely facilitating an introduction to the President.'

'Is Ellen Rometch our agent?'

'No. She has never worked for us. As far as I know she is an innocent woman accidently caught up in some American political intrigue.

'Did you know from the first time we met on Rügen Island that this operation was planned?'

'Yes. It was planned jointly by me and Markus Wolf. We just didn't have the right person for the task until you came to our attention. That was even before Rügen Island. Your interview with Dr Hoffman was the first step.'

'Did you know that I would be required to be intimate with complete strangers as part of this operation?'

Korten hesitated before answering. 'I could not be sure, but I thought it was a possibility.'

'In other words, yes. Do you expect that the President will seek sexual favours from me as part of the process of becoming my 'friend', as you envisage this operation playing out?'

Korten looked slightly uncomfortable but had decided that, in her current frame of mind she would only be satisfied with straightforward answers. 'Based on what we know of his previous behaviour, I would say it is almost certain that he will try. But of course I can't be sure.'

'I see. And that is fine with you and General Wolf?'

'In the circumstances, I cannot see how we can prevent it.'

'Is there some specific information I am expected to obtain from the President?'

'Not at this point, no. We can consider that when we get passed the first phase of the operation.'

'What will happen if Kennedy meets me, talks to me but shows no further interest in me after the first meeting?'

'Then we will reassess the situation. If it cannot be salvaged, you will simply be reassigned to some other work.' But I have every expectation that you will succeed.'

'Do you really Max? Now who is being naive? Neither you nor anyone else could possibly know what will happen.' She paused at looked at him trying to divine some truth or honesty in his face. 'You once said that you loved me Max. Was that ever true? Was everything we shared just part of your preparation for this brilliant scheme of yours?'

Korten looked at her anxiously, his eyes suddenly pleading for understanding. 'No Klara, I never intended to fall in love with you but it happened and I am glad it did. The memory of our time together last year is very precious to me. When I said I loved you then, it was true and it still is. You must know that Klara, it still is. I feel it now more than I ever did.'

Klara avoided his eyes, then glanced at her wristwatch and stood up. I can't sit in this uncomfortable position any longer and I have a train to catch back to Washington. I have to walk I need to stretch my legs.' Korten also stood up picking his coat of the ground. He stretched out his arm to take her by the hand but she pulled away and began to walk briskly back in the direction from which they'd come. Korten hurried to fall in beside her.

'I don't think that anyone in your line of work has any idea of what the truth is.' She said harshly. 'Let me tell you something, Max, something that is true. I loved you once too. In your beautiful little wooden house in Spreewald and all the other places where we spent such blissful days and weekends last summer. I was certainly happier then than I had ever been before. Since going to Bavaria and also here in America, I have missed you terribly, and think about you constantly. Not a single day passed when you were not in my thoughts. But I don't love you now,

Max Korten and I know for certain that I never will again. You're right, I am naive and I've been unbelievably stupid. Maybe that's what love does to a person. I wouldn't know, I have never been in love with anyone but you. But the scales have at last, fallen from my eyes. It took me until this very afternoon to realise who and what you are Max.' She stopped walking and faced him. She spoke with a determination he had never seen in her before. 'You're a professional manipulator and a liar, a chameleon who can change his colours and his camouflage in the twinkling of an eye. If working for the government begins to bore you I am sure you would make a fine actor. You are a man who is so cynical he would make a prostitute out of the woman he says he loves, in order to further his own career. Because I know it's really your career you're interested in. You don't give a damn for socialist ideology. You are no more a Communist than Richard Nixon is. I suspect that goes for your idol General Wolf too. Well I no longer love you Max, and what's more I no longer need you. I'm in America now. I could walk out of this park and into the nearest New York police station and ask for political asylum and I would get it.'

She could see that he was making a superhuman effort to control his anger. 'I am sorry to hear you say that Klara. That would be most unwise.'

'What's that Max, another one of your poorly veiled threats? Well you need not worry. I'm not going to do that. I will go ahead with the operation no matter how misguided I think it is. Believe it or not I will try my best to succeed and I will tell you why. I have three conditions which must be fulfilled and if you don't agree to them I swear to you I will seek asylum here in the US this very day and live with the consequences.'

Korten's face was flushed with rage, this time he wasn't acting. The conversation clearly had not gone the way he had wanted. Klara could see that her personal declaration of independence had shaken him to the core. When he spoke his voice was an inaudible whisper.

'And what are they, these conditions?'

'Firstly, I will return to the Quorum Club only once more. Next Friday night might be a good time to quit that disgusting so called job. Chip Brewster can make his approach to me then. Whatever method of persuasion you have to use on him, you'd better ensure that he is there next Friday. Once that's done I will never walk through the doors of the Carroll Arms Hotel again. Secondly, my parents are to be officially notified that they may leave Dresden and the GDR as soon as they wish and travel freely to the West. You and the HVA will facilitate their move. Finally, I want you to return to Robert Lavelle any incriminating material you have collected about him when you 'persuaded' him to marry me. Someone can deliver it to him personally before next week, so he can dispose of it himself. I won't be going to the White House, with Brewster or anybody else until that material, whatever it is, has been given to Robert and my sister in Berlin informs me that permission has been granted to my parents to leave. These are my conditions, do you accept them?'

Korten was enraged by this ultimatum, but did his best to conceal it. He was gradually regaining his composure. 'I can't authorise all of this myself Klara. I will have to contact higher authorities. There is something I have not told you. Naturally I did not envisage this breach in our relations so I took the liberty of booking a suite for us tonight in the Carlyle Hotel. There are documents I want to show you. There is a lot more to be said concerning the details of the operation, a public park is hardly the place. You could take the train back to Washington tomorrow.'

'I'll tell you what Max. I have other things to do myself. You go and make your calls to your higher authority. I will meet you at the Carlyle at 8.00pm. By then you will have booked a separate room for me, if possible not on the same floor as yours. If my conditions are agreed to and we need privacy to talk, I'm sure the Carlyle will provide us with a meeting room.'

For the first time since she had known him, Klara could see that Korten was flustered and confused, she felt a little sorry for him. 'The hotel should not be a problem but your other demands may not be so easy Klara. This is Saturday. You know how difficult it is to get decisions from Berlin at weekends.'

'Well then, you have some work to do. I won't delay you any further. See you at the Carlyle at 8.00 pm. If you're not there, I'll know we don't have an agreement.'

She turned quickly leftwards and walked towards the Fifth Avenue exit, her heart thumping and her knees trembling. It took an act of will for her to walk away gracefully and erect, knowing Korten was almost certainly watching. Her emotions were in turmoil, shocked at the audacity of what she had just done and said. Had she overstepped the mark, had she gone too far? Her parents were still vulnerable; they were in effect Korten's hostages. She had started this journey two years ago to save her father. She hoped she hadn't put them in greater danger now.

By the time she reached Fifth Avenue, her nerves had begun to calm a little. She had lied of course, she had absolutely nothing to do. She headed towards the Metropolitan Museum, a place she had found restful and quiet on previous Saturdays, when she had finished her meetings with Kosenko. She had discovered a fondness for the emotional excitement in the works of Caravaggio but she couldn't handle the high drama of his paintings today. She went to the section on French Impressionist and sat in front of the calming lily ponds of Claude Monet. Her mind was not on art but on the daunting prospect of a possible meeting with John Kennedy. Despite her indignant response to Max's proposed scheme, she felt more than a tingle of excitement at the prospect of going to the White House. Only now would she admit to herself that this had been an ambition of hers since she began her American studies in the Adler Programme, to meet with this charismatic man. Now, incredibly, it might actually happen. On one level it was frightening while on another, she had to admit to herself she had never been so excited about anything in her entire life.

CHAPTER 20

June 1963

A beautiful woman, known to the few people in Washington who know her as Elsa Kircherr, sat at on a high stool in the bar of the Carroll Arms Hotel, just a stone's throw from the steps of the Capitol. To the casual observer she looked stunning, despite the simplicity of her clothes or maybe because of it. She wore a simple sleeveless, black, knee length dress, with matching high heeled shoes. Her jewellery consisted of a single strand pearl necklace, a gold bracelet and a wristwatch. A faux fur, half length coat was draped over the stool in front of her, a small black evening purse on top of it. She had had her hair cut and styled in Arlington that morning. She knew she looked well because Eric the barman had told her so, at least twice and Eric was quite an expert. It was early Friday evening the hotel bar had not yet filled up. Earlier that afternoon Klara received a call from Bobby Baker at the apartment she shared with Robert Lavelle. Baker told her to be in the bar at 7.00pm and to wait for a visit from 'Senator' Chip Brewster. He was no longer in the Senate but he clung to his former title like a badge of honour. Baker told her in his smooth South Carolina voice, to 'try to make an effort this evening, look pretty and to try to be extra friendly.' He didn't say what the meeting was about but his tone implied that she needed to up her game in the friendliness department, because this was not just a routine rendezvous. Baker also seemed to imply that he didn't have much hope that Elsa Kircherr would do as he asked.

It was exactly a week since the discussion with Max Korten in central park, so Klara knew that this was the call she had been waiting for. She had to hand it to Max; it seemed he had pulled it off. Klara didn't know

Brewster well but she had seen enough of him to observe that he was urbane, smart and witty. He was the kind of man who was equally popular with both men and women. Of course in the milieu of the Carroll Arms Hotel his interest appeared to be primarily in women but like a lot of men of that type, Brewster actually seemed to prefer the more raucous company of likeminded men. He came silently up behind her putting his hand on her bare arm without warning and Klara involuntarily shuddered. 'Sorry darlin', didn't mean to startle you,' Chip Brewster said, smiling broadly at her. He was wearing an expensive looking navy blue suit, a pristine white shirt and striped blue and yellow tie. He was tall dark and handsome in a nineteen forties movie star way. Brimming with a natural easy confidence, he didn't have prefect features, which had the effect of making his tanned face all the more interesting. His eyes looked her over unashamedly.

'Elsa, isn't it.? For some reason you and I have never had a real conversation, which considering how beautiful you are seems very remiss of me. Can I buy you a drink?'

'No thank you Senator I have a soda here, I'm fine for now.'

'Bourbon and branch for me Eric, We'll have it over at the table near the window. Do you mind, Elsa? There's a bit more privacy over there.'

When Eric set the bourbon down on the counter Klara got off the stool and taking her coat, followed Brewster over to a seat by the window. They sat side by side. She laid her coat over the back of the chair opposite.

When they were comfortable, Brewster, who clearly had something on his mind, got straight to it. 'Elsa, have you ever been to Florida?'

'No Senator I haven't. I would like to go sometime.'

Brewster's expression left her in no doubt that he was sceptical of the sincerity her reply. 'You sure you were never there?' He said.

'Of course I'm sure.'

'Ever been to Cuba?'

'Cuba? No of course not.' She said laughing lightly. Brewster still had a puzzled look on his face but he was beginning to believe her. I'll tell you why I ask, Elsa, you see I had a visit down in Miami a couple of days ago from some Cuban gentlemen. We have a large Cuban community in

Miami, almost all strongly anti-Castro. You know who Castro is, don't you?'

'Of course I do Senator. I may be blonde but I'm not dumb.'

'No. I can see that. By the way Elsa, please call me Chip when we're socialising. If we ever bump into each other up there on the Hill or if I'm with my wife, you can call me Senator but here, it's Chip, alright?'

'Sure. Chip it is then,'

Brewster took a dainty sip of his bourbon before continuing. 'Anyway Elsa, these Cuban gentlemen asked me to set up this little meeting with you tonight and I can't for the life of me think why. They were, well let's say they were very insistent that I do so. Now, I don't actually have their names, so I can't ask you if you know them. Now that I think about it they didn't mention you by name but they described you in great detail.

Klara interrupted. 'I can assure you, Senator, apart from you, I don't know a single person from Florida and I don't think I have ever met anyone from Cuba in my life, so whoever you're talking about couldn't possibly know me. You must be mistaken.'

Brewster looked at her quizzically. 'Where are you from Elsa, originally I mean?'

'I'm from Germany, Bavaria, a place called Garmisch Partenkirchen. That's where I met my husband.'

'I've heard of it, a big ski resort, right? That is a long way from Cuba. What does your husband do?'

'He's in the army. He works at the Pentagon.'

Brewster looked a little more comfortable with this information. 'Oh I see that's good. Is he a Republican or a Democrat, your husband?'

'Definitely a Democrat.'

'That so, do you like it here in the States, Elsa?'

'Yes I do, very much but I haven't seen a great deal of it. It's such a big country and there's so much to see.'

Brewster was hardly listening to this banal reply, his puzzled expression returned. 'And yet you've no connection with Cuba or Miami? I just don't get it.'

'Senator, I am sorry, this conversation is very different from the usual kind we have in our little club. I don't really understand what is worrying you or who these people you speak about are but if you would rather not socialise with me this evening, that's perfectly OK. I can see you are worried about something. I have no wish be the cause of your worry.'

'No darlin' it's not that, it's just a puzzle that's all. Do you know what I'd planned for this evening, Elsa?'

'No, how could I?'

'I'm not sure how you could.' He paused, took another drink, clearly trying to figure out what possible connection this woman could have to the people in Miami who insisted on this meeting. Klara could almost hear him thinking. Is she the right woman? Did he get it wrong?

'As a matter of fact I had planned to take us to a pretty special place where security is kind of tight. There will be some interesting people there, well known people. How do you feel about that?'

'I'm fine with it if you are Chip. What is it, an embassy function?'

'Not exactly but I can promise you won't be disappointed. I can see by the cut of that very becoming dress you are wearing that you're not carrying anything that causes bulges in the wrong places. Would you mind very much if I took a look in your purse?'

'My purse, what on earth for?'

'As I said, security is very tight where we're going and photographs are strictly forbidden. I have got to be sure you are not carrying a camera or anything.'

'I don't think a camera would fit in this tiny purse do you? And I can't say I care for your suspicions about me. If you don't want to go out, that's fine with me. I really don't appreciate being searched like a common criminal.'

Brewster smiled apologetically. 'Elsa, I am sorry. I can assure you when you hear where we're going, you will understand. Please just show me the purse and I will explain everything.'

Klara gave every impression of reluctantly handing over the little black clutch. Brewster opened it and glanced inside at the usual female contents of a small evening purse.

'They make very tiny cameras these days Elsa, you'd be surprised.' He closed it, smiled again and handed it back. She tried to look as indignant as she could when she took it from him. The bar was now beginning to fill up with after work Friday revellers, Brewster lowered his voice.

'You know who Jack Kennedy is, don't you sweetheart?'

'You mean President Kennedy, of course I do.'

'Jack and me, we go back a long way. We're pals, I mean real good pals and tonight you and me Elsa, are going to pay him a visit.'

'I don't understand Senator. How do you mean pay him a visit?'

He was amused but gratified by the look of surprise on her face. 'What do you think I mean? We're going call into the White House and spend some time with him. What do you think about that?'

'Sorry Chip, are you joking? I can't visit the White House. I'm not properly dressed. I am not prepared I would not know what to say.'

Brewster emitted a loud guffaw. 'Well if that ain't typical of a woman. Of course you can go. By the way, you're dressed as fine as any woman I've ever seen. Believe me you'll be the best dressed woman there. C'mon finish your soda and let's get out of here.'

'What about the President's wife, how will you explain me to her? I will be too nervous, I just can't do it.'

Brewster looked at his watch. It was funny, he thought, how women always asked about Jackie. It was getting late. 'No, I'm sorry darlin', she won't be there this evening. She's out of town right now. This is not a formal thing Elsa, not a party or anything, just a few friendly drinks in the family quarters that's all. I know this man well Elsa, like he was my own brother. He's very easy to talk to. You just have to trust ol' Chip. C'mon get your coat and let's get going. My car's just down the street.' He stood up and headed quickly for the door, Klara scrambling behind him through the growing crowd, her coat over one arm. Despite the rush, a small smile of satisfaction played on her lips. She was quietly proud of herself. She had managed to get Chip Brewster to persuade her to come to the White House with him. The mysterious Cubans, who had put him up to it, wherever Max Korten found them, seemed to be forgotten already. Maybe she was a better spy than she had ever thought she was or maybe it was just that Chip Brewster was a seriously irresponsible individual. Perhaps a little bit of both. He was waiting at the front door of the hotel when she caught up with him.

As they walked to his car he said. 'I want to warn you about something Elsa. It's not advisable to mention Jackie, when we get to where we're going. He's friendly, don't get me wrong, but he's a very private guy too. No questions about wife or his kids or anything about his private life. That might just spoil the evening. I hope you understand.'

'Of course Chip, I understand completely. Nothing could be clearer.'

CHAPTER 21

June 1963

Charles F. Brewster walked through the South Portico of the White House with all the confidence of a United States Senator, who had been there many times before and was an intimate friend of the President. Klara followed meekly in his wake, her high heels making it difficult to keep up with the long strides of her tall companion. In a hushed carpeted hallway next to a small elevator stood a man with a military demeanour, short cropped hair and an athletic build. An usher wearing a black vest white shirt and a black bow tie stood silently on the opposite side of the corridor.

'Good evening Senator, nice to see you again.'

'Good evening Agent Banner how are you. We're on the list I believe, this is Miss Kircherr.'

'Evening, Banner said. 'May I take your coat and purse please Ma'am? I'll have the usher take care of it till you return.' Klara handed him her coat but held on to her purse. He pressed the elevator button, it opened immediately. Wait a moment please Senator and I'll escort you both up. He gave Klara's coat to the silent usher, who nodded obediently and took it away. Klara and Brewster got into the elevator, which was just about big enough to hold three people, Banner followed them in.

'Where are you from Miss Kircherr?' Banner asked.

'I live in Arlington.' She answered.

'Not far from home then.' Banner said. Klara thought she saw an imperceptible knowing look pass between the Secret Service agent and the Senator. By the time this brief exchange had ended the elevator had reached the second floor. Agent Banner got out first and led them the short distance down a broad parquet floored corridor with 18th century nautical pictures on the walls and a thick blue rug running down its centre. The place was deathly quiet. Klara's sudden realisation of where she was and who she was about to meet raised her anxiety to unexpected levels. She hoped it wasn't obvious to the secret service man. She tried to dispel her nervousness by looking at the pictures and decor with exaggerated interest. At the end of the corridor another Secret Service agent sat on a chair outside closed cream coloured double doors. Banner nodded at the man, who rose from his seat, opened the doors and stood aside to let Brewster and Klara into a long narrow, tastefully decorated room. Three young women stood in the centre of the room around a circular table with a linen table covering. They were drinking cocktails and listening with obvious amusement to a balding middle aged man telling a humorous story. At the far end of the room, was someone Klara recognised, a tall heavy set man in a business suit and horn rimmed glasses he was standing, talking intently to a man wearing a navy blue suit and tie, sitting on a plain straight backed dining chair, his feet resting casually on a coffee table. It was the President of the United States. Chip Brewster placed his hand at Klara's elbow and guided her over to where the other women stood.

'Ah Senator, the bald man said breaking off from his anecdote to shake hands with Brewster. 'Good to see you.'

'And you too Dave. This is Miss Kircherr, a very good friend of mine. Elsa, this is Mr Powers.'

The man gave her a genuinely friendly smile and shook her hand. 'You're very welcome to the White House. I'm sorry what's your first name my dear?'

'It's Elsa.' Klara replied.

'Well Elsa let me introduce you to everyone.'

At that point Klara heard the President's familiar voice call from the end of the room.

'Hey Charlie, get over here will you. Bill's just told me something I find very hard to believe.' Chip Brewster immediately answered the summons. The man with the horn rimmed glasses looked over and recognised Klara. He raised his glass in her direction by way of a greeting. She knew him as Bill Waters, a regular Quorum Club visitor and a notorious pursuer of women. He wasn't a politician he was a lobbyist, something to do with airlines. Klara had successfully evaded Waters' lecherous attentions more than once. He was the last person she expected to see in the White House. The friendly Mr Powers offered Klara a daquerie and introduced her to the three other women with him, all of whom worked in the White House. They traded small talk for a while, until one of the women asked Powers to continue with whatever story he had been telling. The older man obliged. Klara sipped her drink and pretended to listen to the story but could not shake off her disbelief at being where she was. In the background she could hear the President and the other two men talking and laughing, the President's distinctive voice more pronounced than the others. As Powers finished his story, which, as far as Klara could tell, was about a man in Boston who was arrested while trying to vote more than once at different polling stations on the same day, the three women laughed loudly. When their laughter subsided Klara heard Chip Brewster call out to her. 'Elsa, dear, come over here for a minute. There's someone who'd like to meet you.'

She put her glass on the table. Powers smiled at her benignly. 'You can leave your purse here if you like my dear. He said. 'We'll take care of it.'

She placed the purse on the table. She could feel the other three women observing her closely as she excused herself to meet the President. She knew they had no illusions about what she was and why she had been brought here. She tried to dispel the uncomfortable feeling this thought gave her as she walked across the room towards the three men.

Waters greeted her over familiarly with a kiss on the cheek. 'Hello beautiful, good to see you again.' She acknowledged his greeting with the briefest of smiles. Brewster did the introductions.

'Mr President. I would like you to meet Mrs Elsa Kircherr. She's new here in Washington, her husband's at the Pentagon.' He said this, as if her husband had been appointed Chairman of the Joint Chiefs of Staff.

The President offered her his hand but did not rise from his chair.

'Pleased to meet you Mrs Kircherr. My apologies for not standing, my back is bothering me quite a bit today. These hard backed chairs are one of the few things that give me some relief.'

The President's deeply tanned face was a little jowly, his teeth perfectly white. There were the beginnings of crow's feet around his alert blue gray eyes. Klara was suddenly awestruck by the encounter and could not utter a word. She could tell Kennedy was aware of this, it had obviously happened to him many times before. He was good enough to come to her rescue.

'Where are you from originally, if you don't mind my asking?'

'I lived in Bavaria before coming to America, Mr President, a town called Garmisch in the Alps. He was listening to her carefully and seemed to look at her with genuine curiosity.

'Garmisch huh. Believe it or not, I was there once, in 1937, a lifetime ago. I must complement you on your English, you don't sound German. I'm going to Berlin at the end of the month. Do you know Berlin?'

'Yes I do. I know it quite well.'

'Do you think I'll get a good reception there?' He asked his upper class tones combined with a New England accent created a curious kind of voice.

'I think the people of West Berlin will welcome you with great enthusiasm. I presume you are not going to the East, Mr President but I believe they too would welcome you, if only they were permitted to.'

Klara noticed a spark of interest in President's expression at her response. 'Do you think so? Too bad I won't be going this time. It's Elsa, isn't it?'

'Yes.'

'What's your opinion of Dr. Adenauer Elsa?'

'Well he's old, a little bit passed his time and I think West Germany would benefit from a younger leader. But he's honest, he has created a genuine democracy, economically strong and of course he is totally committed to the alliance with the United States. There are not many who could have succeeded in doing what he has done, considering the condition the country was in after the war.'

Kennedy nodded appreciatively at this assessment. 'Who do you think will go down in history as the greatest German statesman, Adenauer or Willi Brandt?'

'I think, perhaps Bismark would beat either of them. But I presume you mean present day statesmen. As of now I would say, definitely Dr. Adenauer. But Berlin is such a volatile place, maybe there are challenges still to come for Mayor Brandt. If he meets them he might overshadow the older man.'

Kennedy smiled broadly at Waters and Brewster.

'Bobby Baker must be running seminars on international politics over there at the Carroll Hotel. Elsa here seems to know more about it than most Senators, Chip.' He said, looking at Brewster.

Brewster and Waters laughed politely. Kennedy took his feet off the coffee table and rose from his chair with some difficulty, a dart of pain from his bad back was visible on his face. 'Now if you two gentlemen will excuse me I think I'd like to give this beautiful young lady here a short tour of the mansion. That is, if you would like it, Elsa?'

'Yes Mr President, I would like it very much that's very kind of you. You don't mean you yourself will be the guide?'

Kennedy laughed. 'Of course I will, don't you trust me? I do know a little about this house, believe it or not.'

'I'm sorry.' Klara said blushing.' I didn't mean to imply.....'

'I'm just kidding.' He turned good naturedly to Brewster and Waters.' Are you fellas still here? Can't you see I have things to do? Chip, I want to talk soon about my trip to Florida in November. You're the only guy I can trust to give me an accurate picture of what's really happening there.' He called across the room to Powers, ignoring the three young women who were with him. 'Dave, I'll see you later.'

Turning to Klara he said. 'Elsa, is there anything you'd particularly like to see?'

'I think I'd like to see the Lincoln room if that's possible. I believe there is an original copy of the Gettysburg address there.'

Kennedy looked at her with renewed curiosity as they left the room. 'Of course you may. As it happens it's on this floor. Come with me. You know ninety nine people out of hundred, I ask that question say they'd like to see the Oval Office. What do you know about Lincoln?'

'Very little, I have read about him, not as much as most Americans of course. I find him a most impressive historical figure. I was impressed by his genuine despair at the numbers of men from both sides who were killed in your civil war. I believe he was a man of real compassion, real humanity. It's a rare quality in a world leader, present company excepted of course. When I first read about Lincoln for some reason his personality reminded me a little of my father.'

They walked a short distance and stopped outside the door of the Lincoln bedroom. Kennedy indicated the corridor they stood in.

'In Lincoln's time, here on the second floor, it was not the private space it is today. This very corridor was constantly packed with an eclectic collection of supplicants and hangers on, many of them timewasters, seeking favours or preferment from Lincoln.' He said. 'Lincoln gave them all a hearing and helped whoever he thought needed it. You're quite right though, he was a humane man and because he was, the carnage of the war pained him terribly. He aged a lot in those four years.' He opened the door to the Lincoln room but before going in he asked. 'What does your father do?'

'He's a Lutheran pastor.' Klara replied, remembering too late, that her cover story as Elsa Kircherr indicated that she had been brought up without a father. The presence of this beguiling man and his obvious interest in her, had thrown her into confusion. Kennedy merely nodded, pushed open the door and walked in ahead of her. The room contained a large ornately carved timber framed bed, a couch and chairs of the Victorian period. In its centre was a small circular table with moulded metal legs. A framed document case sat on the marble table top containing a sheaf of hand written pages. Kennedy indicated the document case.

'This is what you were looking for. It's one of only five handwritten copies of the Gettysburg address. As presidential speeches go it's quite short, it has only two hundred and seventy two words altogether. It took Lincoln a little more than three minutes to deliver it. I studied it closely when I was preparing my own inauguration speech, to see if I could divine its secret.' He said, smiling at the thought.

'It must have worked. You didn't do too badly' Mr. President.' Klara said.

'Well thank you, I'm pleased to hear you say it. Lincoln used this room as an office and sometimes even held cabinet meetings here. I believe Mrs Lincoln purchased the bed. What do you think of the room?'

Klara looked around. 'It's a modest room for such a giant of history but very much in keeping with the man himself.' She walked across the floor to examine a portrait of a silver haired but youthful looking man on the wall. 'That must be President Andrew Jackson. She said. 'I believe Lincoln was a great admirer of his.'

'Kennedy was clearly impressed. Was she overplaying her hand, she wondered.'

'You know what I can't understand? How someone like you ever got mixed up with a slippery character like Bobby Baker. C'mon, I'll show you some more of the family quarters.'

Klara could feel the President's natural impatience. This was a man in a hurry, a man who was easily bored, who wanted to keep the momentum of his life continuously moving forward. They left the room and walked a short distance down the corridor. Kennedy opened another door and this time held it open and let Klara go in before him. They entered a spacious, beautifully decorated bedroom with powder blue walls and furnishings, floor to ceiling windows and a large double bed with a matching blue cover. There were small framed family photographs placed on various surfaces throughout the room.

'This is Mrs Kennedy's room, the President said. It has a wonderful view of the South lawn, take a look.'

Klara went over to the window, pulled aside the sheer curtains and looked out over the lawn. The Washington monument was prominently visible in the distance. It was dusk but not yet dark. Lights were coming on sporadically across the city, the early evening Washington traffic had subsided. Most of the government employees were already safely back in their suburban homes. The city looked beautiful but for a split second Klara inwardly shivered with a feeling that neither this city nor the United States, would ever be her home. As she took in the impressive view, Klara could feel the President's presence in the room behind her and could sense what was coming next. She stood still, staring out of the window until she felt his hands on each of her bare arms and felt the warmth of his breath on her neck. His voice was quiet and soothing.

'You're a very beautiful woman Elsa. I'm sure I'm not the first person to tell you that.'

She did not reply. He touched the zip at the back of her black dress and lowered it a couple of inches. She turned around to face him. He stared intently into her eyes and she stared right back. He took both of her wrists in each hand and guided her gently over to the bed indicating that she should sit down. She did so without a word. As he stood over her he must have noticed a tiny flicker of concern in her expression. He said.

'Are you OK with this, Elsa?'

Her heart was pounding so loudly she was sure he must hear it. From where she sat she could see a framed photograph on the bedside table, of the President's two young children sitting on a beach, the young boy trying to grab an ice cream cone from his older sister's hand.

'I am sorry Mr President, but I'm not.'

He clenched his teeth and tightened his lips in unmistakeable irritation.

'Chip told me you might not be a sure thing. I guess I should have known better than to make a pass at a pastor's daughter.' He said somewhat harshly.

An image of her father was the last thing Klara wanted to think about at a time like this. 'It's not that.' She said. 'It's just that it is not the right time for me, not now. Not on this particular day.' She spoke with what she hoped was the necessary emphasis.

He looked at her again as her intended meaning began to dawn on him. His features softened little. 'I understand what you mean, Elsa. That's a damn shame.'

There was an awkward silence then Klara spoke.' Perhaps we should go now, Mr. President. I am very grateful for the tour. You have been very kind. I was most honoured. I think it is wonderful that Lincoln's memory is so tastefully preserved in this house.'

'That's all Mrs Kennedy's doing. She supervised the restoration of the entire house. We are all very proud of her.'

He reached down, took both her hands again and lifted her gently from the bed. When he spoke again his voice had reverted to the lightness of their earlier conversation.

'It was my pleasure to show it to you. It's a long time since I had such an interested and appreciative guest. Now, let's get back.' He said quickly.

When they returned to the long room there was no sign of the other guests. The circular table where the drinks had been served was cleared away. The small black purse was sitting where Klara had left it. Kennedy said. 'I presume you came with Brewster. I can get you a ride home if you like.'

'Thank you. That would be very nice.'

He picked up a white telephone sitting on a credenza by the wall and without dialling waited for a response.

'Where do you live, Elsa?'

'Arlington, Mr. President.'

There was an audible click then Kennedy spoke peremptorily into the phone.

'Agent Banner, would you arrange for a pool car to take one of my guests, Mrs Kircherr, home to Arlington please. She'll give you the address. If there's a problem perhaps you, or one of the other agents could drive her. She's on her way down now. Thank you.'

When he hung up he took a small gold pen from his inside jacket pocket and wrote on a message pad beside the phone.

'This is my secretary's private line Elsa. Another Mrs Lincoln but definitely no relation to the great man we've just been discussing. She will call you sometime before I go to Europe. I'd like to talk to you again, particularly about the everyday realities of life in Berlin. If I forget to tell her, which I may do, maybe you would call her a week or so before I go and get her to remind me. I travel on June 22nd. Of course this is not a royal summons, it's only if you would like to.' He smiled almost shyly.

She took the slip of paper from him. 'Yes I would like to very much. How will Mrs Lincoln know where to find me?'

'Don't you worry about that, she'll find you. The White house switchboard can find anyone.'

'Thank you Mr President. I can find my own way to the elevator. Thank you for a most memorable evening.'

He laughed. 'Not as memorable as I thought it might be but I enjoyed our talk. Elsa, if you take my advice a smart girl like you should steer clear of the likes of Bill Waters and Chip Brewster, you're way out of their league. And believe me that's a compliment. The agent outside the door will escort you down. Good night.'

He turned and left the room without a handshake or a backward glance. Klara was left alone. She picked up her purse and stood there for a moment taking in her surroundings in silence, then walked to the far end of the room to the door she had entered earlier with Brewster. The same Secret Service agent who had been sitting outside when she arrived was there, waiting to take her down, her fur jacket draped over his arm.

As she sat in the back of the car taking her to Arlington, provided by the White House transport pool, she could think of nothing but her momentous meeting. She glanced at her watch. She had been exactly one hour in the White House but what an experience. She suspected she would never erase the image from her mind of the fascinating, outwardly perfect but undoubtedly complex and flawed man she had just met. There was of course no reason why she couldn't have given in to him, part of her certainly wanted to. The photograph of the children had affected her decision. But some other instinct told her it was not the right thing to do. If she had done so, would he have asked to see her again? It was now dark. A warm glow of satisfaction enveloped her as she looked through the car window at the white marble facades of the capital's most impressive buildings. Was she foolish enough to think that after one hour in his company, she was in love with the President of the United States? If so, she was realistic enough to know she was not the only one. In her hand, like some kind of holy relic she clutched the page he had written on, torn from the note pad. It contained a phone number and the words 'Mrs Evelyn Lincoln, departure Europe, 22 June', written in the President's own spiky handwriting. She was happy about two things. As agreed with Max Korten, she was now finished with the Quorum Club and Bobby Baker. She would never cross the threshold of the Carroll Arms Hotel again. The first part of her mission for Max had been accomplished. Unbelievably she had gone to the White House and she had met the President. She unfolded the little piece of paper and looked at the phone number again. Whatever happens now, she thought, I will go back there before he leaves for Europe. I will see him again.

CHAPTER 22

October 1963

I took the late flight from Washington to Boston on Friday 12th October because that was the day I lost my job. Until 4.30 that afternoon my working day had been as dull and predictable as any other. An hour later, I left the State Department carrying my personal possessions in a cardboard box, escorted to my car by Cy Metcalf, the Department's head of security, who had stood over me as I emptied my desk drawers and relieved me of my departmental ID card and my car park access. He made sure I didn't take as much as a paperclip that didn't belong to me. I sat in the Dodge for about five minutes before driving away, followed by Cy, who was to take possession of any official material I had at home. During the drive home I felt as if I had been punched in the gut by Sonny Liston. On the flight to Boston and on the bus from Logan to Hyannis, I mentally rehashed the bruising and humiliating encounter I had had that afternoon and tried to figure out what my future was going to be.

I got the call at exactly 4.00pm. It was from a Miss Bascombe who said in a clipped no nonsense voice that she was Elliot Markham's secretary and informing me that I was to come immediately to the Dean Acheson Room, the Secretary of State's exclusive conference room on the seventh floor. She ended the call before I had time even to acknowledge the message. The seventh floor, what the hell was this all about? A tight ball of anxiety had developed in the pit of my stomach as I came out of the elevator on seven, just three minutes later. A woman in her fifties with a perm of iron gray hair, wearing austere looking spectacles with heavy pink frames and two sharp points sticking out at each side, stood there waiting for me. It could only be Miss Bascombe but she did not introduce herself. She simply said. 'This way please' and escorted me the short distance to the conference room. She opened the door, ushered me into the high ceilinged wood panelled room without comment and retreated closing the door behind me. If I had any illusions that the summons might turn out to be something trivial, they were quickly dispelled. Sitting at the biggest conference table I had ever seen were four stern but familiar figures. Elliot Markham sat in the centre of the group, at one side of the table. Beside him was Lana Phillips the deputy head of personnel, a woman I knew slightly. She was in her mid fifties, had spent all of her career at State and was regarded by everyone as a genuinely sympathetic and helpful person, ideally suited to her role as a senior personnel officer. Next to her sat Vernon Templeton looking even more haggard and anxious than when I had last seen him. What the hell is going on with him? I thought to myself. To Vern's right, separated from the other three by five or six feet, was the surprising sight of Shirley Beaumont from the German desk, the woman who had given me the copies of the Elsa Kircherr papers a month ago, as part of her office clean up. Shirley would not be in this exalted company for any other reason but to confirm the handover of the papers. So that was it I thought, I've definitely been rumbled. Lana Phillips spoke first.

'Please be seated, Mr Flynn. Our apologies for the very short notice but there are certain urgent matters related to your work which have only recently come to our attention and we would like your help in clearing them up.'

I sat down opposite the four of them on the far side of the wide conference table. Elliot Markham stared at me with the narrow eyes of a hunter who had just sighted his prey. He was clearly itching to speak. Lana Phillips continued.

'I think you know everyone here, Mr Flynn. Miss Beaumont, as you know, works on the German desk with Greg March. We understand Miss Beaumont was in touch with you some weeks ago and passed you certain documents. I am just going to ask her to confirm in your presence what she has already told us. Please Shirley, go ahead and tell us in your own words what occurred.'

Shirley Beaumont looked distinctly uncomfortable, avoiding direct eye contact with me. She may not have known what was going on but she was a junior officer just like me and she knew that whatever she said was going to drop a fellow drone right in it. She had no choice however, so she simply said her piece.

'Well, on the evening of Monday 16th September I was doing one of our regular document clear outs. We accumulate a lot of paper in our area because Greg is a stickler for seeing everything that could possibly have anything of relevance to the German desk'.

'Let's leave Mr March out of it for the moment, Shirley. Just stick to your own role please.' Lana Phillips interrupted politely but firmly.

'Of course, I'm sorry. Well I came across some documents relating to two German women who were to be deported, which the language analysis unit had been asked to translate for the Justice Department. I am not sure how Greg became aware of the documents. I think he had heard about them from someone at the German Embassy, who he talks to quite often. Anyway, he wanted to see them and LAU2 had sent us copies in July. I simply called Jimmy, that is Mr Flynn and asked him if they should be disposed of with a lot of other stuff we were about to send for incineration as confidential waste, or if he wanted them back. He said he did want them and offered to come up to our floor and collect them. But as I was on my way home, I said I would drop them off on my way downstairs. So I did that. I handed them to Jimmy myself, eh, Mr Flynn. He thanked me and I went home. That is all that happened.'

'Thank you Shirley, you have been most helpful. Lana Phillips said. 'We won't detain you any further except to ask you if you are certain of the date when this happened.'

'Oh yes, it was certainly September 16th It's in my diary. That's the day Greg insisted on the clear out of all superfluous papers, as he calls them, being completed.'

'Thank you Shirley, you can go now but please remember what I said earlier. This is a highly confidential meeting. You are not to discuss the matters we have discussed here today with anyone inside or outside the Department. And that includes Greg March. In fact it would be appreciated if you would not mention to anyone that this meeting has taken place. Is that understood?'

'Yes of course, Mrs Phillips, perfectly.' Shirley stood up and walked out of the room, with just the tiniest flicker of a smile in my direction. It was enough for me to register her sympathy for my plight and her obvious relief that she was not the poor schmuck in the firing line. Lana Phillips then turned to me.

'Mr Flynn I have just a few brief questions for you in relation to what's just been said. Do you confirm the accuracy of Miss Beaumont's account regarding these documents?'

'Yes. Of course, that's exactly what happened.'

'What did you do with the papers Miss Beaumont gave you?'

'I took them home?'

'Where are they now?'

'They are still at my home.'

'Did you inform your superior Mr Templeton of their existence, or should I say their reappearance?'

'No.'

'Don't you think that was highly irresponsible of you?'

'Perhaps it was. But I was aware that the matter was officially closed insofar as our Department was concerned, so I did not think Mr Templeton had any further interest in it and my interest in these documents was personal rather than official, because I had been a witness to the murder of one of the women who were the subject of the papers in question.'

Lana Phillips' irritation was sudden and genuine. 'This is the State Department Mr Flynn. It is not a playground where you may indulge your private interests, whatever they might be. To take official documents home, without a specific work related reason and to retain them is an unacceptable breach of regulations. To conceal those documents from your superior is about as unprofessional an act as I can imagine. Mr Templeton will have some questions for you himself, in a few moments and so will Mr Markham. I hope you will answer them honestly and fully. Be in no doubt Mr Flynn that the consequences of your actions, insofar as we already know them, are of the utmost seriousness for you and for your career.' She turned to Vern. 'Mr Templeton, if you will.'

I knew then, if I didn't know it already, that my position could hardly be worse. Lana Phillips didn't use that kind of language lightly. I also knew that there were no mitigating factors. Everything I had done, I had done with full knowledge of the consequences. In all my life I had never felt as humiliated as I was at that moment. I waited for Vern to take his shots. He looked mad and I couldn't say I blamed him. I had deceived him, deliberately kept him in the dark. As I faced him, I was ashamed of my disloyalty to someone who had always treated me courteously, even kindly.

'You will recall, Mr Flynn,' he said pointedly not using my first name. 'That I asked you when we first heard of the FBI investigation on September fourth, the day after Labour Day, whether there were any further papers relating to this deportee Miss Kircherr. You assured me there were not. Would you not agree therefore, that when the copies of the documents relating to Rometch and Kircherr subsequently came to light, that I, as your superior, should have been informed?'

'Yes of course.'

'Why then did you not inform me of their reappearance?'

'I didn't want to bother you with something which was no longer of interest to the State Department. You had said yourself it was now exclusively an FBI matter and I knew they already had the originals of all relevant documents.'

My response was lame and everyone in the room, including me knew it. Vern shot me a withering look. 'How very considerate of you not to bother me. Frankly, your loyalty to me personally, as well as to the Department leaves a lot to be desired. Do you recall me asking on the morning of October 2nd whether you had heard anything further in the matter of the FBI investigation and you said that you had heard nothing?'

'Yes. I'm sorry about that. I was less than honest.'

'You mean you told me an outright lie. There were a number of answers you could have given me to that question but you chose to ignore them all. For example, you could have said that you had met with Herbert Kluge, Second Secretary at the West German Embassy, over an expensive lunch in Harvey's, to discuss his memoranda on the two deportees. You could have said that you had made contact with the late Sergeant Robert Lavelle, husband of one of the deported women. And you could have mentioned that you received from a friend of Lavelle's a parcel containing Miss Elsa Kircherr's personal effects, which had been forwarded to her husband by the FBI. In short, Mr Flynn, you could have told me that you were, in effect, conducting a full scale, time consuming, private investigation into the death of Elsa Kircherr, while you were an employee of the State Department. But you did not admit to any of these activities did you? You lied to me and continued acting entirely inappropriately for a government official. You worked actively against the interests of your own employer by concealing information and putting this Department at risk of serious political embarrassment with respect to other government agencies.'

I was shocked by how much he knew and I could think of no defence which did not sound hollow or just plain dumb. Everything Vern said was true. His anger, if anything, had increased rather than subsided as he spoke. Before he finished he took one last personal shot.

'I need hardly say I am deeply disappointed with you. I was foolish enough to think that you and I had a good working relationship. I can see now how wrong I was. I thought we had a professional understanding, when all the while you were deceiving me, playing amateur detective, having cosy chats in Arlington with Bobby Lavelle about a matter which I specifically and categorically instructed you to ignore and to leave to those whose job it was to investigate.'

Vern stopped abruptly. I thought he might break down. Even in the deep trouble I was in, I felt very sorry for him. I could tell he was genuinely saddened by my stupid behaviour. He put down the pen he had been holding and rubbed both of his eyes with the palms of his hands. He suddenly looked exhausted.

'I have nothing more to say, Mrs Phillips.' He said wearily to Lana, who nodded in acknowledgment. She turned to Markham.

'In that case, Elliot, perhaps you would address the issues which are of particular interest to you.'

Markham had been straining at the leash ever since I walked into the room but now that his turn had come, he feigned a Cary Grant like demeanour. 'Not just of interest to me, Mrs Phillips, but also of keen interest and concern to Secretary Rusk himself.' He said with a condescending smile. Then he began.

'You will recall Mr Flynn that we spoke prior to your meeting with the Attorney General on the evening of October first.'

'Yes I do.'

'On that occasion I specifically instructed you to confine your briefing with the Attorney General to the subject at hand, namely the document which had been translated for him. Is that not so?'

'Yes it is.'

'Would it surprise you to know that the Attorney General subsequently, in fact on the following day, asked FBI Director Hoover, whether the Bureau was investigating an incident on a Cape Cod beach which occurred Labour Day weekend, because he had been told about it by someone working in the State Department?'

'I wasn't aware of that no.'

'Did you mention the incident involving this woman who was deported to the Attorney General?'

'Yes, it did come up briefly in conversation. No names were mentioned, simply that a homicide had taken place.'

'Briefly in conversation, I see.' Markham made a big show of writing a further note on his yellow pad.

'And were you aware that on the same day you met with the Attorney General in Justice, two senior and highly regarded FBI agents reported to Director Hoover that you Mr Flynn, had made a verbal accusations against them as you left the building and accused them of a derogation of their duty with regard to the Labour Day incident?'

'No of course I was not aware of that. And I did not initiate any accusations against them, I merely responded to a provocation of theirs. By the way, Mr Markham, what happened on that beach was more than a mere incident, it was cold blooded murder in a public place.'

'Whatever it was Mr Flynn, it has quite clearly nothing to do with you. You had no business mentioning it to the FBI or responding to their so called provocations. You were sent to the Justice Department to provide a routine briefing, not to act like some kind of juvenile delinquent and enter into arguments with its officers. Did you in fact refer to a lack of progress in their investigation when you had this chat with them?'

'Yes, I believe I did.'

Markham paused again to note this information before proceeding. 'I understand that you are acquainted with Attorney General Kennedy and that you and he were once neighbours of sorts. You omitted to mention this fact when Mr Templeton and I briefed you prior to the meeting.'

'I am not by any stretch of the imagination an acquaintance of Mr Kennedy's. I did summer work as a kid in a local yacht club where he and his family were members, that's all. I can't recall ever having a conversation with him before the meeting in question.'

'And did he allude to your past association?'

'It was discussed very briefly.'

'I see, yet another brief conversation. I thought you Irish fellows had a reputation as prolific talkers? That must be a myth.'

I noticed Lana Phillips bristling at this remark but neither she nor I said anything. Markham was not quite finished.

'I would like you to be very careful Mr Flynn with your next answer. Did you give your friend, the Attorney General, any indication that you would provide further help or advice to him in the future, regarding the Bolshakov document or any other departmental matter? Did you give him any undertaking that you would assist him in any way, without the knowledge or participation of the State Department?'

I took a deep breath before answering. I couldn't tell if Markham knew something or if he was just fishing. I had to hope and trust that Kennedy would not have mentioned to Secretary Rusk or anyone else that I agreed to translate his reply to Bolshakov. My instinct told me he wouldn't have spoken to anyone else about what he intended to write to Bolshakov but how could I be certain? I didn't know anything about how people at that level operated, I was way out of my depth and I knew it but I jumped in anyway.

'No, I did not give him any such undertaking.'

I was lying and it was high risk. If Markham did know that I had agreed to do a further translation for Kennedy without the Department's knowledge, I might as well write out my resignation then and there.

'For your sake Mr Flynn, I sincerely hope that is an honest answer.' Markham said. 'That is all I have for now, Mrs Phillips. I think I have enough'. He said, closing his yellow pad and resting the palms of his hands on the table.

It was Lana Phillips's turn once again. She looked like a judge about to pass sentence, which I guess, in this scenario, is what she was. She cleared her throat and spoke with the serious tone and facial expression of someone who was not the bearer of good news.

'In view of the lamentable litany of transgressions and examples of professional misconduct we have heard from you today, Mr Flynn, the State Department has no option but to carry out a full and detailed review of your recent activities, with a view to ascertaining whether there is a case for your dismissal. I have to say, on the basis of what I have heard so far, your situation does not look particularly good. You will of course be permitted representation when this matter is considered again and I would strongly advise you to avail of it. In the meantime we have no alternative but suspend you from duty, without pay and with immediate effect. You will receive written confirmation of this decision in a few days. I would estimate it will be another eight to ten weeks before we all meet again to reconsider this matter. You will have time in the interim to prepare a defence of your position and of course to consider the other options which are open to you. In the event of a voluntary resignation on your part, we will not pursue this further. The matter will be considered to be at an end as far as the State Department is concerned and crucially there will be no obvious stain on your character.'

So that was it, the Roman Centurion option. Fall on your sword, resign or face the humiliation of being fired. There was no doubt as to what they wanted me to do. Lana continued.

'When we have finished here, Mr Metcalf, our head of internal security, will be waiting outside and will accompany you to your office where you may collect your personal possessions. He will then travel with you to your home in Garret Park, to collect any and all of the material you have in your possession relating to our discussion this evening, including the personal effects of the unfortunate girl who was killed. They will be returned to the FBI. You would be well advised to give Cy everything you have. That is all for now. I hope you have clearly understood everything I have said. The Department will be in touch with you about the formal disciplinary hearing, but not for some weeks. You may go unless you have anything to add to what you have already said.'

I pushed back my chair and stood up but could think of nothing to say. My legs felt like jelly and blood was coursing loudly around my brain. I hoped I could make it to the door with my dignity still intact. Vern too looked miserable, enveloped in self pity. You'd think he was the one being canned. Markham had trouble keeping a triumphant look off his tanned, complacent mug. Only Lana Phillips looked human, now that the harsh words had been said. Her parting remarks were spoken with genuine sympathy. 'I am very sorry about all of this, Jimmy, I wish you the very best of luck.' She said.

'Thank you Mrs Phillips.' I said to her, ignoring the other two. I took the long walk to the conference room door. Cy Metcalf was indeed outside waiting for me. Obviously he had been left in no doubt as to how this meeting was going to end.

I was still replaying the entire disastrous events of the day in my mind, as the bus from Logan pulled into the Almeida bus station just behind Main Street in Hyannis. It was ten forty five at night and dark outside. It's a short cab ride from there to my folk's house on Walton Ave. I was carrying my light blue holdall containing the few things I usually needed for a weekend stay at my mother's, so I decided to walk. New England was enjoying an exceptional Indian summer and the night was unseasonably warm for October. Apart from my other problems, I still had to figure out how to break the bad news to my mother. Walking along the almost empty streets, I noticed the flashing neon light of the Wianno Motel on North Street. The place Elsa Kircherr had stayed the night before she was killed. Although it wasn't exactly on my route I decided, for no particular reason to pay the place another visit, if only to delay going home. The motel was deathly quiet. There was a light on in the reception area but only two cars in the parking lot and no lights on in the rooms. A teenage girl in pigtails and horn rimmed glasses was reading a movie magazine behind the reception desk. She didn't look up as I walked in.

'Excuse me Miss. Would you have any objection to me taking a look at cabin number seven?'

The girl looked up, glanced at my overnight bag and gave me an unexpectedly friendly smile. 'Are you just looking or do you want to book a room?'

'I know it's a little weird but I just want to take a look, if it's vacant. By the look of things they're all vacant tonight.'

'Well that's where you're wrong Jimmy Flynn.' She said, laughing now. 'As a matter of fact we have two bookings tonight and one of them is number seven. So a look at it is definitely out of the question. And you're right it is weird.'

'You know me?'

'Sure I do and you know me. Thanks very much for remembering. I've known you practically all my life. I'm Joanie Marchand. You were in class with my brother Frank.'

'Frank Marchand? Of course, little Joanie, I think you were in elementary school last time I saw you.'

'Well I graduated high school last June, so there. This is just temporary and it's easy work off season.' She said indicating the motel's office. So what is it about cabin seven, is there buried treasure in there or something? The person in it right now arrived yesterday and wouldn't accept any other room but that one.

'Really who is it?'

'Mind your beeswax, that's confidential. We don't give out information about our guests.'

'That's OK I understand. It doesn't matter. I'm on my way home anyway. Nice to see you Joanie, say hi to Frank for me.'

'If I ever see him I will. He's in the service, Navy. He's stationed in

Naples.

'Florida?'

'No silly, the real one, in Italy.'

'Good for Frank.' I said. 'I wish I was in Italy just now. Good night Joanie.'

I walked out into the darkened car park. There was now a light on in the cabin nearest to Joanie's office, obviously cabin number one. All the others were in darkness. I went across to number seven and listened at the door feeling like some kind of peeping Tom. There wasn't a sound from within and the lights were out. I guessed whoever rented it was out. I wasn't really sure what I was doing or what I was looking for. I turned the handle but as expected the door was locked. Suddenly there was a panic stricken voice from inside the room.

'Who is that? What do you want? I am calling the police.'

'Sorry.' I said through the door. 'I've got the wrong room, no need to call the police. I didn't mean to wake you.'

The door was suddenly thrown open and an anxious looking woman wearing a tightly belted bathrobe and a towel wrapped around her head, stood in the half light. He face was covered with some kind of cosmetic mud mask. She looked me up and down before she spoke. The holdall in my hand provided some plausibility to my cover as an idiotic bumbling tourist.

'Yes, can I help you?' She snapped.

'No thank you. My apologies, I thought the room was empty.' I began to step back and walk away.

'Isn't the number of your room on your key?' She spoke with an easily recognisable German accent. Another German in Elsa Kircherr's room?

'Actually I'm not staying here. I just had a particular interest in this room. It's a long story and it's late. Sorry to wake you'

'Why this room, number seven?' She said, genuinely curious now.

'A woman who occupied this room was killed some time ago. I happened to be there when she was killed. I was just curious about the room.' I said, uncomfortably aware that I was beginning to sound like Norman Bates.

'What do you mean? Was she killed here in this hotel, this room?'

'No, she was killed a couple of miles from here.'

'What was the woman's name?' She said with a tremble in her voice.

'Her name was Elsa Kircherr, she was German. You are also German I think.' I said in German.

The woman looked as if she was about to cry but made a gallant effort not to. When she spoke again it was in a quiet whisper.

'That was not her name. Her name was Klara Hartmann.'

'Klara Hartmann, how do you know?'

'Because she is my sister.'

She turned her head away from me and gripped the flimsy door frame as if she was about to faint. Her shoulders shook, the face mask started to run, as tears came, followed by loud, inconsolable sobs.

CHAPTER 23

October 1963

I arranged to meet Anni Hartmann for breakfast at ten o'clock the following morning in a small diner on Main Street called the 'Egg and I'. I wasn't sure how solid the arrangement was because the woman had been crying when I suggested it and I was trying, in an ineffectual way to comfort her, it didn't help that Joanie Marchand had emerged from her little office, full of curiosity, to ask me why I was bothering the guests. We sorted it all out pretty quickly and I simply asked the tearful woman if she would meet me in the morning. I told her Joanie would explain where the place was. Joanie herself seemed greatly entertained by this drama. Obviously there wasn't much excitement on the reception desk of the Wianno Motel. My year in Heidelberg University taught me that Germans are never late for appointments, so I arrived at the diner ten minutes early and ordered coffee while I waited. When I reached home the previous night, my mother had left me a note to say she was spending the night in my sister's house in Falmouth, no doubt to help prepare for the birthday party of young prince Kevin. Thankfully, that meant no lengthy discussion as to how things were going in the State Department. That confrontation could wait for another time.

My Dad's fire engine red Chevy Bel Air, once his pride and joy, was still at the house, so I could use that for the weekend. At one minute to ten precisely, a woman with thick shoulder length auburn hair, in her mid to late twenties, came through the door. She wore a three quarter length brown leather coat over a light blue roll necked top, navy slacks and gleaming white tennis shoes. She had a capacious soft suede bag with a long strap hanging from her shoulder. She looked so glamorous and so out of place among the landscape gardeners, house painters and a sprinkling of fall tourists in the small diner that I wasn't certain if it was the same woman I had spoken to last night. But she recognised me straight away, held up her palm by way of a greeting and came straight over to my table. I stood up and shook hands in the formal European way and offered her a seat.

'My name is Jimmy by the way. Jimmy Flynn. I'm not sure if you remember that from last night.'

'Yes of course. And I am Anni Hartmann. I am sorry for crying so much. I have been having a terrible time since my sister died but I have tried to hold myself together. For some reason it all came out like one giant waterfall or something like that.'

'We can talk in German if it would be easier for you.' I said in German.

She smiled. 'You are the first German speaker I have met in America and I can tell you are good. But if you don't mind I would prefer to speak in English. I work in a department store in Berlin. We often have English speaking customers, so the practice is good for me.'

'OK sure. Before we talk, maybe we should order breakfast.'

'Of course, I am quite hungry.' She glanced around the diner. 'The Egg and I' what a strange name.' She said, as she removed her leather coat and put it over the back of her chair.

'Is it some kind of joke?' She asked.

'Something like that. It's the title of an old movie. It's supposed to be clever I guess.'

Ordering breakfast took a little time with explanations as to what hash browns were and the various ways of making eggs. When that was done Anni Hartmann became serious again, looked me in the eye and said without aggression or casualness but in typically blunt German fashion.

'So, now Mr Flynn, could you please tell me who you are and why did you first want to break into my room and now want to meet with me this morning?'

I smiled at the directness of the approach. 'It's quite a long story and I'm sorry to say it begins with your sister's death. If you want, I will tell you about that. You of all people are entitled to know what happened to her. But if we are to talk, I would like you to call me Jimmy. Is that alright with you?'

'Yes of course.' She said. 'And you may call me Anni.' In Europe we have not quite learnt this casual American way but it's changing.'

'OK Anni. I will begin. Afterwards, if you wish, I will bring you to the place where your sister died. It's not that far away.'

Her eyes filled up but thankfully there was no repetition of the night before. She didn't risk speaking, merely nodded her assent. I began my story. I told her about Robert Lavelle, her sister's husband. She made no comment but listened carefully. When I mentioned that he too was dead, tears came to her eyes again, she seemed genuinely shocked. Our breakfasts were brought and consumed. I spoke and she listened, intervening only occasionally. When I had finished and we had both had more coffee than was good for us, she said she would like to go to Craigville beach and see where Klara had died. I paid the check and we walked out on to Main Street. The day was bright and warm, more like late May than October. I had to get used to the fact that the person I had thought of as Elsa Kircherr, since this murder happened, was someone called Klara Hartmann. Elsa Kircherr didn't exist.

'Before we go there I would like you to come back to my motel room.' She said.

I was not usually such an instant hit with attractive women. But of course it wasn't a come on. She seemed to read my mind and said quickly that she had something she wanted to show me. We drove the short distance to the motel. On the way I mentioned my nephew's birthday party and that I had go to my sister's house in Falmouth later, about thirty minutes from Hyannis. When we got to the motel, Joanie Marchand's shift had obviously finished and a more responsible looking middle aged man was now at the desk. Anni collected her key and we went to cabin number seven. The room was just as I remembered it from my last visit with Tom Noonan, except for Anni's open and perfectly packed suitcase, sitting on the neatly made bed. The bathroom door was open and I could see the usual selection of cosmetics and toiletries arranged on the single glass shelf and around the wash basin. She went to the bedside locker and took a copy of the Gideon Bible from the drawer.

'Does every American hotel room have these Bibles?' She asked.

'Yes, I think so. An organisation called the Gideon Society places them everywhere they can.'

'My father would very much approve, he is a pastor. It is a nice tradition. It would never be permitted in the GDR.' She pushed her suitcase to the centre of the bed and made room to sit.

'Please sit next to me I want to show you something.' I did as I was told. A pleasant odour of expensive perfume hovered between us as she opened the Bible.

'Last night, before you came, I took it out and looked through it. Which I suppose is what they are there for. Inside there was a piece of paper between two pages.' She said, opening the Bible at the New Testament, the section containing the epistles of St Paul.

'You can see that this passage is underlined with a black pencil. It is in fact a woman's eyebrow pencil.' She passed the book to me and I read the underlined sentence. *"Do not be overcome by evil but overcome evil with good".*

'It is part of St Paul's letter to the Romans. It is a favourite quotation of my father's. He often quoted it to me and to Klara when we were growing up. I can remember it so well, Romans, chapter 12, verse 21, he would say. It was a piece of advice he would give us whenever we complained about the government or the state of the world. I think Klara must have looked at this page and underlined it. This is the piece of paper that marked the page.'

She handed me a slip of white paper she had removed from the book. It was a Plymouth and Brockton line bus ticket from Logan airport to Hyannis. Exactly like the one I still had in my pocket from the day before. It was dated 29th August, just two days before her sister's murder. On the back of the ticket, printed with the same smudgy eyebrow pencil that had underlined the scripture passage, were the letters SIO with a large exclamation mark beside them. I showed Anni what her sister had written.

'Yes.' She said. 'I saw that but I have no idea what it means.'

'Was she religious, your sister?'

'Not at all, she constantly rebelled against our father's religious teaching, but she was close to him all the same. She was his favourite, not me. She told me that her decision to work for GDR state security and coming here to America, she did it for him. And for a while it worked, he had been arrested for speaking out in his church against the evils of materialism and Communism. After Klara agreed to work for the HVA, that's the Foreign Intelligence Directorate of state security, my father's position improved and he was eventually released.'

'So Herbert Kluge was right. Your sister really was a Communist spy.'

'Yes perhaps, but for a good reason, if that is possible. Who is Herbert Kluge?'

'Oh, no one, I'll tell you later. You said that Klara helping your father had worked for a while.'

Yes. When she was deported at the end of July, the HVA apparently had no further use for her. My father was arrested again in August and is now in Bautzen. It's a prison in Saxony, not too far from my parent's home. It's a terrible, place. Everyone in the GDR has heard of it and has a fear of it. They call it 'the big yellow'. If he stays there for any length of time he will almost certainly die there. My mother is now alone again.' She sighed loudly, closing the Gideon Bible and replacing it in the drawer.

'My father's philosophy of faith and hope is very hard to accept'. She said.

I was about to throw the bus ticket in the waste paper bin but thought it might seem offhand as Anni obviously thought it had some significance. I stuck it in my back pocket.

'Come' she said, speaking German without thinking. 'Let me get this over with, let's go to this awful beach.'

The drive from Hyannis to the village of Centerville and Craigville beach, took only ten minutes. The beach car park was almost empty. An old lime green Ford Edsel with Rhode Island plates, was the only other car there, pulling in just after we did. I parked the Chevy and we walked to the beach. Despite the sunny morning, there were only a handful of people strolling across the wide expanse of sand. The tide was at its lowest ebb, so it was possible to walk to the approximate spot where Klara Hartmann, as I now had to think of her, had been shot. I explained to Anni, once again, what Tom Noonan and I had seen and heard that day. She was silent as I spoke, staring at the sand as if it would somehow conjure up her sister.

'I'll leave you here if you like.' I said. Maybe you need time alone.'

She looked up and gave me a wan smile. 'Thank you but it's OK. I have thought about nothing else since I heard about all this. To die beside a beautiful ocean, where everyone is happy and gay, it is so sad. Thank you for bringing me here but maybe we should go, there is really nothing to see.'

We started to walk back towards the car. 'How did you come to know about what happened here?' I asked.

'A man called Max Korten visited me in Berlin. I had heard about him from Klara. He told me he was connected to GDR state security. He seemed to be able to cross the border from the East at will. He was a very cool customer, as you say in English. Confident, very well dressed. He made it clear that he knew Klara very well, if you know what I mean. He told me she had been shot by a criminal, probably intending to rob her. He said it happened in Boston. He said this kind of thing was common in the United States, a violent capitalist society. He was unsympathetic and clearly disapproved of me because I was a so called border crosser, someone who had worked in the West while living in the East before the wall was built. I had compounded my crime by staying on in the West once the wall was constructed, rather than returning to live in our glorious socialist homeland.'

We reached the car and sat in. 'If you thought she was killed in Boston what made you come here to the Cape and stay in the same motel as Klara? How did you know she was ever here?'

'It's very simple. She sent me a post card with a picture of the motel on it. You can buy them at the reception desk.'

'Have you got the postcard with you?'

'Of course not, it's still in Berlin.'

'Can you remember what she wrote?'

'Yes, very well, I read it over many times I didn't quite understand it. It said.' *"Liebchen, I have a gift for your friend from Schoneberg. I hope it will be of help to Papa. Back in Garmisch on Tuesday. Love K".* 'It was a bit confusing.' she added.

'Have you a friend in Schoneberg?'

'Yes. Uschi, one of my colleagues on the cosmetic counter where I work, lives there. But I can't remember ever mentioning her to Klara.'

'Where were you on the 29th of June this year?'

'I can't remember, at work I suppose. Why do you ask?'

'Because that was the day President Kennedy spoke in Berlin. It was the day of the famous *"Ich Bin Ein Berliner"* speech. Don't you remember that?'

'Yes, of course, I remember it very well. I was actually there and I saw him. I heard him speak those words. It was a fantastic day. We had never seen anything like it in Berlin'. She looked at me again and it began to dawn on her. 'Of course he made the speech at the Schoneberg Town Hall. I told Klara all about it. She was pleased that I was so enthusiastic about Kennedy's visit.'

'Do you know anything then about Hyannis or Cape Cod?'

'Nothing at all, I know only what you have already told me this morning. To be honest, I never heard of this place until I received that postcard.'

'Well then you didn't know until this morning that the President lives here, in Hyannis Port, just a few minutes from here?'

'Until you told me, I never knew this?'

'How do you mean you told Klara about the speech? I thought you said that you didn't see her since she was deported.'

'We spoke on the phone. She called me from Bavaria, early in August, to tell me she was back from America. Just one phone call and she was trying to be careful what she said because the phone lines from West Germany to Berlin go through East Germany. We assume they are listening. She seemed stressed and excited at the same time. She just said she was well, but she was concerned about Mama and Papa. She said she would explain everything later. I remember now that I told her about Kennedy in Berlin and his speech, how fantastic it all was. She was very interested in this but did not want to say much over the phone. That call and then the postcard were the last times I heard from her.'

We sat in silence for a moment. 'Listen Anni, I have to get to Falmouth, my sister will kill me if I'm late for the kid's party. You're welcome to come with me. You can come to the party or you can look around the town, whatever you prefer. Falmouth is a pretty place. Either that or I can leave you back to your motel.'

She took a guide book from her bag. 'I have already decided to take a tour to a place called the Plymouth Plantation. Yesterday, before you came along, I simply had no idea what to do. So I bought a ticket. A tour bus leaves from the bus station at 1.00 pm it does not get back here until 8.00 this evening.

'OK, if you're sure. I'll take you there right now. How would you like to have dinner tonight? I can meet you when you get back.'

She looked at me with wide brown eyes that would melt an iceberg. The temptation to blow off Kevin's party and to spend the day in Plymouth with this beautiful stranger was almost overpowering.

'Why are you doing this Jimmy?' She asked. 'You don't know me and you never even spoke to my sister. But you have put your job and your future at risk to find out how she died. It seems to me that we will never know what happened. Believe me I want to find the truth. That is why I came. But she is my sister. You may lose everything and for what? To find out what happened to a complete stranger, a lost German girl. And nothing we do will bring her back.'

I looked into her eyes, now tearful as she considered the truth of what she had just said.

'What are you saying? That you want me to mind my own business, to leave you alone?'

She stretched out her hand and put it on top of mine as it rested on the steering wheel. 'No, I am not saying that. I am saying that I have no right to ask you to help me or to accept your help. I have nothing to reward you with. I am spending all of the little money I have on this trip. I must be back at work in KaDeWe before the Christmas shopping period or I too will lose my job. So you can see, I am just as lost as Klara was. I have no friends in this country, and I don't know where to begin to find out what happened to her. But I can't ask you to destroy your life for me and my family.'

She took her hand away suddenly embarrassed at the gesture and gave me an apologetic half smile. I started the engine and reversed the car out of the parking bay and headed for the Almeida bus station back in Hyannis. I noticed that the passenger window of the green Edsel was open. There was a thick fog of cigarette smoke wafting out of it. We drove in silence for the ten minutes it took to get there. I parked the car across the street from the station. A bright yellow 'Plymouth Pilgrim Tours' bus was waiting. This late in the season there was only a small number of tourists waiting to board.

'Anni I have been doing a pretty good job of ruining my life all by myself up to now. I can't really tell you why I am doing this because I don't know myself. It has something to do with the trauma of seeing someone shot in cold blood and no one being really interested in finding out why it happened or who did it. In fact everyone, except you and me, seem very keen not to find out. You mentioned your father's advice to you and Klara. My father's favourite saying growing up wasn't from scripture but it was simple, "finish what you start." Well I've started. It's been a train wreck so far but I'm damn well going to finish it. If you and I worked together, maybe things would improve and maybe we might actually get just a little closer to the truth.' I stopped for breath but she said nothing. 'So, what do you think Fraülein Hartmann?' I asked.

'She looked straight ahead and when she spoke there was a slight catch in her voice. 'I am glad to have met you, Jimmy, but you seem to me to be a bit of dreamer, a romantic, maybe not so practical. And I am not much better. I am just a store assistant after all. Would we really achieve anything?'

'I was just a little stung by the dreamer remark but I let it go. 'Well there's only one way to find out.' I said. 'Why not give it a try.'

From across the street we could hear the tour bus driver start the engine.

'You better go.' I said. 'You'll like the tour. It tells you something about the beginnings of this great country of ours.'

She got out of the car but did not say anything. There was no passing traffic. I watched her cross the street, taking long athletic strides, her shoulder bag rocking back and forth, her chestnut hair blowing in the breeze as she walked. She was a beauty, no question, in that not quite perfect way that is far more appealing than the unblemished fashion model type. She took her place in line. If she looks back, I thought, I may be in business. If she doesn't then she thinks I'm just a schmuck with nothing better to do than drive a lonely tourist around for the day. The small line of passengers presented their tickets to the tour guide as they went aboard. Just before it was her turn to get into the bus she tossed her head around in my direction, gave me a shy smile and one of those finger waves that only women do. I couldn't help smiling myself. Cute, I thought, cute but confident. She obviously knew I was still there and that I was looking at her. A couple of minutes later the yellow bus drove away. Something about watching the tickets being handed up got me thinking. I took the two bus tickets from my back pocket, the one Anni had found in the Bible and my own one from the day before. They were identical apart from the different dates. And of course the letters SIO, written in eyebrow pencil on the back of Klara's ticket. It was the heavily scored exclamation mark after the letters that seemed to say the letters were important.

I started the car and headed for Route 28. As I drove onto Main Street I saw that the car behind me was the same green Edsel with Rhode Island plates that had been parked at Craigville beach. I wondered whether I was being followed but when I got to Route 28, the Ford turned off northwards and for a couple of minutes the road was empty of all traffic, I headed towards Falmouth and the fifth birthday party of the young prince.

CHAPTER 24

October 1963

By evening I was back in precisely the same spot across from the bus depot where I had parked that morning. As luck would have it the Plymouth Pilgrim Tours bus broke down on the far side of the Sagamore Bridge and did not arrive back in Hyannis until almost ten o'clock. By the time Anni and all the other irritated passengers got off the bus, she said she was too tired to eat after a long day. I was tired myself. Kid's parties can take it out of you. We decided to call it a night. I dropped her back at her motel. On the way she told me a little about her trip. I drove into the motel car park, said goodnight and watched her as she put the key in the door of cabin seven. Before she went inside, something I had been thinking about as I waited for the bus to arrive suddenly occurred to me and I honked the car horn just a little too loudly, to get her attention. She closed the cabin door and walked back to the car.

'Sit back in a second Anni.' I said. She got in. I took the bus ticket that had been in the Gideon Bible, from my pants pocket and showed it to her

'While I was waiting for you this evening I had time to think about things, including that postcard Klara sent you. If Klara had a gift for someone, where would she keep it before handing it over?'

'In her room perhaps. Maybe the police have it now?'

'I don't think so. On the day after the murder I was told that all they found was a Canadian bus ticket'

'Well, she might keep it in the motel safe or maybe a bank, or even in her pocket. It depends what it was, how big it was.'

'You're right, although I didn't think of the motel safe. We can ask

Joanie. These letters Klara wrote on the bus ticket SIO. I think they're not letters but one letter and the number ten. I think it may stand for Locker number ten. 'S' for *Schliessfach,* isn't that the word for a locker?'

'Yes.'

Well, there is a small bank of lockers over at the bus station. I noticed them while I was waiting they don't look very secure but maybe that's where she left whatever she had for *"your friend from Schoneberg"*

Anni thought for a moment. 'Wouldn't it be more likely that she would leave something in a locker in Boston or even Canada, wherever she got the bus.'

'You might remember that the Plymouth and Brockton airport bus sell the tickets after the passengers have boarded. I think it's more likely she would note the locker number as soon as she put whatever she had in the locker.'

'Yes but she may have written the number just after she bought her ticket at Logan airport and that is where the locker is. But why don't we go back to the bus station here in Hyannis and see if there is a locker number ten?'

'I intend to but even if I'm right, there is another problem. The locker number is not enough. There should also be a key. If there was a key and the Feds found it among Klara's possessions they probably already have whatever was inside.'

'The Feds?'

'The FBI.' I said. I looked at her face and noticed for the first time, the dark patches under her eyes and her obvious state of emotional exhaustion. 'I'm sorry Anni I can see you're tired. How about we leave all this till the morning? I'll pick you up at say nine thirty and we can over there together and take a look at locker number ten if there is one.'

She nodded her agreement and got out of the car once again.

I arrived at the Wianno Motel at nine thirty precisely the following morning. Anni Hartmann, was waiting outside the door of cabin seven, dressed almost exactly as she had been the day before, except for a navy sweater over a white blouse, instead of the roll necked top. I parked and suggested we walk to the bus station. It was quiet when we got there. Sunday morning. No passengers and no buses waiting outside, nothing due in until ten. A guy I didn't recognise, who looked to be in his sixties, his black rimmed glasses held together with a band aid, wearing a Plymouth and Brockton nylon jacket, sat behind the only ticket counter.

'Hi.' I said. I indicated Anni standing beside me. 'My friend here is over from Europe. Just before Labour Day she left something in a luggage locker here but lost the key. Is there any way she could get access to the locker without the key?'

'Maybe, what's in the locker?'

'Does it matter?' I asked, not expecting that question.

'Sure does. There could be diamonds or gold bullion in there that doesn't belong to you or to this young lady here. I can't let you just walk in here and take it away. But if you know what's in it before I open it and you turn out to be right, that's a different story.'

I was beginning to regret not having rehearsed what I was going to say before I walked in. 'Well it's not gold bullion. 'It's just a, eh, package.' I said taking a wild, unspecific guess.

'A package huh. Which locker are you talking about?'

'Number ten.'

The man got up from his seat and walked over to a board on the wall behind him, keys of various shapes and sizes hung from a row of hooks. 'Well, I can tell you for sure, this young lady didn't lose her key.'

'Oh really?'

'No she didn't, because the key to number ten is still here.'

He returned to his chair holding a key with a cheap orange plastic key ring dangling from it. This time he ignored me and addressed Anni.

'You come all the way from Europe just for this?' He asked, holding up the key.

'No' she said giving him a polite smile. 'I have been travelling here in America and just got back here a few days ago. I had completely forgotten about the locker until I arrived back in Hyannis. Thank you so much for taking care of the key.'

Security at the bus station was obviously not as tight as it seemed at first. As sometimes happens, a friendly smile from a pretty woman did the trick. The man handed Anni the key. 'You are more than welcome my dear. Some people don't like to risk losing their keys, so they ask us to hold on to them until they need to get into the locker. Most people don't leave it as long as you did though. That must be what you did. I guess you've forgotten.'

Anni favoured him with another charming smile as she examined the key. 'Now that you say it that is exactly what happened. I really don't know what is happening to my memory these days. I think I must stop travelling and settle down.'

The man smiled back at her. 'Wait till you get to my age and you'll know all about bad memory. Better check the locker, young lady. See if your package is still there.'

We walked over to a bank of ancient stainless steel lockers in the corner. There were just two rows of five, exactly ten of them. Anni inserted the key, opened number ten and took a look. It was a package. It consisted of a single white A4 envelope, already neatly opened by a letter opener or something like it. It was bulging with documentation of some kind. She picked it up and read the typed address: Mrs Elsa Lavelle, 1200, Cherry Tree Lane, Apartment 3A, Arlington Virginia. The envelope had the words Carlyle Hotel Fifth Avenue, NY, NY. embossed on the upper left hand side. The right hand side had no less than six stamps. Whoever mailed it was taking no chances. It was the kind of envelope that upmarket hotels provide for their guests. The old man was looking over at us from his perch behind the counter with considerable interest. Anni turned to him, holding up the envelope and put his mind at ease.

'Everything is here just as I left it,' she said. 'Thank you for taking such good care of it.'

'All part of the service ma'am,' he said. 'You can leave the key in lock for the next person.'

We left the bus station feeling like two school kids who had just put one over on the teacher. We walked back to the motel and let ourselves in to cabin seven. Anni removed the contents of the envelope to see what we'd got. She spread four separate stapled documents out on the bed.

It only took the briefest perusal of the front cover of each one, to see what we had. The four separate documents were written in German, each had a stamp on the opening page in Cyrillic script saying 'Top State Secret' with a short identical note below the four stamps stating:

These documents have been compiled by Directorate 8 of the Committee of State Security of the Soviet Union with the assistance of Sonata. They are provided to Chairman of the SED Walter Ulbricht and General Erich Mielke, Minister for State Security of the GDR, for their personal information only. Distribution to any other party comrades, irrespective of seniority, or to any other organs of the state is strictly forbidden.

Signed. VW Shelyepin.

We both took a couple of minutes to examine the contents. My first thought was how the hell did Klara Hartmann ever get hold of these? According to the subheadings, each of the documents contained detailed psychological and biographical profiles of four senior members of the US government, namely The President, the Attorney General, the Vice President, Lyndon Johnson and Robert MacNamara, Secretary of Defence. The profiles relating to President Kennedy and LBJ each comprised twenty three pages. The other two were four or five pages shorter. They appeared to have been written as background briefing for the use of anyone likely to be in negotiations with the subjects of the profiles. But a quick glance at the level of detail contained in each one, suggested they went far beyond being merely profiles to be used to assist with negotiating strategies.

Anni was shocked by what she was reading, 'What was my sister doing with this stuff? Is this what she was talking about when she said she had gift for the President?' She asked.

'I think we'd better read it carefully and see exactly what we've got,' I suggested.

'We will have to take these papers somewhere else. The maid will come by soon to clean the room. She is very punctual.'

I began to gather up the four documents and put them back in the envelope they came in. 'I have a suggestion.' I said. 'How'd you like to go to Nantucket?'

'You mean the island?'

'That's the only Nantucket I know. We can take the ferry from the docks, just a couple of minutes away. The trip takes a little over two hours. There won't be many people on it at this time of year. So we will have time to read this stuff. I'll take two of them, read them and you do the same, then we will swop over. By the time we get to the Island we should have some idea what this is all about.'

'How much do the tickets for the ferry cost?'

'Don't worry about that. I'll take care of it. C'mon, I think it leaves at ten thirty, let's get out of here.' We put the papers back in the envelope, which fitted perfectly into Anni's suede shoulder bag and headed for the docks.

The sky was gray and the wind a little high as the ferry headed out of Hyannis Harbour and into Nantucket Sound, just a half hour after we had decided to go. After a cursory look around from the open upper deck we decided to sit down below out of the wind and a light misty rain. As I thought, there were very few people on the boat for a Sunday. Out on the water there was a palpable feeling that the long Indian summer was coming to an end. The fall would be a short one, winter was on the way. We bought cups of coffee and muffins, chose a spot as far away from other tourists as we could and settled down to read. I took President Kennedy's and Robert MacNamara's profiles first and Anni started with RFK's and LBJ's. Once we started reading, we both sat there in silence, sipping our coffee. I found myself concentrating more intently than I ever did for any of my college exams. The Soviet Committee for State Security, more commonly known as the KGB, who had compiled the material, seemed to me to have done a pretty thorough job. It took me just twenty five minutes to read the profile of the President. The contents were so stunning that I went back to the beginning and re-read it straight away. The early biographical material was familiar enough to me. The story of old Joe Kennedy's family background and his rise to riches could have been taken from any Reader's Digest article. It relied too much on press cuttings and recycled magazine profiles. The President's early military and political career was treated in greater detail. Insofar as I knew, it appeared to be accurate and insightful, particularly about Kennedy's fairly lacklustre performance as a Congressman and his higher profile as a Senator. It pointed out his greater than average number of absences from the Senate since 1953, as a result of ill health and because he was busy preparing to run for the presidency. The details it provided of Kennedy's true state of health were shocking. They were enough to seriously damage him politically if they ever became public knowledge. He was said to definitely have Addison's disease, something that was always officially denied. It detailed a plethora of problems arising from surgery on his spine which the document predicted would eventually prevent him walking and confine him permanently to a wheelchair. But it was the psychological profile that was so devastating. It described the President as a reckless, narcissistic, lifelong womaniser. It included a long list of alleged lovers, complete with the dates and the occasions on which he met them. Many of the names, actresses and celebrities, were well known to most Americans. It described an extraordinary risk taker, a charming erudite man on the surface, but according to the KGB, not one with a first rate mind.

The profile suggested that he posed as an intellectual but he did not have a high level of mental capacity in his own right. He made up for this deficiency by ensuring that he was surrounded by the best minds he could hire, to advise him. The document revealed that Lyndon Johnson, who, in 1960 had not contested the presidential primaries, had deliberately spread rumours among Democratic delegates to the convention in Los Angeles that year that Kennedy had Addison's disease and was unsuitable as a nominee for the presidency. When Kennedy won the nomination anyway, Johnson blackmailed Kennedy to obtain the Vice-Presidential slot for himself, by threatening to release to the public, information on his illnesses and his philandering. Kennedy gave in to this blackmail and against his brother Robert's advice, offered the VP slot to Johnson.

As I read all of this, I tried to convince myself that this was just the Russians, what did they know? It was all so incredible that it simply could not be true. The level of sleaze, dishonesty and backstabbing the profiles depicted could not be part of the American way. I thought about what Robert Lavelle had said about my naivete. *Maybe not in*

Main Street USA where you live but in the real world. I thought of Herbert Kluge's surprise at my not knowing the kind of thing that goes on at the Quorum Club. Even Tom Noonan had joked about Kennedy's code name 'Lancer' and I had no clue what he was talking about. Am I some kind of naive idiot? I was beginning to think so. The conclusions of the Kennedy document were that, as an adversary of the USSR, the President was vulnerable to blackmail and security breaches, to manipulation in negotiations, because of the effects on his judgement of the myriad of medications he takes. He was fundamentally a weak man and non-confrontational, it said but he still posed a threat to the USSR and to the interests of the socialist bloc, because he could be influenced by his tougher younger brother, Robert and his father, both of whom had reputations as uncompromising, aggressive individuals, if their interest were threatened. The concluding sentence of the twenty three page profile, relating to the President stated simply:

'The suggestion of Comrades Mielke and Wolf, outlined in their joint memorandum of 14 September 1961, submitted to Chairman Khrushchev and Comrade Shelyepin, concerning the utilisation of the proposed Adler Programme to exploit the vulnerabilities at the highest level of the American government identified in this document is a matter entirely for the authorities in the GDR. The Presidium and Central Committee of the USSR does not express any fundamental objection to the proposal.'

That was it. That was a green light from the GDR's Russian masters to use this damaging information to influence and undermine the American presidency.

The profile on Robert MacNamara contained far less drama or interest apart from the fact that he was identified as one of the people with a formidable intellect that Kennedy had hired. It was clear the Russians thought of him as a highly competent technocrat type and someone with a very keen brain. But the profile was mainly biographical. I had the impression that the author or authors did not really know too much about how the Secretary of Defence interacted with the President or with his own peers. Much of the document was concerned with Soviet impressions of MacNamara's real or imagined role in the Bay of Pigs invasion in the spring of '61. I have to admit I read it with less attention than the previous profile, the contents of which were still reeling around my head. When I had finished with MacNamara, Anni handed me the two papers she had finished reading and I handed her mine. The sky outside brightened a little, the sun was struggling through but we ignored it. The tourist crowd seemed to cheer up as the rain clouds diminished and conversation around us got louder. I looked around and marvelled at the incongruity of the scene. Two people sitting on the Nantucket ferry, a disgraced public servant and a department store sales assistant, reading top secret Soviet documents. I had no real idea what I was doing with this material or what I was going to do with it. I was punch drunk. I had made one badly thought out move after another ever since Klara Hartmann was killed. I needed time to think things out. What was I doing and why was I doing it? Was there any way in all of this, to save my career or what was left of it? It seemed unlikely. I looked at Anni. She was still reading with intense concentration, ignoring me. She at least had a reason for what she was doing. She wanted to find out who had murdered her sister. I, on the other hand, had just about destroyed my life and I had no idea why. I picked up the first of the papers Anni had passed to me. LBJ, I thought, now there was a challenge for any psychological profile.

The LBJ document was as detailed as Kennedy's. It painted a picture of a man full of contradictions, someone manipulative, ruthless, ambitious, financially corrupt and largely ignorant of the world outside of his native Texas and Washington DC. On the flip side of his personality, he was a highly efficient legislator and a highly persuasive salesman when it came to securing congressional and Senate votes. The KGB profilers described a strange conflicted personality. They considered him insecure, given to bouts of self pity, but with a genuine desire to help the marginalised in America, while continuing to curry favour with, and take money from, conservative Texas oilmen, who had no interest in the marginalised. Johnson, who came from a family of modest means, had been in receipt of a public representatives salary for all of his working life but was worth, according to this profile, almost 14 million dollars, many times more than he could ever hope to be paid by the American taxpayer. The document stated categorically that he would not be chosen by Kennedy as his Vice Presidential running mate in '64 because of the likelihood of his exposure for acceptance of corrupt payments and because of Robert Kennedy's hatred for him. A key player in Johnson's various dealings over the years was identified in the document as none other than Bobby Baker, the guiding light of the Quorum Club. The Russians it seemed knew all about it and about Baker. According to the profile, the club was Baker's brainchild, intended as a tool for the manipulation and blackmail of members of Congress and the Senate. The methods used by Baker to secure cash as well as votes for Johnson were set out in considerable and convincing detail.

It was almost one o'clock by the time we got off the ferry at Nantucket town. I had no doubt that what I had read in the previous two hours was enough to bring an end to the Presidency and Vice Presidency of the United States and to create an unprecedented constitutional crisis if it ever became public. The four documents fitted easily into Anni's bag as we walked the short distance from the ferry into Nantucket town. I had been here many times before. Anni was predictably impressed by its quaintness, by its 18th century appearance, pretty houses and cobbled streets. If I was honest with myself there was something about the town and the Island that I disliked. I thought I could still detect in it the remnants of joyless New England Puritanism. The flinty hard eyed Yankee ethos, which I thought of as narrow minded and insular, was still here. But I knew I was in a minority of one. I never met anyone who didn't gush over the peace, the tranquillity and the downright cuteness of Nantucket. We headed for a restaurant I knew well called the Red Snapper on Easy Street, just a ten minute walk from the dock. It had a reputation for imaginative and tasty fish dishes and it was completely empty when we sat down. The owner, a man I knew slightly, called Bill Coffin, from an old Nantucket family, seemed pleased to see us. The walls were covered with black and white photos of the island in the last century. The picture closest to where we sat, showed Nantucket Harbour and it seemed the entire Atlantic Ocean beyond it, frozen solid in the winter of 1898. As Bill handed us menus, he told us that the season was just about over and that he was closing for the winter at the end of the month. We both ordered sea bass, a speciality of the house. After choosing and ordering was completed, Bill Coffin, who was doubling as waiter for the day, retreated to the kitchen and Anni and I were left entirely alone in the small restaurant.

'So, How about we talk about what we've got' I said. Frankly, I am still in shock after reading what we've just read. Not to mention that your sister had this kind of material.'

'Yes', said Anni. 'I am too. It seems to me that the capitalist system has as many flaws as communism.'

'I wouldn't quite go that far'. I said. 'We don't have to build a wall to keep people in.'

'Maybe we can discuss that question another time.' She said. 'For now, let us be logical, let us put together all of the information we both have and see what is sensible.'

'See if it makes sense?'

'This is no time for English lessons, Jimmy.' She said in a serious tone. 'I will begin and you can ask me questions if you wish. Fortunately I don't have very much information, so my part won't take long.'

'OK, shoot.

'Shoot?'

'Go ahead.'

'Ah yes, I see.' She took a deep breath. 'My sister Klara met me in Berlin in August of last year. We spent the day together. She told me a fantastic story. That she had been recruited and trained for something called the Adler Programme, which is mentioned in this document. It was run by the GDR foreign intelligence directorate. She said she expected to be sent to the United States on a special assignment.'

'What was the assignment?'

'She didn't know what it was. Don't interrupt so soon, give me chance to say all of this.'

'Sorry.'

'She said the boss of the Adler Programme was a man called Max Korten, the same man who later visited me in Berlin, who told me that Klara was dead. When we met In Berlin in August of '62, Klara had told me she had fallen in love with this man. She described him to me in great detail and was convinced that he was the love of her life.'

'But you didn't like him?'

'No, and he didn't like me. When he came to visit me, I could tell that he was angry at Klara's death but not sad, as perhaps a lover would be sad. He was angry as if she had betrayed him. I could be wrong but I did not get the feeling that he had lost the love of his life. I had the feeling that he was seeking some kind of revenge against my sister, but of course that was not now possible.'

'You're a perceptive woman, Anni.'

'Perceptive?'

'You are a good judge of people. You're very shrewd. Apart from thinking I'm the impractical dreamer type of course. You're completely wrong there.'

She smiled sympathetically. 'I am sorry. I should not have said that. You are offended.'

'I am not at all offended because it's absolutely not true. But I have no doubt you're perceptive when it comes to others. Please continue.'

'I should tell you something more about my sister Klara. She may have looked like an angel but she was a natural rebel. She was breaking rules all her life. And she was breaking rules by meeting me in West Berlin and by telling me about the Adler Programme and about Max Korten. But we had shared everything all our lives, so this was no exception. But now she was not playing some schoolgirl game. This was dangerous, because she was working for dangerous people. And what was worse, she had been caught. Korten followed her to West Berlin. She was supposed to have escaped over the Wall but of course that was all faked by the Stasi. In West Berlin, he followed her or had her followed and he knew she had made contact with me, which she was not supposed to do. But even after disobeying a strict order, Korten let her continue with her mission, whatever it was and she was sent to Bavaria where a job in a hotel was arranged for her.'

'Maybe Korten was in love with her too, so he let her continue with the mission, although it doesn't seem very professional.'

'Maybe. She was beautiful. Boys were always falling in love with her. She was always the pretty one, not me. I was the eldest, the sensible one.

'I wouldn't let it worry you, Anni. I'd say you do alright.'

She dismissed the compliment with a quick shake of her head and continued. 'There is no question that she had a real love affair with Korten that year. The very first in her life. She told me all about it.'

Just then a couple came into the restaurant. As if by magic Bill Coffin reappeared from the back kitchen to greet them, menus in hand. Bill had placed Anni and me at the only window seat. The couple were seated a few of tables away from us, further back. It allowed us to continue talking while they were doing their 'what will we have' bit with help from Bill.

'When did you last see Klara?' I asked.

'I saw her only once after we met in Berlin. She was afraid to make direct contact with me but she asked someone in Garmisch, a guest at the hotel where she worked who was going to Berlin, to bring a message to me to me. Working in KaDeWe is quite convenient for that kind of thing. Everybody knows where it is and the cosmetics counter is on the ground floor. The person just had to walk in and hand me a letter from Klara. To my surprise it was a wedding invitation.'

'What, she invited you to her wedding with Robert Lavelle?'

'Yes.'

'Did you go?'

'Yes. But I could not be an official witness, in case the Stasi checked the public record and would know Klara was in contact with her family. But I was there in Munich. A very simple civil ceremony, I was the only guest.'

'Did you know that the wedding was part of Klara's cover story?'

'Yes, she told me but not until I got to Munich. I liked Bobby very much and so did Klara. I cannot believe that he is dead. He was a handsome man but we both suspected he was not the marrying kind.'

'Bobby?'

'His friends call him Bobby. Klara did and therefore so did I, although I only met him that one time. About a month or so later, Klara and he left for America. She did not contact me at all while she was here. After she was deported, she called me just once to say she was back in Garmisch and I had to tell her that Papa had been arrested again and was now in Bautzen. She was very upset, of course, and blamed herself.'

'Is that when you told her that you had heard the Kennedy speech at Schoneberg Town Hall?'

'That's right, yes. That call and the postcard from the Wianno Motel, after she came back to this country, were my last contacts with my sister.' She stopped talking for a full minute and then said. 'Now I will never speak to her again.'

Suddenly, she was on the verge of tears. Another family group had arrived, business in the Red Snapper was suddenly picking up. 'Anni, can you ride a bike? I asked in an effort to distract her.

'Of course I can.' She said, as she dabbed her eyes with a Kleenex.'

'OK, let's get the check and get out of here. We'll hire couple of bikes and take a tour of this little island. We can talk as we ride'

Whatever about my prejudices about Nantucket, I had to admit that on this particular day, the island was looking its best in the mild fall air, with the sun sporadically peeking through the clouds. It took about forty five minutes riding along winding country roads to get to the beach at Siasconsett. In the summer, Sconsett, as everyone calls it, is one of the island's most popular beaches. Anni's rental bike had a wicker basket in front of the handlebars. In it she had placed her suede shoulder bag with the envelope containing four top secret KGB documents. The weirdness of this situation struck me again. I had to think about where I would stash the documents when we got back to the mainland and what we would ultimately do with them. We parked our bikes outside a place called Mildred's Tea Shoppe, which was already closed for the winter and walked to the beach, resuming the conversation we had started in the restaurant. A lone woman walking a black Labrador some distance away was the only other person in sight.

'So, the last time you saw Klara was at the wedding which was in December last year, and you spoke to her only once after that, apart from getting the postcard.'

'Yes.'

'She was deported on 29th July and was back in this country by Labour Day weekend. The FBI said she came in via Canada. But nobody mentioned finding her passport. It wasn't with her personal possessions, unless the FBI found it and kept it. She would have needed one to fly from Germany to Canada and she would need one to get into the United States. We can assume that her reasons for coming to Hyannis with the papers you're carrying there in your bag was to give them to the President.'

'Yes, but you said your friend Joe told you that she was turned away from the Kennedy Complex.'

'Compound, the Kennedy complex is a whole other thing. But knowing what you've just told me about her breaking rules, being turned away was not going to deter her. There are two other obvious questions about the papers that occur to me. Who mailed them to Klara in the first place? That was a pretty reckless thing to do with sensitive intelligence information. And secondly, how did they get to the States. Only two top East Germans were supposed to see them, Ulbricht himself and Eric Mielke, who is the Minister for State Security. What are they doing sitting in the Ameida bus station? We could also ask; why did Klara want to give them to Kennedy? They are hardly flattering about him or his family. There is an awful lot of embarrassing detail in there. Anyone with access to such high grade intelligence would in effect be admitting they were a spy.

'I think I can answer the last question.' Anni said.

'You can?' I said. 'Well, go ahead.'

'I think the reason she would have given these documents to your President was that she wanted him to know what the KGB had on him, as you say. She wanted him to be one step ahead of his enemies.'

'If she did that she would be betraying her masters in the Stasi.'

'I told you Jimmy, no one in my family was ever a Communist and certainly not Klara. She probably wanted your government's help to release my father. But I believe she had another reason as well.'

'What was that?'

I could see Anni hesitate before she answered. 'She had met the President and I am guessing she had intimate relations with him.'

'Intimate relations? You don't say. Very delicately put, Anni. Judging by what's in the profile there in your bag, there are very few women in America who have not had "intimate relations" with him. Anyway, how could you possibly know that?'

'You seem angry about this Jimmy. I am only trying to help. Could we sit on the sand for a while? She said. 'You don't realise how fascinating it is for me to see the Atlantic Ocean like this. I was born in one land locked city and now live in another. It's very exciting for me to see the ocean waves crashing in like this.'

We sat down as she suggested and stared at the surf. The woman with the dog had gone. Sconsett was completely deserted, apart from the two of us. 'I'm sorry, I said. I'm not sure why I'm angry. I think it's the shock of reading all of that stuff, Kennedy, Johnson, sex, blackmail and financial corruption at the heart of the American government. I always thought of myself as a patriot. I'm feeling a little foolish.'

Anni smiled sympathetically. 'Remember, these things were written by the KGB. That organisation does not have a great reputation for honesty.'

'I know, but that material was created for their internal use, for the people at the very top. Somehow, as incredible as it seems, the stuff is so specific and detailed that it has a ring of truth. Your friend Robert Lavelle, 'Bobby', accused me of being naive. I'm beginning to think he was right. We can't escape the fact that Klara's mission was somehow to meet with President Kennedy, to take advantage of his particular inclination for sexual shenanigans and to spy on him or influence him.'

'Shenanigans?'

'You know, adultery, as it used to be known.'

'Yes I'm sure your right.' Anni said. But he must have made such an impression on her that she decided he needed to know what the enemy knew about him.'

'Did she actually say that she did have intimate relations, as you call them?'

'No, she did not actually say that. I am only guessing. She said she met him but didn't say where. She said that she had been alone with him and that he was wonderful, a man of peace, of culture and noble intentions. I just assumed she had been intimate with him because she seemed so, I suppose you would say, captivated by him.'

'That must have been some phone call you two had. How long did it last?'

'About an hour, I think.'

'An hour? She called you in Berlin from Bavaria and you spoke to her for an hour? What about the phone lines going through East Germany and the possible bugging of the phone?'

'Yes it was careless perhaps, but it was my sister and she had just been deported. Our father had been arrested again. She was now in trouble with the Stasi and I could tell she was very worried. She wanted to talk to me and I wanted to talk to her. We did not intend for the conversation to go on so long.'

'Anni, you must know that sophisticated bugging will pick up on key words used in conversation. If a conversation contains words such as deportation, Washington DC, President Kennedy, the Justice Department or the CIA, the people listening in are going to pay attention.'

'I don't think we ever mentioned the CIA.'

'Oh great no CIA just everything else. That's not the point. She could have put her life in danger by talking about these things over a phone line going through a Communist country. She had to have known that. After all, she was a trained intelligence operative. Maybe she no longer cared.'

'I don't think she did. She was finished with the GDR and the Stasi and they with her.'

'She may have been but they may not have been finished with her. Now she's dead and the Stasi may have killed her, if she wasn't killed by LBJ, John Kennedy or J Edgar Hoover. Did she mention that she intended to come back here to the States?'

'No definitely not. We spoke mainly about our parents and their difficulties, a little about Max Korten, how bitter she was about him and a lot about, Kennedy, the test ban treaty and the possibility of an end to the cold war.'

'If East German listeners didn't pick up on that they must be useless. Did she mention Korten by name?'

'No she used a code name. She called him 'the Golden Pheasant'. It was kind of a joke between us.'

'Very amusing, where did that come from?'

'It's how Germans used to refer to interfering Nazi party officials during the war, because of their brown uniforms. Korten always had a deep golden sun tan.'

'It looks to me that if Klara came here to give the envelope to the President and it seems clear she did, then the people with the biggest motive to stop her were her own bosses in the Stasi. She was betraying them, or she already had, and was about to hand over secret material which had been provided to East Germany by the Russians.'

'Yes but if the American government, the CIA or the FBI or someone, knew about these papers they too might have a motive to get them back or even to silence the person who had seen them, by killing her.'

'We have no reason to think that they know about the documents. Anyway Anni, the American Government does not kill people. This is a democracy.'

She gave me a pitying look. 'I work in a store, Jimmy, and you work for your government. I thought you would know better. I think Bobby was right, you are very naive.'

I looked at my watch and stood up. 'Maybe we should go, Anni, we've a boat to catch and it's another forty five minutes back to town. She reached her hands out for me and I pulled her up off the sand. For few seconds we faced each other our noses almost touching. She was a beautiful woman and the desire to kiss her there and then was suddenly overwhelming. She looked me straight in the eyes as if she was reading my mind and suddenly bent down again to pick up her bag.

'Yes, you are right. She said, turning her head quickly in the direction of Mildred's, where we'd left the bikes. 'We don't want to miss the ferry back.'

CHAPTER 25

October 1963

We caught the four thirty ferry back to the mainland. The clouds thickened and the sky darkened, the light rain of earlier in the day had returned. This was not unusual for Nantucket, known as the 'gray lady' because of its tendency to become enveloped in fog. As the ferry left the harbour we could see the beginnings of a mist descending on the island. We sat below once more to avoid the increasingly chilly air on deck. 'Did you enjoy the day?' I asked Anni.

'It was a perfect day, Jimmy.' she said.' I have no wish to be ungrateful but I can never really enjoy anything with genuine pleasure when I think about my father in prison and my mother worrying about him. It weighs on me every day, like a heavy stone. Somehow, I was hoping that coming to America and finding out what happened to Klara might help my father's situation. But I can see now that is just fantasy, a stupid, illogical dream.'

'I'm sorry. I keep forgetting about your father's situation. I know it can't be easy.' We sat in silence for three or four minutes.

'Do you know what a three decker Irishman is?' I asked.

'No.'

'That's OK, most people don't. Well my father was one. That means he was born and raised in a three story timber framed house in Charlestown, East Boston. They were known as three deckers. In those days, Charlestown and East Boston were Irish ghettos. As I told you, my great grandparents were born in Ireland.' Anni was now listening with interest.

'Please continue' She said.

'Yesterday, at Kevin's party in Falmouth, I told my mother and sister about losing my Job. They didn't take it well, particularly my mother. My sister thought it was no big deal. She always thought I could do better. Anyway, after the initial shock, my mother said that the only person she knows with any influence in government, is a guy called Dave Powers, a fellow three decker Irishman from the same neighbourhood as my Dad. They lived on the same street in Charlestown and were in the same class in school. I never heard my father mention him, but my mother met him once or twice when she and my Dad were going out. Powers has been involved in Democratic politics in Boston since forever. He's one of those guys who knows everybody. He's a particular Boston political type, pols they call them. Nothing happens in Charlestown without him knowing. He knows every family, their parents, grandparents, cousins, all their sins and their secrets. Of course he knew my father. These guys never forget a friend or neighbour and always help out, particularly if there's a vote in it. That can be good and it can be bad. But it's the way Democratic politics has worked in Boston since 1847.'

'Why are you telling me this Jimmy?'

'I'm getting to that. Last night, my mother called an old neighbourhood friend of hers in Boston. She, the friend, spoke to her husband who gave her Dave Powers' home number. Then my mother called Dave Powers but he wasn't home. But Powers' wife contacted her husband and called my mother back to say that Powers, will contact me next week. Powers no longer lives in Boston he lives in Washington. He works at the White House.'

'Is this true, the White House? Can this man get you your job back?'

'I doubt it. I don't think he has that much influence, but he does work directly for the President. Of course my job is the only thing my mother wants me to talk to him about. I was thinking that if he meets me, I may be able to find out a little more about Klara and the President, maybe something that will help.'

'Don't you think that the subject of the President and women might be a very sensitive topic to discuss with this man?'

'Of course it's sensitive but I'll be diplomatic. I'll just see how it goes. It certainly can't do any harm to talk to him.'

'Do you think such a person might be helpful to my father?' She asked hopefully.'

'I really don't know, Anni, the GDR is a long way from East Boston. But I promise you I will mention his situation to Powers, if I meet him.'

'Thank you.' She said. 'But maybe your mother is right. You should just try to get your job back.'

'We'll see Anni. Talking to this guy is only a tiny straw to clutch at. But I'll try to make the most of it. Anyway, we can't achieve much by hanging around here on the Cape. We have to go back to Washington. Before that I suggest we go to New York and talk to someone in the Carlyle Hotel to find out who mailed those documents to Klara. Possession of these papers must have something to do with her murder. Then we can go on to Washington and wait for Power's call. At least we'll feel we're doing something.'

'I agree action is much better than talk,' she said. I have just thought of something.' She opened her bag and removed the white Carlyle Hotel envelope and examined the stamps in the right hand corner.

'I was wondering if we could make out the date when this was mailed.' She said. She took a small flashlight, about the size of a pen from her bag and shone it on the area surrounding the stamp.

'Yes, Jimmy, look. The date is very clear, 26 May, 1963.'

She was right, there was no smudging on the post office ink stamp. The documents had been mailed to Klara in Arlington from New York on 26th May. Of course there was no guarantee that they had been mailed from the Carlyle Hotel, but there was a good chance that they had been.

'Well done, Anni,' I said. 'That settles it we'll go to the Carlyle this week and ask a few questions. There was something you said earlier that got me thinking. You remember I mentioned my boss Vern Templeton, who was part of last week's kangaroo court?'

'Yes, I remember.'

'Well, in his lengthy critique of my irresponsible behaviour, he mentioned something about me having cosy chats with 'Bobby' Lavelle in Arlington Cemetery. He called him Bobby, just like you did, he didn't say Robert. I didn't think he knew anything about Lavelle. How could he have known we met in Arlington Cemetery? And he would only have called him 'Bobby' if he had known him. And if he knew him, it means Vern, my colleague and boss, knew Klara's husband, which is, let's face it, very strange and a hell of a coincidence.'

'Yes and what is also so strange about all of this I think.' Anni said, 'two people, Klara and her husband both die, within a very short time. One is murdered and one dies suspiciously. That too is a big coincidence. The two things must be connected. If we knew that Bobby's death was not a suicide, as his friend thinks, it would be helpful in finding out who killed Klara.'

'You're right, but finding out who killed Lavelle is just as difficult to do as getting to the bottom of Klara's death. I can't help thinking that Vern Templeton knows a bit more than he is saying. Since the time of Lavelle's death he has been acting kinda strange. You would have to know this guy. He is the essence of cool, never panics never gets excited. But lately he has been behaving like a man under severe strain. He says he is having marriage problems and maybe he is. But the Bobby Lavelle thing is weird. How could he know to call him Bobby and how did he know we met in Arlington?'

'Do you think he could have killed Bobby?'

I laughed out loud. 'No Anni, I don't. Vernon is the kind of guy who stands at a door and waits for someone to open it for him. I doubt if he has ever as much as rinsed out a coffee cup or picked a piece of paper off the floor. He's certainly not capable of drowning somebody in a canal, someone much younger and fitter than he is.'

'Maybe you should ask him if he knew Bobby, what harm can it do?'Anni said.

'Maybe, but first things first. I have some money put by, not a lot. I'm going to use it to cover our expenses in the next few weeks. So we can fly to New York before going to Washington. There's room in the house I share in Garrett Park. It makes sense for you to stay there if you don't object. It won't cost you anything. What do you think?'

Anni replaced the bulging white envelope in her bag and looked at me.

There was something on her mind. 'No, Jimmy. I will use what little money I have to pay my way also.' She paused for a moment and then added. 'There is something I should have told you, which I think I better tell you now before we go any further.'

'Go ahead.'

'I could see her take a breath before she spoke. 'I live with a man in Berlin, Jimmy. We share an apartment and have done for six months. He has helped me with the finances for this trip. I would not like there to be any misunderstanding between us, either about money or about anything else. I thought I should let you know.'

My stomach muscles unexpectedly tightened. 'Oh I see. Do you live with him as a roommate or is there something more between you'

'No, not a roommate, there is something more.'

'What makes you think that there would be a misunderstanding?' I said in a voice that I hoped sounded as cool as Sean Connery talking to Bloefeld.

Even in the poor light of the covered in deck I could see her discomforture as she answered. 'It was just that earlier on the beach I thought you might have, other intentions, but maybe I was wrong. I'm sorry. You are going to a lot of trouble for me and I need to make my situation clear to you. I like you very much, Jimmy, and I am grateful to you.'

'Anni.' I interrupted her. 'Don't worry. I know what you're saying. I started this before I met you and as I said before, I intend to finish it. So who you live with in Berlin is irrelavent. It doesn't matter. All that matters is whether you still want to pursue this with me.'

'Of course I am, Jimmy. It's just that you are being so kind to me and I don't want you to think that I am taking you for granted. If that's how you say it.'

'Yes that's how you say it alright. And you're not, so let's forget it, OK?'

She nodded her thanks.

'What's his name?' I asked casually, 'Your fella in Berlin.'

'His name is Franz Walter. He is a lecturer in Economics at Berlin Free University, a part time lecturer, not yet a permanent employee.'

'He didn't want to come here with you and help with this search for the truth about Klara?'

'No. He disapproved of my coming, thinks I am being foolish but when I told him I was going anyway he gave me a little money and paid my airline ticket. If he left work for any length of time it could prevent him getting a permanent post in the university.'

'He sounds like a sensible fellow.' I said hypocritically. I realized that I suddenly disliked someone I hadn't even heard of just three minutes before. It figured that a girl as nice as Anni Hartmann was unlikely to be alone for long. The ferry's loudspeaker interrupted my malevolent thoughts about Franz Walter with a muffled announcement that we were twenty minutes from our destination. We had been talking all day. We sat in silence for the rest of the voyage.

CHAPTER 26

October 1963

I took the KGB psychological profiles from Anni when I dropped her back at her motel. I told her I knew a safe place to put them. I figured she had told me about her boyfriend in case I had any ideas about being asked in to her room when we got back. We said a slightly awkward goodnight. I told her I would be going to Boston early in the morning to visit an attorney. There was some minor taxation problem delaying finalising probate on my father's will, and I was the executor. I said the meeting with the lawyer wasn't likely to take long and while I was there I intended to call in to Pan Am's Boston office in Copely Plaza and book our flights to New York and Washington. I expected to be back in Hyannis by lunchtime. Before I left I paid a visit to the Wianno Motel reception desk. Joanie Marchand was back on duty. Inevitably, I had some trouble parrying her questions about my connection with the guest in cabin seven, in exchange for a new envelope and a stapler to stitch the flap firmly shut. I wrote the words Miscellaneous Papers − J. Flynn, on the address side of the envelope Joanie gave me. I folded the original Carlyle Hotel envelope and put it in the inside pocket of my short tan jacket.

When I finally escaped from Joanie's interrogation, I drove down Ocean Street. Close to Kalmus beach, there's tiny cul de sac called Owen Street, to the right off Gosnold, where Joe Davis lives. As I'd hoped, Joe was home watching Sunday night sports. He asked me in, gave me a beer. He turned down the volume on the TV and we chatted about this and that. Joe had grown up in this house. He had inherited the detached four bedroom home from his folks who had both passed on. It was neat and orderly and surprisingly tastefully furnished for the house of a lone bachelor. I felt a pang of envy at Joe's stable life in his very comfortable home, compared to my own current chaotic existence, no home of my own and soon, it seemed only a matter of time, no job either. He still had that funny English hairstyle I had seen on Labour Day weekend, if anything his hair was even longer now. As I expected, when I broached the subject he readily agreed to hold on to the envelope until I came to collect it. I knew Joe was dyslexic. The condition was almost unheard of when we were in high school, which explained why he was such a poor reader. I knew he would not be tempted to open the envelope but if he did, the German text would completely baffle him. I didn't mention what was in it but I told him it was highly confidential, that had to do with my job and I didn't want my mother taking a peek at it. He seemed to accept this vague explanation and told me, 'I know the very place for it, leave it to me.'

He took out a record album with an intriguing black and white cover showing the disembodied heads of four young men in half light wearing black polo neck sweaters and four identical looking hairstyles, just like Joe's, against a black background.

'This is the English group I was talking to you about, the Beatles. The record is not even in stores yet It's an advance copy, a buddy brought it back from London. I'll put it on. Let me know what you think.'

I was pleasantly surprised. The music had a joyous enthusiasm, like nothing I had heard before, even the cover songs, which took up half the album and were already familiar to me were done with an exuberance that was totally original. We drank two beers as we listened to the record and reminisced about the old days at the yacht club and some of the crusty old characters who once made up the majority of the membership. We talked about Thurston Bennett, 'thirsty Thurston' a prolific boozer when Joe and I worked at the club. He was an aging bachelor from an old Cape Cod family, who died in '57 and left Joe his ancient twenty eight foot cabin cruiser, 'Hasty Pudding' in his will. The boat was named after an exclusive Harvard Club where old Thurston had been a luminary in his college days. Joe spent three years restoring it in his spare time. Thurston's gesture had been the talk of the yacht club and much of the town. Leaving it to Joe, who was not related to him, was considered typical of Bennett's eccentric personality. When the record album had played we finished up. I left the house at about nine or so, thinking what a decent, reliable guy Joe always was. It was a mystery to me why he hadn't married. He was solvent and sober, always working, there was nothing he couldn't build or repair. I headed for home, tired after a long day. The news of Anni Hartmann's live-in boyfriend in Berlin still rankled. I turned left on to Gosnold Street at the end of Owen Street. It was dark, the street totally deserted. I was not quite out of the short cul de sac when a familiar looking Ford Edsel suddenly cut in front of me. I jammed on the brakes of the Chevy and stopped about four inches from the driver's door of the Ford. A man jumped out of the passenger side of the car and walked quickly over to me. I rolled down my window.

'What the hell do you think you're doing?' I shouted. 'You could have killed us both.'

The guy produced a black wallet containing his FBI badge but I didn't need to see it. I knew who he was. 'Caulfield, what are you doing here? Is this what the Bureau is being issued with now, beat up old Edsels?' I shouted at him, still in shock from the near collision.

'Please pull over to the side Mr Flynn we need to talk to you.' Caulfield said without emotion. He gestured to the driver of the other car. 'Outa the way Larry let him pull around the corner.'

'Larry?' I said. What happened to Verling? J Edgar finally got rid of him?'

'Just pull over and get out of the vehicle please.'

I drove around the corner onto Gosnold Street. Caulfield walked alongside. The Edsel pulled up right behind me. 'I have no intention of getting out of the car until you tell me what this is all about Caulfield.' I said.

He then did something I didn't expect. He pulled a snub nosed thirty eight revolver from a holster on his belt and put the gun through the open window, the barrel six inches from my face.

'Get out of the car Mr Flynn, hand me your car keys and do it now.' He said quietly. I had watched a scene like this in the movies and on TV a thousand times. It's a lot scarier when the gun, a real one, is pointed at you. I decided to do as he asked. He walked me over to the Edsel and put me in the back seat and got in beside me, before he did, I was glad to see him put the Smith and Wesson back in its holster. 'OK Larry', was all he said. Larry was a wiry looking guy with receding hair, slightly greasy and a little long at the collar. He did not look anything like an FBI agent. He started the car and drove us a thousand yards across Ocean Street to the deserted car park of Kalmus Beach. It was deserted except for a single black sedan parked there, with the unmistakable bullet head and close cropped silver hair of Special Agent in Charge Verling, sitting in the passenger seat smoking a cigarette. Caulfield handed my car keys to Larry, got out walked around to my side and opened the door and indicated with his thumb that I was to get out.

'Ten or fifteen minutes Larry'. He said to the driver. 'Take a good look.' Larry drove away.

I was ushered in to the rear of the black sedan. Caulfield sat behind the wheel. The surf seemed to roar in the silence. Verling spoke first. He was his usual charming self.

'Where were you just now?'

'Good evening to you too Agent Verling I said. 'If you must know I was returning a book that Mrs Lacroix, a friend of my mother's had lent her. Has the FBI got a problem with that?'

'What was the book?' Verling said in the same calm monotone.

'Peyton Place.' I said.

'Racy reading for respectable housewives. Who is the woman you were with today?'

'If your guy Larry has been following me for the last two days I guess you know that already.'

Verling threw his cigarette butt out of the window and looked back at me over his left shoulder. 'Tell me anyway, Flynn, and be quick about it. We have a plane to catch.'

'Her name is Anni Hartmann from Berlin. She's a friend of mine.'

Another German. All of a sudden there are a lot of Germans running around here. Hard to believe we won the war. You spent some time there too Flynn, ain't that so?'

'A year yes, it was a long time ago.'

'Is that where you met this girl, Hartmann?'

'Yes.' The lie came easily to me.

'Nineteen fifty eight, not that long ago.' Verling said, letting me know that he had checked me out.

'What was in the package you collected from the bus station this morning? No wait a minute, before you answer that, let me just say this. First off, we know your situation. You have been suspended by the State Department and are almost certainly going to be canned in the next few weeks and I for one am very happy about that. How they ever recruited an idiot like you in the first place I'll never know. Despite this personal setback, you seem to persist in meddling in something that is no concern of yours. In fact you are very close to adding a federal jail term to your resumé, along with your dismissal from State. Nice goin'. As you're such a curious kind o' guy and to speed things up, I will tell you what we're doing. We're aware that the woman, who was killed right here in this town in September intended to provide classified information to the President or to his brother, about a senior member of the Government. We naturally need to know how a common prostitute, let's not mince our words here Flynn, got hold of this information. And then of course we need to plug that particular security leak.

In case you don't know it, that's our job. Director Hoover is naturally anxious to get hold of the information, because it will assist in identifying where the breach in security occurred and we can neutralise whatever damage might be caused by its dissemination. Is all that clear? As I said, I haven't got all night. I will ask you two questions only and I want two honest answers. I warn you, if you are in any way responsible for withholding information or if you are found in possession of documentation which contains classified information, you will go to jail. I will personally see to it and it goes without saying, if you ever get out, which you may not, you'll be lucky to be flipping hamburgers for the rest of your life.'

'So listen carefully to my questions please. What was in the envelope that you and your girlfriend removed from locker number ten at the Almeida Bus station this morning? Secondly, where is the envelope and its contents now? Two simple questions Mr Flynn, now please answer them.'

As I sat in the car I was aware of the empty folded up Carlyle hotel envelope in the inside pocket of the windbreaker I was wearing. 'It was nothing, just general tourist information about North America. Anni is thinking of doing some travelling. It was maps and brochures and travel guides, I assure you, it was nothing that could be described as classified.'

'Where is it now, the envelope?'

'We left it behind in Nantucket. We read through the stuff, junk mail really. There was no need to keep it.'

'Who did you meet in Nantucket?'

'Oh I get it. I guess Larry didn't make it to the ferry. We didn't meet anyone over there. We had lunch in the town, took bikes to the beach at Sconsett, spent about an hour there and came back. That was it.'

'Now listen to me Flynn. I asked you to answer two simple questions and you lied both times. You seem to think this is some kind of game. When you go to jail and believe me you are going to jail, you'll realise it's not a game. Caulfield, get him out.'

Both Verling and Caulfield got out of the front seat of the car. Caulfield came around to my side, opened the door and pulled me out. At the same time the Edsel drove back into the car park. It stopped in front of us, its headlights illuminating the three of us standing in front of the black sedan, like actors under stage lighting. Larry got out of the Ford. Caulfeld held tightly to my upper arm while Verling spoke to Larry.

'Anything?'

'Nothing,' Larry said shaking his head. 'I searched every square inch.'

Verling nodded in my direction. 'Take hold of his other arm.' Larry did as he was told. Verling walked up to me and put his face so close I could smell his smoky breath. 'You are a royal pain in the ass, Flynn, you know that? Let me tell you what's going to happen. You are going back to Nantucket and you're going to get this document you took from the locker this morning. You will call into my office in Washington, at the latest by Thursday of this week, with the document. And don't under any circumstances make a copy. If you fail to appear by noon Thursday, there will be a federal arrest warrant issued and you will go to jail.

What's more your pretty German girlfriend will go too. So you do whatever you have to, to get it. It's very simple, even for a doofus like you. Go back to Nantucket and get the envelope and bring it to me, Thursday morning at the latest. Believe me I have better things to do than to chase morons like you and I have no intention of coming back to this dump of a town ever again. I'm generously giving you a couple of days to do this 'cause you'll be busy tomorrow.'

'What do you mean busy?' I stupidly asked.

'Oh, didn't I say? Tomorrow you're gonna need to get some medical attention. Hold him tight boys.'

Larry and Caulfield tightened their grip on each arm. It happened so fast, I was bent over in excruciating pain before I realized that Verling had punched me hard in the solar plexus. The other two continued to hold my upper arms tight. If they hadn't I would have fallen to the ground.

'Turn him around.' Verling said. They did as he asked. Verling punched me again repeatedly, four or five heavy punches to my kidneys and lower back. 'Let him go.' he said to the other two. They immediately released their grip on me. I fell to the ground like sack of potatoes but Verling wasn't finished yet. My back was facing him so he walked around me and aimed four hard sharp kicks with his heavy polished back brogues at my stomach and ribs. Before each measured kick he said the words. 'Just get me, the fucking, envelope.' I lay on the ground, now balled up in the foetal position, unable to speak or to move. Verling wiped his brow with a large white handkerchief. I could hear him panting as he spoke to Caulfield. 'Let's get out of here. I'm gettin' too old for this.' Verling returned to his car but before he got in I heard Caulfield murmuring to Larry. 'The name is Lacroix, Owen Street. Don't hassle her, just check her out.' Even in my severe pain I knew this was going to be a problem because Mrs Lacroix didn't exist.

Both cars started their engines and began to move out. The black sedan stopped beside me as I lay on the concrete surface of the car park. Verling spoke to me from the open window on the passenger side. 'No later than Thursday at noon Flynn, Washington, my office. Don't make me have to come and get you.'

I heard both cars drive away leaving only the soothing sound of the nearby surf. The pain in my ribs and my kidneys was as intense as any I have ever experienced. I lay there for a long time slowly allowing the pain to subside, fully conscious but not really caring if I never rose again from the cold ground.

CHAPTER 27

October 1963

It took almost an hour before I felt strong enough to stand and to stumble slowly back to where the Chevy was parked on Gosnold Street. Larry had left the keys in the ignition. By then I knew I was badly hurt. I sat in with great difficulty and drove at a snail's pace to the Emergency Room of Cape Cod Hospital a distance of about a mile. The last thing I remember was collapsing on the floor in front of the receptionist's desk, after I had given my name and explained that my injuries derived from an encounter with muggers while I was taking a walk on Ocean Street. I didn't remember another thing until I woke at around ten thirty the following morning in a comfortable bed with a strong scent of starched linen, in a bright clean private room. A young female intern with a name tag telling the world she was Dr Dorothy Stevens was standing over the bed as I opened my eyes.

'Good morning, I'm Doctor Stevens. We gave you a strong sedative last night. You've been in the wars Mr Flynn, how do you feel?'

'Sore.' I said and then stupidly 'I've never been treated by a lady doctor before.'

'Well there's always a first time and you'd better get used to it. 'I'm not surprised you're sore. We'll be taking you down for an X ray very soon. On the basis of my preliminary examination it's obvious you have suffered considerable trauma to your lower back, though not to your spine as far as I can tell. You have also broken or fractured two or possibly three ribs on your left side and one on the right. Your kidneys are certainly damaged. You are likely to pass blood in your urine for the next few days, so don't be surprised when you see it. You told the ER receptionist that you were assaulted on Ocean Street. First time I have ever heard of that happening. Whoever did this to you, Mr Flynn, did a very good job of ensuring that your face or head was untouched. Did you know your assailants?'

'No, I never saw them before in my life.'

Dr Stevens came closer to me, took my wrist in her warm soft hand and felt for a pulse which she timed on her wristwatch. 'This kind of assault is most unusual in my experience. Was anything stolen from you? Your wallet was still in your pants pocket when you were admitted. It's in the locker beside you along with your wristwatch.'

'No, I don't think anything was stolen.' I said.

'Your pulse is fine. Mr Flynn.' She said placing my hand gently on the bedcovers. Anyway, our job is to get you better. The police can get to the bottom of who did this to you.'

'I haven't told the police.'

'No, but we have. As a matter of routine we are required notify the police if a patient is admitted following what appears to be the commission of a crime. I believe someone from Barnstable PD will call to see you sometime to talk to you. But don't worry we won't let them bother you if we feel you're not up to it.'

'There's no need for anyone to call in, Doctor. I will explain everything to them when I'm discharged.'

'I'm afraid they have already told us they will drop by later today, no time specified. In any event Mr Flynn, first things first, we have to get you to X ray. After that we'll have some idea how long you'll be here. But one thing is certain; you won't be leaving the hospital today.'

Fifteen minutes after Dr Stevens left, I was wheeled to the X ray department, where I was put through a number of painful contortions on a gurney to ensure the front and rear of my torso was photographed thoroughly. Back in my room, the nurse on duty told me it would be at least an hour before there were any results from the X rays. In the meantime assisted by a second nurse, she replaced the bandage that had been wrapped around my middle the night before to protect my ribs. She rubbed some kind of balm on my bruised lower back and gave me two pain killer pills with a glass of water. I was still feeling very sore but was beginning to enjoy the attention.

'I'm Judith Packham Mr Flynn and this is Nurse Sullivan.' The nurse said indicating her colleague. 'The good news is that you have nothing to do for the rest of the day except rest.' She indicated a phone on my bedside locker. 'By the way, you are in one of the few rooms here with a telephone. So feel free to make any calls you wish. Just dial nine and you'll get an outside line. Local calls only, mind you. But I'd advise you to rest first.'

Both nurses left the room, closing the door after them. For the first time in a long while I felt totally relaxed, cocooned as I was in a comfortable hospital bed. I had plenty to worry about but for now I was going to take the medical advice I'd been given and rest. Within five minutes I was dozing peacefully. I woke about an hour and a half later, experiencing a pleasant floating feeling from whatever was in the medication. I took the phone and made three calls in quick succession. The first was to my mother to say that I had gone to Boston the night before and was staying there for the meeting with the probate lawyer that had been postponed until later that afternoon. I would stay in town until sometime tomorrow evening and I might even stay over another night. I don't think I had told her such an elaborate lie since I was a teenager. I then called the Wianno Motel and asked the male receptionist, not Joanie this time, to be put me through to cabin seven. Anni picked up the phone on the first ring. I told her where I was and in a general way how I got here. I was pleased to see that she showed genuine concern. She said she would come over there and then to see me. I put her off, told her I had things to do, not to worry but to come sometime later in the afternoon if she wanted.

My third and fourth calls were in breach of the rules as they weren't local. I spoke to a Ma Bell operator and asked to be put through to the US Senate on Capitol Hill. I then asked for Senator Mike Mansfield's office and finally for one of the interns there, my roommate, Steve McKinnon. To my surprise he was at his desk and took the call. I explained to Steve that I was on leave and would not be back in the house in Garret Park until the end of the week. I also told him that I had a visitor from Europe with me and that I might need to let her use the spare room for a couple of weeks, if he and Brad didn't object. After predicable ribbing from Steve when he heard my friend was a 'she', he said he had no problem with it and would check with Brad but didn't foresee any difficulty.

'I had some news for you on Friday buddy.' Steve said. 'I was sorry you didn't come home.'

'You had, what kind of news?'

'You remember our little chat a few weeks ago about Bobby Baker?'

'Sure I do. What about it?'

Steve's tone of voice changed to a lower register as if he didn't want anyone around him to hear. 'Well he's gone, resigned, last week, from his job as secretary to the Senate majority leader. And it looks like there's going to be an investigation into all his activities, financial irregularities, the Quorum Club, the works.'

'I don't believe it Steve. Baker's out. Couldn't he get Lyndon to protect him?'

'No, he couldn't or wouldn't. Apparently Baker got a late night call from Lady Bird, you know, Johnson's wife?'

'She's the only woman called Lady Bird any of us ever heard of, Steve. What did she say?'

'The usual stuff, Lyndon and I are right behind you, that kind of thing. Baker suspected that Lyndon was listening in to the call to see if he, Baker, mentioned anything about ratting him out.'

'You're very well informed, Steve. How do you know this?'

'Man, this place is the biggest gossip shop in the world you should know that. Scuttlebutt city, they thrive on this kind of stuff. Anyway, I do work for the majority leader. Apparently Senator Williams, from Delaware, has piled on the pressure for a Senate investigation. He has a record as a stickler for correct behaviour. He says the integrity of the Senate is at stake. And my guy, Senator Mike, is not that different. He's horrified at what he's hearing about the goings on at the Quorum Club. Mansfield doesn't approve of that kind of stuff. He's strictly old school.'

'That is news, Steve. What's going to happen now?'

'It's hard to know. Baker's resignation was a surprise. He went for a boozy lunch last Monday at the Carroll Hotel. He really tied one on, seems he told his drinking buddies that he had been abandoned by everyone, Mansfield, Dirksen, Lyndon and the entire Senate. Afterwards he stumbled in to Senator Mike's office, I saw him go in myself. He resigned there and then. The Senator tried to talk him out of it, suggested he take leave of absence, but Baker refused. He's hoping resignation will bring his troubles to an end. But Senator Williams is insisting on putting down his motion Wednesday, seeking a full Senate investigation. So, whether he likes it or not, Baker is eventually going to have to face the music. And a lot of people here in DC are worried about what he'll spill.'

'Who do you think has the most reason to be worried, apart from Baker himself?' I asked.

'No question about it Jimmy, it's got to be LBJ. Johnson's up to his neck in everything Baker was involved in. If Baker spills the beans Johnson is toast, no pun intended.'

'Thanks for filling me in, Steve. I have some news for you too, something personal, but it'll keep till I see you. Do me a favour and mention Anni's arrival to Brad, to be sure he's OK with it.'

'Anni huh? You're a dark horse Jimmy and no mistake. I'll talk to Brad, but I don't think there'll be a problem. When are you getting back?'

'I'm not sure yet, Wednesday or Thursday.'

Just then a tray with my lunch was brought by a friendly middle- aged lady. I finished up the call to Steve. I realised I was very hungry, I hadn't eaten anything since the lunch in the Red Snapper on Nantucket the previous day. While I was eating I put in a call to Herbert in the West German Embassy. I told him about my being suspended from duty at State and the reasons why. But I also told him I was still pursuing the Elsa Kircherr matter and if he ever heard anything relevant about her that maybe he would keep me informed. Typically, he had somehow heard about my suspension and wanted to assure me that he had not been responsible for providing State with any incriminating information about me. I'm not sure I believed him. If he hadn't who had? He promised to keep in touch and let me know if anything of interest came his way.

After a very satisfactory lunch I was left to myself for the first time since the assault, to ponder what the hell was going on. I thought about the night before, about Verling and Caulfied and all that had been said and done. Apart from being professionally beaten up for the first and only time in my life, I had actually learned quite a bit from things Verling had said or had left unsaid. He specifically mentioned he was looking for a document relating to someone in government. A single document, not four of them and about one person not four people. I was certain that Verling, for all his bluster, had only the vaguest idea what he was looking for. It was also clear to me that whatever investigation he and Caulfield were engaged in, was unofficial, off the record and highly suspicious. In the first place they beat me up in a public place which can't be routine practice for the FBI. Even for two goons like Verling and Caulfield. Then he told me to go to back to Nantucket and get 'the envelope.' Everything I know about criminal investigations I learned from Joe Friday on 'Dragnet'. For a law enforcement agent to leave a suspect to retrieve a piece of evidence himself and to bring it back personally to the FBI couldn't possibly be in the manual.

Then there was the sleazy guy in the Edsel, Larry. There was no way he was a federal agent unless he was so deep under cover that he had gone native. Verling and Caulfield had obviously been using him to shadow me. I don't think that would be normal practice unless they were running some kind of private operation. Verling was an SAC, There had to be plenty of agents in the Boston office he could have called on for that kind of duty. I tried to comfort myself that Verling's threats about putting me in jail were just hot air. But he was dangerous, that was obvious. He had ordered me to bring the envelope to Bureau headquarters in Washington, so he wasn't being entirely secretive about what he was doing. My musing was interrupted by a polite knock on the door and Dr Stevens came in followed by the duty nurse. Dr Stevens wasted no time with preliminaries.

'Well, Mr Flynn, you will be happy to know that your X rays have not presented us with any major surprises. You have badly fractured three of your ribs, two on the left and one on the right. And you have bruised others. That's where most of your pain is coming from. There is no permanent damage to your liver or kidneys but the bruising is as severe as I have ever seen. I'm afraid there is nothing we can do by way of any further medical intervention, except to allow the healing process to continue. You will need to drink a lot of liquids That gradually reduce the blood content in your urine, which you will have noticed is considerable. As for the ribs there is also nothing that can be done except to allow the bones to knit back over time. Given time, they will do so. You will be prescribed painkillers but I would not recommend you taking them for more than two or three more days. Of course you should be firmly strapped with bandages as you are now, to assist the process. Have you any questions, for me Mr Flynn apart from the obvious one which is usually 'When can I get out of here?''

'No, Doc that was going to be my only question.'

'I thought so. We recommend that you stay here for at least two more days while we keep you under observation. You may then be discharged but it is essential that even at home you stay still, rest as much as possible and do not do anything strenuous for the next few weeks. Do you understand?'

'Of course Doctor, perfectly. Thank you for the information and for the excellent standard of care.' I said nodding in the direction of the duty nurse.

That's what we're here for, Mr Flynn.' Dr Stevens said in a no nonsense tone but I could see she was pleased with the compliment.

She came over to the bed and plumped up my pillows for me. 'If you are feeling up to it there is a detective from Barnstable Police Department here to see you and to question you about the assault. Are you well enough for that?'

'Sure.' I said, not feeling sure at all. I hadn't decided yet how to describe the so called assault, other than I had no intention of telling what actually happened.

'Will you tell the detective to come in, Nurse Packham?' Doctor Stevens said. 'I will leave you now, Mr Flynn, she added. And I will call in to check on you tomorrow morning.'

Nurse Packham returned two minutes later with an elderly man wearing a tweed trilby hat. The detective was none other than Rob Durand, the same cop I had met with Tom Rooney the day after Klara Hartmann's murder.

'Well, Detective Durand, isn't it a small world,' I said.

'Good afternoon Jimmy. I heard your name mentioned when the notification from the hospital came in, so I decided to call in and see for myself. I believe you were attacked by three men on Ocean Street. I have to say that in all my time at Barnstable PD, I can't recall that ever happening before.'

I asked Detective Durand to sit down on the only chair in the room. He did, throwing his hat on the bed and pulling the chair closer to me. I didn't know this man but I had a gut feeling that he was what he looked like, a middle level cop close to the end of his career. He seemed trustworthy and honest. I took a decision there and then to be straight with him and hoped that in the process I might learn something. I decided to tell him everything, or almost everything, including the identity of the people who beat me up. I recounted most of what had happened to me since Labour Day leaving out any mention of the existence of KGB profiles or of Anni Hartmann. When I had finished my story, Rob Durand was quiet for a minute, clearly deciding what he could safely tell me.

'That's a hell of a story Jimmy, I'd even say it was incredible, except that I know a few facts myself which confirm some of what you're telling me. What I am about to tell you Jimmy I am telling you, not as a cop, but as someone who knew your father. I'm retiring before the end of the year and I don't want to jeopardise my pension. You understand?'

'Sure I do,' I said.

Durand took a breath before he spoke. 'As you saw that day, the Feds took over the investigation of the murder of Elsa Kircherr from the get go. We and the State Police were told from on high to butt out and leave it to them. On high being Governor Volpe's office. So we did. The shooting happened, as you know, on Saturday morning. Verling and Caulfield arrived on the Cape from Washington at 6.00 pm that same evening. They landed at the airport here in Hyannis on a small plane belonging to the FBI. That's a rapid response by any standard especially on a Labour Day weekend. When we checked out the contents of the deceased's motel room, all we found was Elsa Kircherr's name in the register, a West German passport and a bus ticket from Rock Island Ontario, on the Canada Vermont Border, to Logan Airport. We informed the Boston FBI Field Office as a matter of routine. We sure as hell didn't expect two agents from Washington to show up within four hours. I have some contacts with the Bureau in Boston and I was told that Verling and Caulfield are not your regular agents. They are both assigned to Director Hoover's office and are used solely for sensitive tasks, reporting directly to Hoover. Verling has a pretty nasty reputation, which I hardly need to tell you, is well deserved. 'He said this with a chuckle.

'That all comes as no surprise.' I said. 'Any idea who this guy Larry is?'

'Yes I know him by reputation. His name is Larry Fiuscardi, a licensed private eye, works out of Providence. Occasionally operates up here on the Cape. He has a mainly lowlife clientele. He's rumoured to be on the fringes of the mob in Rhode Island, but has never been convicted of anything. I can't understand someone like Verling using him, unless he's trying to keep things on the low down and wants to keep his colleagues out of things.'

'That's what I thought. But why would Verling and Caulfield need to do that if they're so tight with their boss?'

Rob gave me a knowing look. 'I have no doubt they're doing exactly what their boss wants them to do. The two agents may be working off the books, but probably under Hoover's orders.'

'That has to mean Hoover is working off the books too, which doesn't really make sense.' Another thought just occurred to me.

'My Friend Tom Rooney - you remember Tom, who was on Craigville with me that Saturday?'

'Course I do, I know Tom of old.'

'He separated out some people who had been standing near Klara just before the shooting. He asked one of the uniformed officers who had shown up, to take statements from them. Did you get any statements and did they throw up anything of interest?'

'Did you say Klara?'He asked, looking at me curiously.

'Sorry I meant Elsa. The statements, was there anything in them?'

'The Feds took all of the statements away'

'All of them? Did you keep copies?'

'Durand looked embarrassed. 'They wanted all copies as well. And we handed them over. But I had a chance to read them before we passed them to Boston FBI. Only one person, a woman tourist from Durham, New Hampshire, noticed anything that could be described as significant. She said that the blonde lady in the blue windbreaker was standing at the water's edge chatting with another woman. That was about three or four minutes before the shot was heard.'

'Did she give a description of this other woman?'

'All the witness said was that the woman wore a bright floral dress, a wide brimmed white sun hat and round sunglasses, like she was on the beach for the day. There was nothing suspicious about it. The witness said it was just another person enjoying the nice weather.'

'Nobody else had anything better than that?' I said.

'Nobody noticed anything until the sound of the shot and the victim fell on the sand.'

'Strange, at least three hundred people running around and no one saw a thing.'

'No, nobody saw a thing, including, you and Tom Rooney.' Before I could respond to the implied criticism, Durand changed the subject. 'Are you intending to press charges against anyone for this assault, Jimmy?'

'I wouldn't think so, would you? I'm in enough trouble as it is. I am mad as hell with Verling but he is the FBI. My Dad used to say, you can't fight City Hall. I think I'll leave it. We all have to take our licks. He used to say that too.'

'Your father was right.' He said, picking up his trilby hat from the bed. Whatever is going on, it's not for the likes of us to interfere. Not with the kinda guys we're dealing with.'

There goes a man two months away from his pension, I thought. There was no way Rob Durand was going to rock any boats. The reason he came here was to make sure that I didn't either. Just at that moment there was a gentle knock on the partially opened door, and Anni Hartmann, appeared carrying a large, expensive looking bunch of flowers. I hadn't mentioned Anni to Durand and would have preferred if they didn't meet. Intuition told me it would only complicate matters.

Fortunately Rob Durand was a gentleman of the old school. He stood up and waved Anni into the room.

'Come in, young lady, I'm just on my way out,' he said, then he turned to me. 'Good talking to you, Jimmy and best of luck with the recovery. By the way I think you're making the right decision about City Hall.'

He looked at Anni with a mixture of a cop's curiosity and male admiration. I had no option but to introduce them.

'Anni, this is Detective Durand from Barnstable PD.' I said not mentioning Anni's surname.

Anni smiled at Durand and shook his hand. 'Very nice to meet you Mr Durand,' she said, her accent was obvious and I noticed that Durand had also taken note of it. But in keeping with his policy of lying low until his retirement he must have decided to say nothing.

'Well I'll be off now and leave you two alone,' he said. Good luck Jimmy and take good care.'

When he was gone Anni came over to me tossing the flowers casually on the bedside locker. She leaned in to me taking my hand in hers while kissing me on the cheek. Did I imagine that her smooth and perfumed skin lingered there just a little longer than politeness required? She whispered in my ear.

'Oh Jimmy, what have they done to you? We must stop all this foolishness, it is far too dangerous. Let us stop now before something even worse happens.'

It may have been my imagination but the pain in my ribs and the soreness in my kidneys seemed to momentarily vanish.

CHAPTER 28

October 1963

We arrived at La Guardia Airport, New York at 12 noon, Thursday. The same day I was supposed to bring the confidential documents to Agent Verling's Washington office. The drive from the Cape to Boston and flight didn't do anything to ease the excruciating pain in my ribs. I was beginning to rely a little too much on the magic pills Dr Stevens had given me on leaving the hospital. She handed me what seemed like a very generous supply as I was being discharged the previous day but I could see now there were not many left and she hadn't given me a prescription for more because, she said, 'It's easy to become much too fond of them.'

I had been just about to leave my comfortable hospital room, having showered and dressed and thanked nurses Packham and Sullivan for taking such good care of me, when the phone rang for the only time since I had been there.

'Hello Jimmy, is that you?' A man said in a voice that was so uncannily like my father's I sat down on the bed in genuine shock.

'Yes it is.' I said anxiously. 'Who is this please?'

'Jimmy, my name is Dave Powers. Your mother spoke to my wife and asked me to call you. Have I called at a bad time?'

'No I said, not at all, Mr Powers. I'm sorry I just got a shock when you spoke, you sound exactly like my father.'

'I was very sorry to hear about your Dad's death, Jimmy. I'm afraid it passed me by. He and I were the same age. I knew him quite well when we were kids but we lost track of each other in our teens. When he was about ten or eleven Billy Flynn was the best stickball player in all Charlestown.' Powers emitted a friendly chuckle at the memory.

'How did you find me, Mr Powers? No one really knows I'm here.'

'Call me Dave please, Jimmy. I asked the White House switchboard to see if they could find you. They can locate anyone anywhere in the world. They got you in about fifteen minutes. Listen, Jimmy, I don't want to keep you. I know from your mother that you have run into a little problem with the State Department. I don't have any special influence there but I would be happy to talk to you about it. I will be in Boston Saturday the 19th, for the Harvard- Colombia game, and then at a Democratic Party fundraiser that night. I'm coming to the Cape on Sunday. I could meet with you in either place depending on what's convenient. Now that I think of it, though, I'll have more time to talk with you Sunday, because my boss will be spending the day with his father.'

'That would be great.' I said. 'Sunday will be perfect. Any preference for a place to meet?'

'Do you know the Mayflower on Main Street, Hyannis?' Powers asked.

'Sure I do. That would be perfect. There are booths there if we need some privacy. I really appreciate this, Mr Powers. Thanks for going to the trouble.'

'It's no trouble for the son of an old friend. I'm not making any promises, mind you, but we can talk. See you Sunday then. Let's say two thirty in the Mayflower. The lunchtime crowd will be starting to leave by then.'

'Sunday it is. See you then and thanks again.'

I replaced the receiver and for the first time in a while I was overwhelmed with the memory of my father. If the man hadn't said he was Dave Powers, I could have sworn it was my Dad.

Anni and I took a cab to downtown Manhattan. While I had been in the hospital she had taken care of the travel arrangements. I had suggested that we might stay in the Carlyle on the corner of Madison Avenue and East 76th. It's where we were headed anyway. It was very expensive and I had never stayed in that kind of place before but I figured it was only for one night. To my surprise and to save money, Anni booked us a double room with twin beds. I asked her if her friend Franz Walter would approve. She answered with a laugh, that as she was travelling with a man with bruised kidneys and three cracked ribs, Franz had nothing to worry about and neither did she. The Carlyle was the most expensive hotel I had ever been in. But by the time we got to our room I was in no position to enjoy it. I felt like there was an elephant sitting on my chest. I kicked off my shoes and lay on one of the beds exhausted. I told Anni I would need to rest for about an hour. She understood and unpacked both her own bag and then mine, putting everything neatly away. The thoughtfulness of the gesture combined with our proximity as she bustled about, gave me a pleasant feeling of intimacy with her. But she was right. She had absolutely nothing to worry about. I had never in my life felt more like an invalid, my ribs were hurting so bad. She told me to take a nap. She would go out and take the opportunity to look around Manhattan. It was one thirty when she left. I fell into a sound sleep and woke at three to see her sitting on the other bed, her shoes thrown casually on the floor, quietly reading a copy of Life magazine.

'So how is our patient? She asked cheerfully when she heard me groan into wakefulness.

'A little better I think, hard to tell. How was your sightseeing?'

'This city is the most amazing place I have ever seen. The scale of the buildings is truly unbelievable.' She put the magazine down before asking. 'Jimmy, have you given any thought to what we are going to do next?'

'Yes, I have. We're going downstairs to talk to somebody at reception as soon as I get off this bed and throw some water on my face. If you agree I will do most of the talking and maybe you will back me up, if it's necessary.'

'Of course, but who will you talk with and what are you going to say?'

'Leave that to me.' Let's take things one step at a time.'

She looked sceptical but said nothing. Twenty minutes later we were sitting in the Carlyle's plush lobby watching four competent, hardworking people behind the reception desk, two men and two women. I selected my mark, the oldest of the bunch, an efficient looking man in his mid forties but not yet a full blown manager. His name tag said he was RP Burns. He adopted a convincing manner of professional obsequiousness when dealing with customers but, I could see that he was a slightly bossy supervisor to his three younger colleagues. I was glad that I'd put on a necktie for the occasion and worn my work suit.

'When there was a lull in traffic at the desk, Anni and I approached. 'Good afternoon Mr Burns.' I said producing my wallet and removing my State Department business card, which informed the reader of my name, my office telephone extension number and that I was an *Analyst* attached to *Language Analysis Unit 2*. The card was all I had by way of credentials. I was relying on the vagueness of the job description to discourage any in-depth inquiry.

'I'm from the State Department, my name is Flynn and this is Miss Murchison. I wonder if you could spare us a few minutes of your time. We are inquiring about a security matter it requires a certain amount of discretion. You're obviously part of the management team here in the hotel.'

Mr Burns looked at the card. 'A security matter you say, can you tell me what this is about, Mr Flynn? If we can be of help we will certainly try.'

'Is there somewhere we can talk in private?' I asked.

Burns indicated a tiny room next to the reception desk and ushered us in. The room was about the size of a walk- in cupboard its contents consisted of a narrow desk placed against a wall and a single chair. A coat rack, with what I took to be the receptionist staff's coats and jackets hung on it stood in the corner beside the door. All three of us stood in a huddle. I produced the, by now dog eared Carlyle Hotel envelope from my pocket, and unfolded it.

'Mr Burns this envelope appears to have been mailed from the Carlyle here on May 26th. You can see the post mark here with the date clearly shown. We were wondering if you could tell us anything about the person who sent it and the circumstances in which it was sent.'

Burns took a minute to examine the envelope carefully and then surprised us with his answer. 'Well I think I can tell you who wrote the address on the envelope because his writing is familiar to me, but I would be very surprised if he was connected with any kind of security problem.'

'Really Mr Burns you recognise the writing?' I tried to sound as professional as I could but I was excited to have hit pay dirt so quickly.

Burns looked at the writing on the envelope once more. 'Yes, unless I am very much mistaken that is Raoul's handwriting, it's quite distinctive.'

'Raoul?'

'Yes Raoul Hernandez. He is one of our porters. We refer to them as Housemen here at the Carlyle. All purpose junior employees. But Raoul is also studying accountancy at New York City College and will be leaving us when he graduates next year. We shall miss him; he is one of our best employees.'

'Do you know if he was working on the date in question?'

'I have no idea, but he may well have been. At that time of year Raoul usually does a stint as night porter as his college course finishes for the summer. You don't think he is mixed up in anything we should be concerned about, do you? If so you will have to speak to our General Manager. In fact, perhaps I am not the appropriate person to discuss this with you at all.'

I was doing so well with Burns, I didn't want to lose him now. And I had no faith in my business card passing muster with the General Manager, whoever he was.

'No, Mr Burns, not at all. Neither your colleague nor the Carlyle has anything to worry about. We are just trying to confirm that the person who sent the letter was a particular State Department employee. Its contents were sensitive and it should have been sent by special messenger that's all. It's a minor breach of Department protocol. It is a potential disciplinary matter for the person concerned so I can't say anything more about it. Isn't that so Miss Murphy?' I said bringing Anni into the conversation.

'As I reminded you already Mr Flynn, my name is Murchison. Perhaps you would be good enough to remember that.'

She said this in pure American with no trace of an accent and maintained an impressive poker face with just the hint of a twinkle in her eye. I had to disguise my irritation at her jokey response. I couldn't afford lose my concentration.

'My apologies, Miss Murchison,' I said, then turning quickly to Burns I asked;

'Is there any way I could make contact with Mr Hernandez just to clear this up? I don't want to waste any more of your valuable time, Mr Burns.'

'Well you can talk to him now if you wish, assuming he's not busy. Would that be of help?'

I could hardly believe my luck. 'You mean he's here in the hotel, working today?'

'Yes I believe he is. Just wait here a moment please, I'll see if I can get him.' Burns left the little room and I immediately sat down on the only chair. My ribs were killing me. 'You don't mind if I sit down for a moment, do you Miss Murchison?' I said to Anni sarcastically. She merely laughed.

'You were the one who gave me the name after all. That man might easily have noticed your mistake. We special investigators need to be careful.'

'Very funny,' I said wincing with the pain. 'Any ideas as to what we ask this man Raoul, if Burns brings him back?'

'Why don't we start by asking how it was that he came to write this particular address on the envelope? Who did he get the address from?'

'Good work, Tonto, why didn't I think of that?'

'What is Tonto'?

'I'll tell you later.' Just then Mr Burns reappeared with a young dark haired man in a bellboy uniform. He looked to be about twenty three or so.

'Mr Flynn, Miss Murchison, this is Raoul Hernandez I have told Raoul you wish to speak to him and I have assured him that there is no question of any impropriety on his part.' Burns said.

'Absolutely not,' I said pulling myself up out of the chair with some difficulty. I shook hands with Raoul, who was a handsome guy not unlike the teen idol Fabian. 'Thanks for your time Raoul. This will only take a couple of minutes. Mr Burns, if you need to get back to work we can probably manage from here on.'

'Oh no,' Burns said quickly. 'I think for the sake of the hotel I had better stay.'

I could see that he was enjoying the cloak and dagger aspect of the drama. I handed the envelope to Raoul. 'This is what we have come about, Raoul. We are trying to ascertain the origin of a letter which was in this envelope. It appears to have been sent from the hotel. Mr Burns here thinks that the handwriting on it may be yours and if that is the case, we wondered how you came by that address and if you had any knowledge of what was in the envelope?'

Raoul gave a cursory look at both sides of the envelope but I could tell he knew exactly what it was, within a couple of seconds. 'Yes.' he said, Mr Burns is quite right. It's my handwriting and I remember very well mailing this letter, but I never knew what was in it.'

Our luck was holding. Despite his Hispanic name and dark good looks, Raoul Hernandez spoke with a pronounced New York accent. 'Can you remember who asked you to mail it?'

'Yes it was a woman, young, very attractive and very polite. I was night porter for that week. I remember it was a Saturday night Sunday morning. Things were quiet, as usual after about twelve thirty. This lady, I forget her name although I think I knew it then, came down to the lobby at about five fifteen in the morning. The place was dead quiet. She wanted to check out, but I'm not supposed to do checkouts. The desk here opens at five thirty am. Anyway I told her that as the room had been booked for her by another guest and payment in advance had already been made, the other guest could check out for her later that day.'

'What was the other guest's name?'

'Sorry, can't remember, something foreign'. Raoul Hernandez said with a shrug.

'We'll have a record of it.' Burns interjected. 'I will get the register for that month.' He left the little room to do just that.

'Did the woman say her name was Elsa Kircherr?' Anni suddenly asked Raoul.

Raoul looked at her for the first time. 'Yes.' He said. 'Yes I think that was it.'

'Have you any idea why she was leaving the hotel in the middle of the night?' I asked.

'No. But she seemed very agitated, worried about something. She was in a hurry, asked me for a large envelope and I gave her that one. We have plenty at reception for any guest who may need one. There are no large ones like that in the rooms, just the regular size along with hotel headed paper. She pulled a bunch of papers from her little overnight bag. Not a letter, a large number of stapled pages. The overnight bag was the kind we sell here in the hotel store. She put the papers in the envelope. Some night clothes came out of the bag when she pulled out the papers, she stuffed them back in. She turned her back to do it. Then she asked me if we had any stamps, which of course we do, and she asked me to make sure to put more than the correct amount on the envelope to be on the safe side. While I was doing that she was zipping up the small overnight bag. She was actually kneeling on the lobby floor doing it, so she asked me to write the address as well. While she was zipping up the bag she called out that name and address in Virginia and I wrote it down as you can see. There's a mail box for guests and residents right here in the lobby, I took the envelope over and dropped it in.'

'Did she say anything else?'

'Well she looked very relieved to see it was gone. She apologised for all the panic. She kept looking towards the elevators as if she was expecting someone to come out but no one did. She and I were the only two people around. She asked me my name and I told her. She thanked me for helping her and gave me ten dollars. We get a lot of rich people in this hotel but mostly they don't tip very well. This lady did not seem rich, though she was quite a beauty but she gives me ten bucks for writing a name and address. I was impressed.'

Burns came back in to the little room carrying a bulky hotel register and some registration cards. He placed them on the small desk. 'Yes, I believe we have the names here.' He pointed at the relevant date in the register. 'Miss Elsa Kircherr's room was booked at four thirty on Saturday 25th of May, by a Mr Maxim Simonov, a guest who had checked in himself the previous day. His room was booked by the Belarusssian Mission to the United Nations. We get quite a few UN related bookings here at the Carlyle, only for very senior government people of course. Mr Simonov checked out on Sunday morning.'

'What time did Simonov check out?'

Burns said looking at the register. 'Eleven thirty five. I see here he had also booked one of the small conference rooms we have on the second floor for a meeting. He booked it from Seven thirty to nine pm.' Meetings on Saturday nights are rare but with diplomats you never know, they seem to work irregular hours.'

'Mr Burns, I should be getting back. Do you need me for anything else?' Raoul interrupted.

Burns looked questioningly at me. 'No Raoul.' I said. You have been very helpful, thank you. Unless there's something else you think is relevant.'

'No, I just hope that lady is not in any trouble. She seemed to me to be very worried about something and she was so nice.'

I glanced at Anni and I noticed her lip trembling. 'No, Raoul, she is not in trouble any longer.' I said, not knowing how else to reply. I shook his hand and thanked him again. Anni reached out and shook his hand also, not trusting herself to say anything. Her eyes glistened with tears. I knew she was thinking of whatever terrible trouble her sister might have been in that night.

When Raoul was gone I thanked Burns for his help. He seemed disappointed that we had nothing further to ask and reluctantly closed the hotel register on the table, said goodbye and brought it back to wherever it was kept. Anni and I repaired to the very comfortable hotel bar to assess what we'd got out of the encounter. The plush Bemelman's Bar was crowded, even at that time of day. We managed to find a quiet corner and sat on two well padded chairs facing one another. I ordered a daiquiri for Anni and a Coke for myself. I wanted to stay away from booze as I was intending to dose myself with more painkillers as soon as I got back to the room. When we were sitting comfortably I said to Anni. 'You go first, what do you think happened that night?'

She took her first sip of the daiquiri before she answered. 'I think that

Maxim Simonov might be Max Korten and that somehow he, assuming it was him, managed to get into the United States to consult with her or something. Whoever it was must have given her the profiles or else she stole them. They probably studied them together in that meeting room. Some kind of crises must have occurred during that night. I don't know what, an argument, a difference of opinion or something. Klara took the profiles, mailed them to herself under her married name. I have no idea why she would do that.' She took another sip of the Daiquiri. Actually until now I had no idea Belarus was a country in its own right.'

'Strictly speaking it's not. It's one of three Soviet Republics that are members of the UN, along with Russia and Ukraine.'

'About that story Raoul just told, what do you think, Inspector Maigret?' Anni asked almost giggling. That drink must pack a punch I thought.

'I agree with you about what happened. They must have had some falling out, but I guess we'll never know what it was about. From what Raoul said, it sounded like she left in a panic and was afraid that this guy Siminov would come after her.'

'I find it so hard to hear about Klara being in trouble like that, alone and so far from home. I want to reach out and protect her, help her but of course it's too late.' Anni said in a whisper her mood suddenly sombre. After a few seconds she added. 'Jimmy, let's think about what we know. It seems to me that Klara decided to switch sides, or if you prefer to betray the Stasi. I told you she was never a Communist anyway. Why else would she take those documents and run out of this hotel in a panic? We know four clear facts. We know she went to Cape Cod to bring something to the President. We know she brought the documents to Hyannis when the President was there. We know she had already met the President sometime before that. We know she was murdered. We don't know who murdered her but I think we can say that the profiles are the key. Therefore we know why she was murdered. Do you agree?'

'I agree with all of that, I couldn't have put it better. But I don't agree that we know who did it. Look we know a couple more things. We know that the FBI also knows of the existence of the profiles, and wants to get their hands on them, and they will resort to violence. We know that Klara's husband Robert Lavelle died in suspicious circumstances not long after she was killed and the DC police are determined that his death be considered a suicide. The Kennedy administration has the most to lose if the profiles are made public. We have got to ask, have they anything to do with Klara's death? We don't know who killed Klara or why Lavelle was killed. Maybe Max Korten did follow Klara to the Cape and shoot her, but I don't think even Communist East Germany, a country crying out for diplomatic recognition by the US and the West, would go so far as to send an assassin to Washington to murder a member of the American armed forces in broad daylight.'

'You are wrong about one thing.'

'What's that?'

'From what you told me the FBI man said, they only know of the existence of one of the profiles, and we don't know which one. Also how is it that they know of one but not the other three?'

'I don't know, Anni. I've been trying to figure that out since Sunday.' I put down my Coke and noticed Anni's glass was empty. 'I have to take a shower.' I said. 'Then I need to wrap this rib bandage around my torso again, I might need some help with that.'

'Don't worry, I will help.' She said. 'I know you're a sick man. What will we do later? Do you need to rest?'

'I think I'm OK. I thought we might go to the place where Buddy Holly proposed to his fiancé. Ever heard of Buddy Holly?'

'Yes, Jimmy, even in Germany we have heard songs like 'Peggy Sue' and 'Words of Love.' Where is this place?'

'It's a Bar called PJ Clarke's on Third Avenue, not far from here. They say they serve the world's best bacon cheeseburger there.'

She suddenly stood up. 'Speaking of fiancés I think I must call Franz. He will be wondering what has happened to me. I will ask at reception how to make an overseas call.'

She walked out quickly leaving me sitting alone in the Bemelman. Fiancé, I thought. She never mentioned that Franz Walter was her fiancé. I had just been brought back to earth. I got out of from my chair with some effort and hobbled out of the bar. I was feeling depressed about Franz Walter, as well as sore. I headed towards the elevators and couldn't help thinking of another Buddy Holly song. 'That'll be the Day.'

CHAPTER 29

October 1963

We were back on the Cape by Friday evening. As arranged with Dave Powers, I arrived alone, at the Mayflower restaurant in Hyannis at 2.30 the following Sunday afternoon. It was October 20th. Earlier that day Anni took a bus to Provincetown, to spend the day in the quaint artists' colony at the tip of the Cape. During the summer season, the Mayflower relied on the tourist trade for the bulk of its business. But it was also a solid family restaurant with a loyal local clientele. As Dave had predicted, the lunchtime crowd had dwindled by that time I got there. Looking around I couldn't see anyone sitting expectantly like they were waiting for someone to join them, so I took a seat in an empty booth and ordered a soda. It occurred to me that I had no idea what Dave Powers looked like. Our brief conversation on the phone had somehow made me feel like I already knew him. A friendly waitress brought me the soda and a free copy of the Boston Globe's Sunday edition, a nice touch for a lone diner. The paper carried an article on an inside page about the resignation, two days earlier, of Britain's Prime Minister Harold Macmillan. Officially he was resigning on health grounds but it was universally accepted that he was a victim of the fallout from the Profumo sex scandal, which had consumed Britain for months. The same page carried a piece about President Kennedy's attendance at the All New England salute dinner, an annual Democratic fund raising event in Boston the previous evening. Powers had mentioned to me that he was going to be there. The article mentioned that the President had literally stopped the traffic on Boylston Street, Saturday afternoon, by jumping out of his limousine, walking down the street and going alone into Schraffts to order a butterscotch sundae. The Globe said the gesture delighted people in the street but that it was irresponsible of the President to evade his Secret Service detail if he valued his personal safety. As I was reading the report of Saturday's Harvard, Columbia game at Soldier's Field, I noticed a man in his early fifties coming in the door and removing his hat to reveal a bald head. Something about his round Irish face told me this must be Powers. I folded the paper, gestured to him and stood up. He came over gave me a friendly smile and a firm handshake. 'So you're Billy Flynn's boy.' He said. 'I can't see a likeness, but maybe you favour your mother.' The uncanny similarity to my father's voice struck me again. I immediately warmed to the man.

'I see your boss is fond of the ice cream in Schraffts,' I said

'Oh that yeah. He created quite a panic. One of the waitresses got such a shock when we walked in, she dropped her order.'

'You were there?'

'Yes it was just him and me.'

We took a quick look at the menu and both of us ordered steak and potatoes. 'This place is owned by a Greek family.' I said. But they mainly serve American food, if that's what you call it.'

'I know.' Dave said, 'Nicky and Jack Joakum, they run a very nice operation. They sometimes do a little catering at the compound.'

I had to remind myself that there was hardly anyone in Massachusetts that Dave Powers didn't know. I can't tell you Mr Powers, how much I appreciate the chance to talk to you. But I have a long story to tell and you're a busy man. Do you have much time?'

'The President is spending the afternoon with his father and is calling on some neighbours later. We don't go back to Washington until tomorrow. For once I have the afternoon off. But as I said on the phone, unless you call me Dave you're going to have to eat two rib eye steaks instead of one. By the way, Jimmy, now that I look at you closer, I can definitely see a resemblance to the Flynn clan in Charlestown.'

'OK, Dave it is. Sorry this story is so long please bear with me and interrupt whenever you feel like it.'

'Go ahead, Jimmy,' he said. 'I'm all yours and all ears.'

I told Dave the whole story, this time without any editing or redactions. Starting with Labour Day weekend and ending with the meeting we were now having. He was a good listener, but he was also curious and asked plenty of questions along the way. I told him about meeting the Attorney General and even the about the Bolshakov letter. When I mentioned the name Elsa Kircherr he raised an eyebrow. I knew he must have heard the name before. He asked for a detailed description of her and when I gave it to him I could tell he knew who I was talking about. When Bobby Baker's name came up he nodded, as if to say, everybody knows about him. I even told him about the contents of the secret psychological profiles and that I had given them to a friend for safe keeping. By the time I was finished and had answered all of Dave's questions, we had eaten our steaks and were on our second cup of coffee. Apart from the staff, the Mayflower was almost empty Dave and I being the last customers.

Powers did not look happy. 'That's a hell of a story Jimmy. I have to say I wasn't expecting all of that. I thought you were going to ask me to help with your problems with the State Department. But you're into something much deeper than I ever imagined. I have to ask you, after all you've said, what is it you want?'

'I want to find out who murdered this woman and why they did it.' I said. 'I guess I want justice for a person shot in cold blood just ten minutes down the road, which someone in government wants covered up and forgotten.'

Powers face showed considerable irritation 'I got to say my first thought is: What's it to you? Is it any of your business? Don't you want your job back? Your mother sure wants you to get it back.'

'Sure I do, Dave. I feel like I am being railroaded out of the State Department. But honestly, if it was a choice between finding the truth about this killing or keeping my job, I think I would prefer to find the truth.'

'OK, Jimmy, cards on the table here. Before I say anything further, you've got to promise that this conversation is between us and nobody else, not your mother, not your sister, no one.'

'You have my word, Dave.'

'I hope so, Jimmy, and I am relying on you. Let me explain something. I'm very low down the pecking order in this administration. My title in the White House is personal assistant to the President. Officially I am responsible for the President's schedule. My job is to see that he gets where he's going to on time, and that he is fully prepared when he gets there. It's not a high level job. I'm not a policy wonk or a security expert. I'm the first to admit that. I don't often deal with classified matters and I don't attend many high level meetings. I love what I do, but I know it won't last forever. Most of all I love working for Jack Kennedy. It's not an exaggeration to say that he and I have a special relationship. He's a great boss. He is by no means perfect. He's flawed just like the rest of us, more than the rest of us in some ways. But he sincerely wants what's best for this country and for the world. He wants peace, an end to the cold war, an end to racial discrimination and to poverty, not just in America but everywhere. What he said in Berlin in June and in his speech at the American University before that, about world peace, he means it, every word of it.'

'I can't help thinking there is a 'but' coming in this conversation somewhere, Dave.' I said.

'Yeah, well there is. Didn't some writer say that the rich are different?'

'Scott Fitzgerald, I think.'

'Well Jack Kennedy is rich, and always has been. He, his wife and most of their friends live a life that townies like me and your father never knew anything about. Their values are different from ours. So that stuff you say was mentioned in the documents, about the President, you know, women and all that: it has more than a grain of truth in it.'

Dave looked sheepish, even embarrassed as he admitted this fact. 'Was Elsa Kircherr ever one of these women?'I asked.

'I was coming to that Jimmy. The answer is no, she wasn't. Which is surprising because believe me, she was a beauty, a beauty with a sweet nature and a good heart, as far as I could tell. Although I say so myself I'm a pretty good judge.'

'Wait a minute, you knew her?'

'I met her twice. The President met her on the same two occasions. She came to the White House with Senator Chip Brewster, one evening in early June I think. As far as I know nothing occurred between her and the President, but he liked her, found her interesting and asked to see her again. He invited her to an informal lunch just a few days before we left for Europe on June 22nd. The three of us ate chowder in the family quarters, while the President quizzed her about life in Germany, particularly about life in the divided city of Berlin, what difference the wall has made and all of that. The girl was smart, she seemed to know a lot about it and the President was really pleased about the level of detail she was able to provide. He loves that kind of thing, the real story behind the headlines. Turns out she was a history buff just like him. He's curious about everything, always has been since the first day I took him on a tour of east Boston, before he ran for Congress in '46.'

'That was it, just those two meetings?'

'That was it, and no hanky panky. I walked her down from the family quarters myself that last time. But something did happen at the end of the lunch which slightly worried the President. The subject of Lyndon came up and whether he would be on the ticket in sixty four. The President was not particularly flattering about him. Elsa picked up on this and mentioned that she was in possession some very sensitive information from a very reliable source about Lyndon's financial dealings and his relationship with Bobby Baker. Of course she hadn't brought anything with her. The President assumed the information must have been something she had picked up at the Quorum Club, so he wasn't keen on turning over that particular stone. He politely declined her offer to bring him whatever it was she had. In fact he advised her to put as much distance between herself and the Quorum Club as she could. She was disappointed by his lack of interest in the Lyndon angle but, they parted on good terms. I walked her out and that was it.'

'So nobody else apart from you and the President heard her mention the profiles or the LBJ stuff?'

'No, we were the only people there. Although when I was saying good bye to her at the West Wing exit, she brought it up with me again. She said the information she had was highly sensitive. I guess the Secret Service agent on duty who escorted her out to the west gate may have heard her.'

'Wasn't a guy called Banner, was it?'

'George Banner? Maybe, I'm really not sure. But now that you mention it, I think that's right. How do you know him?'

'Just a guess. He was the agent that ushered her out of the compound the day before she was killed. She seemed to know his name.'

'Actually he's ex FBI. He transferred to the Secret Service just after the President was elected. It's an unusual thing to do because career prospects at the Bureau are far better.'

I thought of something that hadn't occurred to me before. 'Dave, does the President know she's dead?'

Powers looked solemn. 'I don't think so, Jimmy. If he does he never said anything to me. But then again he doesn't tell anybody everything. That's how he operates, everything in its own little compartment.'

The Mayflower staff were now clearing up after lunch and setting tables for dinner. They were obviously anxious for us to leave. I insisted on picking up the check and suggested to Dave that we might go across the street to a little bar on Barnstable Road called the 19th Hole, for a beer. He looked anxiously at his watch and said that he could manage just one, and then he would have to get back. We sat on high stools at the bar. I ordered two bottles of Sam Adams and Dave asked the question which must have been on his mind since we started talking.

'So these papers, Jimmy, where are they now?'

'A friend of mine here in town, Joe Davis, is taking care of them. He's a reliable guy, he'll keep them safe.'

'You can't leave sensitive stuff like that with a civilian. My strong advice to you is to get them back from your friend and give them to me. Do not hang on to them, that kind of material is dynamite. Its existence may have already killed two people. You could have been the third. Where exactly did your friend put them?'

'I don't know exactly.'

'This is very worrying Jimmy. Let me make a suggestion. I will try and get someone to put in a good word for you at State and see if we can do what your mother wants to get your job back. You get those papers from your friend and give them to me. I will make sure they're disposed of so they cause no more trouble. Once that is done my advice Jimmy is to forget about this whole thing. It can't do you any good. You're dealing with spooks here, the real deal, Well out of your league and mine. I've seen this kind of thing before. You'll never get to the end never get the answers you're looking for.'

'I notice Dave you're not advising me to hand the stuff over to the FBI.'

Dave paused and took a sip of his Sam Adams. 'Contrary to his public image, J Edgar Hoover is not a nice man, Jimmy and he is not a big fan of our President or of his family. Personally, I think he's nothing more than a professional peeping Tom. He loves secrets, other people's secrets. He has dirt on more than half of Washington and he uses it if he needs to.'

'Would he go so far as to plant someone like Banner close to the President to keep an eye on him?' I asked.

Suddenly Dave looked very worried. 'I wouldn't be surprised at anything Hoover might try. Hoover is also very tight with LBJ. They're old buddies from Lyndon's early days in Congress. So your pal Verling may very well be after that stuff because it's damaging to Lyndon, and Hoover wants to get a look at it and use it to his advantage. Or he may even be looking for it on Lyndon's behalf, I don't know. But if he got all four papers, Hoover could do a lot of damage to our team. Lyndon could too, if it turns out Hoover is doing all this for him. So no, I don't recommend giving the papers to the Bureau. Give them to me and I will see they are disposed of for good.'

'My friend is out of town right now'; I lied. I can't speak to him till he gets back later this week.'

'Oh yeah, Where is he?'

'He's sailing up in Maine.' I was becoming a better liar with each passing day.

Dave looked like he wasn't buying my story but he was too polite to make an issue of it. 'Promise me Jimmy you will contact him as soon as you can. We have to get those papers.' Then almost as an afterthought he said. 'I have no doubt you were shocked at some of what you read about the President. But let me tell you, he's a complex person but a genuinely good man. As I said, he wants three things for this country, to lift this nuclear threat off all of our shoulders, to get a Civil Rights Bill through Congress and to do something about eliminating poverty. He will do all three if he's elected next year.'

'I'll take your word for it, Dave.'

He looked away for a minute as if he was trying to conjure up a more convincing argument. 'Did you ever hear a Sinatra tune called *September Song* Jimmy?'

'I don't think so why?'

'It's the President's party piece, if you like. He sings it at every intimate family gathering. He's got quite a good voice. He sang it last week at a party for the Irish Prime Minister in the White House. A friend of the Kennedy's named Dot Tubridy sang 'The Boys of Wexford'. She did it so beautifully it had a strange emotional effect on the President. He responded with 'September Song.' It's a sad, slow ballad about the passing of time, September rolling on to November, that kind of thing. The brevity of life is a subject that's sort of an obsession with the President. He thinks he's never going to make old bones, as my Grandma used to say. It's a secret, but the man is not as healthy as he looks, and he's convinced that his life may be a short one. He wants to achieve whatever he can as quickly as he can.'

I couldn't resist a smile. 'OK Dave, you've sold me. I get it, he's a great guy. It's not just your voice that sounds like my father's. You both have the same politics too.'

Powers laughed. 'We townies, guys from Charlestown like your father and me, we're very particular about who we give our loyalty to. We don't do it lightly, but when we do it's for keeps.' Dave looked at his watch and stood up. 'Jimmy, it was great to meet you, but I have to go.' He took a business card from the breast pocket of his jacket and handed it to me. 'Listen, get hold of your friend and those papers and get them to me as you can. Call me at any of these numbers when you have them. Call me any time, day or night. In the meantime I will talk to someone about your problems with the State Department. But if you get any deeper into this mess than you already have I don't think even Dean Rusk will be able to pull you back out. Do you understand me?'

I nodded, thanked him and promised I would call him. We shook hands and Dave left. Through the window of the bar, I saw him walk to the corner of Barnstable Road and Main and hail Larry Hodges' distinctive maroon and white Packard taxi cab, a permanent feature in our town for as long as I could remember. Dave jumped into the front seat. As the cab drove away I could see him starting to chat to Larry like he was his long lost brother. That was going to be some ride I thought, two compulsive talkers in one confined space. *The President is not as healthy as he looks*, Dave had said. I could have told him that the Russians and the East Germans know every intimate detail about his poor health and had set all of it out in the profiles he is so anxious to get hold of. I regretted lying about Joe Davis to such a decent man, but I needed time to think. I went to the phone on the wall near the bathroom, put in a dime and called the Wianno Motel. Joanie answered at reception. I didn't identify myself just asked for cabin seven. Anni picked up on the first ring. I told her about the meeting with Dave and she told me about her day Provincetown, which she liked very much.

'Do you think this man will get you your job back?'She asked.

'I don't really know, Anni, except that anything he can do can't hurt.'

'Did you mention my father's situation to him? Can he do anything to help?'

I could have kicked myself. With all the talk, I had completely forgotten to mention Anni's father. 'I am sorry, Anni.' I said. I didn't get a chance to say anything about that to him. He didn't have a lot of time.'

'Oh, I see, I understand.' She sounded subdued and disappointed.

'I'm really sorry, but I will talk to him again.' She did not reply. After a long silence I said, 'What would you like to do this evening?'

'I think I will stay here and read. I'm tired after the day. I bought a book in Provincetown. The title is 'The Group' by a writer called Mary McCarthy. I think I will stay here, read it and improve my English.'

'OK, I will call you tomorrow then. I think it's about time we went back to Washington.'

'I'm sure you know what is best. Goodnight.'

She put the phone down before I could say anything else. She had a point I guess. It had never even occurred to me to think about her father, even if it was unlikely that someone at Dave Power's level could do anything to help. I was annoyed with Anni for giving me such a hard time and with myself for being so selfish. My ribs were starting to hurt again.

'JP' I said to the bar tender. 'A Jack Daniels, please. Make it a double.'

CHAPTER 30

October 1963

Dinner at the house in Garrett Park the following Thursday was a great success. Anni Hartmann was proving to be a big hit with my roommates, Steve and Brad since our return to Washington the previous Tuesday night. I had gotten used to having her to myself and was a little disconcerted to see that she quite enjoyed the company of other men and they clearly enjoyed having a pretty woman around the house. Before leaving the Cape, I had been fitted with a back brace at the hospital in Hyannis. It was a contraption similar to a woman's corset, intended to provide temporary support for my fractured ribs. It felt awkward and impeded my sitting and standing and it wasn't making much difference; the pain was still intense. To explain my injury, I told my roommates I had fallen from a bike on Nantucket. Brad was a good cook and that evening he produced a fabulous meal, a tasty chicken and pasta pie with a mixed salad and homemade garlic bread. Two bottles of Chianti were consumed in record time. Anni was full of praise for Brad's culinary skills, which he accepted graciously and which I resented entirely unreasonably. We were still at the table drinking coffee. Brad was enjoying an illicit Cuban cigar that somebody in Harvey's had given him when Steve produced a bottle of vintage port, given to him by a grateful constituent of Senator Mansfield's. He poured a glass for each of us and toasted Anni saying she was undoubtedly the most pleasant sight he had seen since moving to Washington and the most beautiful housemate he had ever had. I knew I was going to have to keep a close eye on both of these guys.

Now well lubricated, Steve was in top form. He was soon regaling the rest of us with snippets of political gossip he picked up on the Hill. It didn't take him long to get to the Bobby Baker scandal, which was now getting increasing, although still discreet coverage in the press.

"Did you guys see that the Chairman of the House Rules Committee told the Post that they are going to call Baker in and question him?' Then he added, 'I know there are quite a few in the House and Senate, wondering where this is all going to end. The formal resolution which Senator Williams sponsored says that that they want an investigation of "possible conflicts of interest or other improprieties." Of course it's the 'other improprieties' that has the press buzzing. Nobody knows what they are, but whatever went on in the Quorum Club has them salivating over the prospect of an American Profumo affair. Senator Mike's office gets a call from a journalist every couple of hours about this. But of course he doesn't comment.'

'It's not just the press that's salivating,' Brad said laughing 'It's you too Steve. You've definitely been bitten by the bug. You can't get enough of this stuff. I can't see you going back home to take the bar exams and practice law in Cheyanne or wherever.'

'That's Wyoming buddy, I'm from Montana. It's a whole other state. But you've got a point. I do find this stuff fascinating. But I can't imagine facing my old man after all he's spent on my college education, telling him I don't want to be a lawyer that I'd prefer to be a journalist or even a politician.'

'When will Baker face the music, Steve?' I asked.

'I'm not sure, but it will be soon. Senators Dirksen and Mansfield have final say on what the Rules Committee will look into. Baker has trouble on two fronts. The first is financial, in the sense that he was allegedly on the take for himself and maybe for others. The second is the Quorum Club and the high jinks at the Carroll Hotel. Of the two, not surprisingly, the press interest is almost exclusively on the second. It's also the most sensitive for the politicians. Mansfield is as straight as an arrow; I think he will be opposed to keeping anything secret or sweeping it under the carpet.'

'What if the President was involved? Brad interjected. 'Would Senator Mike let that go public?'

'How could he be involved? He was hardly hanging out Friday nights at the Carroll Hotel.' Steve said.

'No but I hear he likes female company. Waiting tables in Harvey's you hear quite a bit, nobody ever notices a waiter, it's like we're not really there. As you know the place is full of insiders. Pierre Salinger, the press guy in the White House, is a regular. He's the one who gave me this cigar. I definitely heard him tell Joe Alsop that that his boss had met this German woman Rometch, the papers are all talking about.'

Joe Alsop, I thought, one of Vern's good friends. I noticed Anni's posture stiffen at this turn in the conversation.

'I'd like to think the President of the United States does not have time for that kind of thing. Steve answered. 'Although I hear that when he was in the Senate, Kennedy, Chip Brewster and George Smathers had quite a reputation with the ladies. But they were single then.'

Still an innocent I thought, just like I was a few short weeks ago. Steve would probably give his right arm to see what Anni and I had read in the KGB profiles.

'To answer your question, Brad,' Steve said. 'Mansfield has great affection for Kennedy. So I doubt he would drop him in it. When the President visited Great Falls last month - that's Montana by the way Brad, not Wyoming - he made time to call on Patrick Mansfield, Senator Mike's father who's been ill. Nobody asked him to, but Kennedy went out of his way to call on the old man. He insisted on going to Mr Mansfield's home and he met the rest of the Mansfield family. When Senator Mike heard from the President's advance man that he intended to do that, Mansfield actually had tears in his eyes. I can't see him ever doing anything that would hurt JFK. And as far as I know Dirksen, although a Republican, also likes the Prez. So my bet is nothing in the Baker scandal will touch the White House if either of those two have a say in it, which clearly they do.'

'Spoken like a true and loyal Democrat,' Brad said, blowing his cigar smoke away from the table. Steve stood up and went round to each of us topping up everyone's port. I thought he was becoming a little unsteady on his feet.

'You've got to remember.' He said, sitting down, slurring his words slightly. 'The women that Baker was 'handling' if that's the right word, were real lowlifes. The papers call them party girls and escorts but we all know that's just newspaper code for call girls, hookers. I suspect that only the sleaziest of politicians would have anything to do with them. You'd take your life in your hands if you as much as touched someone like that.'

I glanced at Anni and noticed that her face had suddenly reddened, her mouth tightening. Steve noticed too.

'Sorry Anni.' He said. 'This is not a proper conversation for a respectable woman like you.' He looked at Brad and me as if we and not he had said something offensive. 'Maybe we should change the subject fellows?' He said.

Anni stood up from the table, poised but clearly upset. 'Excuse me please gentlemen I am suddenly very tired. Thank you Brad for a lovely meal, good night everyone, no doubt we will all speak in the morning.' She walked briskly away and upstairs without saying anything to Steve or to me, or looking in our direction.

Steve looked over at me appealingly his hands open in front of him. 'What is it Jimmy, what did I say? I didn't mean to offend her. I assumed a sophisticated European would be more open-minded.'

'Don't worry about it, Steve.' I said. 'She has other things on her mind, family problems. Don't sweat it.'

Brad was re-energised by Anni's departure. He stubbed out his cigar in a saucer on the table and turned to me, an intense and curious expression on his face. 'Now that she's gone, maybe we can change the subject. What exactly is going on with you, Jimmy? You arrive back here with a mysterious woman. You're not working and you're clearly under some kind of strain. You're wearing a back brace, and walking funny because you say you fell off a bike in Nantucket. That sounds a little like the dog ate my homework. Anni seems lovely, but who exactly is she, and what is she doing here in Washington with you?'

The question also had the effect of perking Steve up. Suddenly he wasn't quite as intoxicated as had been just three minutes before.

'Now we're getting somewhere boys. That's a great question Brad. What the hell is going on, Jimmy? Are you and Anni an item or just good friends or what?'

Both of them were now looking at me intently, waiting for my answer? I had to say something. I took a decent swig of my port before speaking.

'I'm in a bit of trouble at work and I'm restricted in what I can say. But I have been suspended and I expect to be notified of a date for a hearing of my case, shortly. Then my future in the State Department will be decided. I stuck my nose into something I shouldn't have, that's all I can tell you. There's a better than evens chance that I'll lose my Job. Sorry guys, at this point I can't tell you what it's about, the Department have warned me not to say anything and as I have already screwed up, I don't want to make things worse.'

Steve whistled. 'You're going to lose your Job? That is serious buddy, sorry to hear it. This doesn't have anything to do with that shooting you saw on Labour Day weekend, does it?'

'Yes, actually it does. The girl who was killed is Anni's sister. That may answer your question, Brad.'

'No, it doesn't, because this is the first I've heard of a shooting on Labour Day weekend. Who did you say was shot?'

I gave Brad the edited highlights of the events of Saturday August 31st and was glad that he listened but asked no questions.

'That reminds me Jimmy.' Steve interrupted. 'Someone called for you here last Friday morning. Tall guy, suit and tie, receding dark hair, said his name was Caulfield, he was not very friendly. He asked all kinds of questions about where you were, when would you get back, none of which I could answer. He said that you should call him as soon as you can. Said you'd know what it's about and where to reach him.'

'You're only telling me this now?'

'I only saw you for the first time last night. Anyway Anni's arrival distracted me, I guess I forgot.'

'Jimmy, can we do anything to help you?' Brad asked.

'Thanks Brad, there is one thing. I have a few things to do here tomorrow. Make some calls and stuff. If one of you could take care of Anni for the morning it would be a great help.'

'It's already in hand.' Brad said casually. 'I asked her would she like to take a look at the campus at George Washington tomorrow and she said she would.'

'Oh', I said trying to conceal my surprise. 'Great Brad thanks.'

'No problem buddy. What are friends for?'

'And I can take her on a tour around the Capitol anytime.' Steve chimed in. 'A lot more interesting than a run of the mill college campus. No offence Brad.'

'Thanks both of you, I appreciate it.' I said. 'Maybe I should point out to you both that Anni is engaged to a guy back in Berlin. I'll grant you that she is beautiful, but she's definitely off limits.'

Steve adopted his best Walter Brennan accent. 'As they say in my part of the world Jimmy, He's there and she's here, so frankly, her bein' engaged don't make no never mind.'

'For once I agree with my colleague from the great state of Montana.' Brad said smiling. I looked at his handsome, self-confident face and knew that of the two of them, he was the one to watch.

CHAPTER 31

October 1963

It was raining heavily on Monday evening when we got to the newly fashionable French restaurant on Cady's Alley in Georgetown, known as the French Paradox. The name is a coy reference to the facility the French seem to have for eating the world's finest cuisine but never gaining any weight. Anni and I arrived early, we were there to meet with Herbert Kluge and his fiancé Gabriella, whom I had briefly met in Harvey's on the day I first met Herbert. The calls I made on Friday morning, while Brad and Anni toured the campus at George Washington University, yielded some interesting results. I also tried to contact Dave Powers but I was told that he was unavailable as he was travelling with the President. I called Richard Powell in Arlington to ask if he knew whether Bobby Lavelle had ever met Vern Templeton and I called Joanie Marchand at the Wianno Motel to ask a question I had not thought to ask before. Had Elsa Kircherr, the guest in cabin seven, had any visitors during her brief stay prior to her death on Saturday September first?' The answer was no, and she added that no one, police or FBI had ever asked her that question. Not for the first time I marvelled at the non-investigation of the only recorded shooting of anyone on a Cape Cod beach.

Ever since that Friday afternoon when I had been blackballed from the State Department, I had wondered how the Department knew so much about my contacts with Herbert Kluge. The information could only have come from Herbert himself. I decided to go straight to the source and ask him about it. Something I had failed to do when I called him from the hospital. I called him at the Embassy and was put through. He sounded embarrassed when I asked him, straight out, if he informed on me. He said that he was not in a position to speak. I thought he was going to snub me but he then suggested dinner Monday at the French Paradox. I instantly agreed. I was reluctant to leave Anni in the clutches of either of my two over-friendly housemates for longer than was necessary, so I told him I had a friend over from Europe and would he mind if I brought her along. He said that was fine with him and would I object if he also brought his fiancé with him. This I had not foreseen, but what could I say. A meeting I hoped would clarify concerns of mine had become some kind of a cosy double date, not what I intended.

The restaurant was small and homely, its staff pretentious. They all seemed to be genuinely French or at least French speaking. The place was almost full despite it being a rainy Monday night. This time I had booked the table in my own name and told Herbert in advance that I would pick up the check. Our table was ready when Anni and I got there but neither Herbert nor his fiancé, whose name I had forgotten, had arrived. We were seated right away and offered a glass of Bas Armagnac liquor while we waited. Anni seemed nervous about meeting our two guests. I suspected that she was uncomfortable knowing that Herbert Kluge knew so much about her sister's fictional life. We had agreed not to bother mentioning that Anni was the sister of the woman who had been killed and simply to say that we knew each other from University days in Heidelberg and that she was visiting from West Berlin. The prospect of maintaining this lie was putting an additional strain on Anni but it was better than having to explain all we had found out about Klara Hartmann's activities to a foreign diplomat. I spotted Herbert's tall figure at the entrance removing his glasses to wipe the rain of the lenses and placing a wet umbrella in the stand beside the door. His fiancé was appropriately wearing a blue French beret. In contrast to him she was short, blond, athletically trim and very pretty. They were escorted to our table. I stood up shook hands with both of them. Herbert introduced Gabriella and I introduced Anni. Two further glasses of Armagnac were offered to the new arrivals, which they accepted. When the drinks were brought to the table along with menus for each of us, Herbert raised his glass as if to propose a toast, but instead he made a short but earnest speech.

'Before we eat I would like to clear the air about something which has been on my mind since I heard about your difficulties with the State Department, Jimmy. I hope I am not being indiscreet.' He looked over at Anni his glass still raised.

'My apologies to you Anni, if that is the case. When Jimmy and I met for the first time in Harvey's, we agreed that our conversation would be private. However, not very long after our lunch, my superior, Berger, the person at the Embassy with responsibility for so called 'cultural relations'- I think we all know what that really means- queried me about my meeting and its purpose. I am afraid I told him that I had met with you. I did not mention what the actual subject of our discussion was, Jimmy, merely that we spoke about foreign policy and the current political situation in general terms. I assure you, my friend that is all I said. So if anything I said to my superiors caused you any trouble, I am very sorry. If there is anything I can do to help you in your current difficulty I will be more than happy to.'

I replied to Herbert's gracious little speech, thanking him for what he said, and suggesting that we treat this evening as a purely social occasion, forget about our work troubles and any of the matters he and I had talked about at our meeting in Harvey's. I suggested that as all four of us at the table speak German, we could continue in that language for the evening. Gabriella quickly interjected that she would prefer to speak in English because it helped her improve her fluency. Naturally we agreed. Once that was out of the way, we ordered our meals and we ate with gusto. The food and the wine were excellent and the conversation lively. We talked about everything under the sun. It was a pleasant relief and by any standards great evening. Herbert was intrigued by Anni and her Berlin background. I enjoyed watching her skirt around his questions about her family and how she had apparently met me during my year in Heidelberg. I couldn't help thinking that she would have made a great spy, so deft was she at fending off Herbert's penetrating questions. I also noticed and resented, as people in my emotional state often do, how much she seemed to like Herbert and enjoyed talking to him.

Gabriella was charm itself, extremely pretty in an all American kind of way despite being European. Her golden blonde hair was done exactly like that of the actress Doris Day. Like the actress, she had the same beaming bright smile and the bluest blue eyes I had ever seen. She was clearly an intelligent woman, very well informed about American politics, and fascinated by life in Washington. She seemed to be very much in love with Herbert, looking over at him lovingly if there was a lull in the conversation or when she thought no one noticed. She told me that she had been born in Berne and raised for the most part in Geneva, in Switzerland's French speaking region. She charmed the waiters by ordering her meal and discussing the wine in beautifully modulated French. She explained that she had worked for the International Red Cross in Geneva but became bored with her home town and had sought a secondment to the American Red Cross to see something of the world outside her own small country. She was cheerful and good humoured and seemed to complement Herbert's earnest nature perfectly. We finished off an outstanding meal with coffee and desserts. Desserts creatively presented were apparently a speciality of the house.

'Oh Nanu! Apple strudel, my favourite.' Gabriella exclaimed in German, as her dessert was set down. The rest of us laughed at her enthusiasm. Anni and I both ordered some variation on lemon meringue pie, which was excellent. And Herbert made do with coffee saying he had already gained ten pounds since coming to America. The 'French Paradox' lived up to its reputation as the best new restaurant in Washington. I know next to nothing about French cuisine but even I could tell that the food was exceptional. Herbert and Gabriella had work the next day, so once I'd paid the check we didn't linger too long. We parted on the pavement in a pleasant haze of good wine and bonhomie, as though we were lifelong friends. While Gabriella and Anni were saying their goodbyes, Herbert told me that he had heard that Senators Mansfield and Dirksen had met secretly at J Edgar Hoover's house, and it had been decided that the proposed investigation into Bobby Baker's activities would be confined to alleged financial transgressions only. Inquiries into the goings on at the Quorum Club would be strictly off limits. I marvelled at Herbert's ability to obtain information about the activities of the US government that most senior American officials would have been hard pressed to get hold of. They were in a hurry to get home, so there was no time to ask him how he knew this. We agreed to talk again. He suggested a drink Thursday evening and said he would call about a venue. I gave Gabriella the customary European two kisses, and we went our separate ways. Since we dined, the rain had stopped and the temperature increased. It was now a lovely balmy evening. We strolled down Wisconsin Avenue. We were taking a taxi back to Garrett Park, expensive but essential, as we had consumed way above a normal Monday night allocation of alcohol. We passed the rows of classic residential Georgetown streets known by letters of the alphabet. It had been such a pleasant evening that in my enthusiasm I was tempted to take Anni's hand as we walked along. She seemed to read my mind and linked her arm in mine, a gesture that was friendly but could be interpreted as romantically neutral. I was more than happy to accept, whatever was intended.

'What did you think of Gabriella?' I asked.

'She was alright I suppose. You seemed to like her.' Anni said. 'I wonder why she didn't want to speak German.'

'Well she is Swiss, from Geneva. Maybe she's not that confident in German. Swiss German can sound comical.' I said.

'Didn't she say she was from Berne? It seems they say 'Nanu' there too just as Berliners do.' As we passed the sign for N Street I noticed a phone booth on the corner and realised it must have been the same one that Robert Lavelle had made his last call to Richard Powell from the evening he died. 'N Street', I said to Anni. 'This is exactly where Bobby Lavelle was just a half hour before he died. He told Richard Powell he was calling from a phone box on 'N' Street.'

I looked down the street of redbrick terraced houses. It was deadly quiet as befits an upscale residential street on a Monday night.

'I know someone who lives here'. I said. 'Let's go pay him a quick visit?'

'Jimmy, it is ten thirty on a Monday night.' Anni said, disengaging her arm from mine. We can't call on someone now. What is the matter with you?'

'Bear with me Anni, this is important and it will only take a minute.'

I marched down the street squinting at the numbers on each house. Anni followed at a distance reluctantly, irritated by my behaviour. I spotted the one I was looking for, number 3047. A light was on in one of the downstairs windows.

'This is it, Anni, come on.'

'No Jimmy I won't, I don't want to.'

I took her by the arm. 'There is nothing to worry about. This could be important. I will do the talking. You don't have to say anything.' We walked up the steps to the front door. I rang the bell which resounded as a loud chime I felt could be heard by every house in the street.

After a long wait, the door was slowly opened by Vernon Templeton III. He was wearing a beige buttoned cardigan sweater, a chequered shirt open at the neck, gray pants and expensive looking leather house shoes. He looked so different from his office persona that I almost didn't recognise him. He stared at me incredulously, ignoring Anni's presence altogether. Before I said anything, he spoke to me in a slow, subdued tone.

'I was about to ask you what you're doing here, Jimmy, but I won't bother. Your presence here is highly irregular and entirely inappropriate. I want you to leave immediately. If you don't, I will call the police. You won't be surprised to hear that they respond to calls from this neighbourhood very rapidly. Please do not say anything to me, just go. At your forthcoming disciplinary hearing, I will have to decide whether to add this particular *faux pas* to the long list of transgressions already being held against you. Goodnight and please do not say another word.'

He went to close the door, far more quickly than he had opened it. Like some frustrated door to door salesman I blocked it with my foot and spoke rapidly.

'Vern, this is Anni Hartmann, Bobby Lavelle's sister in law. I believe you know Bobby and his friend, Richard Powell. I doubt that you need to be reminded, but Bobby Lavelle was found dead just a twenty minute walk from this house. His wife, as you know, was murdered on Labour Day weekend and I was suspended from the State Department for making enquiries into her death. I can't help remembering that at our last meeting, when I was booted out of the Department, so to speak, you failed to mention that you knew Bobby Lavelle, although you mentioned him by name and his association with me. You also failed to mention that he was here in this very house, just a short time before he died in highly suspicious circumstances. I think any future disciplinary hearing might like to hear that part of the story as well, don't you? Do you still want us to leave, Vern? Or may we come in and discuss this in a civilised manner?'

I took my foot away from the door and waited while Vern absorbed what I said. His face sagged and he was suddenly a much older man. He opened the door wider and indicated with his head that we were to come in. When he had closed the door behind us he said quietly. 'First on the left, go on through.' We entered a cosy book lined den, which for some reason made me think of Sherlock's Holmes' rooms in Baker Street, but furnished with what I took to be the most exquisite early American antique furniture. Apart from a small desk and chair there was a two seater mustered colour couch facing two matching well upholstered armchairs. Vern looked exhausted but he did a surprising thing. He walked over to Anni and offered his hand.

'I am Vernon Templeton, Miss Hartmann.' He said. 'My condolences on the death of your sister, please sit down both of you. I'm sorry I can't offer you any food, my wife is out of town and frankly it's very late, already well past my bedtime.' He indicated the two armchairs and we sat. He sat facing us on the couch, a marble topped coffee table between us. Vern's good manners had not deserted him despite our falling out. It seemed like a full twenty seconds before anyone spoke. Vern looked at me and said:

'I hope you are not under an illusion that anything you may say to me this evening can influence the outcome of your forthcoming dismissal hearing. I can assure you it won't. People far more influential than I are apparently determined to see that you get what's coming to you.'

'We haven't come here to talk about me, Vern. We have come to ask about Bobby Lavelle and about his death.'

'How do you know that I knew him, Jimmy?'

First name, maybe he was thawing a little. 'You referred to him as Bobby when you mentioned him at my suspension hearing, if that's what it could be called. I didn't know it, until Anni here told me. 'Bobby' was what all his friends called him. I spoke to Richard Powell and asked him if he or Bobby knew you. He confirmed that you did and in fact that you were all members of the same private club in Alexandria, the Albemarle.'

'Did he tell you what kind of club it is?' Vern asked quietly, his eyes avoiding mine, staring at the bookcase behind me.

'Not specifically, no, but it's not hard to guess. I know the Albemarle Hotel was a haunt of Oscar Wilde's in London in the 1880's.'

Vern's face was impassive. 'Yes, I've always been something of an Anglophile as you know.' He said.

'Vern, I have no interest in sticking my nose into your private life. Whatever clubs you're a member of is none of my business. What Anni and I would like to know is what Bobby Lavelle was doing here the evening he was killed, and who was he meeting?'

Vernon was silent for a moment. He suddenly stood up and walked over to a circular side table arrayed with a variety of bottles and glasses. 'Would you like a drink, my dear?' he said addressing Anni.

'No thank you, we have just had dinner.'

'Jimmy, will you join me in a scotch and soda?'

'Yes Vern I will.' I said. I was not sure whether the wine at dinner had given me a taste for alcohol or I was stressed by the tension in the room. Either way I suspected things would go better with a drink. Vern took some time preparing the drinks, handed one to me in a crystal tumbler and resumed his seat on the couch. 'Are you quite sure my dear? I have quite a selection,' He said to Anni.

'I am certain, thank you.' She said.

Vern looked at both of us in turn for a moment before speaking. 'I am in a position to provide you with some information relevant to your inquiries although why you, Jimmy, persist with all this I do not know. If you wanted to destroy your career you have certainly gone right way about it. What I have to say may be helpful or it may not. But despite your implied threat, I'm quite happy to say nothing at all, to take the consequences and allow you to stew in your own juice, as it were. I will speak to you here and now on a number of conditions. If you agree to abide by them then I will tell you what I know. If you don't, you might as well go home now. Do you want to hear my conditions?'

Before I could say anything, Anni spoke up. 'Yes, of course we do, Mr Templeton she said. Any information that might help us find out who murdered my sister is helpful.'

She spoke in a quiet sympathetic tone which had the effect of putting Vern visibly at this ease, although that may have been helped by the whisky.

'Please call me Vern, everybody does. I am sorry, but in my anxiety I have forgotten your own first name.'

'It's Anni.'

Vern raised his glass to her. *Prost, Gnädige Fraülein.* Welcome to my humble home.' Like everybody else, he seemed to have taken to her.

'You were saying about your conditions, Vern.' I said.

'Yes I was. You see, I entered this profession with the specific aim of becoming an ambassador to a nation of significance on the world stage. I still retain that ambition. Therefore, my first condition is that anything I may tell you now is off the record and I will deny I said it if it is ever attributed to me.'

I was about to reply when Vern held up his hand. 'Please don't say anything until I am finished. I will say only what I have to say and no more. I am not interested in any supplementary questions and I will not accept any. Furthermore, what I may say about my private life is all I am going to say. If either of you attempt to dig any deeper I will terminate our conversation and you can both be on your way. Are you willing to comply with these conditions, and give me your word that what I say will not go beyond the four walls of this room?'

I was reminded of almost the same speech Joe Davis had made to me sitting on the beach on Labour Day. Anni answered immediately. 'Yes of course we are. We will respect your confidences and will not betray your trust.'

'Thank you.' He looked at me. I nodded my agreement.

'Good. Well then sit quietly, listen carefully and don't interrupt.' He took another sip of his whisky and soda before he spoke.

'In my idealistic youth, like many of my generation, I flirted with left wing politics. I attended a small University in western Massachusetts at a time when fascism was on the rise in Europe. I was vehemently opposed to fascism. It's a familiar old story, shared by thousands of enlightened people at the time, so I won't labour it. When I joined the diplomatic service in '39 I did almost three years of home duty before I was posted overseas, first to London and later to the US Consulate in Istanbul. While in Istanbul in the spring of 1944, I was, shall we say, seriously compromised. You don't need to know the circumstances but the effect of my being compromised meant that I was vulnerable to, I suppose blackmail is all it can be called with any degree of accuracy. I was never an agent of the Russians mind you. I was, what is known in the espionage business, as 'a confidential contact.' Very occasionally, since that time, I have been asked to perform some small and relatively unimportant service for the Soviet Union. I should remind you that at the time I agreed to this arrangement, the United States and the Soviet Union were firm allies in the fight against fascism.

In retrospect, I was perhaps a little too easily persuaded to agree to cooperate. I can honestly say that in all my subsequent years I was asked to perform very minor services maybe three or four times. I was never asked to spy, *per se,* to copy documents, to betray a colleague or to reveal secrets or to do anything important. I never would have, had I been asked and I never did. I merely ran the occasional errand.' Vern looked over at Anni. 'As Jimmy already knows Anni, I was a member of the American delegation at the Yalta conference in February 1945. Shortly prior to the conference I worked closely with a well known State Department colleague, Mr Alger Hiss. We travelled to Yalta together and became good friends thereafter. Sorry, Jimmy, but the last time we discussed Hiss, I misled you as to the closeness of my acquaintance with him. In fact I knew him quite well. When Hiss was accused of being a Communist in the late '40's and ultimately forced out of the State Department, I also found myself under suspicion, I presume because of our professional association. As everybody in State knows, from that time on, my career, which, until then, had been fairly impressive, began to fizzle out. Apart from a two year period seconded to the FAO, the UN food and agricultural agency, in Rome, I was never given another foreign posting. Agriculture, as you may imagine, is hardly my cup of tea. When I returned to Washington, I was given responsibility for an eclectic bunch of unimportant departmental activities on the home front, which no one else could be found to manage. No offence Jimmy.'

'None taken.' I said, wanting him to hurry up and get to wherever this story was going. Vern paused, still avoiding eye contact and stared into his cut glass whiskey tumbler like a fortune teller looking into a crystal ball. When he spoke again he seemed to be talking to himself as if there was no one else in the room.

'The truth is, because of my tenuous association with the Soviets, I simply did not have the confidence, or perhaps the courage, to challenge the fact that I was clearly being sidelined at State. I didn't know whether my exclusion was solely because of my friendship with Hiss or because there was a suspicion in the Department of my predicament since Istanbul. I didn't have the courage to challenge my superiors and risk bringing it all into the open.'

Vern stood up, went over to the drinks table and made himself another whisky and soda. He poured a bottle of ginger ale into a tall glass, threw some ice into it, walked over to Anni and handed it to her.

'Just to have something in your hand my dear. Jimmy, a refill?'

'No thanks, Vern.'

He resumed his seat on the couch. The balm of confession seemed to be working its magic on him. He had looked like a hunted animal when we came into the room. He now gave the impression of a distinguished public servant reminiscing with old friends about the vagaries of his career. He resumed his narrative.

'Until a month ago I hadn't heard from anyone in the Soviet sphere since 1956. I was hoping they were gone for good. But a few days after you and I spoke Jimmy, I was contacted by an agent called Kosenko from the Belarusssian Mission to the United Nations, in New York. He called me and asked me to meet him the following weekend. Appropriately enough, he suggested Mount Vernon as a location for a rendezvous.' He said this with an ironic smile. 'Kosenko was pleasant enough initially. We did the tour and he seemed genuinely interested in George Washington and his life. Outside in the gardens we sat down and he asked me, or more accurately, instructed me to invite Bobby

Lavelle here to my home for a meeting on a specific date. I did not have to do anything else, merely had to provide a venue for a meeting for about half an hour. I was not to mention to Bobby that a third party would be present. I was simply to say that there was something I needed to talk to him about and ask him to come to my home. If Bobby agreed to come, the agent and he should be given a private room to chat. And I was to withdraw, although there was no objection to my staying in the house. That was it, and that is what I did.

Bobby arrived first, at about 6.45 on the evening of October first. The agent he was to meet arrived less than two minutes later. They spoke right here in this room. I was across the hall in the living room staying well out of it, as I had been told to. I did not hear any of the conversation and when I heard the front door close, I realised that they had both left. I looked out of the window but could not see either of them. That was it all of it. That's exactly as it happened and there's nothing more.'

Although I had been told to keep quiet, I could not resist one question. 'You are sure that Bobby and Kosenko left together?'

'The agent who came to the house wasn't Kosenko. He merely set it up. He had told me Lavelle was to meet with a colleague of his. A day or so later I called a friend, a member of the Albemarle, who knows Bobby and Richard very well. He told me that Bobby had committed suicide by drowning himself in the canal right here in Georgetown that Monday evening. I could not believe what I was hearing.'

Suddenly Vern put his left hand to his eyes and began to weep. I sat there helplessly staring at him. Anni rose from her seat walked over to him, took the whiskey tumbler from his other hand, put it on the coffee table. She placed her hand tenderly on his heaving shoulder. Within a minute or two Vern had regained his composure. He stood up, wiping his eyes, nodding his thanks to Anni and said. 'Perhaps you would both go now. I have nothing more to say and it is getting late.'

I knew there was no point in asking him any more questions. He walked us out to the foyer without a word and opened the door. Anni walked out first kissing him lightly on the cheek. At the door I stood beside him and offered him my hand, unsure whether it would be accepted or not. Vern had never been a handshake kinda guy. In fact he was the sort of person who does not like to be touched at all. But he took my hand and shook it firmly like a politician looking for a vote.

'Our positions are suddenly reversed Jimmy.' He said in a quiet voice. 'Now my fate is in your hands. Please don't renege on your promise of discretion. May I ask you how you knew that Bobby Lavelle was in this house on October first? Did Richard know?

'No, he didn't, and neither did I. I noticed you were not yourself when you and Elliot Markham met me that day, and you haven't been ever since.   Richard confirmed to me that you knew him and Bobby quite well. They spoke to each other the evening he was killed, from the phone booth at the end of this street. I simply had a hunch that you knew something about it and you have now confirmed it.'

Vern merely nodded. 'Very impressive Jimmy, at the next hearing in connection with your suspension, I assure you I will say as little as possible unless it is likely to be of help to you. It's all I can promise. Goodnight and goodnight Anni, it was a genuine pleasure to meet you.'

'Good night Vern'. She said in a prim voice. 'Thank you.'

He silently closed the front door. We hailed a cab on Wisconsin Avenue and headed back to Maryland through the empty still wet streets of the capital. I asked Anni; 'What did you think of all that?'

'I was sorry for him. I think he is a sad and lonely man.' She said.

'Yes, he is certainly that.' I said. 'But is that all he is?'

CHAPTER 32

October 1963

At ten o'clock the following morning I drove my Dodge down the leafy lanes of McLean in Virginia. FBI Agent Caulfield was in a car right behind me making sure I got safely to my destination. Earlier that morning two unexpected events occurred in quick succession. At eight thirty, a courier arrived at the house in Garret Park with an official letter addressed to me from the Department of Justice. I read it at the doorstep, rubbing sleep from my eyes, while the government courier waited to see if there was a reply. The note typed on Department of Justice headed paper comprised a single paragraph, it read:

Attorney General Robert F Kennedy requests that you to meet with him this morning at 10.30 am at his home at 1147 Chain Bridge Road, Mclean Virginia, with regard to matters previously discussed with him on October 1st 1963. If you are unable or unavailable to attend at that time, please inform the bearer of this communication or call the undersigned.

Signed: EM Fitch

Personal Secretary.

I told the courier that there was no reply and that I would comply with the request contained in the note. By the time I had showered and shaved but before I could have breakfast, there was a further call at the door. This time it was the unwelcome presence of Agent Caulfield, minus his superior Verling but accompanied by another FBI agent, who was not introduced. Caulfield didn't beat about the bush. He had come to ask me for 'the document' that had been the subject of discussion with Agent Verling some time ago and to take me into custody if it was not forthcoming. I told him I had no such document. He then asked me to accompany him immediately to FBI Headquarters.

'I'm sorry Mr Caulfield, I'm afraid I can't do that', I said.

He didn't miss a beat. 'If you refuse this request Mr Flynn, We are authorised to use force to compel you to come with us.'

'I'm sorry, but I have other business to attend to. I have a meeting this morning with the Attorney General, who I believe is your nominal boss, Agent Caulfield. I don't think he would want me to be late, do you?'

Caulfield, still standing at the doorway, hesitated for a moment before saying, 'if that's true, and somehow I doubt that it is, I will drive you right now to Justice, to be sure you get there in time for your meeting.'

'I'm not meeting him at his office. I have been asked to go to his home.'

Caulfield's frustration was obvious, but he was unsure what to do. He pushed the front door open and walked into the foyer. The second agent followed in his wake.

'Where's your phone?' he snapped.

I indicated the phone, which in this house usually sat on the little used dining room table. Caulfield made a call while the other agent and I stood there without speaking. Caulfield turned his back to us and spoke in a mumble to whoever he called. I had little doubt that it was Verling. After listening in silence for about a minute, he replaced the receiver with bang and turned to me.

'When are you having this meeting?'

'Ten thirty this morning, I intend to leave as soon as I have breakfast.

'Forget breakfast. Let's go now.' He said looking at his watch. 'We will follow you all the way. Believe me, I know where the AG lives, so don't deviate by as much as an inch. There will be hell to pay if you're making this up, Flynn.'

'Sounds like a waste of time to me, but hey, I just need to get some papers upstairs, then I'm ready to go.'

I ran upstairs, quickly told Anni what was happening and that I had no idea how long I would be. When I pulled the white Dodge out of the driveway five minutes later, the black FBI sedan driven by the anonymous agent, with an alert Caulfield riding shotgun, took up its position right behind me. About forty minutes later I had found Chain Bridge Road in McLean. Number 1147 was a tall white nineteenth century stone house, built on a hill and surrounded by two or three acres of woodland. There was a regular mailbox with the name Kennedy on it and the name Hickory Hill was displayed on the gatepost. The gate was wide open and there was no sign of security or any police presence. I drove up the long driveway. In my rear view I could see Caulfield's black sedan stop at the gate, the two agents watching me head towards the house. When I had parked and walked towards the front door, I could see that the FBI vehicle was no longer at the gate. They had accepted my story but I knew it would only be a temporary reprieve. I rang the doorbell. A woman in a maid's uniform, with a strong Irish accent, opened the door and invited me in. The house was large but not elegantly furnished. It had a comfortable lived in feel to it. with evidence of childrens' presence to be seen wherever I looked. Tennis rackets, footballs, swimming trunks and similar debris were scattered about. The maid showed me into a relatively small dining room for such a big house. On the dining table was an ancient looking heavy black typewriter with Cyrillic keys, a yellow lined legal pad, a copy of the Oxford English Dictionary, a Russian/English dictionary and a copy of Roget's Thesaurus.

'Mr Kennedy will be with you shortly, Jimmy,' the maid said familiarly, the way people from Ireland often do, particularly if you have a name like Jimmy Flynn. I thanked her and sat at the dining table and waited. I couldn't help thinking about all I had read in the KGB profiles since our last meeting about the young Attorney General. He was portrayed in the documents as the conscience of the new frontier, the indefatigable defender of his brother's reputation and of his entire family. He was certainly instrumental in the deportation of Ellen Rometch and presumably of Elsa Kircherr too. The profiles said he was a man who had a prickly relationship with FBI Director Hoover and hated Vice President Lyndon Johnson with a passion, because he believed he had blackmailed JFK in 1960. Kennedy's hatred was reciprocated by Johnson, who believed that the Attorney General was secretly behind the investigation of Bobby Baker's activities, in order to discredit Baker's former patron, Johnson himself. These were the thoughts going through my mind when the Attorney General, wearing a gray business suit, white shirt and narrow striped tie, suddenly came into the room.

'Good morning Jimmy. Nice to see you again, thank you for coming at such short notice.' He said.

I stood up momentarily startled. 'Hello sir. Good to see you again.'

'I thought I was going to have time to stick around this morning and go over this letter with you. But I'm afraid something urgent has come up and I have to go to the office. It looks like I'll be tied up for most of the day.'

He took a neatly folded sheaf of paper from the inside pocket of his jacket and laid it on the table. This is my reply to Georgi Bolshakov. I would like you to translate it as best you can, it's not very long. Who was it who said, I apologise for writing such a long letter but I didn't have time to write a short one?'

'I think it was George Bernard Shaw.'

'Whoever it was got it right. This took me a long time and many drafts, but in the end I decided just to keep to the essentials. I am also worried that the whole thing could be KGB provocation to get me to make potentially embarrassing revelations. We can't be certain who wrote it. So I have kept things fairly non-committal. I intend to send both versions to Bolshakov, your translation and my original. Please don't let either copy out of your hands. When you're finished call my wife- she's around somewhere and knows you are here- or have one of the maids get her but give both versions to her. My advice is to get it done before our kids get home from school. It's impossible to work in this house once that whirlwind comes through.' he said smiling.

He shook my hand. 'Thank you again. I hope you remember that this is a personal letter, just between Bolshakov and me. Let's keep the State Department well out of it.'

Obviously he had no idea that I was no longer on speaking terms with the State Department. When he had gone I was left standing in the dining room alone. I closed the door, sat at the table and picked up Kennedy's reply. It was typed very professionally on domestic headed paper bearing the names and private numbers of Robert and Ethel Kennedy, Hickory Hill, Virginia. The entire letter took up only a single page. I began to read.

My Dear Georgi,

It was so good to hear from you after so long. I hope you have adjusted to home life after your stay here in America. I greatly miss our regular meetings and the many stimulating conversations I had with you and so enjoyed. Thank you for your letter and for your summary of the current political situation. I have discussed it with the President. You can be assured that the administration here will do what it can to make political life easier for your Chairman and for the elements within your government who are supportive of creating a new relationship between our countries based on mutual respect and increased understanding.

Last year's Cuban settlement, for which you personally deserve a great deal of the credit, and this year's Nuclear Test Ban Treaty have had the effect of reducing tensions between the Soviet Union and the United States to a level unseen since 1945. This new reality allows us all to move forward. As I think you know, the President regards the lessening of international tensions between nations with nuclear capabilities, to be the paramount aim of his administration's foreign policy. I believe his future policy in respect to Vietnam will be seen to reflect the reality of our new relationship. I don't expect that you will see any significant build-up of US military advisers in that country in the years to come.

If there is anything the administration can do to be of practical help to you, please let me know. I would very much like to keep this line of communication between you and I open.

The President sends his warm personal regards to you and your family, as of course, do Ethel and I. I hope it won't be long before we meet again face to face. Until then, take care of yourself and keep in touch. I found your letter to be insightful as well as informative. I hope it will be the first of many more.

Yours very sincerely

Bob.

I was a little disappointed with the letter and its contents. It bore all the hallmarks of bureaucratic caution in response to Bolshakov's original letter which was open, honest and even indiscreet. The personal references in the reply were formulaic, lacking any genuine warmth. Someone must have advised Kennedy to be careful. That maybe the original letter had not come from Bolshakov at all. Was there a suspicion that maybe someone in Moscow is trying to wheedle similar indiscretions from the AG. Either way it wasn't my business. All I had to do was translate it into Russian. Judging by its blandness, its length, and its lack of subtlety, it wasn't going to be a particularly difficult job. I sat down at the table and began the task. Within an hour I had a version I was satisfied with. I typed it out one final time on the Russian Cyrillic typewriter and pinned it to the back of the English language version. I placed it in the envelope left on the table for that purpose. By way of a souvenir, for no particular reason, I took a spare copy of the high quality personal headed paper, which was lying on the table, folded it and stuck it in my inside pocket. I went out of the room to look for someone to give the translation to, wondering how this letter was going to be delivered to Moscow. Out in the yard, which was more like a big field, there was a young woman throwing a stick for a large dog to fetch. The dog was some kind of Pyrenean mountain dog or St Bernard. I walked through the French doors and out to the yard. The woman on closer inspection wasn't as young as I thought. I told her I had something to give to Mrs Kennedy.

'You must be Mr Flynn.' she said. 'Mrs Kennedy is out for a short while. She told me you would have something for her husband. I'll take it from you if you like. I'm Emmaline Harper, the children's nurse.'

I handed the envelope to her. I'll see myself out.' I said.

Forty minutes later I pulled into the driveway of the house in Garrett Park. There was no sign of the FBI car. I knew it was only a matter of time before Caulfield would show up again. I noticed Anni standing at the open door waiting for me to come in. I could tell by the look on her face that something was wrong.

'What's up?' I said as I came into the house.

'It's that girl from the motel in Hyannis, Joanie. She called, said she wanted to talk with you urgently.'

Joanie? That is strange. How did she know where to find me? Did you ask her what it's about?'

'Yes but she said she will only speak to you. She sounded strange. Not as friendly as usual. I think she was surprised I answered your phone. She wants you to call back as soon as you can.'

I picked up the phone and dialled the number for the Wianno Motel which by now I knew by heart. While I waited for a reply I looked at Anni's anxious face. 'Don't worry.' I said. 'It's only Joanie, it can't be that bad.'

She took quite a while to answer, and when she did she sounded out of breath. 'Hi Joanie, it's Jimmy Flynn. You were looking for me.'

'Oh Jimmy it's you. Have you heard the news?'

News? No I haven't heard the news, that's why I'm calling. What's happened?

'It's Joe Davis, Jimmy. He's a friend of yours right?'

'Joe? Yeah sure what about him?'

'He's dead Jimmy. He's been murdered, in his house on Owen Street.'

I couldn't speak for about five seconds. 'Murdered? How do you know this Joanie?'

'Everybody knows it, it's all over town.'

'How did you know he's a friend of mine?'

'Because he called here Saturday looking for you and that German lady you used to visit. I think that was her who answered your phone today, am I right?'

'What did Joe want, Joanie?' I said, ignoring her question.

'He wanted to talk to you. He seemed worried and was kinda sore that you weren't around. He had already been to your Mom's house and your sister's in Falmouth.'

'Do you know when he was killed?'

'They think Sunday night. He was shot in the back of his head. But his body wasn't found until last night. Joe's sister Beth, the one who lives in Harwich, called in and found him. His entire house was ransacked, drawers opened, clothes thrown around, even the attic was open and stuff pulled out. But it was worse than just murder, Jimmy.'

Joanie started to cry. I tried to get her back on track but I just had to wait it out.

'How do you mean worse?' I said when she calmed down, my voice trembling a knot of anxiety gripping my stomach.

'He was kind of tortured, Jimmy, before he was shot, hurt real bad they say. Whoever did it wanted to hurt him. They did something to his hands. That's all I know.'

I was so stunned by this news I couldn't think of anything to say.

'Thanks Joanie. I said finally. It was real good of you to call me. This is the worst thing I ever heard in my life, but thanks for telling me.'

Joanie's response before she put the phone down was a tearful whimper. 'You're welcome Jimmy, bye.'

Anni looked at me with something like fear in her eyes. 'It's something very bad, isn't it?'

'Yes.' I said. As bad as it gets.'

I took out my wallet and removed the business card Dave Powers had given me. There were three different numbers listed. I called the first of them and Dave himself answered straight away.

'Hello Dave, this is Jimmy Flynn. I have got some bad news. My friend, who was holding the items we discussed recently, has met with a serious accident. I'm afraid he's dead. It's possible that the items we talked about may now be gone. My friend's house was broken into. I suspect whoever broke in was looking for those items.'

There was a long tired sigh on the other end of the line before Dave spoke. 'Jimmy, I expected you to get back to me a long time ago. I was very disappointed not to hear from you. It's a week last Sunday since we spoke. I simply couldn't wait any longer, in view of the sensitivity. So I spoke to a colleague here in the White House about the matter. I remembered you mentioned the name Joe Davis. It was easy to get his address. We arranged for a trusted senior officer in the Massachusetts State Police to call, unofficially, on your friend Mr Davis, to retrieve the documents. He called to him Friday, but Mr Davis said he would not hand anything over until he had spoken to you. Obviously he failed to reach you. When did this tragedy happen?'

'I think Sunday last. He spoke to someone I know on Saturday, but was dead by Sunday. They didn't find the body until yesterday. I have to ask you, Dave, would somebody in the administration have had anything to do with this?'

Powers sighed again. 'Jimmy, I am very disappointed that you would suggest such a thing. The answer is no. So now these very sensitive and damaging documents are in someone else's hands. If they are, believe me, they will become public knowledge sooner or later.'

'I'm sorry Dave. I don't know what to say. But maybe Joe held out. Maybe he didn't tell his killers where he put them.'

'I think that's highly unlikely, don't you. Do you know where he kept them?' Dave asked.

'No, he never said'

'Jimmy, the administration may fall if this stuff is made public. At the very least it's certain we won't win in '64. I'm sorry, but I really can't help you anymore. We in the administration will have to pursue the matter ourselves. I will repeat what I said to you when we last spoke. Keep your nose out of this. You have caused enough trouble. Your government career is certainly over. Whatever you do now, do not, under any circumstances, involve yourself in the matter of these documents again. Have you got that?'

My father's voice rang in my ears. 'Yes, I understand.' I said.

'Good.' Dave said more in sadness than in anger. 'I guess we won't be speaking about this any further. Goodbye Jimmy.'

He hung up. Anni was sitting at the dining room table, her hands clasped over her mouth, her eyes wide with anxiety.

'Your friend, the one you gave the papers to, he's dead?'

I nodded as tears came involuntarily to my eyes. 'He's dead.' I said. 'And I killed him as surely as if I shot him myself.'

'What are we going to do now?'

I sat down myself, suddenly exhausted. Heartbroken over the death of an innocent man, a friend I had knowingly placed in danger.

'If we stay here, Anni, I am certain I will be arrested by the FBI within a couple of hours. I can't let that happen. Let's get out of here right now. We're going to a funeral.'

CHAPTER 33

November 1963

Joe Davis's funeral took place at St Andrews Episcopalian Church in Hyannis Port, Saturday November second, a cloudy gray day with rain threatening. The little stone clad church on the small hill above the ocean stood out in contrast to the timber and clapperboard houses surrounding it. The church was packed to capacity and about thirty or forty people stood outside. Quiet and introspective Joe Davis was more popular than he ever knew. This show of genuine affection for him only magnified the guilt I already felt over his violent death. As far as I knew, Joe himself was never conventionally religious, but his sister Beth was and she had made all of the arrangements. Although Beth lived ten miles away in Harwich, she had chosen the church in Hyannis Port because of her brother's long association with sailing and the yacht club nearby. I was distraught at the funeral service, something which surprised those who noticed me. It was common knowledge in town that before he was shot, the fingers on both of Joe's hands had been crushed with a heavy object. Whoever did this to him knew that a man who made his living with his hands would barely survive if he couldn't use them. Everyone, including the police, assumed that the intruders caused the injuries in order to steal Joe's cash or other valuables. I alone knew what they were after. How casually I had put this man in danger, without once thinking of the consequences.

Anni and I had left the house in Garrett Park within twenty minutes of my conversation with Dave Powers that Tuesday. Before we left I made a quick call to Herbert Kluge to tell him a friend had died and that I had to attend a funeral and cancel our planned meeting for Thursday. I left an uninformative note for Brad and Steve, saying simply that we were going out of town for a couple of days. We threw our bags into the Dodge and drove north, stopping at a hotel in Danbury Connecticut that night and another one in a little town called, Rehobeth outside Providence, the following night. My back brace was killing me with each successive mile. I couldn't drive through the night. We felt like a pair of desperados, an updated Bonny and Clyde, sticking to secondary roads and avoiding the main highways, part of me wondering if I was I was being melodramatic thinking that the Feds were that interested in a nonentity like me. But when I thought of Joe, the third person connected to this event to be murdered since Labour Day weekend and my own violent run in with Verling and Caulfield, I knew we couldn't be too careful.

Anni's and my relationship was as chaste as that of Clarke Gable and Claudette Colbert in 'It Happened One Night.' We took separate rooms in both of the small hotels we stayed in. As we crossed the state line from Rhode Island into Massachusetts Thursday afternoon, I raised the issue of our accommodation in Hyannis.

'How would you like to stay in my mother's house for the next couple of days? We'd save a few bucks.' I asked casually. Her answer took me completely by surprise.

'Jimmy, I would prefer to stay in the motel just as before. I will pay myself, of course. I still have some money and you have been paying for everything. But I don't want to complicate things any more than we have to. I think it is time for me to return home. We are not getting any closer to knowing who killed Klara and we seem to be getting into more trouble. The next person to die might be you. We must stop all of this.'

'Are you serious?'

'Yes, of course I'm serious. I made a call to Franz in Berlin from that little hotel. I told him I would come home in the next week. You have been very good to me, but you must admit that neither of us knows what we are doing and it is getting dangerous. I have to agree with that policeman who came to you in the hospital. We will never get to the bottom of this. The waters are too cloudy. The truth about Klara's death will never be clear.'

I was so disappointed to hear this that we barely said ten words to each other until I pulled the car into the car park of the Wianno Motel less than an hour later.

When the funeral service was over, Joe's body was taken for burial to St Francis Xavier Cemetery, not far away in Centerville. Anni and I and a small group of others, Joanie Marchand included, accompanied Beth and her husband to the graveside. Afterwards, as arranged, many of the mourners gathered at the Hyannis Port Golf Club, right next to the church for canapés and coffee, and to hear people paying tribute to Joe. The occasion left me numb with grief, knowing that I had played an unwitting part in the untimely death of a fine man. The final few words were spoken by Beth, Joe's sister, who thanked us all for coming and for the warmth of the tributes paid to her brother. She mentioned his love of sailing and of his pride in the restoration of his cruiser 'Hasty Pudding' which had been left to him all those years before by Thurston Bennett. A knowing chuckle went around the room at the mention of the late eccentric Thurston, a legend of the Hyannis sailing community. As Beth spoke, it suddenly hit me where Joe was likely to hide something where he thought no one might find it. '*I know just the place to keep it,*' he had said the night I gave him the envelope. I looked over at Anni who was listening intently to Beth's tearful words. I took her arm and ushered her towards the door.

'I have an idea where Joe may have hidden the documents, assuming they weren't found by whoever killed him,' I said. 'It's not far, come with me.'

We went out the club's front door only to see agents Verling and Caulfield get out of a black sedan in the little car park just a few yards in front of us. I saw Caulfield stopping at my Dodge and checking the license plate. I pulled Anni back into the clubhouse and into a small sitting room off the vestibule marked, 'members only'. It was only a matter of seconds before the two FBI men came in the main entrance and walked briskly passed us, into the function room, where the funeral party was still gathered. When they had passed by, we slipped out of the clubhouse door and down the steps. I left my car where I had parked it. If Verling spotted it on his way out he would assume I was still there.

It was a ten minute quick walk to the little archway which marked the entrance to the yacht club. I knew the place as well as I knew my own back yard. We walked along the beach, past Ambassador Kennedy's house and the stone breakwater, and towards the long wooden jetty. The clouds were low, heavy with moisture, the day was cold and the harbour almost deserted. The only sound was the tinkling of the metal halyards against the masts of the moored sailing boats. I ran along the jetty, Anni following in mystified pursuit. There, moored near the end of the jetty, was an old but pristine sailing cruiser with the words 'Hasty Pudding' emblazoned on its stern. I jumped aboard and reached out to help Anni step onto the wobbling deck. The teak door to the cabin was closed but unlocked. We went inside and down the three steps into the cabin itself. Typical of Joe, the small cabin with gleaming brass fittings, comprising galley, eating and sleeping area, was as neat as a new pin. There were polished hardwood cupboards and presses at every turn. There was a navigation table on the port side covered by sailing charts, a shiny antique red and brass fire extinguisher was pinned to the wall above the table.

'I'll take the left side and you take the right.' Anni said. She knew what was on my mind without my actually saying so. It didn't take her long to find what we were looking for. In a wide thin drawer under the navigation table, sandwiched between sets of nautical charts, was the large white envelope Joanie Marchand had given me to hold the KGB profiles on same the night I had given them to Joe. A quick glance confirmed that all four documents were still inside. I heaved a massive sigh of relief but before I could say another word, I heard a strangely familiar voice from outside the boat, calling me.

'Jimmy, is that you? Jimmy, are you there?'

Still holding the envelope, I climbed up the three short timber steps from the cabin to the deck. 'Who is that?'

Incongruously, standing on the jetty was a woman I had noticed earlier in the church. She was wearing a black overcoat, black stockings, high heeled shoes and a wide brimmed black hat, perfectly dressed for a funeral. To add to the slightly theatrical effect, she also wore large round sunglasses.

'The woman was looking at the envelope in my hand. 'I see you have found what you were looking for. How clever of you. I think I had the same idea as you when I heard the Mr Davis's sister mention the boat. But of course I don't know my way around, so I had some trouble finding this place.'

I stepped further out onto the deck. 'Do we know each other?' I asked.

'Oh yes I think we do.' The woman suddenly kicked of her high heeled shoes, leaving them on the jetty and hopped down on to the deck beside me in one fluid athletic movement. She removed her sunglasses and her hat shaking loose golden blonde hair which had been carefully tucked in under it. Without her shoes I could see that Gabriella Darnovsky, Herbert Kluge's girlfriend, was a very small woman.

'Gabriella, what are you doing here? Did I see you at the funeral?'

'Sit down, Jimmy, but before you do, hand me that envelope.'

'What will you do if I don't?' I said, like some kid in a school yard standoff.

She walked across to the open cabin door and glanced in, taking a tiny pistol from the pocket of her coat as she did so. I moved away from her to the stern of the boat.

'I will shoot you is what I will do.' She said turning to me, now giving me her full attention. 'Hand it to me, now.'

I handed the envelope to her, moved further back to the stern of the boat and sat down. Gabriella stood with her back to the cabin door.

'A Beretta 950, with the lift up barrel, the same gun that killed Klara Hartmann,' I said.

'Where is Anni?' Gabiella said sharply.

'She is still up at the club. She will be wondering where I am.'

'She won't have to wonder for long. Is she staying at the same motel as last time?'

'I really couldn't say.'

'So she is then. I'll pay her a visit when I am finished here.'

'Did you kill Joe Davis, Gabriella? I know you killed Klara.'

'Klara Hartmann betrayed her country. Your friend Davis could have survived if he had simply given me these papers.'

'Is Herbert in on this with you?'

She smiled. 'Poor Herbert, yes, actually he is in on this with me. He just doesn't know it.'

She looked over to her right as a slightly larger, more modern cruiser with a middle aged couple on deck, puttered close by, its sails being lowered and engine running. It manoeuvred into place to tie up to a floating mooring about seventy yards from where we were. The couple on board began the business of tying down the sails, tying on fenders and locking up their boat. They waved over at us, gesturing at the sky and the prospect of imminent rain. I waved back from my seat in the stern. The friendly exchange clearly worried Gabriella. She spoke in a low, threatening voice.

'Don't speak to them or make any further gestures. Stand up, go down to the cabin and I will follow. If you say a word, or do anything to attract the attention of those people, I will shoot you.'

I stayed exactly where I was sitting, at the back of the boat, feigning a calm I certainly did not feel. 'One way or another Gabriella, you are going to shoot me. I would prefer to be shot in the open air, like Klara, than down in a cramped cabin. I don't think you're going shoot anyone while those people are there, so if you don't mind I will stay where I am for the moment.'

'You know, you are an insufferable fool. I thought so from the first moment we met. Why did you involve yourself in all of this? Love for Klara? What a joke. You actually fell in love with a corpse. It seems she had a power over men alright, even when she was dead.'

'You must have known her.'

'I knew her, but she did not know me. She thought of me as an ugly duckling, which I suppose I was. But as you see, I am now a swan. Only one person discerned the beauty within. Klara, in her arrogance, never did.'

'You mean Max Korten. Sounds like you killed Klara out of personal jealousy, not for your country or for the Communist cause, how disappointing.'

I glanced over anxiously at the sailing couple. They were working fast, worried about the impending rain. I saw them preparing to get into a small rubber dinghy which they had towed behind their boat. They would soon be gone.

'So you know about Max, I'm impressed.' Gabriella said. 'He trained us well. He taught us that personal feelings must never influence our work. Klara seemed to be unable to learn that basic lesson.'

'I suppose you also killed Robert Lavelle?'

'I am not a monster, if that's what you're getting at. Lavelle was more affected by Klara's death than we expected. He was showing signs of strain. Klara had almost certainly told him too much.'

The couple were now stepping into their dinghy. The man leaned against the hull of his cruiser to steady the dinghy as his wife stepped carefully aboard. Behind Gabriella, who was facing me, the tiny pistol still pointed in my direction, I could see Anni's head emerging slowly up the cabin steps. Joe's boat began to rock slightly as she moved. I had to say something to hold Gabriella's attention so she wouldn't turn around.

'Did you know that Max Korten called on Anni in Berlin to tell her about Klara's death? He said that Klara was the love of his life.'

To my left I could hear the splashing of the dinghy's oars in the water. The couple were moving off heading toward the shore and away from us. Gabriella took a step in my direction.

'You are a liar, Jimmy, and a bad one. Max always was, and still is, in love with me. He played Klara for a fool. She had the beauty, but no skills, no brains and was ideologically suspect. State Security should never have taken a chance on a clergyman's daughter. I was Max's star pupil, but I was more than that to him. All of last summer we were together. We laughed at her behind her back. She would never for a second have imagined that Max and I were lovers.'

Gabriella looked past me towards the beach. 'Your sailing friends have now gone Jimmy, walk forward slowly and go below.'

Anni had now reached the top step. She stepped forward onto the deck. I saw she was holding the long narrow antique fire extinguisher with both hands. She raised it over her head like a battering ram. Gabriella sensed her presence and turned towards her, Anni, by far the taller of the two, smashed the base of the cylinder at her face with all her might, hitting Gabriella full on her forehead. The blow knocked her backwards. There was a loud thud as the back of Gabriella's head cracked against the brightly polished brass winch on the starboard side of the boat. The Beretta and the envelope slipped from her hands onto the deck. I picked them both up. Anni raised the fire extinguisher as if she was going to strike again. But there was no need. Gabriella wasn't moving, though she was still breathing. A single bright blue contact lens had dislodged on impact and was stuck to Gabriella's cheekbone revealing one natural brown eye. Anni dropped the fire extinguisher, a look of savage anger on her face, as she stood over her sister's killer. We lifted Gabriella off the winch and laid her flat on the deck of the boat, blood seeping copiously from the back her head.

'I knew she wasn't Swiss.' Anni said, panting after her exertion. 'There was something wrong from the start.'

'Now you tell me,' I said.

'I tried to tell you before, but you didn't listen.'

'If she's not Swiss who is she?'

'I am almost certain she is Hedwig Schaeffer, Hetty to her friends. Klara was one of them, or thought she was. She is another protegée of Max Korten's, another participant in the Adler Programme. He must have sent her here to murder my sister.'

I leaned down to check Gabriella's pulse. She was breathing but blood was still oozing from the back of her skull, seeping into the pristine teakwood deck

'We have to call an ambulance' I said. I climbed off the boat onto the jetty, and pulled Anni up after me. We walked towards the yacht club. I put my arms around her. I knew she was thinking that she had somehow avenged her sister's murder and realised it would make no difference. It would not bring Klara back. I could feel her trembling with shock as she leaned into me. The low gray clouds opened over Hyannis Port, and the rain came.

CHAPTER 34

November 1963

As we drove northwards from the Cape over Sagamore Bridge that evening, the local radio news mentioned that an unnamed Swiss citizen, an employee of the American Red Cross, was declared dead on arrival at Cape Cod Hospital. She died of injuries caused by trauma to her head. The report said that late that afternoon, an ambulance had been called from a public phone booth outside the Hyannis Port Post Office. The anonymous caller described where the injured woman was located but did not answer any other relevant questions. The news reader said that the police suspected foul play and that the matter was under investigation. Another unsolvable puzzle for Detective Rob Durand, I thought, on his last few weeks on the job.

We had made call from outside the tiny Hayannis Port Post Office within five minutes of leaving Gabriella lying on the deck of Joe's boat. Anni and I walked from there in the rain to the Brass Rail at the west end of town. As we walked, we heard and saw the ambulance and a police car speeding towards the yacht club. We sat at the bar, had a much needed drink, and discussed the most traumatic day either of us had ever had. Relieved at the sudden unravelling of the mystery of who had killed Klara Hartmann, and why, I was conscious of an unsatisfactory anti-climax about the whole thing. We stayed in the bar waiting for darkness to fall and the rain to stop. At about six thirty, I called a cab for Anni to take her to the Wianno Motel in North Street to collect her suitcase. While she was gone I walked back to the Hyannis Port Golf Club, the clubhouse was locked. It was dark and still raining. There was no sign of Verling or Caulfield or anyone else. I picked up my

Dodge, the only car remaining in the car park and drove to the Wianno to collect Anni. As we headed north for Boston, the only thing I was sure of was that the FBI was still looking for me and for the documents in my possession. The death of Gabriella Darnovsky would only have muddied the waters further. I was bound to be their star suspect. My sore ribs were killing me, my nerves shot and Anni's weren't much better. After crossing the bridge it was a one hour drive to Boston. In that hour we agreed a plan to try to get out of the unholy mess we had landed ourselves in. It was after 8.00pm when we arrived at the Parker House Hotel on School Street, across from the State House. The Parker House was a beautiful old world hotel and, surprisingly for a Saturday night, there was no shortage of rooms. It was expensive, I had never stayed there before but after the events of the day, I didn't care anymore. I was in the process of booking two singles when Anni joined me at the reservation desk.

'Why don't we make it a twin Jimmy?'

The reservations clerk didn't bat an eyelid. 'Go ahead' I said to him. 'You wouldn't believe the day we've had.'

After a light dinner in the themed hotel restaurant called the 'Last Hurrah', we returned to our room. I lay on one of the two beds in my socks, looking at the single sheet of headed paper I had taken on Tuesday from Hickory Hill. I placed a call to the private home number of the Attorney General, written on top of the page. A voice I presumed to be that of a young teenage girl answered the phone very politely and without any hesitation handed the phone to her father when I told her who I was. The voice of the Attorney General was distinctly unfriendly.

'Yes, what is it?'

'Sir, this is Jimmy Flynn, my apologies for calling you at home on a Saturday night, but I need to see you about a matter of considerable urgency. Do you think that would be possible?'

'That depends on what it's about. I don't have much time this evening, we are hosting a dinner party. Is this about the Bolshakov letter?'

'No but it's something just as sensitive, maybe more so. I can't say too much about it over the phone. Dave Powers at the White House knows about it. He would be able to fill you in on the details.'

'Dave Powers, what's this got to do with him?'

'I talked about this matter with him he's an old friend of my father's.'

'Frankly, Mr Flynn, you are talking in riddles. And furthermore this is a very unorthodox approach from an officer of the State Department. However, as you have been helpful to me, I guess I must give you the benefit of the doubt. I will talk to Mr Powers, depending on what he says I will decide whether it's worth meeting with you or not. This better not be one of Dave's hopeless cases from East Boston, because right now I have got a lot more important things to worry about. Where are you calling from?'

'I am in Boston, at the Parker House. I'll just get you the number.'

'Don't bother. I'll get it if I need to call you back.'

He hung up before there was time to say anything else. So all of a sudden it was Mr Flynn, not Jimmy. This guy and his sense of entitlement, was beginning to get on my nerves. I was in possession of documents that would sink the lot of them if they were made public and all of a sudden the 'General' won't give me the time of day.

'That didn't seem to go that well?' Anni said, already tucked up in the other bed.

'No it didn't. If he's not careful I'll take this stuff to the Boston Globe or the Washington Post.'

'Well it's difficult for him when he doesn't know what it is you're talking about.'

'Whose side are you on, anyway?' I said.

'I'm on yours Jimmy, yours and nobody else's.'

'What about Franz Walter?'

She raised her head and looked over at me purposefully. 'I will have something to say to you about Franz later, but now I need to be quiet and to sleep. Today I have taken the life of another human being. I never thought I would ever do such a thing. I doubt if I will ever get over this terrible feeling.'

'What I don't understand is how someone as small as Gabriella, or whatever her name is, was able to murder your sister, Joe Davis and Bobby Lavelle, particularly Joe, he was wiry but as strong as a bull. They must have trained her well. She was a killer Anni, a trained killer. You can't blame yourself for what happened. If she hadn't hit her head on the metal winch, she might still be alive.'

'Even so, my behaviour is hardly in keeping with my father's scripture quotation "Overcome evil with good." Killing someone, even a killer, cannot be described as doing good.'

'Don't forget you saved someone's life too, mine. I for one am happy about that even if you're not. By the way I don't think I ever thanked you.'

'There is no need. I didn't really know what I was doing. But I am glad you are still here. Now let's stop talking and sleep.'

'If you didn't know what you were doing then you didn't kill Gabriella. It was an accident. If you feel bad I could come over there and comfort you till you fall asleep.'

She pulled up the bed covers and turned her back to me. 'Thank you for the kind offer Mr Flynn but no. Maybe another time;' she said with a discernable smile in her voice.

I wasn't sure I had heard her right, but I let it go. I had my own demons to deal with. Joe Davis was dead and I was, at the very least, complicit in his death. How was I going to live with that for the rest of my life? How was I going to tell Joe's sister Beth what I had done? We lay there silently on our respective beds until we both simultaneously drifted off to sleep.

At breakfast the following morning, the dining room manager came over to our table. 'Mr Flynn, there is an urgent call for you. I can bring the phone to your table if you wish.'

'Do you know who it is?'

'I couldn't possibly say.' The man replied knowingly but not answering my question. The phone was brought to our table the manager handed me the receiver with a conspiratorial smile. A familiar voice came on the line its tone was markedly different from last night.

'Jimmy, Bob Kennedy here, can you talk?'

'Sure Bob.' I said before I had time to correct myself.

Kennedy chuckled at my accidental informality. 'With regard to our conversation last night, I have just got off the phone from speaking to Dave Powers. I think you and I should meet as soon as possible. I will be in New York tomorrow evening for an event. Could we meet briefly in the Oak Bar at the Plaza Hotel, let's say seven thirty?'

'Yes of course, sir.' I said.

'Good. My office will book a room for you at the Plaza for Monday night. So you will be well rested when you travel back to Washington Tuesday. Dave confirmed to me what I had already surmised about you Jimmy. You're one of us, and Dave tells me your father was before you.'

'Well I would like to think so sir.' I said lamely, not knowing exactly what the hell that meant.

'In the meantime I trust you will keep our meeting to yourself and that you will come alone.'

'Of course I will. Thank you for agreeing to see me.'

'You're welcome. And thank you for your help with the other matter. That letter we discussed and your translation have already arrived at their destination. Anyway, I will see you tomorrow evening. Goodbye for now.'

'Goodbye sir.' I said into the mouthpiece but as before, the Attorney General had already hung up at his end, obviously not a man given to idle chit-chat over the phone.

I put the phone down. 'Well, the General sure has changed his tune.' I said to Anni. 'Dave Powers must have told him what exactly we have in our hot little hands. He wants to meet me in New York tomorrow night.'

'Now you call him Bob?'

'That was an accident. But so what, he's not God almighty. He's just a regular guy like you and me.'

'Of course he is.' She said sceptically. 'Does this change anything that we have already decided on, Jimmy?'

'No, absolutely not, once we have checked out of here we will drive to Logan and see if we can change your ticket for the earliest available Pan Am flight to Frankfurt. The sooner you are out of the country the better for you. Depending on the time of the flight, if we manage to change the ticket, we can come back into town and take a stroll around down town Boston, just like regular people. We can pretend we're tourists and that we didn't kill an international spy yesterday.'

'What will you say to Kennedy tomorrow?'

'I don't honestly know yet. I'll work it out as I'm driving to New York.'

'You realise that you have his future and his brother's in your hands?'

'Yes I do but I have to figure out the best way to play it.'

'Are you sure you don't need my help?' She said with a grin.

'Actually I'm not. At every crucial part of this, you have done and said the right thing and I have done the dumb thing. But I think we'd better stick to the plan.' I paused for a minute and looked her in the eyes, as she used the starched napkin to wipe a trickle of maple syrup from her lips. 'I'm really going to miss you Anni,' I said.

'Yes I know.' she said. Suddenly getting up from the table, she scurried from the room holding her napkin to her mouth, leaving me sitting there alone.

It was just after noon by the time we got to Logan Airport and almost one o'clock by the time we reached the top of the line at the Pan Am desk. At the desk the woman dealing with us said that it would be no problem to change Anni's ticket. There was in fact a Pan Am flight to Frankfurt leaving in forty minutes and Anni could check in her bag there and then. The downside was that the flight was already boarding. There would not be another flight to West Germany from Logan that day. I looked at Anni and she looked at me. She spoke first.

'I think we should do it, Jimmy. I should go now?'

'OK.' I said. 'I can't think of any reason why not, except that I don't want you to go at all.'

Anni ignored this and turned and spoke to the reservations lady. 'Thank you. I would like to proceed to change the ticket and check my bag through.'

It was another ten minutes by the time the bag was checked in and a new ticket had been issued. We walked to a quiet corner of the terminal. As we sat down, an announcement for the boarding of Frankfurt flight came over the loudspeakers. Everything was happening too fast for my liking. I handed Anni the Hickory Hill note paper.

'I want you to write down your father's full name, his date of birth, your parents address in Dresden, the name of that prison in Saxony that you mentioned and his prison number, if you know it, and also the name and address of the church of which he is pastor. And write down anything else of relevance that you can think of, for example, the charges that have been made against him.

'There have been no charges made against him'. Anni said. She began to write. As she was writing her face was showing clear signs of strain. 'What's this for?' She asked.

'I am going to see if I can persuade some people in high places to do something for us for a change. When I say us, I mean you and your family. You have all suffered enough. It's the least we can do for Klara. 'That's why she came here wasn't it, to help your father? She died trying to do the right thing for him.'

There was silence as Anni finished writing and stood up. She handed me the paper. There were tears in her eyes. A final call announcement for the Frankfurt flight rang out through the terminal. 'I love you Jimmy,' she said.

'What?'

She laughed nervously on the verge of crying. 'I think you heard me. When I get home, I have decided to tell Franz that I do not believe that we should continue to be together. Of course, I am not asking anything of you. I am just telling you what I feel.'

I walked towards her and took her in my arms. 'Anni, you can ask anything of me you want. You must know that I feel the same way.'

She began to laugh and cry at the same time. 'I hoped you would but I was not sure.'

'And there I was I thinking you were the smartest woman I've ever met.'

The announcement of the final call for the Frankfurt flight rang out through the terminal. 'C'mon' I said. I grabbed her hand and ran with her to the gate for the flight. When we got there we stopped, kissed for the first time, passionately and unashamedly for a long time in front of two bemused ticket checkers, until one of them coughed politely and said: 'Doors closing in three minutes.'

I reluctantly pulled away from her. Anni showed her boarding pass to the attendant, walked through the doors, down the steps and out onto the apron to the waiting Pan Am Boeing 707. I went to the nearby viewing window and watched her walk away. She was leaving but I was suddenly happier than I had ever been in my life. When she got to the bottom of the aircraft steps I could see a stewardess at the top gesturing impatiently to her to board. Half way up the steps she turned around, waved in my direction and in true Marilyn Monroe fashion, put her hand to her lips and blew me a kiss. I watched her until she went through the door. The steps were quickly pulled away and the aircraft door closed. I turned to go. I floated through Logan Airport and out to the car park like someone standing on a magic carpet. When I sat into my car, I slapped the steering wheel and roared to the heavens my delight at this turn of events. Feeling like Superman I decided, there and then, not to go back into Boston but to drive straight to New York. Before I did though, I got out of the car, pulled up my shirt and removed the painful back brace, throwing it on the back seat. My ribs would heal without help. They were already beginning to feel better.

Monday night, the Oak Bar at the Plaza was packed with middle aged men. Apart from the waitresses, I couldn't see any women. The Oak Bar was famous for its men only lunches on weekdays, and it seemed as if they were extending this practice to dinner. All the men were dressed in dinner jackets and black bow ties. A sign at the entrance to the room informed me that the Samuel Seabury Memorial Dinner hosted by the New York City Bar Association would commence at eight that evening. The guest speaker was to be Attorney General RF Kennedy. I was wearing an open necked gray, buttoned down shirt, navy sports jacket and khaki pants so I was seriously underdressed for this kind of function. Under my arm I carried a slim faux leather document case, which I had bought in the Plaza's gift shop. When I entered the Oak Room the only other person there not wearing a tux approached me.

'Are you Flynn?' He said in an unmistakeable Boston accent.

'Yes, can I ask who you are?'

'My name is O'Donnell. Please follow me. 'We've been given a room on the second floor we can talk in private there.'

'I followed him to the elevator. When we got in he said. 'So your Dad was a friend of Dave's. Where did you go to school?'

'BC. And you?'

'Harvard.' He said without a smile.

O'Donnell looked wiry but tough. He was medium height, dark haired, sharp featured with a small tight mouth. He was a stark contrast to the jovial bonhomie of Dave Powers. When the elevator door opened we walked directly to the room opposite. O'Donnell didn't knock, simply walked in and held the door for me to follow. The room was a regular hotel bedroom. Robert Kennedy was there wearing a black bow tie and dress shirt, his dinner jacket was thrown on the bed. He was sitting in an easy chair reading what I presumed was his speech for the evening. Two other straight backed chairs were placed to face his. Kennedy rose briefly and shook hands.

'Hello again, Jimmy, thanks for coming. Please sit down. You've already met Kenny. He and I go way back, same year in college. Anything you say to me you can say to him.'

As I suspected, this was the legendary Ken O'Donnell, some kind of senior aide to the President. The clan were keeping this very tight. Powers and O'Donnell were deep inside the inner circle, personal friends as well as professional aides. No career government officials were being consulted. 'Thank you for seeing me sir, I said. I have a long story to tell you and I know you are pressed for time. If it's OK with you I will start at the beginning.

'Go right ahead,' Kennedy said. As I had done with Dave Powers and others, I went through the events since then with as much detail as I could remember. Both men listened with great attention. Kennedy held his chin in his hand, remaining silent throughout. He shook his head in disgust when I mentioned the antics of Verling and Caulfield and visibly winced and rubbed his eyes in sorrow when I told him about the fate of Joe Davis, whom he had once known from the yacht club. When I had finished, Kennedy was the first to speak.

'You say these documents are detailed and thorough. Who exactly has had sight of them?'

'Here in the US, only me. Klara Hartmann, who is dead and her sister Anni Hartmann now back in Germany. I can't say who has seen them in East Germany or Moscow, although it seems from the preamble that they are highly restricted. Even members of the East German government apart from Ulbricht and Mielke, were not given access to them.'

'Did these two Bureau goons specifically mention the Johnson material? From what you say they seemed to think there was just one document?' O'Donnell astutely asked.

'They didn't mention Johnson specifically but I think that's what they were after.'

Kennedy and O'Donnell exchanged a brief understanding glance.

'Can the sister, Anni Hartmann, be trusted to keep this information confidential?' Kennedy asked.

'Yes she can. I can vouch for her.'

'Where are the documents now?' He asked.

I tapped the slim case on my lap. 'They are right here.' I said.

Now I had their full attention. 'Are you planning on blackmailing the administration with these papers?' O'Donnell asked aggressively.'

I looked him in the eye. 'No I'm not Mr O'Donnell. I am planning to hand them over to the Attorney General here. That's why I came. There is a considerable amount of sensitive information here, some of it potentially very damaging, a lot of it very personal. I have no intention of taking advantage of anything contained in them?'

'May I see them?' The Attorney General asked. I passed the document case over to him and he removed the contents. 'They are in German.' He said with some surprise.'

'Yes, they are a translation from the Russian original. The translation work was done in Moscow and passed to the East Germans. Somewhere in Moscow I presume, there are Russian originals. If you have someone trustworthy to translate them into English for you that's fine. If not, I can do it for you. As I have already read them. But it's a big job it will take a few days.'

Kennedy looked at O'Donnell. 'What do you think, Kenny?'

'I think circulation of this kind of stuff should be kept to an absolute minimum. Mr Flynn here is a qualified translator and has he said, he has already seen the material. If he does the job quickly and he hands over the originals without taking a copy, I don't see why not. But that's essential, no copies.' He looked at me with unmistakeable suspicion. We'll have to take your word for it that you haven't already copied them.'

This guy obviously didn't trust me an inch. 'Yeah, you're just going to have to take my word on that.' I said with equal assertiveness.

'I am going back to Washington as soon as we finish here.' O'Donnell said to Kennedy. 'I would like to hold onto the documents for now. I can return them to Mr Flynn to work on when he gets to Washington himself. Security is the key thing with this kind of stuff.'

'That's very sensible.' Kennedy said. 'Do you have any objection, Jimmy?'

'That's fine with me.'

'Is there anything else you want to tell us?' Kennedy asked me.

'No sir, that's it.'

'I find it hard to believe you're doing all this and not asking anything in return,' O' Donnell said.

'You're right I'm not asking anything in return. You now have the documents. So that's the end of that. But I'm not being entirely altruistic either. I do want something and if I'm honest, that's really why I'm here.'

Kennedy shifted uncomfortably in his chair. 'What's that?' He said.

I took the folded Hickory Hill headed paper from the inside pocket of my jacket, containing Anni's details about her father, written in her clear neat hand writing. I handed it to the Attorney General. He stared at it, puzzled as to what I was doing with his personal notepaper. Now I had to make my pitch.

'Bolshakov, in his letter to you said he would do anything he could to be of assistance. Well now I have a problem. It's not a simple one. In fact it's very difficult. It might be something that Bolshakov or his bosses could be consulted about. Frankly sir, I badly need your help and I'm here to ask you for it.'

'I haven't got a lot of time,' Kennedy said. You'd better spell it out for me.'

CHAPTER 35

November 1963

Two days after my meeting in the Plaza Hotel, a man with the colourful name of Muggsy O'Leary, called at the house in Garret Park and handed me the same mock leather document case I had given to the Attorney General the previous Monday. There was a sealed envelope inside it and nothing else. I read the short typed note on Department of Justice headed paper contained in it, simply saying:

Mr J Flynn,

Room 417 on the fourth floor of the Justice Department has been reserved for your use for two days for the special task assigned to you by the Attorney General. Please call to the undersigned tomorrow morning, November 7, at 9.00am. The relevant documentation and a key to the room will be provided to you. Documents and papers associated with this exercise, when not in use, must be secured at all times in the safe provided in room 417 and returned to the undersigned at the end of each day.

E M Fitch

Personal Secretary

The following morning I took the train into the city and walked to the Pennsylvania Avenue entrance of the Justice building. At the Attorney General's floor, Mrs Fitch handed me a set of three keys and a slim metal briefcase, containing the documents I had given to O'Donnell at the Plaza Hotel. She made no comment except to tell me how to get to Room 417 and to say that I was to return the locked briefcase and contents to her when I was finished. I spent the rest of the day there working alone, translating the four papers. Reading the profiles again and examining every word from a translator's viewpoint brought home to me the toxicity of this material and the damage it could do the reputation of American democracy if it was ever made public. The prurient details of the President's love life were fascinating but his behaviour, contrasting so starkly with his public image as an American hero, was sometimes hard to take. In order to retain my objectivity I had to remind myself of Dave Powers' praise of his boss and his belief in the President's genuine commitment to civil rights and to world peace. I wanted to believe as Dave and my father did, but it wasn't easy.

The details of Lyndon Johnson's methods of extracting cash for political favours from a variety of sources over his entire career also provided unsettling glimpses as to how American politics actually works. I wasn't naive enough to think that this kind of behaviour was confined to Texas. I had no doubt that the Boston politicians of my father's generation were just as shady as their Texas cousins. There was a lot more to the political system we so revered than most Americans could ever know. It was my new best pal, the Attorney General, who emerged as the most admirable of the four individuals profiled. Soviet animosity to him was largely based on his opposition to Communism and his perceived aggressive tendencies. But they contained a grudging approval of his pursuit of organised crime. The picture of him, the profilers inadvertently painted, was of a man who was loyal, hardworking, idealistic and as honest as it was possible to be in the world of politics. His most thankless job was to protect the reputation of his older brother, whom he obviously revered. He seemed to be selfless in his loyalty to the President, a man who lived a reckless life secure in the knowledge that his younger brother would always be there to watch his back, to conceal his transgressions and protect his reputation.

I was careful with the work, and when I was finished with the translations I considered I had done a good job on all four of the profiles. I was left entirely undisturbed in room 417 and completed the job to my satisfaction by noon Friday, a few hours ahead of schedule. When I had packed all the papers in the metal briefcase and locked it, I placed a call to Herbert Kluge's number at the West German Embassy. I was put through to him instantly. Without any preamble I asked him would he meet me that evening on the steps in front of the Lincoln Memorial. A very subdued sounding Herbert said he would see me there at five thirty. I locked the door of room 417, called in to Mrs Fitch and handed her the briefcase along with the keys. She said very little except that the Attorney General would be in touch with me in due course.

Herbert Kluge was a changed man when we met on the white granite steps in front of the seated Abraham Lincoln. His face was pale his eyes bloodshot. He had the demeanour of hunted animal. He said he couldn't stay long. We walked down the steps toward the reflecting pool. It was already beginning to get dark. Herbert spoke in an anxious whisper. He said the West German Ambassador had been informed confidentially on Tuesday evening by a call from a man named Tolson, Deputy Director of the FBI, that a woman, identified as a foreign agent, had been romantically involved with one of the embassy's diplomatic staff. The woman in question was now deceased. Herbert said he had been summoned to the office of the embassy's head of security Wednesday morning and questioned for more than an hour about his relationship with Gabriella Darnovsky. He was told that there would be a full security investigation of the matter. Less than two hours before Herbert left the embassy to meet with me, he had been summoned again this time by his Ambassador. He was told that he was to be recalled to Bonn with immediate effect and reassigned to a home posting for the foreseeable future. Poor judgment and a lack of vigilance on Herbert's part was the reason for this decision but nothing other than gullibility was being held against him on security grounds. I decided not to tell Herbert how Gabriella had died or that I had been there when it happened. He didn't ask me about it and I didn't volunteer the information. He was a broken man and I felt very sorry for him. As well as being a killer, Gabriella had been an arch manipulator. Clever but naive Herbert, with his academic gawkiness, his big spectacles and his trusting nature was putty in her hands. Apparently the HVA had targeted him for recruitment and Gabriella was both the bait and potential controller. There was something in particular I needed to ask Herbert.

'Herbert, when I called you from the hospital a few weeks ago, did I mention to you that I had left something with a friend of mine? Did I mention the friend's name?'

'No, you didn't say anything like that and you didn't mention anyone's name.'

'I never mentioned the name Joe Davis?'

'Yes, you told me about him the first time we met in Harvey's.'

'Did you say anything about him to Gabriella?'

'I don't think so,' he said without much conviction. Then something came to him. 'She once asked me who your friends were, which I suppose is an unusual question.'

'What did you tell her?'

'I said I had no idea, I told her that the only people I had ever heard you mention were Tom Noonan and Joe Davis, your school friends from Cape Cod. The two names you mentioned to me when you first told me about the shooting.'

That was it, I thought. That must have been enough for Gabriella to check up on Joe. What a fool I had been to confide in Herbert, and what a fool he had been to trust such a cold blooded killer. But Herbert wasn't to blame for Joe's death, I was. Much as I wanted to I knew I couldn't pin this on anyone else. We walked silently around the long pool and back towards honest Abe. When we reached the bottom of the steps we shook hands. I wished him luck and said I hoped we would meet again. He said the same, but neither of us really believed we would. We walked away in opposite directions.

I spent the following week in a state of high anxiety but nothing at all happened. I hung around the house in Garret Park and visited the Library of Congress and the Smithsonian, thinking about what I would do with the rest of my life once I was formally kicked out of State. I spent a lot of time composing a suitably romantic reply to a beautiful letter I had received from Anni Hartmann in Berlin. I heard nothing further from the Attorney General and nothing from the State Department To add to my worries, I had just about run out of money. Fancy hotels don't come cheap. My financial chickens were coming home to roost. The first hopeful sign of a change in my luck came ten days after my meeting with Herbert. I got a call from Lana Phillips of the State Department's personnel section. We hadn't spoken since my suspension hearing. This time she sounded friendly, even cheerful.

'Jimmy I have what I hope is good news for you. Secretary Rusk himself has informed us here that the hearing in relation to your suspension need not now proceed due and I quote, "to new information which has come to his attention." It's all very mysterious but it seems that your suspension may be lifted and though it has to be confirmed, it looks like you may be able to come back to work.'

'I'm glad to hear that Lana. Thanks for letting me know. When is this likely to happen?'

'We don't exactly know. We are waiting for the paperwork from the Secretary of State's office. Elliot Markham called me about it and told me I could inform you, off the record, of this development. Written confirmation will follow. But he wouldn't tell me anything else. It seems all very hush hush.'

I could tell Lana was dying to know what was going on but I wasn't in a position to enlighten her. 'It's as much a mystery to me as it is to you Lana, but I'm very relieved all the same.'

She could tell I was holding something back. 'Well congratulations anyway.' She said disappointed with my minimal response. 'When I know more I will call you again. I hope you know, Jimmy, I was rooting for you.'

'I know that Lana. I said. 'I sensed it on the day of the hearing and I very much appreciated it. Thanks so much for calling.'

I put the phone down and for the first time since Labour Day I felt like a huge weight had been lifted from my shoulders. I would call my mother in Hyannis, as soon as I caught my breath, to tell her the good news. I would have to give her the impression that Dad's childhood pal, Dave Powers, had successfully delivered the goods. Maybe he had.

I had another piece of unfinished business. That evening I drove into the city and parked outside the Templeton residence on N Street in Georgetown. Within a minute of ringing the loud bell, the door was opened by a tall elegant lady of about sixty, with carefully coiffed blue gray hair, wearing an expensive looking black dress which flattered her slim figure. This must be the legendary Bunny T, I thought.

'Good evening Mrs Templeton, is Vern in?' I said. 'I am a colleague of his, Jimmy Flynn.'

'Ah yes, Mr Flynn, I believe I have heard of you. Please come in. Vernon is in the study. You may go on through.'

I walked into the same room Anni and I had sat in just two weeks before. Mrs Templeton did not follow me in or announce my arrival. Vern had been reading, he stood up, half moon glasses on, book still in hand, which I noticed was Barbra Tuchman's, *'The Guns of August.'* When he saw me, he suddenly looked very worried.

'Jimmy, it's you.'

'I'm not staying Vern, I won't sit down.' I said. 'I have something important to say, but I'll be brief. I have had sight of some classified material recently which mentions the existence of a Soviet agent codenamed Sonata.' Vern took off his glasses, his face visibly paled, I knew then I had hit a bull's eye. 'I have good reason to believe Vern, that you are 'Sonata', or part of it, that the work you do for the Soviets is of a far higher level than the impression you gave me in this very room a couple of weeks ago. I need to ask you: were you involved, either directly or indirectly in the deaths of Klara Hartmann or Bobby Lavelle?'

Vern took a deep breath, put his glasses in his breast pocket but did not sit down. He took his time answering. He spoke in a whisper. 'I wasn't Jimmy. I swear to you on my family's honour I wasn't. I have never knowingly put the life of any American or any other person for that matter, in danger, ever.'

'Someone told those who killed Lavelle that he was about to crack and reveal things he shouldn't. Was that you Vern?'

'No, Jimmy, it wasn't me. I would never have done anything to harm Bobby Lavelle, never.'

'I hope that's true, Vern, I really do. I suspect high level information and gossip is more in your line. But I find I can't let this go. A person like you cannot remain in the State Department or in government service, given your activities since 1944, whatever they were. I have always liked you Vern, but I can't just forget what I know. You need to hand in your resignation from State right now and bring your diplomatic career, not to mention your espionage career, to an end. If you do, I will not take this matter any further. But if you don't leave now and quit the game, I will go to the FBI with what I know.'

Vern sat down, dropping his book on the floor beside him. 'Are you saying the FBI doesn't know about Sonata?' he asked.

'They know Sonata exists. I don't think they know what or who it is. I have no doubt they will investigate the matter themselves, if they haven't already started. There's nothing I can do about that. They don't know it's you and I won't tell them.'

'Why Jimmy? Why are you offering me this reprieve?'

'To be honest, Vern, I'm not sure. Maybe it's because I can't see the point of someone like you languishing in a high security federal prison for the rest of his life. You'd never survive that and I don't want to be responsible for it. You've always been fair to me and you gave me a break giving me the Bolshakov translation. I appreciated that. I just hope I am not making a huge mistake.'

'How did you know that I was part of Sonata? Where did you see the name?' He asked, speaking so low I could barely hear him.

'I can't tell you that, it's a long story. It helped that the Russians, somewhat carelessly, give code names to their spies which are appropriate to the individuals they're running. Given your penchant for classical music, that part was an easy guess. And of course what you told me about Istanbul the last time we spoke confirmed your political bias. Actually until I came here tonight I wasn't a hundred per cent certain.'

I opened the door to leave. Vern remained seated, still in shock. 'I meant what I said, Vern. Leave now, as soon as possible. If you don't, I've no option but to go to the Feds.'

I left the study, closing the door behind me. The elegant Mrs Templeton was standing in the vestibule outside, a pained look on her face. I had no doubt she had heard every word of our conversation. I let myself out the front door saying good night to her as I went out. She didn't reply.

I drove home to Garrett Park wondering if I was letting Vern off too easily. I had no idea what kind of damage his treachery may have done in the past. The covering note to the KGB profiles mentioned that the information contained in them was provided 'with the help of Sonata.' I was betting that the Attorney General would not be so irresponsible as to conceal the existence of such a person or a network, even if he was going to conceal the contents of the profiles themselves. So Vern might not be out of the woods yet. I spent the following day waiting in vain for any news from State or Justice but nothing happened. It was Wednesday almost noon before I got a call from the DOJ. It was from Mrs Fitch, who for the first time introduced herself on the phone by her first name.

'Mr Flynn, Edith Fitch here. The Attorney General has asked if you would be available to meet with him here in the Department at four thirty this afternoon.'

'Yes, of course, Mrs Fitch. I'll be there.'

'Oh, and you have been asked to bring an overnight bag with you. Will that be a problem?'

'It's not a problem no, but why? Am I going somewhere? I don't quite understand.'

'I don't understand either Mr Flynn, I haven't been told anything. Can I take it that you will be here at four thirty?'

'Yes of course. I'll be there thank you.' I put the phone down.

As Sherlock Holmes or maybe it was Doctor Watson, used to say, the game is afoot. But I had no idea what game or where it was being played. Packing an overnight bag would not be a problem. I still hadn't fully unpacked since my last trip to the Cape.

CHAPTER 36

November 1963

At four thirty I was ushered in to the conference room next to the Attorney General's office. There were three men already there seated next to one another near the top of the table, one of whom, Elliot Markham from Dean Rusk's office, I recognised. Another of the three wore an army Colonel's uniform. The third man was in a gray business suit. Markham greeted me with a cautious smile but typically took charge.

'Come in, Jimmy, sit down. The Attorney General will be with us shortly.'

I dropped my overnight bag in the corner of the room and sat opposite Markham. I was reminded of our last hostile confrontation across a similar conference table. I could tell that the atmosphere this time was more benign. Through the walls I could hear a cheerful group of revellers singing 'Happy Birthday to You', followed by mumbled speeches, laughter and a prolonged round of applause. Markham did the introductions. Indicating the man in the gray suit sitting next to him with a pleasant face and sharp intelligent eyes Markham said:

'Jimmy Flynn, this is Cartha De Loach, FBI liaison with the White House. Next to him is Colonel Mike Holbrook. The AG will explain what we are all doing here when he arrives.'

The table was too wide for handshakes. I nodded hello to the other two and sat down. There was a minute or two of awkward silence as the four of us sat there with nothing to say. The sharp eyed De Loach broke the silence. 'It's the General's birthday today.' He said, in a warm, deep bass, southern accent.

It took me a couple of seconds to register that the General in question was Kennedy. Presumably he and his staff were celebrating the event in the room next door. 'How old is he?' I said, for want of something to say.

'Thirty eight.' De Loach said. 'Young for an Attorney General'

As if on cue the connecting door between the conference room and Kennedy's office opened and he briskly walked in taking his seat at the head of the table, while putting his jacket on and straightening his tie at the same time. Gentlemen sorry for keeping you, as you probably heard, I had an important commitment.' He flashed a brief smile. 'Thank you all for coming. We can get this over with quickly. I know that you all have a lot to do. I take it, Jimmy, you have met everyone here. Perhaps we could get right to it. Can we start with you, Mr Markham?'

Markham had a thin batch of papers in front of him. He was all business as usual, sleek as a thoroughbred racehorse. 'Certainly, General, on my instructions, Mr Flynn has already been informed verbally of the decision by the State Department with regard to his current employment status. Following an internal review, he has been fully exonerated of any misconduct on his part. Secretary Rusk has instructed that he may resume his duties in the Department at the earliest possible opportunity, without any loss of pay for the period of his temporary suspension. The Secretary also understands that Mr Flynn has been of considerable help to the Department of Justice and to the Bureau in relation to an undisclosed, classified matter. In that regard I am very pleased to be in a position to inform you, General, and this meeting, that Secretary Rusk has accepted a recommendation for Mr Flynn's promotion to Second Secretary.' Markham paused here for effect. Kennedy simply nodded his approval. 'Regrettably this will mean that his services will no longer be available to LAU2 in the Department, where he is currently assigned but his exceptional language skills will no doubt be put to good use in his future diplomatic career. I took the liberty of bringing the letter of offer in respect of the promotion, to this meeting. If Mr Flynn wishes to sign it now, he is free to do so. His revised pay scale is payable from the date on which the promotion is stipulated on the letter, which is today.' Markham looked at me questioningly and pushed a single typed page and a gold pen across the table at me.

'Jimmy, you may wish to give this some thought, but if you don't need to, then you may sign the acceptance here and now.'

I had to hand it to Markham. He must hate every minute of this but he hides it well I thought. As for me I was shocked and excited in equal measure, but I had no doubt what I was going to do.

'Thank you, Elliot.' I said. 'I'm very happy to sign right now.' I picked up the pen without hesitation and signed.

Markham looked affronted at my use of his first name but he nodded his approval. 'I should add that there is a current vacancy for a Second Secretary at our Embassy in Vienna, where of course your knowledge of spoken and written German would be of great help. I believe consideration is being given to a possible appointment for you there.' Promotion and exile I thought. How convenient for all concerned.

'Thank you, Mr Markham.' Kennedy said. Please convey my thanks to Secretary Rusk for his assistance in this matter and for his understanding. I appreciate it very much, as does the President. I am sorry that I could not be more forthcoming about the nature of Mr Flynn's assistance to my Department and to the FBI. As the matter remains part of an ongoing investigation. We can't say more at this time. Secretary Rusk will be fully informed in due course.'

Markham smiled a thin smile of acknowledgment, but he wasn't fooling anyone. He was out of the loop and he was going to have to stay there. Kennedy then turned to De Loach. I noticed the army Colonel at the end of the line watching all of this with keen interest.

'Deke have you got an update?' The Attorney General asked.

De Loach spoke as quickly as his southern drawl allowed him. 'Yes sir, I don't have too much to say. But as you have already pointed out, there is an important ongoing investigation under way, so I cannot say too much. I just want to inform Mr Flynn here that Director Hoover is fully aware of the difficulties he encountered in the course of his recent dealings with the Bureau. Misunderstandings arose from what might be described as, eh, an unplanned confluence of events. In light of what has transpired, the two agents with whom Mr Flynn has had some interaction with in recent weeks are being re-assigned. Special Agent in Charge Verling will now head up the investigation the Attorney General has already alluded to. Agent Caulfield will shortly be re- assigned to our New York Office.'

If this was supposed to be an apology from J Edgar Hoover it seemed to lack a certain amount of contrition, *'an unplanned confluence of events'* my ass. The two guys who put me in the hospital were being well looked after. Caulfield was being sent to the most prestigious FBI office outside of Washington and Verling was assigned to investigate 'Sonata'. I thought about Vern, his troubles were not over yet, I didn't envy him grappling with Verling, but there was nothing I could do. As for me, I had just been catapulted into the diplomatic career stream with a hike in pay. The Attorney General, as usual, seemed impatient and clearly wanted to get the meeting over with. He nodded in De Loach's direction.

'Fine thank you Deke. Maybe we'll leave it there. I believe I will see you both at the White House Judicial Reception later this evening. Mr Markham, thank you again and give my personal regards to Secretary Rusk.'

Markham and De Loach stood up, Colonel Holbrook remained seated. Markham spoke as he put his papers away in a thin expensive looking alligator skin briefcase.

'You are more than welcome, General.' He said. 'I will certainly pass on your kind remarks to the Secretary of State.' Then looking at me he said congratulations on your promotion Jimmy. You may not have heard that your old boss, Vern Templeton, has resigned from the diplomatic service with immediate effect. I got word this morning. He and his wife are going to live in Venice, I believe. Some people have all the luck.' Markham was the best poker player I had ever seen. I doubted that he had any idea what was behind all of this, and he certainly did not want me back in the Department. But somebody got to him so he put a brave face on it. He even managed to look as if he himself had orchestrated my miraculous return from the dead. When he and De Loach left the room Kennedy quickly got down to business.

'Jimmy, Colonel Holbrook here is with US Army, Berlin, stationed in eh, where is it, Colonel?'

'The Allied *Kommandatura,* Berlin- Dahlem, sir.'

'You are travelling there with him tonight.' He said to me.

'What, to Berlin?'

'Yes, tonight as soon as this meeting is over. There's a plane waiting at Andrew's. Colonel Holbrook will be travelling with you. I took your advice. I had someone contact our mutual friend Georgi in Moscow. He managed to pull some strings over there. It seems that Khrushchev is almost as enthusiastic as the President for a new beginning between both our countries. Anyway, someone very senior in Moscow has put a little pressure on the East Germans. The upshot of all this is that Pastor Hartmann is to be released from prison and allowed to travel to the West, along with his wife. Colonel Holbrook here is an expert at this kind of thing. He has handled a number of transfers like this in the past. There is no reciprocation this time. Because of their age and their poor health the Hartmanns are simply being permitted to cross over. I understand the pastor is not very well. Where and when will this take place Colonel?'

'Glienecke Bridge, sir, in a couple of days, same place Gary Powers came over,' Holbrook said in a clipped military voice.

'Colonel, you can brief Jimmy on the nuts and bolts of this thing on the flight. I have spoken to General Clay to thank him for all the help you've given us with this. It's very much appreciated.'

Holbrook suddenly stood up from the table, stood to attention and saluted. 'You're welcome sir.' He said.'

'If you wouldn't mind waiting in the corridor for a minute, Colonel, I need a quick word with Mr Flynn.'

Holbrook left the room, closing the door after him. Kennedy looked at me with an intimidating intensity. 'I have three things to say to you Jimmy. Firstly, do I have your word of honour that you are unaware of any other copies of the KGB documents?'

'All I can say with certainty is that none were made while they were in Klara Hartmann's possession, Joe Davis's or mine.'

'Good. Secondly, as you have no doubt gathered, I have told Director Hoover about the existence of Sonata, whatever or whoever that is. But he knows nothing about the source of my information or of the contents of the profiles and he's not happy about that. I don't want you to mention this matter ever again, are you clear on that? Not to anyone, and not a word to Holbrook. You and he will share a long flight and he's bound to be curious. Have you got that?'

'Of course.'

He stood up and I did the same, he walked towards me and then seemed to relax. 'Finally I want to thank you sincerely, for everything, the translations and everything else you've done. I appreciated you handing over the documents to me at the Plaza before asking for help for the Hartmanns. If you had done it the other way around, it might have been a different story. From what I have been told since then about this man, Pastor Hartmann, we're doing the right thing.' He held out his hand.

'I'm told Holbrook's a very good man. Good luck in Berlin and thank you.'

'Thank you for everything sir, I can see you've gone to a lot of trouble over this.'

'You're welcome Jimmy.'

'By the way sir, many happy returns of the day,'

He gave me a broad friendly smile, pointed to my overnight bag in the corner. 'Don't forget your bag, Jimmy,' he said, turned and left the room through the connecting door.

CHAPTER 37

November 1963

I had plenty of time to think during the long overnight flight aboard the Douglas Cargomaster that Colonel Holbrook had managed to hitch to a ride on to Berlin. I didn't have a passport, but Holbrook said it wouldn't be a problem. The huge four engine propeller plane took off from Andrews Air Force Base at seven thirty that evening. It would stop for refuelling in the Azores and then go on to Berlin. The expected arrival time in Berlin was 11.30 am the following day. There were about twenty five other officers and men aboard, returning to Berlin from leave, most of whom Holbrook seemed to know. The rest of the aircraft was packed with miscellaneous cargo for the US Army, Berlin garrison. Joe Davis's death was still preying on my mind. I had the feeling if I lived to be a hundred it would never go away. As Holbrook and I drove to Andrews after the meeting I had time to think. I had no illusions about what had happened. I knew I had just been offered the biggest bribe I was ever likely to be offered and I had grabbed it with both hands. The price I had to pay for my promotion was silence. I was to keep my mouth shut and to forget whatever I had read in the Sonata profiles. The only way I could justify this was by convincing myself that accepting the bribe might help get an innocent man out of prison.

Holbrook was an interesting guy, not without humour. He insisted on me calling him Mike. Not yet forty, he was stationed at the *Allierte Kommandantura,* which had been the headquarters of military governing body for Berlin since the end of the war. It was situated on Kaiserwerther Strasse in the upscale suburb of Dahlem in the west of city. I was provided with a room on the same street, in a VIP army guesthouse, for the duration. Like me, Mike Holbrook spoke Russian and German. As part of his duties, he frequently crossed over and back between east and West Berlin virtually at will. He had Russian colleagues in the *Kommandantura* with the same freedom in West Berlin, as well as British and French, the two other occupying powers. He asked me about the Hartmann family. I told him what I knew but I had the impression that he knew a lot more about them than I did. He said he expected the hand over at Glienecke Bridge to be routine. It was scheduled to happen at dawn Friday morning before the normal business of the day began. He never asked me what the charade we had both been party to in the Justice Department earlier that day was all about. At about 2.30 in the morning, in a dismal windswept air base in the Azores, we got out and stretched our legs while the plane was being refuelled. Sitting in a shabby café, the only one in the terminal building, I asked Holbrook if he had had ever heard of Max Korten. His answer surprised me.

'Yeah I know him. Word is Korten's on the way out. Blotted his copybook, as the Brits say, but no one knows how. He is said to be close to Markus Wolf, the top Stasi guy, the so-called spy without a face, so he was always protected. What I hear is that he screwed up in a big way and his career is now on the slide. What do you know about him?'

'Not much, I just heard his name really. It's a long story'. I said.

'I get it, part of that ongoing investigation the FBI guy was talking about today, or was it yesterday?'

'Yeah, something like that.'

'Don't worry, I won't pry. I deal with spooks like you every other week. If I don't need to know, I know better not to ask.'

'I'm not a spook, just under orders.'

'I hear that, me too. But you'll get your chance to see Korten for yourself on the bridge Friday morning. He's the one delivering the Hartmann couple over.'

At three o'clock, Thursday afternoon I walked down the Kurfurstendamm and through the main door of KaDeWe. I was wearing the same suit and plain tie I had worn to the meeting at Justice the day before. It was freezing in Berlin and I hadn't thought to bring an overcoat. I saw her at the cosmetics counter the moment I walked in, but she didn't see me. I had forgotten how beautiful she was. I stood for a few seconds staring at her, knowing she had no idea she was being observed. She looked different at work. Her normally long chestnut hair was pinned up like an air stewardess. The women working the cosmetic counter were obviously supposed to wear the products they sold. I walked up to the counter while she had her back turned and said:

'Excuse me Miss. Can you recommend a nice perfume as a gift for a beautiful young woman? I want it to be a surprise.'

She turned around, speechless for five long seconds, her hands held to her mouth. Ten minutes later in a coffee shop on the top floor of KaDeWe, I gave Anni the news about her parents. She was incredulous. She said she was happier than she had ever been, but it was hard to tell. She began to sob so loudly the other coffee drinkers gave me threatening looks. She was too overcome to go back to work. With permission from her sympathetic boss we were out of the department store by four o'clock. We crossed the street and took the U Bahn to her small, cosy, well heated apartment in Charlottenburg. All signs of the existence of Franz Walter seemed to have been removed. The following morning Anni and I appeared, as arranged in Mike Holbrook's office in Dahlem, at the appointed time, five am. It was pitch dark outside. Holbrook looked glum and it didn't take long to find out why. The East Germans had cancelled the handover for that morning at the Glienecke Bridge and had informed Holbrook that they would be in touch. No time or date for a future contact had been mentioned and no reason for the cancellation was given.

'This is par for the course for these guys.' He told us. 'Hard to know if its incompetence or just sheer cussedness, but they love to yank our chain like this, to let us know they are the ones running the show.'

Anni was devastated by the news. 'They will never let them out,' she said. 'They have no compassion, no humanity. I should have known it was too good to be true.'

It was heartbreaking to see this cloud of depression come over her. She insisted on going to work that day, as it was Friday and a busy day in the department store. She asked me to call in to her on the Ku Damm if I heard anything further. Holbrook said there was nothing more to do for now. To kill time, he said that he would get me a military guide to take me on a tour of the city. There was nothing else for it but to wait. That afternoon, back in the guest house after my tour, I placed a call to Steve McKinnon in Garrett Park, guessing, given the time difference, he would not have gone to work yet. I hadn't told Brad or Steve where I was going or how long I would be away but I had been absent from the house so much lately maybe they didn't care. The army guest house came complete with a switchboard in the lobby downstairs, manned by a soldier operator. He did not demur when I asked to place a call to the States. When I got through, I told Steve I was in Europe on business and got the predictable response.

'You know, Jimmy, you really are becoming an international man of mystery. What the hell are you doing there?'

'It's a very long story Steve but it's coming to an end. I promise I will fill you in when I get back. By the way, that problem I had with the State Department has gone away. I have been reinstated, as of this week. I have a lot to tell you both but I'm not exactly sure when I'll get home.'

'Weirder and weirder, Jimmy, is all I can say. Can't wait to hear about this. By the way have you heard the latest on the Bobby Baker saga?'

'No, what's new?'

'They're zeroing in on financial malfeasance and whether there is direct link to LBJ. The investigating team are bringing in a witness this afternoon. He is expected to say that Baker asks people looking for favours from Johnson to purchase advertising time on a TV station Johnson owns in Texas. That way the money is ostensibly for a legitimate reason. But why would small businesses on the east coast want advertising on a local station in Texas? Senator Mansfield thinks that if this kind of allegation sticks Baker may go down and Johnson will almost certainly be dropped from the Democratic ticket next year. Word is Bobby Kennedy badly wants to dump Lyndon. This is almost definitely curtains for the big Texan.'

'That is incredible, Steve. Are you saying it's happening today?'

'Yeah, the witness, some guy from Maryland, is coming in today. It will be a closed proceeding, investigators and witnesses only. As expected, all discussion of the Quorum Club is now off the table. But it looks like Lyndon is yesterday's news.

'If I have time I'll call you tomorrow to see how things panned out. I gotta go Steve, talk to you later.'

I hung up. The time lag from the overnight flight was catching up on me. I was exhausted. I lay back and dozed in the surprising luxury of the army guest house. The bed was covered with a thick eiderdown, warm and cosy. It felt like something snow white might have slept in. Two hours later an unfamiliar ringtone aroused me from my half sleep. It was dark outside. I picked up, it was Holbrook. He spoke rapidly.

'We're on.' he said. We have to be at Charlie at nineteen hundred hours. We need to be early. If they arrive before that and we're not there, they'll most likely nix the whole thing.'

'Who's Charlie?'

'Checkpoint Charlie, Mr Diplomat, ever heard of it? You sure you're ready for your new role Jimmy? Get over here pronto.'

'Sorry Mike, I'm not quite awake,' I said, but he was already gone.

Forty minutes later we were driving from the *Kommandantura* in a green military sedan followed by a four door jeep with its canvas roof firmly battened down. We headed north east towards the Ku-Damm to pick up Anni at KaDeWe. As far as I could tell, American forces vehicles parked and stopped wherever they liked in Berlin; no one questioned them. We arrived at the department store at six pm on the nose, stopping right outside the main door just as Anni's working day was finished. I got out and went inside the store to collect her. She was carrying a large bulging paper shopping bag when she got in the car. We headed east towards Friedrichstrasse and the wall. Progress was agonisingly slow Friday evening traffic in this fashionable part of town was exceptionally heavy. It was six thirty by the time we got to the Friedrichstrasse intersection and Checkpoint Charlie, which, when looked at beyond the bright searchlights on the Eastern side, gave a view into a dark East Berlin canyon. This was my second time that day to see it. I had taken a look at it on the guided tour of the city I had been given that morning by a Sergeant on Holbrook's staff. It looked far more ominous at night. Armed guards were plentiful and visible on the other side.   The searchlights shone on the so-called death strip in front of the wall itself. On our side, there was a simple white wooden hut and a number of inattentive GI's, who looked like they would rather be anywhere else but here on a weekend. We got out of the army car and were joined by two civilians who had been riding in the jeep behind us. It was bitterly cold. When Anni got out of the car she took the shopping bag with her, removed a thick green Loden overcoat and passed it to me.

'It's for you, Jimmy'. She said. 'You must be freezing. I noticed yesterday that you have no coat. I got this at the store. We have a staff discount.'

All the men who were gathered round chuckled at the incongruity of the scene, none more than Mike Holbrook.

'Go ahead, Jimmy, put it on, you do look cold.' He said, then to know one in particular. 'Some guys have all the luck. I don't know where I go wrong.'

As I put on the warm coat the two strangers who had travelled in the jeep were introduced. One of them was Amos Webster, whom I had heard of, a State Department liaison officer, assigned to the Berlin Mayor's office. The second man, introduced simply as Mr Schulze, shook hands without speaking and was clearly CIA. Holbrook was very much in charge. He spoke to us all.

'I am under orders to personally receive the two people crossing over this evening. On specific instructions from Washington, I will be accompanied only by Mr Flynn here from the State Department. Everyone else is requested to stand well back from our side of the checkpoint, at least ten metres, and to remain silent. Mr Flynn and I will walk through and meet with the GDR representatives. I expect the whole transaction to be very brief.'

This was all news to me, but I was pleased to have been singled out like this. I suspected I owed this honour to Robert Kennedy, and was grateful to him, whatever his motivation.

'Miss Hartmann' Holbrook said to Anni in German. You are asked to stay back, conceal yourself in the darkness and stay silent. The other side expressly said they did not want you to participate in any way. If you intervene at any stage it could jeopardise your parents' position. That is the last thing we want.'

Anni nodded in acknowledgement. On the Eastern side of the border, cars could be heard coming to a sudden stop, doors opening and slamming shut. A junior officer standing at the barrier on the American side called over to us. 'Colonel Holbrook, sir, I spy strangers.'

'Be right there Lieutenant.' Holbrook said, indicating I was to follow him. We walked over to the checkpoint. The barrier was raised, but Holbrook stood on the Western side until it was clear what was happening over there. We could see cars switching off their lights on the eastern side and hear a mumble of voices, but the searchlights prevented us seeing what was going on. After a short delay a tall blond man wearing a coat with an Astrakhan collar, walked confidently forward. Close behind him was a middle aged couple, arm in arm. The man, tall and thin was wearing a shabby coat and the kind of black peaked cap that is common everywhere in Germany. The woman, looking around her anxiously was not old, but had gray streaks in her hair. She wore a black hat and long coat as if she were going to a funeral. Neither carried a case or any personal possessions. Beside them was a uniformed General of the Border Police and a metre or so behind him, a heavy set man dressed for winter in a thick woollen coat and scarf, complete with a Russian style fur hat. The blond haired man stopped about twelve metres from the American barrier. Holbrook and I walked forward to meet him. By the time we got there, the couple and the Grepo General had caught up. The stout man in the fur hat stayed some distance behind, almost in darkness. The blond man, who I presumed to be Max Korten spoke in English.

'Good evening, Colonel Holbrook, good to see you again. As agreed between our two Governments, I have the honour of escorting two of our citizens, Richard Hartmann and his wife Helene Hartmann, over the frontier, in keeping with their wishes to reside in another part of Berlin.'

He said this as if he was a boy scout escorting two old people across the street. Turning to the couple he said in German. Herr Hartmann, Frau Hartmann you are both free to go.'

Holbrook turned to me and also spoke in German, 'Mr Flynn, would you escort our visitors through please.'

Korten nodded his approval and the couple stepped warily forward. I shook their hands and for some reason simply said *Wilkommen,* welcome. As I was doing so, I heard a loud holler from the rear. It was the voice of the young Lieutenant on duty. 'No ma'am, don't.'

I had no time to turn around. I felt a rapid movement behind me. Running forward past me and past her parents, was the figure of Anni Hartmann. She went up to Korten and slapped his face so hard the sound seemed to echo in the surrounding buildings.

'You murdered Klara, Korten. You and your whole rotten gang are nothing but a bunch of thugs.' She hissed the words at him, with all the venom she could muster. Immediately, out of the darkness from behind the searchlights four steel helmeted border guards emerged, working the bold actions on their machine guns as they did so. The Grepo General waved them forward.

Holbrook shouted at me. 'Get them out of here now, go. I'll take care of this.'

I linked arms quickly with both the Hartmanns and ushered them rapidly back toward the wooden hut. *'Kommen Sie schnell, bitte.'* I said as we moved away, glancing back to see what was happening with Anni. The Lieutenant at the barrier and an MP came forward and helped me walk the couple over the line and into the safety of the west. I turned to go back to Holbrook, but he must have had eyes in the back of his head. 'Don't come back Jimmy stay where you are.' he roared at me, while still facing Korten. Then to Korten, who was holding both of Anni's wrists tightly, he said calmly,

'Let her go Max, this is bigger than you or me.' The border policemen, machine guns pointed at Holbrook, had almost reached Anni and Korten. Suddenly the man in the fur hat, standing in the background bellowed out to the Grepos, in unmistakably Russian accented German.

'Stand down, that is an order. Comrade Korten, release the girl we have done what we came to do.'

Korten let go of Anni's wrists while looking intently into her eyes, he released her, leaned toward her and whispered something in her ear. Then turning back quickly he walked away out of the light, swallowed up by the dark streets of East Berlin. Holbrook took Anni by the arm and escorted her slowly towards the barrier. She didn't look at me as she passed under the barrier. Five or six metres beyond the white hut, Anni's parents were waiting, looking around them as bewildered as if they had just arrived on the moon. Anni went over and embraced them, tears flowing freely from all three. The rest of us moved away to where the two army vehicles were parked. 'Goddamn civilians.' Holbrook shouted angrily, to no one in particular, incensed at what had just happened. 'When will I ever learn?'

Twenty minutes later, after we had successfully gotten rid of Amos Webster and the mysterious Mr Schulze, we were seated at a corner table of a classy restaurant on Clayalee in Zehelendorf, the *Kaiserin Augusta*. Zehelendorf, a desirable part of town, was not far, nor as far as I could tell, very different in character from Dahlem, where I was staying. As we walked from the car into the restaurant, I held Anni back and asked.

'What did Korten say to you before he let you go?'

'He said, "I'm sorry, I truly loved her." 'Jimmy, don't tell my parents. Hetty Schaeffer may have fired the gun, but Korten is Klara's murderer. I never want to hear his name again.' She spoke with a bitterness I had not seen in her before.

The Hartmanns were still in a state of shock gazing at the restaurant's plush surroundings as a waiter took our coats. They told us that they had only been informed that very day that they were being released. Anni's father had spent the previous night, as usual, in a cold damp cell in Bautzen prison in Saxony and had been escorted only that morning to Berlin, without being told what was happening. Anni was radiant with happiness, clinging to both her parents as if they might somehow be taken from her. Mike Holbrook was good at putting them at their ease. He had managed with great restraint to swallow his anger at Anni's behaviour at Checkpoint Charlie, which could easily have blown the entire exchange. In deference to her parents he didn't want a public fight about it. He explained the background to his negotiations with the GDR insofar as he could, and told them about the financial assistance that would now be available to them from the West German government. The excitement of the evening had not yet abated. None of us were particularly in the mood to eat. We were still waiting for a waiter to come and take our order when there was a series of gasps from various diners and a sudden loud crash as a full tray of food and plates hit the floor in another part of the restaurant. A buzz of conversation started up at every table. I looked around and saw some women diners taking out handkerchiefs and dabbing their eyes. The waiter who had dropped the tray scurried past our table towards the front door, muttering to himself.

'What the hell is it now?' Holbrook said, as he rose irritably from his seat and went over to the maitre'd to ask what was going on. He returned less than a minute later his face was ashen gray 'It's President Kennedy.' He said in a stunned monotone. 'He's dead, shot in Dallas, Texas, less than an hour ago. It's official.'

None of us said anything. The sobbing around the room was audible. Since his visit in June, the people of Berlin felt a special affinity to the young American President. Pastor Hartmann broke the silence.

'This is a terrible loss for all of us. He was a man of peace. Blessed are the peacemakers, they shall see God.'

Frau Hartmann, tears in her eyes, took her husband's hand and rested her head on his shoulder. Holbrook, still standing ram rod straight, his hand gripping the back of his chair, stared blankly ahead. I reached across the table to Anni, seated next to her mother, and squeezed her hand. Neither of us could say a single word.

Less than half an hour earlier on a fine bright day, beside the swimming pool at Hickory Hill in Virginia, Attorney General Robert Kennedy had taken a call for the second time that afternoon from J Edgar Hoover, on a secure White House line, which Hoover rarely used. He knew before he picked up the phone that something terrible must have happened. Although the Attorney General was nominally Hoover's boss, the FBI Director did not utter a greeting or a single word of sympathy. 'The President is dead', he said and immediately hung up. Hoover's friend, Lyndon Johnson, was now President. Robert Kennedy's power and influence had vanished in the six seconds it had taken to fire three bullets in Dallas. None of us knew it then but our world had changed forever.